Unconventional Love Affair

Unconventional Love Affair

Should Age Difference
Really Matter to Make You Happy

Robert Miller

To order additional copies of this book, contact:
Xlibris
1-888-795-4274
www.Xlibris.com
Orders@Xlibris.com
737016

The story takes place in August to December 2005. As the story opens, twenty-five-year-old Brad Wilson has recently returned to the United States from three years of combat duty with the U.S. army in Iraq. He will be attending Cal State University somewhere in the Los Angeles area. The army will pay his college expenses for the two years needed to complete his bachelor degree. Upon graduation he is obligated to return to active duty in the army for a minimum of four years as a commissioned officer. Brad was on a junior college football team four years ago, which qualified him for a walk-on tryout with State University. He makes the team initially as a special team member and a backup linebacker.

The other principal character, recently divorced thirty-seven-year-old Linda Wallace, is also returning to college at Cal State University to complete her bachelor degree, started twenty years earlier at Stanford University. Her eighteen-year-old daughter, Diane Wallace, is starting freshman year at Stanford. Diane's education and living expenses are being paid for by her father, Larry Wallace, who now lives in the San Francisco area. Larry and his new trophy wife, Cindy, will be looking after Diane while she is at school.

Brad and Linda sign up for a required Environmental Auditing class, where they are assigned the same project team. Brad and Linda have trouble relating to other classmates. However, while working on the project, they find they are attracted to each other. Linda initially wants to foster the platonic relationship, thinking Brad would be a good find for Diane.

However, within a short time they become intimate and initially try to hide their relationship at Linda's request because of the age difference. This results in many unpredictable and humorous situations.

Linda eventually loses most of her inhibitions and blossoms into a confident, self-reliant, contented woman. A trip to Las Vegas with Brad provides many new experiences for her. She even develops a sharp, witty sense of humor. Brad is happy with the status quo but realizes major decisions concerning Linda and himself will have to be made in the near future.

Their relationship is put to a test in December. Linda's parents move in with her after her father retires and sells the family house in Chicago. Then Diane unexpectedly shows up saying she is dropping out of Stanford. To add more complexity, Larry lets Linda know he is divorcing Cindy and wants to remarry her. This leads to many serious detailed one-on-one discussions involving all the principal players.

At the end of the story, Linda and Brad decide to stick with their earlier plan to spend the Christmas holidays in New York City. The story ends without any decisions being made on these serious issues.

CHAPTER 1

Blackjack Dealer Wins

Blackjack. The win by the dealer caused a spot to open at the Las Vegas blackjack table, allowing Brad Wilson to take the third base seat, so called because the player sitting there gets the last card dealt each game. Brad immediately felt eyes of the players at the table and the dealer focus in on him. He braced for the questions he knew would follow. Brad had an unusual suntan that made his body look like it was painted in two different tones. Both hands up to the wrists were dark brown; the front of his face and neck were dark brown except for the area around the eyes where he had worn protective glasses, giving his face an appearance similar to that of a raccoon. His arms and the rest of his visible body were pale white.

The dealer started to reshuffle the four decks of cards, giving the players time to start the questions.

"Where did you get that tan, son, over in Death Valley?" asked an older man wearing a Vietnam ball cap, who sat in the first seat at the far end of the table.

Brad glanced at the other players before answering. A small older lady with butterfly glasses sat at the next seat and then a man about Brad's age or maybe a few years older. At two seats to Brad's right sat a middle-aged couple, probably tourists.

"No, I just got back from Iraq and haven't had time to even out my suntan," Brad finally answered. It's best to just tell them what they want to hear now than to wait for more questions, thought Brad.

However, that comment simply opened the door for more questions. Brad was asked how long he had been in the army, how old he was, if had he been wounded, if he fought in Baghdad, and what he is going to do now. The small lady at the other end of the table was staring at Brad. He assumed she was with the man with the ball cap. They made a strange pair, so he figured they were not married but simply companions out of default or desperation. The lady had a serious look on her face. Finally she asked, "Honey, did you have to shoot any of them Commies?"

Brad answered most of the questions as briefly and succinctly as possible. He had been in the army just about four years, he was twenty-five years old, and yes, like all combatants he received some minor shrapnel wounds. As of the first of August he is on inactive reserve status and will be enrolling in State University in California for the fall semester in order to finish the last two years of college. He didn't mention that he also hopes to make the football team.

Brad also purposely failed to mention any of the unpleasant conditions he had encountered in Iraq. He didn't talk of having to hunker down for two days with almost no food to wait out a severe desert dust storm. He didn't mention the many times after getting out of a helicopter, having to run through a thick dust storm made up of cow manure and goat turds being sandblasted at him by the helicopter wash. He didn't mention having red mist spray his clothes after a suicide bomber vaporized himself only several yards away. He also didn't talk about the many times he said good-bye to his arms and legs, just in case he got hit by an IED, every time he went out on patrol. He also failed to mention that the army was paying for his college and living expenses since he had signed a contract to return to active duty as a commissioned officer upon graduation.

As the questions were being asked, a small crowd had gathered behind the table. Although over a minute had passed, John Sullivan, the dealer, was still shuffling the cards. About that time, a tall distinguished-looking man walked up behind Sullivan. Brad noticed his name tag, which read Art Bartoo Gaming Executive. Brad sensed that even before playing his first hand, he would be asked to leave the table.

Earlier that same Saturday, several hundred miles away in California, two ladies were having brunch at their club after finishing morning exercises. In a little over a week, one of the pair, Linda Wallace, was going to unexpectedly meet and become good friends with Brad, very good friends.

Linda, who will be thirty-seven years old next month, is a very pretty recently divorced brunette. She has a well-proportioned body on a five-foot, eight-inch frame. Linda's eighteen-year-old daughter, Diane, is currently living with her but will soon be moving to the San Francisco Bay Area to start school at Stanford University. Shortly after divorce proceedings started, Linda began getting phone calls from different middle-aged and older men who said they just happened to be in the area and were asked by her ex-husband to look in on her. Linda feels Larry, her now ex-husband, is trying to help her find someone to marry so he can stop paying alimony.

She has also received phone calls from several husbands of friends who just wanted to see if she was getting along all right and if she would like someone to talk to. She has received invitations to play a round of golf, go sailing, go to a baseball game, or to go bowling. Bowling? So far she has politely refused all such invitations.

Linda has not tried dating anyone yet. After all, it has been over eighteen years since she had a romantic date with anyone but her husband. Although she is quite worldly in many respects, her sex life has been somewhat sheltered. She knows that once Diane leaves, she will not have anyone to talk to at home. However, she has a plan that she wants to let her friend, Joan Belson, in on today.

Joan is Linda's best friend. She and her husband, Henry, live next door to Linda with their fourteen-year-old daughter, Hannah.

"So, Linda, what is the big surprise you wanted to tell me?" asked Joan.

Linda decided this probably was as good a time as any to let her friend in on her plans.

"Well, you know next week I'm going to help Diane move into her new student housing apartment close to Stanford University. She will be starting college there the week after next. We are driving Diane's car up there, and then I'll fly back home later that week," said Linda.

"Yes, I know that. Is there something else you want us to tell me?" asked Joan.

Linda continued, "Since I'll have plenty of time to do anything I want while Diane is in college, I've decided to go back to school myself and finish my last two years so I can get a BA degree."

"What's this, you are going back to Stanford along with Diane?'

"No, no, I'm going to enroll at State University here in the city," answered Linda. "I was accepted for classes this fall, and almost all of my units from Stanford can be transferred. I'll only need two more years for a degree." She continued, "Please don't tell anyone else yet. Remember this is a secret. I don't want Diane to know until she comes home for Thanksgiving. I'll tell her then."

Joan looked surprised. She didn't speak immediately, but her face said all she was thinking. Isn't Linda a little old to be going back to college, and if she wants a degree, why not finish at Stanford. Maybe since her divorce, she just wants to hook up with a professor near her age or maybe even a young stud. She will probably drop out after a couple of weeks when she finds out how different college is now from when she started at Stanford eighteen years ago.

Back in Las Vegas, Brad was not asked to leave the table. Instead Art Bartoo wanted to know how long Brad would be in Las Vegas, if he was staying in the casino, and if he was with any friends.

Finally Sullivan started dealing. Brad knew he probably would not last long with only a $100 buy-in and a minimum bet of $5 per hand. However, it was taking time to play the hands due partially to the full table and partially to the lively chatter that was directed toward Brad by Sullivan, other players, and some onlookers standing behind the table. Brad seemed to be holding his own, winning some hands and losing some but staying about even. He noticed that on a couple of occasions his bet was purposely not collected on losing hands. Most of the other players must have also noticed this, but if they did, no one said anything.

The next time play stopped for Sullivan to shuffle the cards, Art Bartoo came back to the table.

"Brad, the casino would like you to be our guest for dinner tonight," said Art as he handed Brad his business card with some writing added. "If you need any help with anything, let me know," he continued.

After thanking him for dinner, Brad noticed that Art had authorized dinner and drinks for two at the casino steakhouse. Brad realized this was the casino and Art's way of thanking him for his service in Iraq.

"Did you get a free buffet?" asked the man wearing the ball cap.

"No, this is for dinner and drinks for two at the steakhouse," said Brad.

As expected, a number of people wanted to know if he was with someone that he would take to dinner. When Brad said he wasn't with anyone else, the table came alive with recommendations on how he could find a nice girl to join him and some hints by a few about not having any plans themselves that evening.

"Hey, Brad, Annie here said she would be willing to have dinner with you," said the man with the ball cap, pointing to the small older lady sitting next to him.

"Yeah, I'm ready. I just have to go home and get my false teeth. I'll even wear my girdle, if I can find it." Annie laughed, happy to go along with the joke.

About that time, the cocktail waitress came back to take drink orders.

"I thought you might be ready for another beer, so I brought you one. I understand Mr. Bartoo gave you a comp for dinner at the steakhouse tonight. That is a really nice restaurant. My ex-boyfriend took me there once," the cocktail waitress said with a big smile.

Brad had taken note of her the first time she stopped at the table. She was a beautiful blonde with a great figure only partially hidden in the skimpy outfit she was wearing. He felt her big boobs on his shoulder as she set the beer in from of him. Her name tag said she was Kandi Kolinsky, although that probably wasn't her real name. Brad knew what to do next, ask her if she would like to have dinner there again with him. However, he hesitated.

Brad was thinking fast, but at the same time, everything around him seemed to be moving in slow motion. It was similar to his Iraqi experiences, during the first seconds of a firefight after being attacked. You know you are in trouble, and you know you have to make quick decisions, but you want to be careful to not make the wrong decision, or it might be fatal. The moment passed without the question being asked. Kandi moved on to the others at the table, taking more orders. *She will come back as soon as I finish this beer, and I'll chug-a-lug it if I decide to ask her to dinner*, thought Brad.

Fortunately a change in dealers allowed Brad to think out the ramifications of any action he may take. Sure he would like to take a beautiful girl to dinner; however, an advice made in army orientations in Iraq and again during his army separation processing just a few days ago popped into his head. Sex has become so casual that there is no time to know what you might be getting into. Transmitting a disease is common now, and almost as common are allegations of rape, so it pays to be a little careful. After considering this, Brad decided to ask Kandi to dinner anyway and then see if can get her up to his room so he could fuck her brains out all night long. *Yeah, that is what I want to do*, thought Brad.

"Place your bets," said the new dealer.

This brought Brad back into focus in real time. He became aware of a silly grin on his face that he quickly dropped. He moved his eyes but not his head to see if anyone at the table had seen his expression. No one said anything about the grin. As is often the case when your turn your attention from inner thought to what is happening around you, Brad remembered hearing a number of comments directed his way earlier. It was almost like hearing backward.

"The cocktail girl said she wanted to have dinner with you. You ought to jump on that offer," someone said.

"I'd sell my car to get enough money to take her to dinner," said the young player.

"Brad, honey, I already told you I'm ready. You can even bring her along if you want to, I won't mind. I haven't had a lobster dinner since 1992," said Annie.

The new dealer, a young woman, now came into focus and was looking really good, as good or maybe better than Kandi. Her name tag said Melissa Queen. Maybe she would like to go to dinner, thought Brad. *Now what should I do.*

Back in California, it was now a little after 2:00 p.m. as Linda arrived home. Diane was anxious to tell her about a change in plans. In one long sentence, Diane told Linda that she had just finished a long phone conservation with her father, Larry, and they have a new plan. Instead of driving to the Bay Area they would fly up on Friday. Larry and his new wife, Cindy, found a perfect student housing apartment, so there would be no need to search for one next week. Larry would rent the apartment for Diane, and then they all could help Diane move in over the weekend. They could go shopping on Saturday. On Sunday they would all have an early breakfast, and then Linda would fly back home.

The change in plans was like a knife in the back. Linda didn't like anything she was hearing and had a hard time not screaming that the change was not acceptable and very inconsiderate since no one had discussed any changes with her. First of all, Linda wanted to spend some quality mother-and-daughter time with Diane on their leisurely drive to the Bay Area. Second if they weren't going to drive, how was Diane going to get all the clothes, household items, and books she said she would need for her new apartment. Third, they won't have much time to find another apartment if Diane doesn't like the one Larry and Cindy found. Also if she was to come home Sunday, who would help Diane register for school the next day.

However, the most troubling aspect of what Linda was hearing was the unmistakable message that Diane was now accepting Cindy as her mother and that Linda was on the verge of, at best, becoming just a friend. Linda also realized there was nothing she could do to change anything at this time. Diane had always been her daddy's little girl. She had made it known that she thinks the divorce was Linda's fault. To make matters worse for Linda, Diane thinks Cindy, who is only eight years older than her, is cool and fun to be with because they understand each other.

Larry is going to pay all of Diane's expenses while she is in college. He can well afford it. His law practice is booming since he took over his father's law practice and transferred his business to San Francisco. Because Diane will not be living with Linda, the child support Larry is paying Linda will stop at the first of the month. That will not be a problem; Linda always spends a lot more for Diane than the $2,000 per month of child support she is getting.

How do I respond to this? thought Linda. Any negative comment made by her would immediately end any further discussion. She knew Diane wouldn't agree to any change of plans that were primarily formulated by her father and stepmother. Linda does not have an aggressive personality, and putting up any kind of a fight would be out of character for her. However, fighting for the love of your daughter is something every mother will do. The coming weekend would see fireworks coming from a feisty Linda.

"Well, Diane, how will you get your clothes and household effects up to your new apartment?" asked Linda, trying to speak in a normal voice.

"Oh, Mom, I can always come back for anything I might need, but Dad said he would buy whatever supplies I need for the apartment and Cindy is going to take me shopping for some new clothes for school," responded Diane.

"Are you sure you don't want me to stay another day so I can help you register?" asked Linda.

"Dad said he will help. I sent him the list of classes we made. Dad said he can fix it so that I don't have to waste classes on remedial English and math," answered Diane.

This was like a punch in the stomach to Linda.

"Those remedial classes are prerequisites for other classes you will need, and your SAT score was not high enough to avoid taking them your first semester," said Linda.

"Well, Dad said he knows some officials that will approve bypassing the requirement. Besides, he said that is done all the time for smart kids who have trouble taking exams, and remember I didn't feel well when I sat for the test," said Diane.

There was no use pointing out any more problems with the new plan. Diane would have an answer for everything, and nothing about the plan was going to change.

"Okay, Di, I can see you know want you want. Let's go to a movie tonight. We haven't seen a movie together for a long time," said Linda. Maybe Diane would respond to her pet name, which she liked her father to call her, thought Linda.

"Mom, you know I have a date with Mark Dominick tonight," said Diane.

"Yes, I remember now, but can't you cancel it since Mark isn't your boyfriend any longer and you said you were just going to hang out for a while," said Linda.

"I can't do that. Mark thinks this is the last time we can be together before I go away to college," said Diane.

"You can hang out on Sunday or a later day now that we won't be leaving until Friday," said Linda.

"No, I can't do that. I don't want Mark to know I'll be leaving later in the week," said Diane.

"Okay, then maybe we can catch a movie tomorrow night," said Linda.

"Yeah, okay. Oh, by the way, I'll need $50 for tonight," said Diane.

Linda felt another verbal blow. After being stabbed in the back and being punched in the stomach, Diane's comments felt to Linda like she was being kicked in the head while she was down. After making new plans without consulting her and then wanting to go shopping with Cindy instead of her real mother, Diane now would rather go out with an old boyfriend using money provided by her mother than spending time with her.

"Why do you need any money? Didn't Mark ask you out, and aren't you just going to hang out?" asked Linda.

"You know Mark, he is always broke, and I think we may go to the movies and then get something to eat," responded Diane.

After getting the money, Diane went to her room saying she had to get ready for Mark. Linda wondered why she had to get ready four hours before the date with Mark.

In Las Vegas Brad had made up his mind. He quickly finished his beer and looked around for Kandi. Melissa was still dealing, but Brad hadn't been able to talk to her. He didn't want to suddenly ask her to dinner without knowing anything about her, especially with half a dozen strangers listening.

A new cocktail waitress appeared and started taking drink orders from the players. Brad asked what happened to Kandi and was told that she was off duty. By this time he was down to $20, and he didn't want to lose any more than that, so he decided it was time to go.

Brad knew he had missed an opportunity for a dinner date, so he thought he would spend a couple of hours trying to even out his tan at the casino swimming pool. As he started to leave, most of the players at the table and Melissa wished him well. Brad thanked them and noticed a smiling Annie, who was still staring at him. Great, he thought, Annie turned out to be his best chance for a dinner date this evening. Just then Annie called out that she would see him later.

"Yeah, maybe," answered Brad

Brad had picked up that phrase in Iraq. It seems whenever one of the Iraqi interpreters wanted to politely say no, he just said, "Yeah, maybe," which usually meant no. Brad remembered asking him if it was safe to enter a house while on patrol. The interrupter said, "Yeah, maybe." As soon as Brad pushed in the door, AK-47 rounds started flying through the doorway, which Brad had fortunately just cleared.

After changing into a swimsuit, Brad headed to the pool. He figured that if he put a towel over his face and lie down on his hands, no one would stare at his unusually colored body.

As he lay on a lounge chair trying to sleep, Brad's mind wandered back to an advice given him at his army separation proceeding. Many soldiers become extremely depressed soon after arriving back in the United States from a war zone. If this happens, you should seek medical attention. Most individuals that get this feeling do not seek help, often with tragic results. Brad never bothered to pay much attention to these comments since he felt he didn't have anything to be depressed about. It just makes sense that leaving a combat zone and getting back in the United States should make everyone feel pretty good, not depressed. Now he wasn't so sure about not having anything to be depressed about.

After receiving army separation orders in Iraq, he was flown to Germany. He spent a couple days there getting a discharge physical examination and then a lengthy back-to-civilian-life orientation. A government-contracted jet flew Brad to McGuire Air Force Base in New Jersey. He was able to collect his back pay and travel pay to his home in Kansas, where he initially enlisted in the army. He then took a commercial flight to Kansas City, Missouri, where he spent a couple more days visiting with his older brother and his brother's family. After a few hours of discussing events of the past year, it became apparent that Brad was in the way of the family activities. Brad's brother had asked a few questions about Brad's Iraq experiences, but it was obvious Brad's sister-in-law did not want to hear anything about that. She went out of her way to announce that her two boys would never be allowed to join any branch of the military. The sister-in-law was pleasant enough but kept busy keeping the children away from Brad.

The second day of his visit, Brad used some more of his separation pay and savings to buy a new economic Ford Focus. After loading up the car with clothes and other personal effects his brother had been keeping for him, Brad headed to his small hometown.

It was at this time feelings of despair begin to creep into his mind. Brad drove by the farm his family owned when he was growing up. The farmhouse, barn, and all farm equipment in sight were in good shape, probably better that when Brad lived there. He thought about stopping at the house to visit with the current owners but then decided against doing that. The next stop was the cemetery where his parents were buried. As soon as he found the grave sites, a strange unexplainable feeling came over him. It was as if his parents were standing beside him and he was twelve years old again. Brad figured his imagination was just playing tricks on him. Suddenly he didn't want to relive any memories.

Brad's mother had died of cancer when he was thirteen years old. His only brother was ten years older than Brad and had just finished college. He had starting his own family and was not able come home and help run the farm. Brad and his father did the best they could, but old medical bills and bad weather prevented the farm from producing any meaningful income. Then during the middle of his senior year, Brad's father was killed in an automobile accident. Brad's brother did help Brad sell the farm for an amount only slightly more than mortgage and other debts. Brad's half of the net proceeds were barely enough to get him through the end of the school year. In order to help support himself, he started working the swing shift after school at a local fast-food restaurant. In addition he volunteered for extra weekend work in order to make a little more money. This, for the most part, ended his social life. Most of the girls he knew at high school started going steady with other boys. His friends that he had played on the football team with for four years were now involved with other sports and didn't have much time for Brad.

When Brad graduated, he was able to negotiate for a partial football scholarship at a junior college about one hundred miles from his hometown. By working at a local fast-food restaurant, he was able to make ends meet but again missed out on normal social activities for someone his age. By the time he had completed three years at the junior college, the Taliban had been driven from Afghanistan, and the military was gearing up to go to war with Iraq. Brad couldn't afford to continue college for another two years, and he was sick of working in fast-food restaurants, so he decided to volunteer for the army. He could sign up for a three-year enlistment that would entitle him to use government funds to complete college when his enlistment was up—that is, if he managed to keep from getting killed in combat.

Brad did drive through the small town where he worked his senior year at high school. He thought maybe he would recognize someone as he walked along the town's main street, but that didn't happen. After he had spent less than an hour in town, he headed out to the junior college town. He didn't have any luck running into anyone he knew there either.

The next few nights Brad had trouble sleeping because of weird nightmares. He would dream of a range of people he had known in the past from high school, junior college, and men he knew in Iraq. Seeing the faces of friends that had died in combat was especially depressing.

As Brad relaxed by the pool in Las Vegas, he realized that he was pretty much alone in the world. He would soon meet many new people at

State University but didn't relish the idea of having to make friends with people that had vastly different worldly experiences from him. Of course, making friends with Kandi or even Melissa would have been all right. He knew he really missed out on an opportunity to get better acquainted with one of them.

Suddenly just like magic, Brad saw Kandi walking toward him. Fortunately, he hadn't put a towel over his face, so he was hoping Kandi would see him.

"Hi, Brad, remember me?" said Kandi

"Well hello, Kandi. I was hoping I'd see you again," Brad answered.

"I thought you might not recognize me now that I'm not wearing my hostess uniform," Kandi said.

Brad thought about what she would look like without a uniform or the casual clothes she was now wearing. She would even look good in a burlap bag. He decided to not let this opportunity slip away even if he risked looking foolish.

"I'd recognize you anywhere with or without your uniform. If you have a couple of minutes, maybe I can buy you a drink for a change," said Brad as he continued to picture her in his mind without a uniform and without a burlap bag.

Kandi did sit down and asked for a long island ice tea. Brad keep trying to get an opening to invite her to dinner, but she apparently wanted to talk about herself. Within a few minutes Kandi had explained that her job at the casino was only temporary until she could get an acting part in one of the casino shows. She continued while Brad tried to find an appropriate time to mention dinner. Finally during a pause in Kandi's rambling Brad got the question out. Surprisingly this seemed to be what Kandi was waiting for. She quickly accepted the invitation and said she needed to go home to change. They agreed to meet at 8:00 p.m. outside the steakhouse. That left about four hours for Brad to spend a little more time at the pool, make reservations at the restaurant and get ready for what he hoped to be a big night.

A little after 7:00 p.m. in California, Mark stopped by for Diane who for some reason was still not ready for her date. Mark and Linda made small talk for several minutes before Diane was ready to go. Mark mentioned how sad he felt about Diane leaving for college and not being able to see her again for several months. Linda asked what their plans were for the evening. Mark mumbled something about probably going to a movie and then getting something to eat. By then Diane was ready, so she and Mark left.

Linda suddenly felt very lonely. She wanted to talk to someone, but it was a little early to call Joan as she frequently did around 8:30 p.m.

As soon as Linda turned on the TV her mind began to wander. How she managed to get herself in this position? Linda grew up as an only child in a middle-to-upper-class family. Her father was a corporate attorney. Her mother never had a real job, other than taking care of Linda and the family finances. After graduating from high school in a Chicago suburb, Linda was accepted at several big-name universities. Going against her parents' wishes to enroll at Northwestern University, she felt it best if she got farther away from home so she could find herself. Stanford University business school seemed like a natural for her. As it turned out Linda was quite a bit more naive than she or her parents thought. The few weeks went fairly smoothly mainly because her mother spent most of that time living with her. Then she was able to move into a dorm room with another girl. At the urging of a couple of girlfriends, Linda tried drugs and alcohol but managed to initially avoid any intimate sex. However, at one of the weekend parties she met Larry Wallace. Her life changed completely from that point forward.

Larry was a second year law major. Having an upperclassman take an interest in her caused Linda to lose any inhibitions she may have had. After a few months of dating without actually realizing it she assumed they would just naturally marry. When she got pregnant reality set in. Larry said he would pay for an abortion. That started their first serious argument. Eventually they convinced themselves that they truly were in love and should keep the baby. They agreed to get married at the end of the school year in June. The baby, Diane, was due in September.

After getting married, Linda continued at school one more year. Larry's parents who lived in San Francisco took care of the baby weekdays, After her second year she dropped out of college in order to take care of the baby full time. After graduation Larry started Stanford law school. His father, who at the time was a senior partner in a prestigious San Francisco law firm, agreed to lend Larry the money needed for law school. Larry and Linda were responsible for their living expenses; however, the Wallaces frequently helped them out during the next three years and often bought expensive gifts for Diane. Linda worked part time in a bookstore near the college and Larry taught some undergraduate courses to make ends meet for the next three years.

For the next fourteen years or so, life was good. Larry and another young attorney opened their own firm specializing in real estate law in Los Angles. Larry and Linda bought an expensive house in a gated community overlooking the ocean near the airport. This included membership in a prestigious community social club. They made many friends and social acquaintances. For a number of years the family was able to travel quite a bit for vacations and in connection with Larry's business trips. The traveling pretty much stopped for Linda about four years ago when Diane decided she didn't want to go on any more family trips.

For the first time Linda realized that is when her marriage started to deteriorate. Larry continued take business trips alone and more frequently. Small things Linda noticed caused her to suspect that Larry might be having one night affairs on many of his trips however, since she had no real proof she choose to convince herself that the affairs were only her imagination. Later she would find out it was not her imagination.

During that time Larry had bought out his partner and now was sole owner of the law practice. Larry's father had also taken full ownership of a large highly successful law practice in San Francisco.

Then two years ago Larry suddenly said he wanted to move his business in order to San Francisco and consolidate it with his father's firm. His father wanted to retire and would give his practice to Larry. That would of course require a move to the Bay Area. Despite Linda's feelings against that, Larry went forward with his plan and by the middle of last year has completed the consolidation of practices. It was agreed that they would not move until Diane finished high school. Larry worked at the San Francisco office during the week and usually came home on the weekends. It was several months before Linda became aware that Cindy came with the San Francisco office. It seems she was the office manager who, of course, was required to work closely with Larry. Once Linda found out Larry and Cindy were living together during the week she gave him an ultimatum, her or Cindy. Larry chose Cindy and divorce papers were filed the first of the year.

Divorces are always messy; however, this probably went better than most. Larry and Linda pretty much agreed upon the allocation of assets between them. The stocks and bonds were split evenly. Linda would get one-half interest in the law practice and in their home. She would get the BMW 760 and Diane's car, which by coincidence was a Ford Focus. Larry would get the Cadillac Escalade. Linda would get custody of Diane and alimony of $40,000 per month plus another $2,000 for Diane's upkeep.

Around 8:00 p.m. in Las Vegas Kandi met Brad at the restaurant. She was wearing expensive looking clothes featuring an electric blue miniskirt. She apparently had time to have her hair and nails done. Brad thought she looked really good just like a high price hooker. He suspected that Art Bartoo had included Kandi as part of his comp.

Inside the restaurant Brad told the hostess they had reservations and asked for a nice table outdoors if possible. The hostess seemed to be impressed when Brad handed her the complimentary dinner card indicating they were the guests of Art Bartoo. They were seated outside overlooking a large reflecting pool. The night air was pleasantly warm and soft music was being played by a nearby pianist. Brad knew Kandi was his kind of girl when she ordered a Stinger instead of one of those multi colored drinks that comes with an umbrella or some kind of fruit. Brad ordered a gimlet even though he wasn't sure exactly what that was.

The hostess come over to the bar as the waitress was placing the drink orders.

"That couple, the working girl and the two toned guy, are guests of Mr. Bartoo. Nothing on the menu is off limits. You and one of the busboys should be close by at all times to make sure they don't have to wait for any service," said the hostess.

For the next two hours Kandi and Brad enjoyed a very nice romantic dinner of steak and lobster with all the extras including after dinner drinks. Kandi seemed to talk nonstop during the entire dinner speaking mostly about herself but occasionally asking Brad some things about him. She also took several cell phone calls but limited the conservation to letting the calling party know where she was and that she would call back the next day.

For the most part Brad was able to tune out a lot of what Kandi was saying and concentrate on what he would like to have happen after dinner. He had to keep reminding himself to not form a stupid grin on his face and not to chuckle to himself at inappropriate times as he pictured what he hoped would be upcoming events.

Brad knew that even though the dinner and drinks were complimentary, he was responsible for the gratuity. His hadn't given this much thought, so his quick calculation of a fair amount to leave was a shock to him. He figured dinner must have cost at least $300 with taxes, so 20 percent of that would be $60. Unfortunately, he wasn't sure he had that much money with him even counting all the change he had including dimes, nickels and pennies. After checking all of his pockets he was able to come up with $45. He kept back $8 but he wasn't sure why since that wouldn't buy even one drink outside of the restaurant. He had left more money in his room thinking that if he would only take what he could afford to lose gambling.

As they left the restaurant Brad came up with the best line he could think of, which conveniently fit the situation.

"Kandi, have you ever seen any of the hotel rooms in this casino?" asked Brad.

"Oh yeah, I've seen a lot of them," answered Kandi. The implication that she has spent a lot of nights with a lot of different men there didn't seem to bother her.

"Well, I'd like you to see the room they gave me," Brad said, hoping she would understand what he really wanted.

"Okay, let's go," said Kandi.

As soon as they got to the room Kandi gave Brad a big hug then she went into the bathroom. When she came out of the bathroom she had her purse with her but otherwise was completely naked.

"Well, what do you think?" she asked as she struck a pose.

Brad had a little trouble forming words but blurted out something about looking great. Brad did notice that Kandi had a great body and all the right parts. He's seen a lot of naked women, but never before had he seen one with a big blue handbag slung over her shoulder.

"I left some rubbers in the bathroom. You'd better put one on or maybe two if it's been a while," Kandi said.

In the bathroom Brad noticed that Kandi had stacked her clothes and shoes in a neat pile at the end of the long marble sink top. *Boy, that Kandi is a real professional*, thought Brad. He did put on two condoms and then headed out the door. By that time Kandi was already in bed. Fortunately, her handbag was on the floor beside the bed.

After hugging and wrestling around for a couple of minutes Kandi asked Brad what he wanted to do first. Brad said they better get right to it before he blew a hole in both condoms. It turned out that Kandi was a screamer. Besides moaning and groaning she seemed to be shouting move by move details.

"Boy, it must have been a long time for you," Kandi said when they finished.

"Yeah, if you don't count sex with camels," Brad said.

"You don't really mean that, do you?" Kandi said as she gave Brad a funny look.

"No, I was just kidding. Even the Arabs don't have sex with camels. They prefer goats."

Kandi wasn't sure if that was true or not, but even so, she thought that was funny. A few minutes later they were fast asleep.

Earlier while Kandi and Brad were having dinner, Linda was talking to her best friend, Joan Belson. Linda quickly blurted out the story about the change in plans and how unfair it was to her. For some reason that made her feel better. She always was able to confide in Joan who was good at keeping their discussions confidential. Linda and Joan were a lot alike they were about the same age, both married young and both had only one child, a girl. They both seem to be in the doldrums of life. Their accomplishments seemed to be behind them and there didn't seem to be anything exciting to look forward to except grandchildren someday.

Linda felt the need to finally tell someone more of the problems she was having with Diana. In the next few minutes Linda expressed her concern that Diane was experimenting with sex. About a year ago Linda discovered that Diane had birth control pills that were approved by the school nurse and proscribed by a local doctor. When Diane was confronted with this, her unbelievable comment was that all the girls are taking birth control pills in case they get raped. Diane also said she was not concerned about getting any social disease. If that should happen she could always get medication to keep it under control.

Joan tried to console Linda by saying that Diane is no different from most girls at her age. They want to be independent but also want to be around people near their own age. Joan could see some of the same circumstances starting to develop with her daughter, Hannah.

"What should I do?" asked Linda.

"Well, you don't have to just take all that crap. Since your plans were changed without your approval why not change them back?" offered Joan.

"You know I can't do that. Diane will simply not get in her car for the trip with me. If I did order her to come with me that would definitely the end of any civil relationship we could ever have in the future," said Linda.

As she was speaking, a thought came into Linda's head. Maybe she could make some changes in the weekend plan without letting anyone know ahead of time.

The phone conservation with Joan continued for over an hour. A talk with Joan always made Linda feel better. A number of ways to change the plan to get what she wants and what she knows is not what Larry and Cindy want raced through Linda's head.

Linda continued to watch TV until around midnight when Diane came home. She did not look very happy. Diane said she was tired didn't want to talk about her evening. She then went straight to bed.

Sunday morning came quickly for Brad. Everything went well during the night; he didn't have any trouble remembering what to do. Kandi was just getting ready to leave. She had to start work at 9:00 a.m. for her six hour shift as a cocktail waitress. Brad wanted to get an early start to California in order to get ahead of the traffic that would be on the road a little later in the day. Brad offered to buy breakfast, but Kandi said she would get something in the employee lounge before she started work. Before they parted, they exchanged cell phone numbers and promised to see each other again sometime soon. After a long passionate good-bye kiss Kandi was gone.

It took a little over five hours to get to his destination as Brad was not in a hurry and stopped for a leisurely breakfast. The army had arranged for Brad to stay in a military transit facility near the airport and not far from State University. The facility was quite large but pretty much deserted when he checked in. The duty sergeant knew he was coming and was happy to have someone that would be staying more than a couple of days. The sergeant explained that occupancy fluctuated from almost empty as it currently was to booked full up, which meant some soldiers had to be checked into civilian hotels. The facility was mostly used for men or women waiting for air transportation to new duty stations.

Brad knew his vacation was over. There would be a lot to do every day for the next several months. On Monday Brad would apply for a debit card from the Armed Forces Credit Union where Brad has his checking and savings accounts. He had credit cards in the past but canceled then when he got orders for Iraq. This time he figured that a debit card would keep him from spending more than his monthly income. He had a lot of shopping to do and wanted to complete all of it on Monday. Tuesday he was the first day of football practice, which would take up most of his time until school registration day the following Tuesday. Brad decided to take a short afternoon nap and then catch an early evening movie.

Sunday passed uneventfully for Linda. She went to church in the morning; Diane stayed home because she wasn't feeling well. Most of the afternoon Linda spent thinking of how she wanted the events at the end of the week to play out. Diane spent a lot of time on the phone talking to friends. During the day Linda was able to get bits and pieces of information from Diane about their trip to the Bay Area. Diane named the hotel in San Francisco where Larry would make reservations for them. She was able to provide only some detail about the airline and flight schedule other than Larry had make reservations for them. Diane was even vaguer on details about the new apartment or anything else scheduled for the weekend. That evening Linda and Diane did go to an early movie near their home.

Linda was busy week the following week. Over the next few days she had finished making changes in the weekend plans. She had changed plane reservations for the flight to San Francisco from 1:00 p.m. to 9:00 a.m. By getting there about four hours earlier, Larry and Cindy would not be able to meet them at the airport. Knowing this, Linda reserved a rental car. That would allow her more control of her movements over the weekend and would mean less time with Larry and Cindy. Linda also reserved a hotel room for her and Diane near the university. Late Thursday she cancelled the arrangements Larry had made for their stay in San Francisco. Once again, staying near the university would reduce the time spent traveling with Larry and Cindy. Linda had several other plan adjustments in mind for the weekend. *This will be a really fun time after all*, thought Linda.

CHAPTER 2

Tuesday morning Brad made his way to the athletic field house for the first day of football practice. A small crowd was already milling around the entrance by the time he arrived. Several small groups of three or four had formed, but most individuals seemed to be pretty much by themselves. Brad was a little self-conscious about his looks but figured that his coloring had evened out a little over the weekend.

"Did you play here last year?" Brad asked a tall slim young man.

"I practiced with the team last year, but they hardly ever let me play in a game. If I would have played more, we wouldn't have lost all our games," said Warren West. "Are you transferring in from somewhere?" Warren continued.

"Yeah," Brad said, suddenly not wanting to continue the discussion.

"What's the matter with your hands and face?" asked Warren as he looked Brad over.

"It's just a special suntan. Do you like it?" responded Brad.

"Yeah, man, it's definitely something," said Warren with a big smile.

This is just great, thought Brad sarcastically. *It looks like Warren and I are going to become the best of friends.*

Just then the locker room door opened and everyone headed inside. A big burly guy in a white tee shirt with Coach Buster Stewart written on it started yelling out instructions. All scholarship and returning players were sent to one side of the room. Brad and the rest of the group were told they were the meat squad and they should wait on the other side of the room. The first group were weighed, measured and then issued equipment and lockers. About half an hour later, Brad's group was asked to line up in alphabetical order by last name. The players slowly arranged themselves in proper order with some difficulty.

"Who are you?" asked Coach Stewart when Brad got to the head of the line.

"Brad Wilson, transfer from junior college," Brad answered.

"If you have college playing experience, you should have been with the other group!" Stewart yelled even though Brad was less than a foot away from him. "Did you let anyone here know you were transferring in?" he continued.

"Yeah, I received a confirmation to be here from Coach Kruger," said Brad.

Stewart grabbed a different clip chart and started scanning the names. When he found Brad's name he looked up and started at Brad for what seemed like several seconds.

"You're the army guy?" Stewart seemed to ask.

"Yeah, I just got discharged the first of this month," answered Brad.

For the next few minutes Stewart tried to find out more about Brad's army experience. He asked the same questions the people in Las Vegas asked. Stewart then spent more time asking about Brad's high school and junior college football experience. Finally he seemed satisfied and wrote down Brad's height at six feet, three inches and weight as 225 pounds. Brad knew he was measured at only six feet one and weighed only 190 pounds. Stewart seemed to see the questioning look on Brad's face and said that Brad would weigh 225 pounds if he wanted to play for State University. Fortunately Stewart didn't say Brad would have to somehow grow two more inches in the next few days.

"Okay, go see the equipment manager and then suit up and get out on the practice field," Stewart said.

Shortly after Brad got onto the practice field, Coach Sam Kruger blew a whistle and yelled for all the players to line up for loosening up drills. After about fifteen minutes the players were told to run around both goal posts and then get in groups with their respective assistant coaches according to their playing positions. Brad hadn't had any real physical exercise for over a month, but he felt he was keeping up with the other players so far.

Brad played a linebacker position in junior college, so he headed to the group forming around Assistant Coach Hal Curtis. Brad's chances of making the team seemed good since only six men including Brad were trying for four positions. Then Curtis called out Brad's name and seven other names for a total of eight. It seems two returning starters from last year's team were going to show up later in the week. Getting a position on the team didn't seem as good now.

"When I call your name, I want you to let me know your best position: outside or inside linebacker. I also want to know what you think is your specialty: run stopping, pass coverage, or blitz. I do not want to hear anyone say they can do it all. I do not want to hear anyone say more than one position or one specialty!" Curtis yelled.

"Coach, what if I want to change to a different position later?" one of the group asked.

"Anton, Mokie!" yelled Curtis, completely ignoring the question.

"Ah, outside linebacker, but I am also really good at the inside," answered Mokie.

"Your answer is outside. Did you forget the second question?" Curtis snarled.

"Oh yeah, I'm good at run coverage," Mokie responded with an almost correct response.

A couple of names later Curtis called out, "Michael, Paul."

"It's Paul, Michael, Coach. Michael is my first name," Michael corrected.

"Are you telling me you have two first names?" yelled Curtis. Coaches don't like to be challenged, ever.

"No, Coach, Paul is not my first name. It is my last name," answered Michael.

"What the hell is the difference? You're both of those guys aren't you? What do you want to be called?" asked Curtis.

"Michael," answered Michael.

"Okay, Mike, now are you going to answer the questions?" snarled Cutis.

When the last linebacker candidate had been called upon, Curtis sent the group to a set of temporary bleachers that had been set up at one end of the practice field. Soon all the players were sitting there together.

At that time Coach Sam Kruger walked to the front of the bleachers and began speaking into a microphone. "All right, listen up, I'm going to tell you what we are going to do this season and how we should win all—I said all—of our games. First, I have a few administrative comments.

"You guys know this is our second year on NCAA probation. That means we can only have eight games this season, four here and four away. We will not be eligible for any after season invitational games. Everything we do is being watched by the NCAA goons. By we, I mean me, all other coaches and each one of you individually. We cannot afford to have anyone mess up and cause us to not get off probation at the end of this year. You all know the rules. No drugs, no alcohol, and no arrests or any other trouble with the law. The coaches are going to go over all the rules in detail with each of you individually this afternoon. Anyone breaking any one of the rules will immediately be dismissed from the team for the remainder of the season. Let me give you an example of one bullshit infraction that was held against us. For several years some of our players misused the parking lot. Yes, the parking lot. That is what was written in the NCAA complaint. Some players parked their cars in the handicap stalls, double parked or parked in no parking zones. Anyone caught doing that this year will be kicked off the team. The school security people monitor the parking areas and have been asked to be especially careful to report any violations by any of you players to my office. If you have any trouble in the parking area call the security, the coaches will give you the phone number. Do not think you can handle any situation by punching somebody's lights out.

"Now, about our schedule. Our first game is only a week from this Saturday. That means, counting today, we will be allowed to practice for only nine days. We will practice twice a day 9:00 to 11:00 a.m. and 2:00 to 4:00 until classes start. Practice will then be 3:00 to 6:00 p.m. Be sure not to schedule any classes after 1:00 p.m. We will be playing the same teams we played last year. On September 24, we play at Stanford. This is the only division one team we have this year and we will win that game. Our homecoming game is October 15 against Idaho teachers, and we will win that game. In order to be prepared for our first game with Newmar, which we will win, we will hold a full contact, game condition intersquad game this Saturday. Today there are sixty-five of you guys that want to play for State University. By Monday night we will be down to fifty-five or fewer. NCAA rules allow us to carry up to fifty-five active players, but we will carry less if necessary. The best way to be one of the remaining fifty-five next week is to show what you can do in practice and in the squad game Saturday. The best ways to not be one of the fifty-five is to dog it in practice, dog it in the game, or break any of the NCAA and team rules.

"One more thing, you get six units for being on the team, and I get to give out your grade. Don't pull your weight, and you'll get an F for a grade."

Kruger finally stopped talking, and everyone headed to the showers. In the next few days Brad learned a little more about the NCAA sanctions. It seems the big ticket infractions concerned illegal recruiting, exam cheating, grade manipulation, and illegal use of department funds. Although proof is still pending all indications are that Coach Sam Kruger was aware of and in fact facilitating most of this illegal activity. Before the start of last season half of the returning players were either ruled ineligible or transferred to other schools.

Brad got acquainted with most of the players and made friends with a few. He also had chances to meet some of the girls who hung around the practice field. A few of the girls were waiting for their boyfriends, but most were trying to latch onto a jock. Most of the girls looked quite young and were not very careful about their dress or hygiene, so Brad quickly decided he did not want to get involved with any of them.

In order to help assure that he didn't get cut from the team, Brad volunteered for the so-called suicide teams, which covered punts and kickoffs. The practices that week went well, but the intersquad game Saturday was going to be the real test.

Later that week on Friday morning Linda and Diane got up early to get ready for their flight to San Francisco. Linda said they had to leave the house no later than 7:00 a.m. or they might miss the plane. They left for the airport at 7:15 a.m. because Diane was a little slow getting ready.

The hour flight went quickly, but there was some time for some mother-to-daughter talk. When Larry and Cindy were not at the airport to meet them, Diane called her father's cell phone. After a few words Diane handed the phone to Linda saying Larry wanted to talk to her.

"It would have been nice of you to let me know of your early arrival," said Larry.

"We wanted some time to look at other student apartments in case Diane didn't like the one you picked out. I also wanted to show Diane where I lived many years ago. I know how upset you must be Larry. I felt the same way when you didn't have the curtsey to discuss this weekend plans with me," Linda said in an unemotional voice.

"I already signed a lease for an apartment, so don't even try to talk Diane into selecting some other apartment," fumed Larry.

At that point the conversation was beginning to turn into a name calling argument, so Linda said they should all meet at her hotel around 3:00 p.m. Larry objected to the change in hotels, but there was nothing he could do about it now.

Diane was very unhappy that she wouldn't get to see her dad and Cindy until the afternoon. She said she didn't want to look at any other apartments since her dad had already signed a lease on the one he and Cindy found. Linda then suggested they take a short walking tour of the university before checking in to the hotel. For some reason Diane seemed to like that idea.

It was a little after 2:00 p.m. when they checked into the hotel. A little before 3:00 p.m. Larry called to say he and Cindy were waiting for them in the hotel lobby.

In the lobby, Diane gave a warm hug to Larry and then to Cindy. Linda received a cold reception, no hugs and not even a handshake. That pretty much set the tone for most of the weekend.

The apartment was within walking distance of the university, but it was small and sparsely furnished. The bathroom had a tub shower combination. The bedroom had one double bed, one table by the bed, two pieces of furniture with drawers for clothes and one non-walk-in closet. The larger room served as a living room separated from the kitchen area by a built-in four-foot-high counter. Diane immediately said she loved it. Cindy said they would go shopping tomorrow for bedding, kitchen utensils and a better TV. Linda felt that several of the apartments she had found on the internet would have been much larger, much better and probably rented for less per month. Linda didn't want to comment on this in front of Diane, but she made a mental note to be sure to point this out to Larry and Cindy when she had an opportunity.

Larry suggested they walk around the university before dinner not knowing Linda and Diane had done that a little earlier in the day. Diane quickly agreed and said maybe they could see some of the sorority houses just in case she was asked to join one. Linda could see that she would not be comfortable with the other three, so she said she would wait in the library. About an hour and a half later Larry called Linda's cell phone and told her to meet them in the parking lot by his car.

Dinner was what Linda expected. She initiated pleasant comments to both Larry and Cindy who responded politely. The majority of the conservation was between Diane and Cindy with occasional comments by Larry. Cindy kept telling Diane how much fun it will be for her in college and kept repeating how important it is to get the best, meaning easiest, professors. Linda thought Cindy's advice about college was a little odd since Cindy had never taken any college courses. Larry managed to comment that the hotel restaurant in San Francisco where he thought they were going to dine would have been so much better. The implication was that if Linda hadn't changed hotel reservations dinner would have been more enjoyable.

Linda knew what was coming but wasn't able to come up with a good defense. As she expected at the end of dinner Larry suggested that Diane stay with him and Cindy that night since they would be shopping in the San Francisco area the next day. The worst case scenario would mean there would be no need for Linda to spend the next day shopping with Diane and Cindy. She would, in essence, not be needed any longer and would be free to return home a day early. Linda didn't want to risk demanding that Diane stay with her that night because she feared Diane would not go along with her demand. That would make it very clear that Linda had lost any close relationship she may have with Diane. However, Linda was saved from that unpleasant situation by an unexpected source. Cindy spoke up and said because it was so late, it might be better if Diane stayed with Linda that night. Sunday after Linda left for home Diane would move into her own apartment. Larry would stay with her Sunday night in order to be ready to help her register for school the next day. He said he wouldn't mind sleeping on the sofa.

Saturday morning Cindy met Linda and Diane at a large shopping center about half way between her house and the hotel. The day passed quickly as all three women seemed to really enjoy shopping. This was the most time Linda had spent with Cindy and the first time she saw Cindy without Larry being present. Linda decided that Cindy wasn't so bad after all but would never make a good mother to Diane or anyone for that matter. Larry showed up late in the afternoon in time to take everyone to dinner.

Dinner was much more enjoyable than the night before. The three women discussed the days shopping experiences and how they could improve Diane's new apartment. Larry seemed happy that the three women were happy and decided he could handle a third glass of a Chilean Merlot red wine.

That night Linda and Diane had a very pleasant length discussion about what college life would be like. Diane seemed to finally realize that this was probably the last time she would be together with her mother until Thanksgiving. As she had done many times before, Diane promised she would study hard and not get pregnant. Linda repeated several times that Diane should call her at least a couple times a week and that she would be available to help out in any way Diane might need. Neither Linda nor Diane could imagine how much each would change over the next few months.

Earlier on Saturday a small crowd was in the stands to watch the intersquad football game. Brad was to play for the red team, which was made up of second stringers and members of the meat squad. The white team players were designated as the best players and were supposed to win by a large margin. Coach Kruger said the game was to be played under actual game conditions. That of course was not the case. Coaches served as referees and time keepers. Many penalties were not called against the white team and many phantom penalties were called against the red team. Two favorite penalties against the red team were offside and delay of game.

Several red team players including Brad were told to play positions they had never practiced. Even more bizarre instructions had Brad playing defense for both the red and the white team on punts and kickoffs. When playing linebacker Brad made several key tackles and covered his area well on passing plays. However, none of the coaches seemed to notice Brad's efforts. Most of their comments were criticisms of the white team players. The white team did win the game by a score of 21 to 14.

Sunday morning Linda, Diane, Larry and Cindy met for breakfast at the San Francisco airport. Larry made a point of telling Linda that they would have to get discuss some changes in the property settlement. After breakfast Linda went to catch her plane by herself and Diane left with Larry and Cindy.

By the time Linda got home she was in deep depression. She felt she had recently lost a husband and now she was losing her daughter. She could hardly wait to talk to Joan even though she didn't think that would make her feel any better. Linda didn't eat dinner that evening. She wondered if she would ever feel like eating again. Finally it was time to call Joan. Linda talked almost nonstop for the next fifteen minutes or more, detailing minute by minute the weekend events. Joan tried to console her by trying to change to a different subject.

"When do you register at State University?" asked Joan.

"This Tuesday, after that I still need to do some shopping for school clothes and supplies," said Linda.

"Well, I'm not doing anything this Wednesday. Would you like me to go along?" asked Joan.

"Yeah, that would be a good idea. The clothes we bought for Diane just don't seem right for me. I'm not sure I'd like to show up wearing shorts and a tank top with no bra," Linda commented.

"Hey, you'd look good. You have to start thinking and acting like a college girl now. Besides the shorts and tank tops, you definitely need to get lots of condoms as well as before and the after pills. My husband, Henry, goes to the gym Wednesday night. Maybe we can hang out at a bikers bar and practice chug-a-lugging beers." Joan laughed.

"Joan, do you know how long it's been since I drank a beer? I guess it would look a little out of place if I ordered a glass of cabernet sauvignon in one of those places," Linda said.

"Look, Linda, maybe we could pick up a couple of studs. It's always dark in bars, so no one would be able to see how old we are. Besides, after a couple of beers, the guys don't care anyway. I think it would help if we don't wear bras," Joan continued.

"Let's just go shopping Wednesday and worry about bar hopping later. I'll see you over here early that morning for coffee," Linda said before ending the conversation.

By now it was close to 10:00 p.m., so Linda called Diane's cell phone. After about four rings, Diane picked up the phone.

"Hi, Mom, I thought you'd be calling about now," Diane said as she answered the phone.

"I just called to see if you got moved in okay," said Linda.

"Yeah, Dad and Cindy helped me get everything set up. Dad is here now," said Diane.

The bland conservation continued for several minutes before Diane said she needed to get to bed because the next day would be busy for her.

Linda spent most of the next day fighting the urge to call Diane. She knew Diane would be busy registering, so she knew it would not be a good idea to call until at the earliest the afternoon. Maybe Diane would call her as she had promised, thought Linda.

A number of questions kept running through her head. Will Diane be all right the first night she will be spending alone in her new apartment? Will she be able to make some reputable friends? Will she study as promised?

Linda slowly realized how much time she had spent each day for the past eighteen years worrying about Diane. It was difficult enough keeping abreast of Diane's activities, but doing so without letting Diane know she was doing this made the task even more difficult. Diane had always wanted to be the center of attention with any group she was involved with. That made things difficult at home as Diane grew older since she wanted independence and didn't want nosy questions being asked. On the other hand she wanted people to pay attention to her and to listen closely to whatever she had to say.

The comments Joan made during their last phone call also kept running through Linda's mind. Joan has a good sense of humor, but perhaps she is serious about wanting to have an affair. The Belsons moved into their house about the same time as the Wallaces moved into theirs. The families became good friends. They joined the same social club, often went to shows together and dined together. Larry and Henry often played golf together until Larry filed for divorce. By that time Henry had worked his way up to the regional head of a large national accounting firm. When Larry and his divorce lawyer started talking about finances, Linda turned to Henry to help her make sure she was treated fairly. That meant that Larry and Henry were advisories, so they broke off their social relationships. The Belsons remained friends with Linda.

Joan Belson was about Linda's age and about her size but a little heaver. Like Linda, Joan had pretty much devoted her life to being a good wife and bringing up her daughter, Hannah. Linda had been telling Joan that the romantic attention she was getting from a number of men was beginning to make her think about getting involved with someone. Perhaps Joan was thinking this would be a good time to join in on the fun.

When practice started Monday Brad was relieved to find out that he would not be cut from the team even though he still didn't weigh anywhere close to 225 pounds. However, he wasn't sure he would make the traveling squad for the upcoming game against Newmar on the following Saturday. The morning practice was devoted entirely to reviewing film of the intersquad game. Almost all of the coach's comments were about the white team offense. Coach Kruger felt the white team should have scored many more points. The fact that the red team defense played well seemed to irritate him.

The team was given the next morning off so they could register for school.

Tuesday morning Brad decided to park in the school bookstore parking lot while he was registering for school. After he completed registering he would have to buy a lot of books and a laptop computer, so he didn't want to carry that load across the campus to the parking lot by the practice field.

As he was parking his attention was drawn to a beautiful lady getting out of a BMW. Great body Brad said to himself. He figured she was an instructor or staff member. The beautiful lady was Linda and she was on her way to register just like Brad.

As Brad walked to the registration area he noticed the way the other students were dressed. Most of the men were wearing baggy calf length shorts, tee shirts with names or numbers on them, and untied oversize tennis shoes. Anyone who had a ball cap was wearing it either backward or sideways. Most of the girls wore ragged overalls or shorts, sandals and sleeveless shirts. For some reason all the girls had lots of underwear showing. It seems like everyone had a back pack and almost everyone was either talking or texting on cell phones. Brad made a mental note to himself about getting some different clothes in order to blend in with the other students. At least most of his body was nearly the same color now, so he didn't have to worry about people staring at him. He didn't like the idea of having to wear a back pack again, but at least he wouldn't have to put on an armor vest like he wore in Iraq.

Students were instructed to line up in front of one of several booths according to the first letter of their last name. As Brad was walking toward the line for Ws, he was surprised to see that Linda was also heading that way. By coincidence, or maybe by fate, Brad got in line just behind her.

Linda wore a clean, wrinkle free dress and was actually wearing real shoes. The dress was the proper length; not mini skirted and not a granny dress. She didn't appear to have any tattoos and none of her underwear was showing. Instead of a backpack she had an expensive looking handbag.

"This is the W line isn't it?" asked Brad trying to start a conservation.

"Yes, it is. Are you a returning student?" Linda commented.

"No, I'm transferring in. I'm Brad Wilson and I haven't met many people here yet," Brad said, forgetting that his football team members were students.

"My name is Linda Wallace, and I'm transferring in also," Linda said.

"Well, it's nice to make your acquaintance," Brad said.

Brad and Linda continued small talk as they moved up in the line. They seemed to be comfortable talking to each other. Linda was surprised to hear herself mention that she was recently divorced. That didn't seem to register with Brad at the time, but he would certainly recall her comment at a later time.

"Hey, Brad, aren't you supposed to be at football practice?" said Tina Williams, who had just walked up beside him.

Brad recognized Tina as one of the girls that frequently waited by the practice field after football practice. They had exchanged comments on occasions, but Brad didn't know her name and wasn't sure how she knew him. Tina's shorts were low enough to expose the top of the thong she was wearing. When she bent forward or raised her arms up, the thong slid down so that the crack of her butt was exposed. Tina seemed to enjoy showing this to anyone in the area.

"We don't have practice this morning, so everyone can register. Are you all checked in?" asked Brad

"No, I just got here. I didn't know the line would be so fucking long. It's a good thing I saw you," Tina said.

"Well, you better get to the back of the line before it gets any longer," Brad said, realizing that Tina was trying to squeeze in the line ahead of him.

"Oh, you can let me in nobody will mind," said Tina

Brad didn't answer Tina but instead turned to Linda. "Do you know anything about this Environmental Auditing class we are required to take?"

"It is a core requirement for all majors. I figured I'd take it this semester to get it out of the way," said Linda.

Before Brad could answer, Tina called out as she sauntered away, "Fuck you, asshole."

"I've seen that girl waiting for someone outside the practice field, but I don't know her name. I guess she just wanted to get near the head of the line," Brad told Linda.

"Are you on the football team?" asked Linda.

"Yeah, well, at least I play some. I'm also going to register for the environmental class," said Brad not wanting to continue the discussion about being a football player.

"I hope there is still room for us. I understand the only open class meets Tuesdays and Thursdays from 9:00 to 11:00 a.m.," said Linda.

By this time it was Linda's turn to sit down with a school counselor to complete the registration process. A few minutes later Brad sat down with a different counselor. He had a little trouble explaining that the U. S. government would pay his tuition but was finally able to get the counselor to sigh off.

As soon as he finished Brad hurried off to the school bookstore. He quickly picked up all the text books he would need and went to look for laptop computers. He saw that Linda was just finishing making a selection. Brad noticed she has a small shopping cart, something he had not thought to use.

"I see you found the laptop required for the environmental class," said Brad as he walked up beside Linda.

"Yes, it looks like they have some left if you haven't got one yet," said Linda.

Brad put his books down on the counter while he waited for a salesperson to get a laptop for him. Noticing this Linda said he could put his books and laptop in her shopping cart until they got to the cashier.

After paying for their purchases, Brad and Linda stopped at the exit door.

"It looks like we'll have to carry our things outside," said Linda, noticing that carts were blocked from leaving the store.

It quickly became apparent that it would be difficult to carry all of their purchases to the parking area in one trip.

"If you can wait here for a couple of minutes while I put my stuff in my car, I can come back and help you carry your stuff to your car," said Brad.

"That would be nice, I'll wait for you right here," said Linda.

As Brad was putting his purchases away in his car he noticed that a car was blocking Linda's BMW. Linda had parked at the end of a closed row and another car had backed to the end of the row and was now blocking a couple of cars from being able to back out of the parking place. Remembering what Coach Kruger had said, Brad called the school security phone number he had been given and asked to have the car towed away. Almost immediately a security officer walked over to Brad from the next row where he had been patrolling.

"Are you the guy that called for a car to be towed?" asked the officer.

"Yeah, we need to get the BMW out," Brad said.

"You know the car driver is probably in the bookstore. Why don't you just go over there and have him paged?" asked the officer.

"I'm not going to do that. I don't want to wait for some half-wit to take his time shopping. Besides, once you get to the cash register, it takes another half an hour to pay for your purchases," Brad answered.

"By the time a tow truck gets here, the guy will probably have left already," the officer said.

The officer's comments reminded Brad of circle talk used by Iraqis when they didn't want to do what was requested. By continually coming up with reasons or excuses for not doing something they eventually begin to either repeat or contradict themselves. Brad didn't have the patients to continue along this line.

"I'm making a proper request as I have been instructed to do if some idiot causes a problem. Get the damn tow truck over here now, or I'll file a formal complaint with the Security Department and the Athletic Department," Brad said in an unmistakably authoritative tone.

The officer then called for a tow truck and asked Brad if he was one of those football guys. Brad said he was and if Kruger hadn't ordered the players to use security he would have waited for the driver and then knocked his teeth out.

Brad then went back to the bookstore to get Linda.

"I'm sorry it took so long, but someone was blocking your car, so I had to call security," Brad told Linda.

When they got to Linda's car the tow truck, the car driver and his friend were all there along with the security officer. The car driver was a little shorter but a little heavier than Brad. He looked like he was about twenty years old. His friend was about the same age but shorter and even heavier. Both of them were wearing the standard uniform for kids of their age.

The driver was telling the officer it wasn't necessary to have the car towed since he was now going to drive away.

"Once a tow truck has been requested and has arrived I cannot cancel the tow," said the officer.

"Well, that's kind of stupid. How the fuck am I supposed to get my car back?" asked the driver.

"The car will be towed to the security lot at the north end of the campus. Once you show that you are the registered owner, pay a $50 towing fee and a $10 fine the car will be released to you," said the officer.

"I don't have sixty fucking dollars and the car is registered to my dad," said the driver.

"Well, you better call your dad then because you will not be able to retrieve the car," said the officer.

"Oh shit, that's not fair. I'm here now and can move the car myself. Who the fuck asked for the car to be towed?" said the driver.

"I did and I'd do it again if you or some other dumb ass blocks my car from moving. Unless you're a complete idiot you must have known you were blocking two cars. Or maybe you thought you could bully anyone who asked you to move your car like you are trying to do now," said Brad, not waiting to be pointed out by the officer.

"Fuck you, asshole," said the driver as he shaded his eyes with his hand to look at Brad.

"If you had any brains you would screw your hat around so the brim blocks the sun. That way you wouldn't have to keep holding your hand above your eyes. Of course, you wouldn't look nearly so quite. Certainly your mom must have taught you that, or do you even know who your mom is?" said Brad.

As Brad was talking he noticed the driver's friend who was behind the officer give him the finger.

"You better watch the chubby stooge over there. It looks like he's getting his finger ready to pick his nose. The way he's wearing his hat looks really darling, but he wouldn't look so good with his finger up his nose," Brad said to the driver.

"You better fucking hope I never see you without an officer to protect you," the driver shouted to Brad.

"About 6:30 p.m. this evening I'll be coming out of the field house. If you want to continue to talk to me, be there. If you don't show up, the stooge here will have to tell all your buddies you can't back up your big talk," answered Brad.

The tow truck was about to leave, so the driver and the stooge started to get in the truck.

"Fuck you, asshole," they both said as the tow truck drove away.

"Sorry for the inconvenience," Brad told Linda.

"I hope you don't get into any trouble because of me. Do you think those guys will show up tonight?" asked Linda.

"No, they were only trash-talking. Those kind of guys never try to back up their tough talk," said Brad.

With that Linda got in her car and left. As she was driving away, she wondered what Larry would have done in that situation other than threatening to sue the driver. She could hardly wait to talk to Joan and tell her she found the perfect boyfriend for Diane, so she called to suggest they meet for lunch somewhere. Joan said she had to stay home to babysit

Hannah, who was grounded for the day, so they would have to eat at her house. This meant Hannah would have lunch with Linda and Joan. For some strange reason, Linda didn't want to talk about Brad at lunch in front of Hannah.

Joan was anxious to hear what Linda had to say about the day's activities. Hannah asked a lot of questions about the students and the campus. This seemed a little odd since Hannah has made it clear that although she will be going to college after high school, she will definitely not be going to State University.

Linda mentioned that she signed up for only two classes: *Library Science II* and *Environmental Auditing.* The classes meet Tuesday and Thursday mornings, so she will only have to be on campus two days a week. She said she met some guy who would be in one of her classes. Later she mentioned some guy helped her carry her books and computer to her car. She also mentioned that someone had blocked her car in the parking lot and some guy helped her get the car towed away. Linda was careful to remind Hannah to keep her secret about going back to college. Fortunately Hannah and Diane were not that close, so the secret should be safe from Diane, at least for a while.

After lunch Linda said she would help clean the dishes, so Hannah could go back to her room to listen to her iPod, text on her cell phone, or google on her computer. As soon as they were alone, Joan asked Linda who "some guy" was that she mentioned three times.

"Oh, was it that obvious that I was talking about the same person all three times?" asked Linda.

"Yes, it was, which means that within an hour of going back to school, you've already found a boyfriend," said Joan.

"No, it's not what you think. I just talked to someone that would make the right kind of boyfriend for Diane. If things go right, maybe he can meet her this Thanksgiving when she comes home," said Linda.

"So, tell me about this right kind of some guy," said Joan.

"Well, I think his name is Brad, he's kind of big at least he is a little bigger than Larry. He is on the football team and here is the best thing. All during our conservations he never, not even once, used the F word," said Linda.

"You mean he never said fuck? Listen Linda, even Hannah uses that word in every other sentence. It is like saying you know every four of five words. Every college student says fuck at least once every sentence and jocks usually say it at least twice every sentence. By the way can he speak in complete sentences and has he shown you his tattoo yet?" asked Joan.

"Of course he can speak in complete sentences, at least most of the time." Linda laughed, trying to keep the conservation from becoming too serious.

Linda continued to talk about Brad. She mentioned how he would not let Tina in line, how he offered to help her carry her books and computer to her car, how he got security to tow the car blocking her car and how he stood up to the car driver and driver's friend.

Joan commented what Linda had thought earlier, that if Larry had confronted the driver of the car blocking Linda's he no doubt would have simply threatened to sue the guy.

"Look, Linda, let's forget about Diane. Just give him my phone number and tell him to call me when Henry is not at home," Joan said in jest.

Linda confided in Joan that she was a little uncomfortable being around kids Diane's age. She wasn't able to open conservation with any of the girls because they were either talking to a friend or talking on a cell phone. Like all women she was convinced she wasn't dressed right and would have to get some different clothes before class started.

After Linda left the parking area Brad had some time left before practice. Since it was a little late for the team lunch, he headed to the campus cafeteria. The food line in the team lunch room would be a mess and the room would smell of fresh farts. Besides, Line Coach Jumbo Harrison would still be there. He was always the first one at lunch and dinner and the last to leave. Harrison was in charge of collecting $2 per meal from nonscholarship players. Brad suspected Jumbo keep most of the money or maybe split it with the other coaches, including Kruger.

During practice sessions Wednesday afternoon Brad did draw the attention of Coach Kruger. Unfortunately it was not the way Brad wanted. The offense was running plays against the defense in noncontact drills. On each play the linemen were supposed to hold their position and more or less push against each other. The defense was supposed to wait for the play to come to them and then tag the ball carrier as he went by. That is what Brad did on a particular play, which drew the following comment from Coach Curtis.

"What kind of a love tap was that, Wilson? Next time a player comes at you let him know you are there," yelled Curtis.

A couple of plays later a similar play developed only this time Brad gave the ball carrier a push hard enough to knock him off his feet.

"What in the hell do you think you're doing idiot? You, come over here!" Coach Kruger yelled as he pointed at Brad.

It may not be against NCAA rules, but school policy says that no derogatory comments of any kind may be made against any player. Apparently idiot was not considered derogatory.

Kruger continued, "Didn't you hear that this is noncontact? Stupid acts like that cause injuries. Make another mistake like that and you're off the team."

Brad got the feeling that Kruger was going to stay mad at him for the rest of the season and that actually turned out to be the case.

Wednesday Linda and Joan did go shopping. They did not wear shorts and tank tops, but they did wear bras. Linda bought some less conservative clothes than she normally would wear but did not bother with the condoms. After shopping they did stop for drinks at the club and had wine coolers.

Thursday afternoon Linda's mother, Ethel Dowling called. When she answered the phone Linda realized she hadn't talked to her parents for almost two weeks. She was as bad about calling them as Diane was about calling her.

After apologizing for not calling her mom, Linda went over all of the activities for the last two weeks. The next several minutes were spent repeating almost word for word past conservations. Linda and her mother told each other how they were feeling, what the local weather was like and that they were both exercising enough and taking vitamins.

She purposely did not mention her plan to start college the following week. Finally they got around to the same subject Larry needed to talk to Linda about, the divorce property settlement.

It seems that Linda and Larry each were given 50 percent of the house Linda was living in and 50 percent of Larry's new law practice. Linda would maintain the house using alimony money and Larry would foot all of the business expenses. Linda would get 10 percent of any annual business profit above $1,000,000.

Ever since Linda's father, Ralph Dowling, had retired from work her parents had been planning on moving away from the winter cold of Illinois to a warmer climate. When the parents learned the details of Linda divorce Ralph talked to Larry about swapping interest in the business and house even up without any cash or boot going to either party. The Dowlings could then move in with Linda and Diane before finding a place of their own. Ralph had talked to Larry before consulting Linda. Larry was all for doing just that.

When Linda found out what was being planned she wasn't sure she wanted that to happen for many reasons. One reason was that she didn't relish the idea of living with her parents again. She was beginning to enjoy being able to make decisions herself without having to get approval from anyone else. Another reason was that Diane would most certainly move in with Larry and Cindy rather than share the house with the Dowling grandparents.

The most important reason the plan was not acceptable to Linda, however, was a financial one. At the time of the divorce Larry's lawyer suggested that Linda get the house and Larry get his law practice. In addition Larry was to receive one-half of the excess value of the house over the law practice

Fortunately Henry Belson spoke up for Linda. He pointed out that within a few years the value of the business would certainly be greater that the house value. Henry also pointed out the business might currently be worth more now if questionable and creative accounting practices were not being used to inflate business debts and at the same time undervalue projected profits from open legal cases. Because of this Henry had negotiated for the potential profit for Linda as an incentive for Larry to swap his share of the house for Linda's share of his business when it was agreed that the value of the house and business were equal.

After Linda pointing this out to her father, he then suggest that he just buy out Larry's share of the house and that Linda keep 50 percent of the business. Because of the clause for Linda to potentially receive part of the business profit, Larry didn't like that proposal. However, he was now interested in swapping business for house interest without any boot to either party. Linda was still uncertain if this is what she really wanted to do.

The phone discussion with her mother ended with Linda saying she and Larry would be discussing the latest proposal soon and that Linda would let them know if any agreement were reached.

During the next several days Linda kept busy getting ready for college and worrying about Diane. Linda tried not to keep score, but she knew she called Diane seven times in five days and Diane called her only twice.

Also on Thursday the traveling squad list for the football team was posted. Brad made the list, twice. His name was shown as a special team member and as a defensive player. This caused quite a bit of confusion Friday morning when the team assembled to take a bus to the airport.

"Coach, we have a problem. We are supposed to have forty-four players, but I counted only forty-three," Coach Stewart said to Coach Kruger.

"Well, find out who is missing and hurry up," said Kruger as he got on the bus.

"Everybody quiet down and listen up. I've got to call roll because some idiot that is supposed to be here isn't!" yelled Stewart.

Stewart then proceeded to call out the names of the offensive, defensive and special team players.

"Coach, you called my name with the defense already," Brad said when his name was called the second time as a special teams player.

"Are you here or not?" asked Stewart, apparently not understanding what Brad had said.

"I'm here," Brad answered, wondering what Stewart would do if he said he was not there.

"Ah jeese, I sill count only forty-three players. Which one of you idiots answered that's not here!" screamed Stewart.

At that time Coach Curtis, realizing what the problem was, grabbed Stewart by the arm and said he just recounted and all forty-four players were now present. With that, everyone got on the bus and headed to the airport.

Friday afternoon the football team arrived early enough to make a walkover of the Newmar football field. They then checked into a hotel for the evening. Brad and Warren West shared a room. Warren did make the traveling squad and he was actually going to get to play in the game. Brad thought Warren performed well in practice and wondered why he didn't get into a game last year. That would become clear the next day during the game.

CHAPTER 3

Saturday the football game started with State University kicking off to Newmar. As a member of the suicide squad Brad ran down the field as fast as he could only to be knocked off his feet by a giant wearing number 72. As he picked himself up Brad was thinking that was almost as bad as some of the concussions from IEDs he'd been hit by in Iraq. For the next several minutes he sat on the bench as Newmar proceeded to methodically march down the field and score a touchdown. Brad and the other members of the suicide squad took the field again this time to receive the kickoff. Brad looked at Newmar players hoping to see number 72 so he could give him a little payback. Unfortunately that player was not in the area Brad was assigned to defend, so he picked out someone else to upend as the kick was being returned.

At the half Newmar was ahead by a score of 21 to 10. Brad had only played on special teams, and Warren West had not played at all. Warren did finally get in the game around the middle of the third quarter for nickel back defense situations. Warren played a cornerback position and did well when Newmar was in passing positions. Late in the third quarter Mokie Anton limped off the field and Brad replaced him as a weak side linebacker. Warren West continued to play corner playing behind Brad.

By the middle of the fourth quarter after State had scored another touchdown Newmar was driving to get into scoring position. Brad and the other defensive players had pretty much held Newmar in check until they started the current drive. A critical third down was coming up for Newmar. They needed eight yards for a first down, so they were expected to try a passing play. State felt that if they could stop Newmar from getting a first down they would have a chance to score once again and win the game.

When the play started Brad saw Warren flash by him on a surprise blitz. It was a surprise not just to Newmar but to State as well since that had not been called by the defense. On this play Brad was supposed to delay to make sure no Newmar receiver was crossing over into his area. If the play was a run he had to move up to attack the ball carrier. Finally he could rush the passer if no receivers or ball carriers were headed his way. Warren had the responsibility for covering the wide receiver and anyone else coming into his area behind Brad. Of course, when Warren decided on his own to be a hero he left his area unprotected. Knowing this Brad, after checking for receivers or runners coming into his area, ran back into Warren's area trying to catch up with Newmar's wide receiver that was now in the open. Newmar's quarterback saw the open man and heaved a pass toward him just before Warren flattened him. Fortunately the pass was a little short, which allowed Brad and Lightning Joe Resnick the free safety to run the receiver out of bounds after he had made the catch for about a twenty-five-yard gain. Lightning Joe was able to get to receiver only because he was very fast: the fastest player on the team. Because of his speed he was not able to stop before the receiver stepped out of bounds. Lightning was not only fast, he was a good football player and knew better than to run into the receiver and have a penalty tacked onto the gain, so instead; he wiped out a sideline cameraman. Brad then hit the ground beside Lightning Joe and the cameraman. However, at the end of the play Newmar was in position for a field goal, which iced the game for them.

Warren was immediately invited to the sideline by coaches Curtis and Kruger, who looked like they were doing an Irish jig. Time-out was called mainly in order to allow Curtis and Kruger to, among other things, tell Warren he was an idiot. This type of spontaneous action by Warren last year in practice kept him out of most games. This year he had promised the coaching staff that he would control his urge to win games single-handedly.

The plane ride back home was not a happy one for the team. Warren who sat next to Brad still didn't seem to feel he had made a mistake.

"You know, Brad, if I had been just a fraction of a second quicker, I know I'd have caused a fumble," Warren said to Brad.

"You are right, Warren, and if your mother had not met your father, you would be somebody else," answered Brad.

This kept Warren quiet for the remainder of the flight as he thought about Brad's comment.

Sunday afternoon was spent reviewing the Newmar game film. Warren's spectacular play was shown many times with many comments from the coaches about how something like this will never happen again. Brad was surprised to hear Coach Kruger yell out at him several times that it was his responsibility to cover the wide receiver and not to just follow him down the field. Kruger also said that play probably cost State the game. Mokie took this opportunity to comment that he had fully recovered from his injury and would be ready to start the game this Saturday. This was an obvious attempt to indicate that if he would have been in the game when Warren made his unsuccessful blitz, Mokie would have been able to cover the receiver and prevent the catch.

There was no practice for Brad Monday because it was Labor Day.

Tuesday morning Brad stopped by the practice field for some weight room exercises. At noon he decided to eat at a nearby fast-food place that was opened and be ready for the new practice schedule at 3:00 p.m. When he got to the restaurant he saw Warren West.

"Hey, Brad, want to join me over here?" Warren said as he waved toward an empty seat at his table.

"Yeah, what are you doing here?" answered Brad.

"I was going to stop by the weight room but decided to stop here first," said Warren.

Warren went on tell Brad about the classes he would be taking this semester. He said he had completed all of his major and core requirements and just need about eight units this semester of fill in studies besides the six units for being on the football team. He was taking *Emancipated Women Studies* and *Self-Nurturing*. His last semester he was planning on taking *Yoga and Relaxation* as well as *Protecting Our Animal Friends*.

"Wow, Warren, those classes really sound exciting and really practical," said Brad sarcastically.

"Yeah, well, Zeke Solum took the women studies class last year and by then the end of the semester he had screwed every girl in class and could have stuck it to the lady instructor if she wouldn't have been so old. It seems the class is about telling girls they should take control of their lives and do whatever they want and not what some man wants them to do. That is really a laugh. All the girls should have flunked the class because they all did what Zeke wanted them to do. Of course they all thought it was their idea, not Zeke's, to get laid," said Warren.

What Warren said may be true in part, but Zeke Solum was probably successful because the girls did what they wanted to do—get laid by the star quarterback. Warren will be in for a big disappointment, thought Brad.

"How were you able to sign up for the women's study class? I thought that would be restricted to women only," said Brad.

"Some smart-ass lawyer threatened to sue to get into the class, saying it was in the U.S. Constitution that men couldn't be barred from women's study classes," answered Warren.

"Damn, those lawyers are really smart. I've read the Constitution but have always missed the part about men being able to go to women's college classes," said Brad.

"Hey, Brad, I just stopped by the locker room and saw Coach Kruger. He wants to see you in his office before practice today," said Lightning Joe who had just sat down at the table with Brad and Warren.

"Do you know what that's all about? I hope he doesn't want to tell me again that I should have covered for the superstar here when he made his failed blitz," said Brad.

"No, I think he wants you to pay for the $800 camera that you broke when you ran over the cameraman. It seems the guy sent a bill to the Athletic Department," Lightning Joe said.

"Why does he think I should pay for the camera? All of us are covered by the school insurance for things like that. Besides you're the one who ran into the guy. Did you tell him that?" Brad asked.

"Well, Kruger thinks it was you and you know how he is when he makes up his mind. He never listens to anyone else. You do know that he has picked you to be the team scapegoat, don't you? He even believed the superstar's story about telling you he was going to blitz and that you should cover for him," said Lightning Joe.

"Why the hell did you tell him that?" Brad asked Warren.

"Well, I had to say something, He was about to kick me off the fucking team. I knew you would be safe, so I said that to save my ass," answered Warren.

That pretty much spells out the character of my teammates, thought Brad. No one in his army squad or platoon would have thought of blaming someone else for any mistake they may have made. Apparently Warren and Lightning were no different from most college students, however. All their lives they have been subject to motion pictures, TV stories, comedian jokes and even instructor actions, which glorify cheating, lying and making fun of others. Neither of them seemed in the least ashamed for falsely pointing blame for their actions to Brad.

After finishing lunch, Brad hurried over the see Coach Kruger. On the way he was wondering how he should react to Kruger's acquisitions. Apparently it would not do any good to deny anything. Kruger probably wouldn't believe him and it would make him look like a wimp. He didn't really think Kruger would ask him to pay for the camera, but if he did, Brad could give Kruger a government requisition to be filled out in triplicate and then sent to the U.S. Defense Department for payment. Instead of that Brad thought he should just claim an equally absurd injury to his feelings due to the incident and ask for lots of money to feel better.

Brad was intercepted by Coach Curtis as soon as he entered the locker room.

"Brad, I understand Kruger wants to talk to you about not covering for Warren and about running into a cameraman in the Newmar game," Curtis said.

"Yeah, that's what I've been told," said Brad.

Curtis explained that he had talked to both Warren West and Lightning Joe Resnick. He knew that Warren never said anything to Brad about his intended blitz and the films clearly indicated that Lightning had run into the cameraman. However, he suggested the best action for Brad was to listen to Kruger and not say anything. If he tried to correct Kruger the coach would probably go crazy since he never wanted anyone to correct him even when he was plainly wrong. Curtis continued saying Kruger may be an offensive genius but that he doesn't care diddle shit about defense. Since Curtis was the defensive coordinator in addition to being linebacker coach, he had the last say about defensive players and would not allow Brad to be kicked off the team.

Just as expected Kruger went into a tantrum when Brad got to his office. He talked for about ten minutes explaining that running into anyone out of bounds was stupid and avoidable. He went on to comment that things like that could jeopardize State getting off NCAA sanctions. Fortunately nothing was mentioned about who was to pay for the broken camera. As Kruger was yelling at him Brad remembered some of the players talking about somebody called mad dog. Brad immediately figured out the players were talking about Kruger.

Practice went pretty well that afternoon. Brad got to practice some with the first team defense and by now was an official member of the special teams. Warren West spent most of the practice watching from the side lines. Mokie Anton was especially active during practice trying to make it known that the weak side linebacker position was his and no one was good enough to take his place unless he was injured. The team seemed almost ready for the West Wyoming game coming up Saturday, which was an away game for State.

Wednesday was the first day of classes for Brad. He signed up for *Managerial Accounting* from 8:00 to 10:00 a.m. and *Working with the Media* from 10:00 a.m. to noon on Mondays and Wednesdays. About twenty men and five women showed up for the accounting class. Brad noticed that everyone dressed better than the students he saw at registration. None of the women had underwear showing, which was nice; however, Brad thought most of them looked a lot like men. He had been hoping to meet a Kandi Kolinsky–type girl in one of his classes, but that wouldn't happen in accounting.

The media class was balanced the other way in favor of women: fifteen women and seven men. Brad noticed several women that he felt could compete with Kandi. Maybe he could get something going with one of them. He hadn't had much of an opportunity to meet any women since leaving Las Vegas. A few nights he had spent drinking a few beers with a couple of the older players, but he seemed to enjoy being alone most evenings. The class let out shortly after 11:00 a.m., giving Brad time to get to the lunch early.

As he left class, he noticed Zeke Solum, who also had signed up for the media class. They walked to the gym, where the training lunch table has been set up. Brad didn't know Zeke very well since Zeke spent most of the practice time with Kruger and other offensive coaches. However, Brad was surprised that Zeke seemed to know quite a bit about him.

During the conservation Brad learned that Zeke was studying to be either a coach or a sports journalist. The media class fit into his major. He also found out Zeke was in his fourth year but was in fact a junior classman as far as his school year was concerned.

"I heard Kruger had a talk with you yesterday," Zeke said to Brad.

"Yeah, he thinks I knew Warren was going to blitz and should have covered for him. He also thinks I ran into the cameraman and broke a camera," answered Brad.

"Well, we all know Warren has problems with his mind and that Lightning ran into the cameraman. So don't let that bother you. Kruger is okay when you get to know him," Zeke said.

Zeke went on to give Brad a little history of Kruger and State football. It seems Kruger came to State in 1997 and by 2002 had built a very powerful football team. That year they won eleven games. Their only loss was to a division one team by three points. They went to a bowl game, the first time for State. Zeke was recruited by Kruger and promised he would get a good opportunity to compete for the starting quarterback position for the 2003 season. Then before the start of the season, things started to unravel. Five players including the returning quarterback were dropped from the team for drug use. Two more players quit the team before the first game. Despite that State won four of the first five games with Zeke playing in all five games. Then the NCAA investigators slapped some restrictions on State, which meant no bowl game that year among other things. In a desperate attempt to keep more players from leaving, Kruger did what many other coaches do; he arranged for some under the table money to be given to several players and helped arrange for special tutoring for some other players. The investigation uncovered this and forced four more players off the team. State lost the remaining seven games that year and the eight games they were allowed to play in 2004. This means Kruger's future as a coach is shattered. He was ready to sign a big dollar contract with a division one school, but that is gone now. He will probably lose his job at State at the end of the year if State doesn't win at least one game. No school would hire a coach that has lost eighteen games in a row.

Zeke then asked Brad, "What did you do in the army?"

"I was just an infantry guy like most other soldiers," said Brad.

Brad wondered how Zeke knew he had been in the army since Brad had not mentioned it to any of the players. *One of the coaches must have mentioned it when Zeke was in the coaches office*, thought Brad.

"So Zeke, Warren said you took the emancipated women's class last semester. Was that a lot of fun?' Brad asked wishing to change the subject.

"No, that was a big mistake. My counselor said I needed to know more about what women think and want now days. He said that would help me better relate to them as a coach or sports writer," answered Zeke.

"Yeah, but Warren said you screwed all the girls in class and could have made the instructor," Brad said.

"That's not exactly true. I did get together with a couple of the girls, but most of them were dogs. Actually that's not right either. They were all very nice, but they just weren't meant to be movie stars. The lady teaching the class would have been great except I don't think I could have gotten anywhere with her. I'm sure she knew she could have had me, but she apparently wasn't interested. I don't think the instructor liked me being the only man in the class because I probably intimidated some of the women and kept them from speaking freely about their feelings. As I said, taking the class was a mistake. I should have known better," Zeke said.

When they got to the lunch room, Zeke said he had to sit with coaches to go over the plays for this Saturday's game.

The next day, Thursday, was Linda's first day of classes. She arrived at school a little early so she could find where her *Library Science II* class would be taught. She was careful to park in a row that had access at both ends so that she wouldn't get blocked in again. She was early enough to get a cup of coffee in the school cafeteria before class and was surprised to realize that she was hoping to run into Brad there.

There were about twenty women and about ten men taking the library class when class started. The instructor spent the first hour of the two-hour class talking about what they would be studying and what was required to get an A for the class. From what Linda heard the class appeared to be an exact repeat of the *Library Science I* class she took twenty years earlier. The class was given an assignment and then was let out early.

Linda's next class was the environment class that wouldn't start until 10:00 a.m. She went back to the cafeteria hoping to see anyone she might recognize from the library class or maybe she would run into Brad. Unfortunately Linda didn't see anyone she might know. She felt a little self-conscious since she seemed to be the only one sitting at table by herself. Besides that she knew she looked a lot older than any of the other girls. She pulled out one of the library text books and stared at it pretending that she was reading. So far school was not what she had envisioned. She couldn't help thinking she had made a bad mistake in starting back to school. Finally it was about time to go to the environmental class.

Linda picked a seat just inside the front door to the classroom. As soon as she sat down she realized she was in the front row. As the room started to fill up Linda felt more and more uncomfortable. Most of the students were coming in a second door toward the back of the room and everyone was sitting behind her. She fought the urge to turn around to see if Brad had shown up. Instead she continued to look straight ahead hoping the class would start soon. Suddenly she became aware that someone had sat down beside her after coming from the opposite end of her row. This is a chance to finally meet someone, thought Linda as she turned her head to introduce herself to the person sitting next to her.

"Hi, Linda, I almost didn't see you sitting up front here," said Brad as he was adjusting his seat next to Linda.

"Hi, Brad. Boy, am I really glad to see you. I haven't met any other students yet, and I feel lost without anyone to talk to," Linda blurted out.

She immediately felt a little silly making such an emotional and telling comment to someone she hardly knew. Brad didn't seem to notice any extra feeling voiced by Linda. However, he did notice that Linda smelled good. She had a faint clean smell, which Brad really appreciated after being in Iraq where nothing smelled good.

Just then the instructor called the class to order. He introduced himself as Dr. Scott Watson, but said it was okay to call him Scott. He then spent the next half an hour explaining the purpose of the class and what would be expected of the students. He pointed out that the class was a requirement and that no student could graduate without passing this course. He said protecting and improving the environment was the most important activity humans can undertake.

Scott then told the class teams of four students each would be formed and then each team would be assigned an environmental audit project. Each team would be required to research a large corporation or business organization. The team was to audit the environmental or lack of environmental practices of that company. A report would then be prepared and discussed with top management spelling out perceived strengths and weakness of the company's environmental practices. Final grades would be based upon the team report content and feedback that Scott would receive directly from the companies audited. Scott said he had a lengthy list of companies willing to participate in the audit. The class had been purposely limited to thirty-two students so eight teams of four students each could be formed. Teams would be assigned one of four programs to audit. This meant that two different teams would be assigned the same program and they would therefore be in competition with each other for the best grade. The company programs to be audited are:

- Adherence to Company Environmental Policies
- Company Environmental Training Practice
- Company Waste Avoidance Practice
- Renewable Energy Source Usage

Scott then gave the following assignments:

- Before leaving today the students need to form themselves into eight groups of four students each.
- Then each team should meet outside of class sometime before next Tuesday to decide which audit program they would like to select for their project.
- At next Tuesday's class, a team spokesman needs to give an oral report to Scott and the class explaining their audit choice and what they feel the audit will accomplish. If more than two teams wanted to audit the same practices, the best presentations would get their choice, and the other team or teams would be assigned a different practice.

"Okay, finish the first assignment here and then class will be over for your team," said Scott.

Suddenly it seems like everyone in the room started talking and walking about in an effort to form teams. Some teams formed quickly leaving several individuals wandering around looking for someone to join up with.

"Let see if we can find a couple of bright people to join with us," Brad said to Linda, assuming that they would be on the same team.

"I'm afraid we will just have to wait for whoever is left. No one seems interested in us," said Linda.

That is actually what happened. Within a few minutes six teams had been formed. One group of six students were trying to decide which four would make a team and which two would have to find another team, which, of course, would be with Brad and Linda.

After several minutes two students from the group of six came over to where Brad and Linda were standing.

"Would you like to join us?" said Kathy Dougan.

"Yeah, we need two more team members. I'm Brad Wilson, and this is Linda Wallace," said Brad, making it clear that he and Linda were going to be in charge of the team.

Brad then asked the names of the new team members.

"I'm Jason Olson. I've got notes from a friend that took this class last year. This class is going to be a piece of cake," said Jason.

"Hi, I'm Kathy Dougan," said Kathy.

Jason and Kathy both looked like they were about twenty years old. They were both dressed casually in oversize clothes. Brad noticed that Jason and Kathy appeared to be boyfriend/girlfriend. Despite that, he thought Kathy looked pretty good. Even if her feet were dirty, her toe nails were nicely painted. Neither of them seemed to be very happy to be teamed up with Brad and Linda. Brad thought being on the same team with Kathy may lead to something.

It took almost half an hour to reach agreement on where and when to meet to discuss the assignment. Brad had to reveal that he couldn't meet on Saturday because he was on the football team and had a game to play that day. It took some fast talking to explain to Jason and Kathy why it would not be a good idea to meet in a pizza shop. Finally, Linda offered to host the meeting at her house on Sunday. Everyone agreed this would be okay after Linda said she would fix brunch for the team. It would be a late brunch since for a number of reasons the meeting was scheduled at 3:00 p.m. The meeting would not be like anyone expected.

As the group was preparing to leave Linda felt a warm hand on her shoulder. She turned to face Scott who had walked up behind her.

"Don't worry about the class, I'm sure you will do well," said Scott with a big grin on his face.

This took Linda by surprise. She wasn't sure how to react. She didn't want to believe the instructor was making a pass at her on the first day of class, but that is what it appeared to be. Within a few days she would know for sure what Scott's intentions were.

"Well. I hope so. It sounds like this is going to be an interesting class," Linda finally responded.

"I'm sure you'll find it very interesting," Scott said as he walked away.

Linda was glad to see that none of the other team seemed to notice the special attention Scott had just given her. Maybe she was over reacting to an innocent comment.

A few minutes later Linda backed her car out of the parking lot without any trouble and headed home. She was feeling quite a bit better than earlier in the day. In the afternoon she intended to complete her assignment for the library class. Friday she intended to spend all day thinking about the environmental assignment.

Around 8:30 p.m. Linda called Joan to tell her about the day's activity. It took Linda about fifteen minutes to explain the environmental assignment. Then she described the unusual comments by Scott. Joan thought it was great that the instructor might be interested in Linda.

"You should take advantage of a good opportunity to skate through the class. Of course it means you would probably have to sleep with him three or four times a week," said Joan.

"I could do that except for all the other guys that are lined up in front of my door every night," Linda said, going along with the humor.

Just before 11:00 p.m. Diane called. Linda and Diane had reached an agreement that Diane would call at least three nights a week before she went to bed and more often if anything unusual happened. That way Linda's wouldn't interrupt Diane's activities with her phone calls. It also meant Linda would know about what time Diane would be going to bed. Of course that assumed Diane would go to bed after calling home as promised. This was Diane's second call for that week.

Their conservation was cordial and low keyed, not the typical mother/daughter happy exchange of information. Linda kept thinking of ways to tell Diane about Brad, but she couldn't think of a way to explain how she met Brad and how she got to know him well enough to talk about him. Diane didn't want to talk about school, which seemed to indicate that she was not happy there. She did talk about being with Larry and Cindy on both of the last weekends and how Cindy often visited her during the week.

As she had with almost every phone call, Diane asked Linda to send her some more personal effects. Linda resisted the urge to scream at Diane. She wouldn't have to continue sending her things if they had packed everything Diane is now asking for in a car she had driven to Stanford. Instead Linda asked if Diane would like her to come up there for a visit. Diane said it wasn't necessary since she was getting along well enough. The phone call lasted only about ten minutes and ended with Linda reminding

Diane how much she was looking forward to Thanksgiving when Diane would come home.

Thursday's football practice was pretty routine for Brad. The team ran a series of plays for Saturday's game in light contact drills. Because the opponent, West Wyoming, featured a strong running attach, State would use four linebackers most of the time. This meant Brad would have more playing time than he had in the first game.

Coach Curtis caught Brad as he came to practice Thursday afternoon and asked him to speak with him in his office. Brad wondered if he was going to be kicked off the team for some reason.

"Brad, do you want to earn some extra money?" Curtis asked Brad.

"Yeah, if it's legal," answered Brad.

Curtis then went on to explain that a regional manager of a nationwide shipping company offered part time work for football players. The manager was a State graduate and former football player. The NCAA was aware of this practice and had indicated it is not a violation of their rules. The job involved manual labor loading and unloading boxes at the airport. The pay was union scale, so a shift was worth almost $100 after taxes. The bad part was that the shifts available to football players were from 7:00 p.m. to 3:00 a.m. Sunday and Monday. Another player worked the Sunday night shift. This meant the open shift was from Monday night to Tuesday morning.

"How come the shift is open?" asked Brad.

"Tommy Foster said he has to concentrate on his studies and needs that time for studying," answered Curtis.

"Yeah, it sounds good to me. What are the job requirements?" Brad asked.

"You need to be able to read," answered Curtis.

"I'm okay so far," Brad said with a smile.

"I mean you have to be able to read big words like Baltimore and Chattanooga," said Curtis.

"I can handle that," Brad responded.

"Can you spell Chattanooga?" asked Curtis.

"No, but I can recognize it when I see it," Brad answered, paraphrasing something he had read a U.S. Supreme Court judge had said in another context.

"I'll set up an interview for you this evening. You should get together with that Matt Lister who works the Sunday shift. Matt will take you over to meet the shipping company regional manager, Gregory Alexander," said Curtis.

After practice Brad and Matt got together at the training dinner table. Matt said the interview was for 8:00 p.m., so they had time for a couple beers after dinner. Matt suggested they stop at Tony's Pizza parlor where a lot of students hung out. When they got there the place was already crowded and it looked like they may either wait for a table or stand at the bar. Matt had a better idea.

"Hey, good-looking, how about seating us with those two girls who just sat down?" Matt asked the hostess who he happened to know quite well.

"We can give it a try, but if they have any brains, they'll ask you to sit somewhere else," answered the hostess.

Matt's plan worked. The girls may not have wanted Brad and Matt to share their table, but they probably didn't know they could say no. Matt tried another ploy to make the girls feel a little more comfortable.

"Thanks for letting us share the table. We'll buy the beer," Matt said.

The girls said that would be nice even though neither one of them looked like they were old enough to drink. They did appear to be students, however, and probably were more interested in meeting a couple of guys than they were in eating pizza.

"So, you girls look like seniors," said Brad, trying to make the girls feel grown up.

That seemed to break the ice, and soon after the beer arrived, the four of them were talking like old friends. The girls admitted that they were only sophomores but maintained that they drank beer all the time. The girl sitting next to Brad was Megan Albers; the other girl was Kimberly Bailey.

Matt quickly found a way to mention that he and Brad were jocks. The girls then joked about what kind of basket weaving classes they were taking. When Brad mentioned the environmental class, it opened the door for lots of questions since the girls knew they would have to take the course.

It was nearing time for Brad and Matt to leave, so Matt decided to press his luck. He came up with a couple of clumsy lines to Kimberly indicating that the two of them should get together later that night. This caused both girls to giggle a little and play like they thought he was kidding. The girls then went to the restroom.

"You blew it, Matt. When they come back they will tell us they have to leave," Brad said.

"Maybe, but Kimberly is going to give me her phone number before they do leave," said Matt.

"We have to go," said Megan as she and Kimberly returned to the table.

With that Brad stood up, drained the last once of beer in his glass and put his arm around Megan's shoulder and looked her directly in the eyes.

"Okay, where are we going," Brad said, playing like he thought Megan was talking about him leaving with her.

"Oh no, I meant Kimberly and I are leaving," said Megan before she realized Brad was not serious.

"Well, I guess that means we'll never see each other again. It's been nice talking to you, so I guess I'd better kiss you good-bye. I'm not sure how to go about it, have you got any ideas? I know, first I'll pucker up," Brad said as he formed an exaggerated lips pucker.

This caused Megan to start laughing. That stopped when Brad planted a quick kiss on her lips.

"That worked out well. We'll have to do it again sometime," Brad said. After a few seconds he kissed her again, this time for a longer time.

Before leaving, Megan scribbled down her phone number and gave it to Brad, saying he should call her sometime so she could buy him a couple of beers. Kimberly said good-bye to Matt and quickly left not waiting for Megan to catch up with her.

Matt wanted to know why Brad got a phone number and why he didn't. Brad said it was simply because he paid for the beer and pizza and the girls just wanted a patsy for their next time-out.

Matt and Brad left shortly after that each in his own car. Brad followed Matt to the commercial side of the airport and then to a big hanger type building. Matt took Brad through the work area to an office on the second level and introduced him to Gregory Alexander. Matt then left.

Gregory briefly explained the job duties. He emphasized that the job was not a make work job but an integral part of the shipping department. A full time employed worked the job five days a week and temporary labor filled in the other two days of the week. Gregory then surprised Brad by asking him to talk about his major and what he would do after graduation.

Brad was careful to refer to the manager as Mr. Alexander when he answered questions. He wasn't intending to talk about going back in the army when he graduated. However, he now had to divulge that information.

Gregory then said that Curtis recommended Brad because he felt anyone who had spent time in the army should be dependable. With that the interview was over. Brad was told to show up a little early Monday to fill out all the employment forms.

A number of unrelated thoughts keep going through Brad's head as he headed home. He was trying to think of when best to call Megan and what to do if he asked her out for a date. Then there was Kandi's phone number, which he still hadn't followed up on. He also was wondering if he could manage working one night a week and keep up his studies. Finally he was worried that the environmental class would take up a lot of time and that it would be difficult working with Kathy and Jason. Another thought came into Brad's head as he drove by the school. It was still early, and he didn't feel like going to bed yet, so he decided to stop at a bar near the school a few times for a beer but also to watch the news on TV. He still hadn't bought a bought a set for his room.

"Wilson, get over here." The voice belonged to Coach Curtis.

Brad hadn't noticed Curtis and Coach Curt Alvey, who was the offensive coordinator sitting at a table in the dark part of the bar.

"Good evening, gentlemen. I didn't know you would be here," Brad greeted the coaches.

"I'll bet you didn't. Aren't you supposed to be in bed by now? You know we're traveling to Wyoming tomorrow morning, don't you?" Curtis said slightly slurring his words.

"It's not 10:00 p.m. yet, and I'll be home well before then," answered Brad.

"You can make it to bed in time if you live in your car, I guess. Sit down, we'll buy you one beer if you're old enough," said Alvey.

The invitation surprised Brad. In the army, officers and enlisted men never socialized together in any way. The coaches were like officers to the players in Brad's mind. Nevertheless, he did sit down at their table.

Brad knew there was no curfew requiring football players to be in bed by a certain time the night before a game or any other time. That rule had been challenged several years ago by some player claiming that a curfew was treating players like boys instead of men. That same player may have been the one who told a sports writer that he liked a new coach because the coach treated the players like men and let them wear earrings.

After Brad sat down, Curtis asked him how the interview with Gregory Alexander went. Brad said he got the job but was worried that it might take away study time for him. He said he may want to talk to Tommy Foster to see why Tommy thought it might be a problem.

"You don't have to worry about that. Tommy didn't quit, he was fired for being incompetent. Besides being late for work and leaving early, he was so lazy he didn't even try to keep up with the work, which put a burden on others. I told Alexander you were in the army. He could depend on you to be productive," said Curtis.

"What did you do in the army?" asked Alvey.

By that time Brad had finished half a bottle of beer and was a little more relaxed. Although he didn't want to get into a lot of details he did give a general description of what the war in Iraq was like to him.

Brad said he went into Iraq at the start of ground operations as part of an infantry company. He spent a lot of the time traveling to Baghdad as a machine gunner atop a personnel carrier. After Baghdad was captured the mission of his outfit changed to be pretty much patrolling parts of the city looking for bad guys. A bad guy was defined as someone with a weapon firing at you. Little was accomplished on patrols since the real bad guys never carried guns in sight of the American army.

Later on Brad's company was transferred to a remote base several hundred miles from Baghdad. The mission then involved helicopter movement to areas of known insurgents. This involved many firefights that Brad did not want to describe.

Brad's unit was ordered to stay past their normal rotation home date. Just before he was finally scheduled to rotate back to the United States he volunteered to extend his tour in Iraq until his original enlistment was over. Brad applied for the officer educational opportunity that he learned of during normal briefings by a senior enlisted sergeant.

Alvey then asked Brad about his experience playing for a junior college. Again Brad didn't want to go into a lot of details, but he did mention that at times he also played a tight end position on offense. Alvey would remember that bit of information at the game the next day.

By then Brad felt it was time to leave. Curtis and Alvey ordered another round of beer as Brad left.

CHAPTER 4

Saturday Linda met Joan for brunch at the club after their morning exercises. Joan mentioned that she would be taking her husband to the airport the next day. It seems Henry attends his company's executive meeting in New York the second Monday of every month. Henry flies to New York City on Sundays and then flies home Tuesdays. Joan always likes to mention that some Monday when Henry is away she is going to have a one night stand with someone.

Finally Linda was able to tell her friend about inviting her environmental team to meet at her house on Sunday. Linda said there were three other members of the team: a boy, a girl, and Brad—or as Joan liked to refer to him, the jock. She said she still didn't know what food to fix. Wine and cheese probably wouldn't be appropriate.

"Why not just order pizza and beer?" asked Joan.

"No, no, I can't do that. I don't think a couple of them are old enough to drink yet. Besides, I had to say I didn't like pizza in order to keep from meeting in a pizza parlor," answered Linda.

"Well, if the jock is coming, you better order a lot of food. The first thing you will want to do when he comes in the door is to hand him a loaf of bread. He'll know what to do with it. Why bother fixing anything? You can just order from the deli and have everyone make their own sandwich. It's best to just serve ice tea. Most teenagers drink a Coke a minute when it's free, so if you serve soft drinks, buy a lot. You better order enough for twelve people just in case. One serving for you and two each for two of the team. That leaves seven servings for the jock," said Joan.

"Yeah, I can do that. Joan, why don't you and Hannah plan on having dinner with me tomorrow after the team leaves? That way we can eat up any leftover food, if there is any," said Linda.

"Hannah is having dinner at one of her friend's house so they can watch some important TV show, but I'm available," said Joan.

"Okay, we should be done by 6:00 p.m. I'll call you when they all leave," said Linda.

"I might come over a little early. I want to see what the jock looks like," Joan commented.

"You don't have to do that, Joan. You can see his picture that I have hanging on my bedroom wall," joked Linda.

Linda felt better after talking to her friends, but she still was a little apprehensive about tomorrow's meeting. She decided ordering deli food was a good idea. She also wanted to shop for some special dessert and a couple dozen soft drinks. In the morning she would have time to straighten up the house and then think about the team assignment after church.

Saturday's football game was with West Wyoming. About midway through the first quarter West scored on a short drive after recovering a State fumble deep in State's end of the field. On offense, State seemed unable to be able to move the ball down the field. When West was on offense they played their favorite style. The West line was big and beefy, just right for run blocking. Because of this West ran most plays between the tackles. This eats uptime and keeps the ball away from State as long as West can keep making first downs. It also takes a toll on the defensive players.

State started using a four linebacker formation early in the second quarter. This meant Brad was put in the game as one of the inside linebackers. In addition Brad still played on all special teams. After a few series, Brad wished he really did weigh 225 pounds or more so he could fight off the blockers a little easier.

The game had turned into a defensive struggle without many spectacular plays. This upset the home crowd and they began to boo their team's offensive. Fortunately for Brad, State's defensive was now playing well. Of course that's partially due to the fact that they pretty much knew West was going to run the ball on every play.

By the fourth quarter the score was still 7 to 0 in favor of West. State finally started to have a little success mixing run and pass plays. About midway through the quarter they reached a critical down. After all their time-outs had been used, State faced a third down eight yards away from the first down marker. Brad moved up to the sideline anticipating State would not make a first down and that he would have to go in the game for a punt State would make on fourth down.

Suddenly, Tommy Foster who played tight end limped off the field. If he was injured he should have laid down so that the referee would call a time-out. That would have allowed Coach Alvey to get a replacement ready. Instead the clock kept running and State was short one player. Coach Alvey then grabbed Brad by the arm and told him to go in as a tight end to replace Tommy. Alvey then looked over the team bench to find another tight end that he could substitute for Brad on the next play if State made a first down.

This is just great Brad thought sarcastically. I don't know the plays and am probably going to do something stupid on the only offensive play I'll ever get.

In the huddle, Quarterback Solum called a pass play and then told Brad he just needed to block because the pass would be a quick out to the other side of the field. Brad could do that. As a member of special teams, he was required to be a blocker on field goal and extra point tries as we well as punts. Coach Alvey must have known that when he asked Brad to go in on offense. The second tight end was already in the game as State had been operating with a mostly run or short pass offense, which required two tight ends.

The pass play worked for eleven yards and a first down. Brad started to the sidelines but was waved back on the field. State had a few extra seconds before the next play as the referee was waiting for the down markers to be set. During these seconds, Solum called the next play, a pass, and had time to tell Brad he was to hold a block for a second or two and then drift downfield as a possible second choice receiver.

The pass did go to Brad and mostly by pure luck he caught it for a twelve-yard gain. State continued moving down the field and finally scored a touchdown and extra point to even the score. Things were looking good for State as they forced West to punt on the next series. With time running out, State changed to a passing game. This meant Brad was not required to play offense. Unfortunately, Solum threw an interception, which West turned into a field goal as the game ended.

Brad wondered what Coach Kruger would have to say Monday. He was sure Kruger would criticize the offense but not say anything about the good defensive game.

Saturday night Linda waited for a call from Diane, which never came. About midnight she decided to go to bed but was not able to get to sleep right away. She wasn't worried about Diane. She figured Diane was with Cindy and not in any trouble. Instead Linda was worried about school. She still had doubts that starting school again was a good idea. It didn't look like she would be able to make any new friends except for the environmental team members.

Sunday morning Linda went to church. She felt uncomfortable being by herself. Even though she knew most church members it seems that, except for greetings, no one wanted to talk to her. At the end of the service the pastor, Ed Rogers, said it was nice to see her again and said he may stop by her house for a visit sometime soon.

At home Linda checked the place over several times to make sure it would look nice for her guests. The caterer arrived around 1:00 p.m. as expected. Linda put the food in the refrigerator to keep until 3:00 p.m. Then she sat down to watch TV but soon fell asleep. She woke around 2:30 p.m. and had to hurry to get ready for the guests.

About twenty minutes later, the doorbell rang. When she looked through the door peek hole she saw that it was Brad.

"Hi, Brad, glad you could find the place," Linda said as she let Brad in.

"Hi, your instructions got me here without any trouble. I hope I'm not too early," said Brad.

"No, I'm surprised you got through the gate without having to call me to open it," said Linda.

"I followed someone through the gate. I hope I don't get into any trouble for doing that," said Brad.

"That's not a problem. A lot of people do that," said Linda.

Linda then told Brad that the team could use a big table in the family room to discuss the assignment. Brad offered to help her set up the food and drinks when he saw her start doing that. By the time they finished it was a little after 3:00 p.m. Linda wondered if Jason and Kathy were having trouble finding her place or if they just decided not to come.

While they waited Brad took notice of the house. It was obvious the furniture was good quality and probably very expensive. The room was decorated tastefully. Brad then noticed a picture of Diane that Linda had set prominently in front where Brad was asked to sit down. He was hoping that maybe Diane was somewhere in the house. Brad suddenly remembered Linda saying she was divorced. He then wondered if Linda had a live-in lover or maybe just a favorite boyfriend.

"Who is the lovely lady in the picture?" Brad asked even though he figured it must be Linda's daughter.

"Oh, that is my daughter, Diane. She is starting college at Stanford," answered Linda.

"She is not here today then?" asked Brad.

"No, her classes started last week just like ours," answered Linda.

"You know we play Stanford up there the week after next," said Brad, meaning the football team would play Stanford's team.

Linda was about to tell Brad all about Diane when the phone rang.

It was Jason calling to say he and Kathy were at the gate and needed Linda to open it for them remotely from her home. A few minutes later they arrived. After the usual greetings and compliments about the house they decided to get something to eat. It took until almost 4:00 p.m. before they started discussing the assignment.

The discussion dragged on for almost an hour. Part of that time was spent by Jason and Kathy answering phone calls. Jason had a call from a friend who wanted to talk about a move he had seen Saturday night. That took almost ten minutes. Kathy received three phone calls. One appeared to be from a boyfriend that she didn't want to talk to in front of Jason. The other two calls were from other friends wanting to know what she was doing. When she was not on the phone, Kathy smiled and giggled a lot. She seemed interested in looking the house over, which caused her head to be in almost constant movement.

Finally they all agreed that their audit should be about Waste Avoidance. Jason thought his friend's papers from a previous class were on that subject. The friend had not given the papers to Jason yet, however. Everyone agreed that Brad should give the presentation at class Tuesday. Jason suggested that Brad put an outline together for the group to review. While Brad was doing that Linda gave Kathy a quick tour of the house. Jason turned on the TV to watch an old movie, which was just ending. The local news came on TV next and Brad heard the announcer say that some highlights of State's football game would be shown.

"Hey, Brad, there're going to show your football game on TV. Let's watch to see if we can find you. What number do you wear?" asked Jason.

"Look for number 54," answered Brad.

It took a few minutes before film of the game was shown. By that time Linda and Kathy were back.

The game film started with the critical third down in the fourth quarter. The first pass play was shown with the announcer correctly identifying the State players. Brad said the next play would show him catching a pass, which it did. However, the announcer incorrectly said the pass was caught by Tommy Foster.

"Hey, Brad, I thought you said you wore number 54. It looks like that is Foster's number and looks like he caught the pass," Jason said mockingly.

"Yeah, it looks that way, but Tommy wears number 84, and he was on the bench for that play," answered Brad.

"Yeah, right," said Jason.

The next scene of the game showed Solum throwing the interception. After that the scene showed West kicking the field goal to win the game.

"Brad, are you going to tell us you were you one that threw the interception?" asked Jason.

"Yeah, that was me. I was trying to throw a pass to myself, but I threw it a little too hard," Brad said, going along with the ribbing.

By that time it was close to 5:30 p.m. Jason and Kathy said they had to leave and did so after using the bathroom, for the second time each, but before reviewing the outline Brad had just completed. Linda then offered to help Brad finish preparing for the presentation. They worked well together and within minutes felt comfortable with what Brad would present to the class Tuesday.

When they finished Linda was surprised to hear herself ask Brad to stay for dinner. She said she would fix some spaghetti and then went to the kitchen. Brad started to watch the news on TV but soon fell asleep. After getting back from the game the previous night he spent a couple of hours with a few of his teammates trying to forget about the game in a local bar.

While Linda was in the kitchen, Joan called to see if it was time for her to come over for dinner.

"Joan, I'm glad you called. I've got a strange man sleeping in my house and I don't know what to do with him. You better come over and help me," said Linda jokingly.

"Should I bring a gun? Before I get there, you better hide in the bathroom, or maybe you'd prefer to hide in the bedroom just in case," Joan answered, going along with the joke.

"I think I'll be all right, until he wakes up anyway. I told him I had invited you and that you were a horny little sex kitten," said Linda.

Linda then went back to the dining area. She rattled the dishes a little when she was setting the table to see if Brad would wake up. That did the trick. Brad sat up, blinked his eyes a couple of times and seemed to be trying to figure out where he was. After a few seconds he was alert enough to offer to help with dinner. Linda said he could open the wine bottle if he didn't mind. That got Brad into the kitchen with Linda.

"Wow, this is really good wine, I think," said Brad, trying to remember something about a wine-tasting class he attended once while in junior college.

"It's from Chile," said Linda, realizing that Brad knew nothing about wine.

As they moved about the kitchen they bumped into each a couple of times maybe by accident, or maybe not. Then the doorbell rang.

"That must be my friend Joan at the door. I hope you don't mind I had invited her for dinner when I saw her yesterday," said Linda, who really hadn't told Brad Joan would be joining them.

When Brad answered the door Joan had to stop herself from saying something like you must be the jock Linda's been talking about.

"Oh, hello, you must be Brad," Joan said instead.

"Yes, and you must be Joan," answered Brad.

Joan gave Brad the once over and decided he looked as good as Linda had described him. She wished Linda had been serious about describing her to Brad.

"My husband is out of town, so Linda invited me to dinner. I hope you don't mind me joining you," Joan said to Brad.

"No, I hope you don't mind me butting in. I hadn't planned on staying, but the meeting lasted a little longer than I expected," Brad said.

The next few minutes Brad and Joan engaged in small talk until Joan said she should be helping Linda fix dinner.

"Boy, Linda, that jock is really a hunk," whispered Joan as soon as she was in the kitchen.

"Yeah, I think he might be interested in Diane. You should have seen him look at her picture," said Linda.

"Yeah, well, Diane is not here, and I am, so I'm going to put the make on him," joked Joan.

At dinner Joan talked about the trouble she had getting Henry to the airport. She made it sound like this was the first time she had ever made that trip. Linda talked about the environment class. She wanted to know what Brad thought of Jason and Kathy. Brad answered as diplomatically as he could that he thought they were nice. Finally Linda was able to change the subject to Diane.

"I wonder if my daughter, Diane, has to take an environment class at Stanford," Linda commented.

"I don't think she is worried about that right now. Her main concern is probably about which boys to go out with. You haven't met her have you Brad?" Joan said trying to help get Brad into the conservation about Diane.

"No, but I'd like to someday," said Brad, obviously trying to be polite.

"You know she will be coming home at Thanksgiving. You can meet her then," said Joan.

"Don't let Joan scare you Brad. By then you'll probably have a steady girlfriend, if you don't already," said Linda.

"I haven't had a chance to meet many of the girls at school yet," said Brad.

"What kind of girl do you like?" asked Joan.

"Oh, you know the usual—two arms, two legs, one nose," answered Brad, trying to keep the conversation light.

At this point the conservation turned toward Brad. Joan wanted to know where he went to junior college. She continued to ask questions about the classes he took and if he played football at the junior college. Brad could see then next question coming and braced for it.

"What did you do for the last couple of years after you finished junior college?" asked Joan.

"I joined the army," answered Brad.

This seemed to surprise both ladies. By the look on their faces you could tell that they were trying to decide if they should ask the next question.

"You didn't have to go to Iraq, did you?" asked Linda.

"Yes, I spend some time there," answered Brad.

"How long were you there?" asked Joan.

"Almost three years," Brad said.

The expression on the faces of the ladies was similar to that of most people when they hear Brad was in the army and had spent time in Iraq. They seemed to be thinking he was either stupid for joining the army or a very mean person.

"I thought you only had to stay for one year. Did they make you stay another year?" Joan wanted to know.

"Yeah, everyone's tour was extended for a few months. By then I figured I might as well finish my enlistment there, so I volunteered to stay for a second tour," said Brad.

Brad went on to explain that the army is paying for his college tuition and since he is still in the inactive reserve he also gets some extra money. In addition to that he is living at the army transit quarters near the airport for $5 a day. He left out the part about having to spend two weeks each summer on active duty training and that he is obligated to return to active duty for at least two years after he graduates.

The ladies asked what Brad's job was in Iraq and if he had anywhere near the war. Brad answered that after he got to Baghdad he was mainly used for patrol duty. He purposely left out any detail about combat operations. Instead he said the worst thing about being there was that, other than a few female army personnel, there were no American women to talk to.

"Didn't you get any mail from girls here in the U.S.?" asked Joan.

"No, the army did sponsor a Mail and Meet program for single personnel, however," said Brad.

Brad then went on to explain how the program worked. He said he made a video of himself and sent it along with $20 to a company that promised to forward the video to a dozen or more single women. They promised they would send a response to him from at least one girl or he would get his money back. After about a month Brad said he got his money and the video back with a note saying no girl wanted to answer his video.

"Gee that's really too bad. Did they say why no one wanted to contact you?" asked Joan.

"Yeah, they gave me a phony excuse. I probably would have felt bad except the reason they gave me was so absurd that I knew they probably didn't even forward my video," said Brad.

"What excuse did they give you?" asked Linda.

"Well, this is hard to believe, but they said all the girls liked the video, but they thought I sounded like a pig snorting when I laughed," said Brad.

"That's funny," said Joan as she laughed a little.

"Yeah, you think they could have thought of a better excuse," said Brad.

With that Brad faked a laugh and purposely exaggerated a loud snorting sound when he took a breath. Both women stopped laughing and shot quick glances at each other. No one said anything for a few seconds.

"I wonder why they came up with that excuse," Brad said as he eyed the women.

Linda and Joan didn't laugh but couldn't help looking at each other with a big silly grin on their faces.

"I think I got you on that story," Brad finally said.

He went on to explain that his story was an old one and that he was surprised that neither of them had heard it before. He said he honestly did not snort when he laughed and that he really never did send a video to anyone.

"You shouldn't fool us like that," said Joan as she playfully punched Brad in the arm.

"Ooh, that's my sore arm," said Brad in jest.

"Gee I'm sorry I didn't know your arm hurt," said Joan, not realizing Brad was kidding.

"Yeah, I'm sore all over from yesterday's game," said Brad, continuing the joke.

"Did we win the game?" asked Linda

"No, but we came close. I think we might actually win the game this Saturday. It should be a pretty good one to watch, you should go see it. I can get four good tickets if you two are able to make it," said Brad.

"Yeah, we'd like to go. Henry used to go to every game a couple of years ago when State had a good team. He would take clients to the game and write off the cost to the company. I'm sure he and my daughter, Hannah, would like to go with Linda," said Joan.

"Yeah, I'd like to go," said Linda.

The message Brad got was that Linda apparently did not have a live-in lover and maybe not even a favorite boyfriend to take to the game.

With that Linda said it was time for dessert. As an afterthought she asked if she should open another bottle of wine. Joan quickly replied that yes that would be a good idea especially since she could walk home from Linda's house. The women then went to the kitchen.

"This gets better and better, Linda. He's not only a jock, but now we find out he is a hero," Joan said to Linda.

"He's not a hero, he's just a soldier," said Linda.

"Anyone that goes to Iraq to fight for our country is a hero, especially anyone that volunteers to stay past the time he is able to go home," said Joan.

"The dessert was supposed to be for the team, but I forgot about it before Jason and Kathy left. Do you thing I should save some for them?" said Linda when she returned to the table.

"Yeah, maybe," said Brad.

Linda shot an inquisitive look at Brad wondering if he was serious. Brad noticed this and thought he better explain his comment.

"I picked up that expression when I was in Iraq. It seems that whenever an Iraqi wanted to politely say no they just said yeah maybe. If you asked them if was safe to go down a street and they said yeah maybe, you knew it was not safe. So I really didn't mean you should save any dessert for Jason and Kathy," said Brad.

"Well, I hope ice cream and cake go good with wine," said Linda as she poured everyone another glass.

"It's great. Just don't let me drink too much. If I start talking about how good the sise ream is, you'll know I've had enough wine," said Brad.

Joan and Linda wanted to know where Brad grew up and how he got along with his family. Brad explained that when he was little he lived on a farm in Kansas with his parents and a brother that was ten years older than him. Brad said his father was a good story teller and often told funny stories at dinner. Brad said his brother was good to him but also liked to tease him a lot.

"One of the reasons I never learned to eat fish is because of my brother. When fish was served at home, my parents told me to be careful not to eat any of the little fish bones that were in the fish meat. Away from the dinner table, my brother told me if I did eat a fish bone I would die within an hour. Because of that I tried to sort out bones in the fish before eating. My mother, not knowing what I was doing, told me to eat the fish and stop playing with my food. I remember chewing the fish for about five minutes before swallowing. I figured if I crunched any bones in the meat into small pieces, that maybe I'd live for up to two hours after eating it. That's when I decided it would be better if I just didn't eat any fish," Brad said.

"That's cruel," said Linda.

"Yeah, but it is funny," said Joan.

"My brother had another way of teasing me. When someone told a joke at the dinner table we all laughed of course. Now I don't do this anymore, and I'm not sure I ever did. Anyway, my brother would mimic me by moving his head back and forth when I was laughing. He said when I laughed like, ha-ha, my head would bob back and forth," said Brad.

Linda and Joan thought that was funny and had to laugh at the sight of Brad moving his head as he explained the story.

"What are you looking at? I told you I don't do that anymore," said Brad as he caught Linda looking at him.

That comment caused more laughter just as Linda put a spoonful of ice cream and chocolate syrup in her mouth.

"Look, Joan is doing it now." Brad laughed.

This caused Linda to laugh so hard her mouth came open. To go along with the joke Joan purposely bobbed her head back and forth. When Linda saw Joan doing this she started laughing so hard some ice cream and chocolate syrup spilled out of her mouth and started sliding down the corner of her mouth. Seeing this Brad reached over and gently with the back of his hand pushed Linda's mouth shut. Linda gagged when this happened and then unintentionally but forcefully spit out all the ice cream and syrup she had in her mouth spraying Joan across the table. Fortunately Joan and Linda thought this was funny and laughed and then giggled for the next several minutes. Both of them laughed so hard tears came to their eyes.

"That's not fair, Brad. You shouldn't tell jokes when my mouth is full," joked Linda.

"Hey, Brad, can you show me again how you got Linda to do that." Joan laughed.

Just then Joan's phone rang.

"Hello, dear, how was your trip?" Joan asked her husband, Henry, who was calling.

"The trip was great only I had trouble getting a cab again, just like last time," said Henry.

Henry went on to explain that he just finished an hour-long phone conversation with the G. Randolph Kelso, the managing partner of Henry's firm. Kelso said Henry's region was in line for the Kelso award, which was presented to the top producing region of the national firm. Among other things the winning regional manager and spouse will be given an all-expense paid two week trip to Europe. Henry was excited about the possibility of winning the award and the trip that goes with it. He explained that is why he was calling so late in the evening.

"Let's try to win the trip. We haven't been to Europe for over ten years," said Joan, who then had to hiccup.

"Where are you at, Joan?" asked Henry.

"I'm over at Linda's place. We are drinking up all of Larry's expensive wine, and boy, are we having a good time," answered Joan.

"Where is Hannah?" asked Henry.

"She is staying over with her girlfriend tonight. That's why Linda and I decided to celebrate with spaghetti and wine. The wine goes good with sise ream we're having for dessert," said Joan who was now giggling.

"Are you going to be able to get home all right?" asked Henry.

"Yesss, I can walk home from here you know," said Joan.

"Well, don't you think it is about time to head home?" said Henry.

"Yeah, maybe," said Joan and then burst out laughing remembering Brad's definition of that phrase.

"Maybe I'd better talk to Linda for a minute," said Henry.

"You can't do that, she is pissed out, I mean passed out, on the floor with a brown beard on her chin." Joan laughed.

"I'm not passed out and I'm not pissed off. For your information my brown beard doesn't look nearly as bad as Joan's brown freckles," yelled Linda as she heard what Joan had just said.

"Okay, Henry, we are about done with the wine, so there is no use for me to stay any longer. I'll be home in about fifteen minutes," said Joan.

That pretty much finished the phone call from Henry. Joan apologized for talking so long, but she wanted to make sure Henry knew she was all right.

"I'm not sure Henry is glad he called. It's a good thing you didn't tell him Brad was here," said Linda.

"Sorry to not mention you Brad, but Henry would never understand," said Joan.

"You did the right thing. One thing I don't ever want to do is to make some husband jealous," said Brad, being careful to not say he had done it in the past.

Brad and Joan helped Linda load the dishes in the dish washer and then Brad got ready to leave. He thanked Linda for the brunch, dinner and helping him with the assignment. Joan said she was glad to meet Brad and wished him and Linda well on the assignment.

As Brad got to the front door, Joan gave him an unexpected big hug. Brad noticed Linda standing next to Joan and wondered if he should give her a hug. He didn't think about it long. As he hugged Linda he got a warm feeling and realized this is was only the second time he had ever touched her intentionally. When he turned to leave Joan grabbed him for another hug. This time Brad knew what to do immediately when Joan let go; he then gave Linda a second hug only this time a little longer. He noticed she didn't seem to mind. He then quickly squeezed out the door before Joan could grab him again.

Linda and Joan stood shoulder to shoulder in the doorway watching Brad get in his car and drive away. Both waved good-bye and watched until his car was out of sight.

"Geeze Joan, look at us. We're both acting like a couple of high school girls," said Linda.

"Well, you are a schoolgirl now, Linda. You should start acting like one," said Joan.

"You know, Joan, this is the most fun I've had in a long time and to think we weren't even drunk," said Linda.

"I know. I have never laughed so hard, not even on my wedding night," said Joan.

Linda wasn't sure what Joan meant by that remark but decided it best to not ask her.

On the way home Brad thought the old ladies were very nice. He enjoyed talking to them and appreciated the fact that neither of them felt the need to use crude four-letter words. He realized that was about the only discussion he had with any students since starting school where almost every sentence contained at least one of those words.

Linda and Joan also said they enjoyed the evening and discussed having Brad over some time in the future. Joan joked about going a little bit farther

"Tomorrow I'm going to ask him to dinner," said Joan.

"Why not breakfast?" asked Linda.

"Yeah, that would be a good idea. Do you think he heard me say Henry wouldn't be home until Tuesday?" asked Joan.

"He may have missed a couple of times you mentioned it, but I'm sure he heard at least one of the four times you made that announcement," said Linda.

By then it was time for Joan to go home. She didn't crawl, she walked.

By now it was just past 10:00 p.m. Linda decided to wait for Diane to call before she went to bed. She was sure Diane would call tonight as she had only called once that week. When Diane hadn't called by 11:00 p.m. Linda decided to call her. To her surprise a recorded message told Linda that Diane's number was no longer in service.

A number of thoughts raced through Linda's head. Diane could have lost her phone and had her phone service cancelled. If that were the case she may not have a new number yet. Linda didn't want to believe that Diane changed phone numbers and didn't let her know. Just to make sure, however, Linda called Larry to see if he had a new phone number for Diane.

"Yeah, what do you want Linda?" asked Larry who was obviously annoyed to be getting a call from her.

"I can't get a hold of Diane. She changed her phone number and hasn't given me her new number. I'm calling you to see if you have her current cell phone number," said Linda.

"Why do you suddenly need her phone number at 11:00 p.m.?" asked Larry.

"I haven't heard from her all week and she was supposed to call me tonight. I just want to make sure she is all right," said Linda, trying to keep an even voice.

"She is all right. Cindy and I saw her earlier today. You have to leave her alone. She is eighteen years old now, you know," said Larry.

"Look, just give me the number, and I'll leave you alone," said Linda.

"Okay, wait a minute while I get it," said Larry.

Linda wondered why Larry didn't just look up the new number on his cell phone directory instead of putting her on hold. *He probably is explaining to Cindy, the bimbo, why I'm calling*, thought Linda. After a few more seconds Larry came back on the line and gave her Linda's new phone number.

"You're not going to call her tonight, are you?" asked Larry.

"Yes, I am. I haven't spoken to her in a week, and I want to talk to her about a few things," answered Linda.

"Speaking about talking about a few things, we need to sit down and resolve the house ownership problem. I have to be down there for business sometime next month. Let's plan on getting together then," said Larry.

"Yeah, just let me know a couple days ahead of when you'll be here," said Linda.

"Are we done now?" asked Larry.

"Yeah," Linda said as she hung up.

Linda then immediately dialed Diane's new phone number. The phone rang four times and then rolled over to voice mail.

"Hey, tell me what you want, and I may get back to you," said Diane's recorded voice.

"Listen Diane, this is your mother, your real mother, and I want you to call me the minute you get this message. If you're listening now, pick up the phone, and so we don't start a phone tag game," Linda said to the recording.

"Hey, Mom, it's me. You woke me up," said Diane said as she answered her new phone.

Linda was madder at Diane that she had been for a long time; however, she tried to control her voice. She told Diane it was very rude to not give her the new phone number and that Diane was not living up to her part of the agreement they had. Linda continued that if Diane didn't feel the need to call Linda when they agreed then Linda was going to feel free to call Diane whenever she wanted to. Diane apologized saying she just has been busy at school and that everything was all right with her. The conversation lasted only about ten minutes, and Linda talked for about nine of those minutes.

After the phone call ended Linda started thinking about her relationship with Diane. It was evident that she was losing touch with her daughter. Linda realized that Diane was old enough to start taking care of herself, but Linda felt that shouldn't mean that Diane should shut her out completely.

Linda was surprised to find that she wasn't unduly depressed about the situation. As a matter of fact after only a week, Linda was beginning to enjoy not having to look after Diane.

A new thought came into Linda's head. Maybe she should visit Diane the week after next and watch the football game with her. Of course that would mean she would have to let Diane know that she had started classes at State University. *I'll have to tell her sometime time*, thought Linda. I might as well tell her next time we talk. The more Linda thought about visiting Diane the more she thought the football game would be a good excuse to get together with Diane for a whole afternoon. She could tell Diane one of her instructors gives extra credit for attending State football games and double credit for attending away games.

Linda then got in bed and went immediately to sleep.

There is a little more to the reason Diane changed her phone number. Diane didn't mention this because it wouldn't have reflected well on her. It seems Diane wanted to have her cell phone in her name when she moved. That way Linda who had been receiving the bill wouldn't know who Diane was talking to. But being Diane, she neglected to pay the phone bill until the phone company just turned off her phone. Larry had to open a new phone for Diane in his name since Diane's credit wasn't good enough to get a regular phone. The phone company could only offer her a prepaid phone with limited minutes.

CHAPTER 5

Monday morning Linda slept late. By the time she got up and dressed for the day it was almost 10:00 a.m. That afternoon she was scheduled to do some volunteer work from 11:30 a.m. to 3:30 p.m. at a local bookstore. She had been doing this for about four weeks. The store owners, Eric and Freda Cushman, needed someone to man the store while they ate lunch, ran errands, and completed weekly administrative tasks. Monday early afternoon was normally the least busy time. This provided an opportunity for Linda to get out of the house and talk to someone other than Joan.

About 1:30 p.m. Malcolm Edwards came into the store to browse and to talk to Linda. Malcolm had developed the habit of buying a magazine and then engaging Linda in a lengthy discussion. When no other customers were in the store Linda and Malcolm would sit at a reading table talking. A couple of times these conversation would last for half an hour or more until either a customer came into the store or Linda excused herself to look busy doing something behind the counter.

Over several visits Linda had learned Malcolm entire life story. He always seemed to find a way to mention that his wife had died last year and that he was all alone now. Linda for the most part was a good listener and had some sympathy for him however; she really didn't want to get too involved in his personal life.

This day Malcolm got around to asking the question Linda knew was eventually coming. Malcolm suggested they have dinner some evening. Linda had anticipated this and had given it quite a bit of thought. She had decided that it couldn't do any harm to have a dinner with Malcolm. He looked like he was in his sixties and didn't appear to be someone to be afraid of. However, Linda was surprised to hear herself thank Malcolm for his offer but say that she just recently started seeing someone. Malcolm was visibly surprised and hurt by Linda's answer but said something like, "Well, that's all right, I hope you don't mind me asking." A few minutes later, Malcolm left. By that time it was almost time for Linda to end her shift. She did have a few minutes, however, to ask herself why she had changed her mind about having dinner with Malcolm and whom she had in mind that she might be seeing.

Shortly after arriving at home, Linda got a phone call on the house phone from Mark Dominick. Mark wanted to know if Linda had Diane's new cell phone number. He said he had tried to call her several times and left messages, but she had not called him back. The last time he called, he got the recorded message that her phone number was no longer in use. Linda told Mark she would ask Diane to call him next time she talked to her. She also said that Diane was busy at school since this was the first week but should have time to talk to Mark later this week.

When the call from Mark was over, Linda remembered that she had not asked Diane why she changed phone numbers. Linda hoped it wasn't just to stop any calls from Mark.

After talking to Mark, Linda decided it might be a good time to call her mother. Ethel Dowling, as always, was happy to hear from her daughter. After the usually small talk, Ethel said that she and Linda's father, Ralph, would like to visit Linda after the Christmas and New Year holidays. Linda agreed that would be nice especially since she not seen them since her divorce. Then Ethel brought up the possibility of moving to California permanently and the possibility of buying Larry's half of Linda's house. Linda explained that Larry wanted to talk to her about that subject in the next week or so. She said after talking to Larry she would be in a better position to decide what to do with the house ownership. By the tone of Ethel's voice Linda could tell she was disappointed that Linda had not agreed with her suggestion. Linda said she was sorry not to be able to make a decision at this time but thought a hurried decision may not be in the best interests of all concerned.

After the phone conversation Linda wondered how she could tell her parents as nicely as possible that she would like them to move to California but that living with her would not be a good idea. Linda was certain she did not want her parents moving in with her and Diane.

Early that evening Diane called and explained why she changed her cell phone service and number. Although she used a lot of filler words she lied that she didn't want to keep getting calls from Mark and certain other people. Despite that Linda kept her promise to Mark and asked Diane to be polite and call him. Diane said she was getting alone well at school and was able to visit with Cindy and Larry every weekend.

Diane was surprised to hear her mother had decided to go back to school but didn't seem to be upset by the news. Unexpectedly she said she would be happy for Linda to visit her the week of the State and Stanford football game. She even offered to get tickets to the game for the two of them.

There are a number of things that Diane did not mention to Linda however. Cindy seemed to be spending an unusual amount of time on campus supposedly waiting for Diane. Cindy liked to sit in the cafeteria trying to strike up conversations with some of the male students. Cindy liked to take Diane to a local pizza shop where a lot of the students hung out. She also liked to take part in all of Diane's conversations with classmate. This was beginning to bother Diane especially since Larry didn't seem to notice or maybe just didn't see anything wrong with this.

Diane also had a new boyfriend of her own that was beginning to be overly protective and maybe even possessive. Wellesley Goldstone first met Diane in their history class. He is tall, thin, and fairly good-looking. Wellesley's family is very rich, which means he has a nice car and lots of spending money. He is also a freshman.

Wellesley started helping Diane with her history homework and now is pretty much doing all of her homework for all of her subjects. That means he and Diane are together almost all of the time. Wellesley had said it would be a lot easier if he just moved in with Diane. So far she has resisted living with him but is not reluctant to having him stay overnight with her frequently. The fact that Cindy also seems to be around a lot has helped Diane fight off the urge to go along with Wellesley's proposal for him to move in with her.

Then there is the school work. Despite what Larry may have told Diane she had to sign up for both remedial English and math? It's even more of a problem for Diane since she is having trouble keeping up in both subjects. History is boring and political science doesn't make sense to her. The one subject she excels in is Female Assertiveness. Problems. Most of her classes are frustrating to Diane since she was a straight A+ student all through high school. Although Diane wants to keep her problems confidential, it will all come out during Linda's visit.

Brad got through his two Monday morning classes without any problems. He used the time between his last class and the start of football practice to eat and organize his homework.

Monday football practice consisted only of watching the game film, no one was required to suit up for field practice. As Brad walked by the locker area on his way to the film room he heard a number of players talking excitedly about something. Brad stopped to see what the big commotion was about. It seems everyone was gathered around a commode.

"Hey, man, it's moving!" Brad heard one player shout.

"It won't go down when I flush the toilet," said someone.

"Hit it with a stick. Maybe that will finish it off," said another player.

"Whoever put that one in there is a really big asshole," someone said.

Brad went over to see what everyone was looking at expecting to see a rat or some small animal in the commode. Instead he saw a pear shaped turd, which appeared to be almost four inches in diameter swirling around in the commode. Finally a player used a stick to break the turd apart so it could be flushed away.

"Mokie, did you drop that bomb?" asked Lightning Joe Resnick.

"No, it wasn't me. It was there when I got here," answered Mokie Anton.

"It must have been Kruger. He was the only one here when I walked in," said a player.

"Well, I knew Kruger was going to shit all over the place when he looked at the films of Saturday's game, but I never thought it would all come out as one big piece," said Warren West.

From that day on Coach Kruger would be known as the turd champion although no one ever knew who really left the deposit in the commode.

Later as the game film was being reviewed, almost all of Kruger's comments were about offense missed opportunities. He called out Tommy Foster several times for not laying down when he was hurt instead of just coming out of the game on his own. By falling down on the field the referee would have stopped the clock giving State time to get the correct replacement for him in the game. Kruger rarely mentioned the defensive play even though Brad thought they played quite well. At the end of the film Kruger mentioned that the coaches would be making some changes in the offense for Saturday's game. The film finished just after 5:30 p.m., allowing Brad time to eat and get to his new job around 6:30 p.m.

The shipping company shift supervisor, Chad Jackson, had Brad fill out several forms and then started to explain the job to Brad.

"Your assignment is to load and unload boxes from trucks and airplanes. Boxes are either taken off a truck and put on a conveyor belt or taken off a conveyor belt and put into trucks.

"Yeah, it sounds easy," answered Brad.

"You get paid for eight hours from 7:00 p.m. to 3:00 a.m. If you finish early, you get to go home. If you are not finished by 3:00 a.m., you work until you finish. You get overtime pay for any work past your normal quitting time. You take your breaks between loads," continued Jackson.

By that time it was a little after 7:00 p.m. Brad started picking out packages to process. Jackson watched for several minutes before he seemed satisfied Brad was performing well enough to be left alone.

"You're going to have to be a lot quicker or you won't be finished until noon," said Jackson as he walked away.

Brad did pick up some speed after several minutes and was able to process all boxes from the first truck load bin within two hours. About that time Jackson came around to tell him that the next load for would be coming in about fifteen minutes. This gave Brad time enough for a short break and time to meet some of the regular workers who mentioned that this night was unusually light, so Brad should be finished before normal quitting time. They also mentioned that the last load normally is delivered before 1:00 a.m.

Brad did finish early but by only about fifteen minutes. By the time he got to bed, he would only have about three hours of sleep before he had to get up and get ready for school. That didn't give him any time to rehearse his environmental class presentation.

As it turned out Brad's first work day would be his last. Later that week Coach Curtis informed him that the NCAA had changed their opinion saying because of hours the job could not be allowed for athletics.

Tuesday morning Brad's cell phone rang at 7:00 a.m., waking him up. It was Kathy Dougan who told Brad she had heard that a lot of environmental teams were going to use a PowerPoint presentation, and each member of the team would take part giving it. Brad said it was too late to restructure his talk, but if Kathy or anyone else wanted to interject comments, they should feel free to do so. It sounded to Brad that Kathy thought their presentation would be a failure and it would be Brad's fault.

Brad and Linda got together in the front of the class room a little before the environmental class started.

"Hi, Linda, did Joan get home all right Sunday night after drinking a whole bottle of wine by herself?" asked Brad.

"Yes, she got home all right. How about you?" responded Linda.

"I think I got home okay. I don't remember much after we started drinking. Wine does that to me sometimes," said Brad jokingly.

"Okay. I hope you don't think Joan and I knock off two bottles of wine every night," said Linda.

"You know I really enjoyed talking to you two. The spaghetti and ice cream were also really good. By the way thanks for helping me finalize the presentation. I hope it goes well, but I'm a little concerned. Kathy called me this morning to let me know that some teams are going to use a PowerPoint program for their presentation," said Brad.

"Kathy also called me to see if we should postpone our talk until Thursday. I told her I reviewed your talk and felt it was going to okay because of the content," Linda said.

About that time Kathy and Jason arrived. Kathy repeated her concern that they were not making a PowerPoint presentation. Jason seemed to agree that they were in trouble as he commented, we're fucked.

Professor Scott called the class to order and repeated the ground rules for the presentations that he had given last week. Each group would only be allowed ten minutes for the presentation and up to two minutes for Scott to ask questions. That way all eight team should be able to finish and Scott would have time to assign audit subjects to each team.

Scott then pointed to Linda, who was seated in the first seat in the front row, and asked her to stand up.

"Your team will be Team 1. Please introduce yourself and your other three team members," instructed Scott.

Brad was then asked to give the team presentation. He talked for the full ten minutes in a clear loud voice using as many power buzz words as he could think of along with some business premises that he learned in junior college. Brad was also able to work in an example of not wasting time. He pointed out that anyone that would be using a PowerPoint presentation should set it up before they are called upon to begin their presentation. That would save some of their allotted ten minutes to talk about their chosen subject. Scott and the other students seemed to enjoy his closing comment in which he said that in keeping with the team subject of waste avoidance, he had used his allotted ten minutes and would not waste any more of the class's time.

The next team presentation lasted twelve minutes before Scott said time for them was up. The third team did use a PowerPoint presentation; however, the slides were simply outlines of the talk without any graphics. Two additional similar PowerPoint presentations were made. Brad counted two other teams that wanted the waste avoidance subject for their audit. Jason commented something that his other team members must have been thinking. He said it looked like their team would be assigned the Reward and Punishment subject since no one else seemed to want it.

There were only about five minutes of class left when the last presentation ended. Team 1 was surprised to get their requested subject of waste avoidance.

Scott then pointed out that all teams except Team 1 went over the allotted time. He the class would have to learn to manage time better. He then gave a reading assignment of two chapters from the class text book to be completed by Thursday's class. With that the class was dismissed.

Team 1 congratulated each other on getting their requested audit assignment. As they were about to leave, Scott stopped the group and said he had a few comments and complements for them. He then said there was a lot of meat in their presentation and that they could provide a very real and valuable service for the company they eventually will choose to audit. He said he had some suggestions he would like the team to consider and that maybe he could discuss them over lunch in the cafeteria with one of the team members. No one spoke for a few seconds allowing Scott to follow up with what he really wanted.

"Linda, maybe you can spare some time and then get back to the other team members later this week," Scott said.

"Okay, I guess I can do that," answered Linda, not knowing what else to say.

"Good, let's go by my office so we can drop off our books and then go to the cafeteria," said Scott.

"Maybe you can call us tonight and let us know what is discussed," said Brad, who sensed the real reason of the lunch offer to Linda.

On the way to Scott's office they passed several students that smiled and greeted Scott, all the students were girls. When they got to the office, Scott carefully positioned himself beside a copy of his doctorate diploma as he shuffled some papers on his desk. He quickly scanned a note addressed to him and did his best to look gravely concerned.

"Looks like we've lost another battle to the environment. This memo indicates the most recent study shows we are losing the polar ice cap much more rapidly than previously thought," Scott said to Linda, hoping she would be impressed with his concern.

The cafeteria was crowded when they finally got there. As Scott followed Linda through the line she wondered if he would offer to pay for her lunch or maybe she should offer to pay for his meal. When she got to the cashier she opened her purse preparing to pay for her meal.

"I'm paying for both lunches," Scott said to the cashier.

Linda weakly offered to pay for her meal, but Scott insisted it would be his treat.

Scott saw two open seats at a table where two other older men were seated.

"May we join you?" Scott asked as he motioned for Linda to sit down.

"The lovely lady is welcome, but I don't know about you, Scott," said one of the men at the table.

"Gentlemen, this is my friend. Linda Wallace. Linda, the man with the big mouth is Professor Kindle of the math department. My other friend is Professor Schultz of the physic department," Scott said as he sat down.

Both professors said they were glad to meet her and then mentioned that they hadn't seen her around the campus before now. Linda then had to explain that she was a student in Scott's class. The professors were perceptive enough to realize, that since Scott's class was an upper level one that this must be Linda's first year on campus. Linda must have transferred from some other school.

"Did you transfer in from another school this semester?" Kindle asked.

Linda figured the best response would to tell the whole story instead of having it drug out of her question by question. The professors seemed impressed when she mentioned that she had completed two years of study at Stanford University. Linda had an idea that somehow Scott already knew this.

Small talk continued through most of the lunch. Linda took note of the fact that Scott seemed to enjoy letting his associates know that he had talked a good-looking woman into having lunch with him. She also noticed that both professors appeared to be several years older than Scott.

Linda felt uncomfortable for a number of reasons. Just being asked to lunch by your instructor on one of the first days of class didn't seem right. Then having a couple of older men grill her on what might be considered personal matters was a little upsetting. The biggest concern however, was the way Schultz continually started at her. Schultz had a half smile frozen on his face. He had what Linda felt were bug eyes and his yellow teeth showed behind his smile.

Finally Scott said he had asked Linda to join him for lunch so he could go over some suggestions for her audit subject. The professors took the queue and quickly excused themselves and left.

"Linda, I was impressed by your team's presentation this morning, particularly the comment about the most important function of a leader. Most teams miss a lot of what was in your talk. I assume you were instrumental in putting the presentation together," Scott said.

"Actually, Brad Wilson put the presentation together pretty much by himself. I only helped him with some of the wording. You know we were all worried about the fact that we did not use a PowerPoint program or any visual aids for our presentation. We were concerned a simple talk would be pretty bland and hard to follow," said Linda.

"Let me tell you about the PowerPoint programs. I've seen the ones shown this morning at least half a dozen times. It seems every year students give or sell the entire presentations to future students. It always amazes me that no one bothers to incorporate the suggestions I make to improve the presentations before handing them off to the next class. I suppose I should make the students work up new presentations if I suspect they were using someone else's work. Unfortunately, most students wouldn't be able to come up with anything nearly as good on their own. By letting them plagiarize someone's work they at least get a feel for what is required. It is similar to asking a student to complete some math problems and letting them use a computer. The information being reported may not require any original thinking on the part of the student, but the information itself is what is important. Does that make sense?" Scott asked.

"Yes, except that I would still consider it cheating. Don't you think you should at least let them know that you know they are cheating?" responded Linda.

"Well, years ago I would have agreed with you, but today it's pretty much agreed that in education it's what you learn, not how you learn it. In essence we don't subscribe to Christian values any longer," said Scott.

"I think our team wants to do the right thing and come up with our own ideas," Linda said.

Scott then told Linda he had applied for a government grant of $1.2 million to study the growing concern over global warming. He said he would be able to take a sabbatical leave from school for a year or two to complete his research starting after the next semester. The research would require him to travel to all parts of the world including the Arctic and Antarctic circles. The grant would provide for him and an assistant's travel and living expenses.

Scott went on to say that as he was completing his research he would be writing a book of his findings and that a chapter or two would be about waste avoidance as a way of preserving earth's resources and possibly of helping to control the global warming effect. Because of that he would be interested in directing Linda's team in their assignment this semester.

By this time it was well past 1:00 p.m., so Linda said she would have to discuss Scott's idea with the other team members. She then thanked Scott for lunch and left. As she was driving home she thought over Scott's comments. It was obvious that Scott somehow knew a lot about her, he never asked if she was married but seemed to know she was divorced. He also seemed to think that Diane may not be coming back to live with Linda.

Linda felt she was being screened as a possible candidate as Scott's companion while he would be traveling for his research. Somehow she did not feel flattered about this. If that is what Scott was thinking his approach was too direct and too quick. She also didn't like the idea that he apparently had found out so much about her personal life. On the other hand, traveling the world could be fun if she didn't have to live in tents.

The cell phone rang and interrupted Linda's thoughts. It was Ed Rogers, the pastor from her church, who asked if he could stop by her house around 3:00 p.m. that afternoon. Linda said that would be fine wondering why he wanted to talk to her. Fortunately she would have time to straighten up the house, which of course didn't need it, before Rogers arrived.

Pastor Rogers did show up at Linda's house right at 3:00 p.m. After exchanging pleasantries Rogers came to the main purpose of his visit. It seems the church needs another youth counselor and Rogers thinks Linda could fill that role.

"You know, Linda, you have had a lot of exposure with the younger crowd through Diane. I've noticed you relate well to younger people. I'm sure you could provide valuable advice to that group. This would only involve a couple hours Monday evenings when the youth group meets at the church. Of course it may involve some individual counseling if some of the group asks for individual attention," Pastor Rogers said.

"You know I haven't done anything like this before, and I've never had any training in this area," said Linda.

"The church will send you to one on one training classes with state-certified counselors, and you will work with another church counselor before going out on you own. I'm sure you could do the job," said Pastor Rogers.

"Let me think about it for a couple of days. I'll try to give you an answer this Friday," said Linda.

With that the visit was over and the pastor left.

Linda was surprised by the pastor's request. She hadn't seen anything like that coming her way and wasn't sure if she wanted to be a counselor.

After dinner Linda decided to call the other team members and let them know what Scott discussed with her at lunch. The main point she wanted to express to the team was that Scott wanted to be heavily involved in their environmental audit. She assumed that the other members would be thrilled to have Scott help out, but she wasn't so sure it would be a good idea.

When Linda picked up her cell phone to make the calls she noticed that she had a phone message from Brad. Her cell phone had been turned off for the visit from Pastor Rogers and she had not turned in on until now.

"Hi, Linda, this is Brad Wilson from your environmental class. A couple of things, I'm interested to hear what Scott had to say about our team. I'm going to be tied up this evening with football practice and then something else later, so I have what I think might be a good idea. I owe you a dinner to repay you for Sunday night, so I thought maybe you might be able to have dinner with me at a nice little French restaurant tomorrow night. The restaurant is the La Vie En Rose, and it is not too far from the campus but far enough so that not many students go there. I understand they have a good wine selection. If you are available, let me know. I can stop by your house or meet you at the restaurant, whichever is better for you. Oh, by the way, I also want to give you four tickets to this Saturday's football game. I hope you can make dinner, because I need a little cheering up. I also have some concerns about Scott and our audit program that I'd like to discuss with you," said the message from Brad.

After listening to Brad's message, Linda sat down and tried to sort out all the requests for her attention she had recently received.

Malcolm Edwards seemed like a nice man, but she didn't want to get mixed up with his family of grown children or his grandkids. It's evident he loved his wife, which means he would naturally continue to talk about her whenever he was with Linda. Even though he was very nice he just didn't seem exciting. If she did go to dinner with Malcolm, even just once, it would be difficult to not get further involved with him.

Linda wasn't sure what to make of Scott's comments about the research project he wants to undertake. She was even less sure of how much Scott wanted to be involved in the team audit assignment. About all she knew of Scott was that he is handsome, intelligent and apparently well-off financially. However, just like Malcolm once she got a little involved with him it would be difficult to not get further involved.

Then she gave some thought as to why Pastor Rogers would think she could be a counselor. Some not so nice reasons came to mind. The pastor knew she had to quit college when she was in her twenties because she became pregnant. He also knows that she is recently divorced. It's possible the pastor thinks she should point out her errors as examples of what not to do. Linda didn't like that idea. The thought of being a youth counselor might be appealing but not if she has to use herself as example of what not to do. However, she wasn't sure if she could turn down the request.

Then there was the question about what to do with Brad. Linda was pretty sure he just thought of her as an older friend. She felt comfortable talking to him probably because he didn't make any sexual innuendos. He was fun to talk to and she felt safe with him. She continued to think of him as a nice boy that she hoped Diane would fall in love with if she could somehow arrange for them to meet.

The only decision Linda was able to make at this time was that she definitely wanted to have dinner with Brad the next night.

"Hi, Brad, this is Linda Wallace. I just got your phone message. Sorry I wasn't able to call sooner. Yes, I can meet you for dinner at the La Vie En Rose restaurant you mentioned, but I'm not going to drink any wine.

I've been there before, so I'm sure I can find it. I'll be there at 8:00 p.m.," Linda said to Brad's cell phone voice mail.

Linda then called Kathy and Jason to bring them up-to-date on her talk with Scott. Both Kathy and Jason thought having Scott help them would be a good idea. Linda felt Kathy and Jason were thinking that Scott would, in essence, complete the entire assignment for the team. Linda didn't think that would happen and if it did it would not be ethical.

The next call was to Joan to bring her up-to-date on the day's activity.

Joan first wanted to tell Linda that Henry was told he was almost assured of winning the trip to Europe. The announcement would be made at the December meeting of his company at the New York City Headquarters. Joan said she wanted to start planning the trip but was worried that something may happen to cause them to not win the prize.

"Joan, why don't you go ahead and start planning? I'm sure you'll win, but if you don't, you can tell Henry you don't want to waste all the planning you've done, so he should take you anyway," Linda told Joan.

"Yeah, I could do that, and Henry would probably tell me to go ahead and go to Europe if I had enough of my own money to finance the trip," answered Joan.

Finally, Linda got to tell Joan about her busy day.

"You know I feel bad about turning down Malcolm, but I just don't want to get involved with him," said Linda.

"How did he take it when you told him you never wanted to see him again?" asked Joan.

"I didn't say that. At least I didn't use those words. Anyway he seemed to understand. I wonder if he will ever come into the bookstore again," said Linda.

"By the way who is the mystery someone else that you have just started seeing, as if I don't know?" asked Joan.

"It's not what you think. There isn't anyone else that I'm seeing. I just wanted to give Malcolm a polite but final answer about having dinner with him," answered Linda.

"Yeah, right and the man you are having dinner with tomorrow, you are not seeing," Joan said.

"Well, you know what I mean. Tomorrow is not a romantic dinner by any stretch of the imagination," said Linda.

"Going to a small secluded French restaurant is not romantic? Maybe you don't think so, but I'll bet Brad does," said Joan.

"Joan, what do you think I ought to do about the church thing?" Linda asked trying to change the subject.

"Well, you know that you will be spending far more time than just a couple of hours every other Monday. Those kids are always planning trips to learn more about God and to have a chance to screw each other. As a counselor you will have to chaperon all those trips. You'll spend all night checking bedrooms," said Joan.

"I guess you may be right. I remember going on some of those trips with Diane to help out the lead counselor. I was drained of energy by the time I got home, and I didn't have to do any of the planning," Linda said.

"I think your best bet is to suck up to Professor Scott Watson and invite yourself on an all-expense paid trip around the world. I assume he is not married," Joan said.

"That's a good idea, Joan. I'll have a chance to get to know him better over the next couple of months. If he isn't what I want in a man, I'll have time to change him. Of course, I would have him make a few concessions before I go anywhere with him. As an example, I will not sleep in a tent or have to pee in a pot," Linda said jokingly.

"Look, Linda, if you don't want to go, tell him you know a hot sex kitten who is raring to go anywhere, anytime," said Joan.

"Who would that be Mrs. Belson?" asked Linda mockingly.

"Never mind. I don't like sleeping in tents and peeing in pots either," said Joan.

"Okay, I'm pretty sure I'm done with Malcolm. I'll just have to wait and see what develops with Scott. As far as church is concerned I think I'll ask to wait until after the first of the year to get involved. How does that sound?" Linda asked Joan.

"I'm Okay with Malcolm and Scott, but do you really want to start counseling next January? If you tell the pastor to ask you after the first of the year he will assume you will accept then. Then there is the big question, what are your intentions with Brad? Are you going to lead him into an immoral lifestyle?" Joan said.

"I'm reserving Brad for Diane. I just came up with a great plan on how to get them to meet each other. The weekend after this one I'm going to visit Diane. She has agreed to go to the Stanford and State football game with me. I'm sure Brad will have time to stop by and visit with us after the game ends," said Linda.

"Oh, you didn't tell me about this. Did you tell Diane you are taking classes at State because you wanted to find the perfect mate for her? Have you have you discussed this with Brad yet?" said Joan.

"Yeah, I did tell Diane I'm starting school again. She didn't seem to care. Tomorrow at dinner I'll work our arrangements with Brad on how to talk to him after the game. I understand many of the players spend several minutes talking to fans or family members after football games," Linda said.

"This is going to be good. I might go along with you just to watch and see how your plan works out," said Joan.

"That reminds me. Tomorrow Brad said he will give me four tickets to this Saturday's football game. Do you think Henry and Hannah will go to the game with us or should we try to pick up a couple of studs in the local bar?" asked Linda.

"Henry said he wanted to go as soon as I told him the tickets were free. I told Hannah we would be sitting with a bunch of college boys, so there is no problem with her. Incidentally, I had to tell Henry you are going back to school," said Joan.

"That's okay now that I told Diane. Tomorrow I'm going to take out a full-page ad in the newspaper announcing that old Linda Wallace is going back to school to meet a stud," said Linda.

"I'll let Henry and Hannah know we are all going to see Linda's new boyfriend play football," said Joan.

"Okay, can we meet at my house at 11:00 a.m.? We should get there early to find parking and get some hot dogs before the game starts," said Linda, ignoring Joan's last comment.

"Yeah, Henry said he would drive. Your idea of getting there early is a good one. That way you'll have a lot of time to watch Brad practice," said Joan.

"That's not what I was thinking of, and you know it." Linda laughed, ending the phone call.

After that Linda then waited for Diane's phone call, which never came before she went to bed around midnight.

Earlier in the day Brad had some time after lunch to complete some reading and homework for his other classes before going to football practice. His big plan was to go to bed before 8:00 p.m. that night to catch up on some needed sleep.

He left the phone message to Linda just before practice at 3:00 p.m. After leaving the message he wondered why he seemed to be so concerned about what Linda and Scott had discussed at lunch.

"Hey, Brad, I just checked all the toilets. No new bomb from the turd champion today," said Warren West as Brad came into the locker room.

"Nice of you to keep me informed. Better not get too close to Kruger today. If he starts walking bull legged, you'll know it's coming," answered Brad.

At the start of practice Coach Alvey called Brad over to the offense end of the field.

"We want to try you out for some limited time as a tight end. Today you'll be practicing with the receivers and offensive line," Alvey told Brad.

"Okay, I still get to play defense and special teams don't I?" asked Brad.

"Yeah, we're only getting you ready for possible spot action on offense," said Alvey.

The rest of the practice went well, and Brad was able to get home around 7:00 p.m. He talked to the duty sergeant at the barracks for a while and then decided to follow through with his plan on going to bed early.

Just as he got to his room his cell phone rang. Brad didn't get many calls, so he wasn't sure who might be calling. He decided to see if the caller would leave a message and answer it later. The call was from Linda who did leave the message about accepting his dinner invitation.

After Brad listened to the phone message he decided to wait until morning to call Linda back to confirm the dinner. He thought it strange that the first woman he was having anything like a date with was someone who was old enough to be his mother. Of course he didn't really consider the dinner invitation to be a date.

Brad also tried to think of when he could line up a real date. Kandi Kolinsky would be great except that she is in Las Vegas. It didn't look like Kathy Dougan was interested in him. He would have contact with her as part of the environmental team, so he would wait to see if anything promising developed with her. That left Megan Albers who was somewhat of a mystery. Even though she was quite young, Brad thought he should plan on calling her before she forgot all about him.

CHAPTER 6

Wednesday morning Brad spent most of his first class thinking of what he should say to Linda when he called her. He wanted to wait until dinner to talk about the environment class and Scott Watson. He also didn't want to give Linda a chance to back out of dinner, so he hoped he could just leave a phone message.

At a break in the class a little after 9:00 a.m., Brad figured it was the right time to call. As he had hoped, Linda didn't answer, so Brad was able to leave a voice mail message. He said he would make reservations and was looking forward to seeing her.

The rest of the day seemed to drag by. Brad spent a good deal of time day dreaming about what he should and should not say during dinner. He thought he knew why Scott was showing so much interest in Linda and for some reason felt he should warn her of the mess she could be getting into. However, it really was none of his business. Linda was obviously a grown, mature woman. She probably understands Scott's attention and maybe welcomes it. Brad convinced himself that his concern was not jealousy but concern as a big brother would have for his younger sister. The trouble with that was that Brad was more like a meddlesome little brother.

Football practice kept his mind off dinner as he ran plays with both the offense and the defense. When practice finally ended, Brad showered, put on clean pressed clothes, and started to leave for the restaurant. He wanted to be there early enough to try some mixed drinks at the bar before Linda arrived. He remembered a senior army sergeant explaining that a martini was the best before dinner drink for men, the best social drink was a scotch and water and the best after dinner drink was Grand Marnier. Brad knew he shouldn't try them all, but he thought he could at least test one drink or maybe two. His plan was scuttled however, because Coach Alvey wanted to talk to Brad for several minutes before he left. By the time Alvey was finished talking to him he had to hurry to get to the restaurant on time.

Brad and Linda both got to the restaurant right at 8:00 p.m. Brad met Linda at the front door. Linda was wearing a perfectly tailored dress with what looked like expensive accessories. Brad thought she looked great she smelled good too. As he approached her he was trying to decide if he should give her a friendly hug or maybe just shake her hand. Instead he gave a silly wave of his hand.

"Hi, Linda, glad you could make it. Did you have any trouble finding the place?" Brad asked.

"Hi, Brad, I've been here before, so I knew how to get here. I like this place it is nice and cozy," Linda answered and then immediately thought cozy was more suggestive than she had intended.

As they were being seated Linda thought of the last time she had dinner at the La Vie En Rose. Larry met her there shortly before their divorce was final. Although the restaurant was nice the evening wasn't enjoyable for Linda. Larry said he and Cindy were going to be married the day after the final divorce decree. This forced Linda to recognize that she and Larry were not going to reconcile and that she would be on her own from then on. The rest of that dinner Larry kept trying to talk her into swapping her interest in his business for his interest in her house. Linda left as soon as she finished eating. Larry was still eating and had just ordered another drink for himself. She was hoping the waiter would not recognize her from the last time she was there.

Brad glanced at the menu when they were seated and was shocked by the prices. He was trying to add to his savings each month so he could afford to buy a new Corvette at the end of next semester and travel around the United States all summer long. He figured the cost of would wipe out any savings this month, but he figured dinner with Linda would be worth it.

Linda didn't want a drink but did order an appetizer.

"Before I forget, I want to give you these four tickets to Saturday's game," said Brad.

"I've asked Joan and her family to go to the game with me. Let me reimburse you for the cost of the tickets," said Linda as she opened her purse.

"No, no, the tickets didn't cost me anything. The school gives up to four tickets to all the players for family members and friends. The seats aren't the best, and you'll be sitting next to the student section. I hope you don't mind," said Brad.

"That is just where Hannah wants to sit. I think she will spend most of her time looking at the boys instead of the game. Henry is a real football fan, however. He said to ask you to be sure and win the game. Joan and I know enough about the game to know if State is winning or losing," said Linda.

"Well, you know we have a good chance to win this time. We've had good practice sessions this week. I may play a little offense in addition to defense and special teams," said Brad.

Linda wasn't quite sure what special teams meant, but she was pretty sure she knew the difference between offense and defense. She decided to take a chance and ask a safe question that would make her look like she knew what she was talking about.

"What position do you play on offense, and what number will you be wearing this Saturday?" asked Linda

"My number is 54. It is the same if I'm on offense or defense. On offense I will play a tight end position. That means I'll normally be the last guy on the line of scrimmage. Most of the time I'll just block, but sometimes I may have a chance to catch a pass," answered Brad.

"You know, I'm really glad you thought of getting tickets for us. It will give me an opportunity to brush up on football terms. I'll need that information because next week I'm going to visit Diane and she suggested we watch your football game with Stanford," Linda said, trying to work in a request for Brad to meet Diane after the game.

"That's great. You may be the only one in the stadium cheering for us. If you let me know where you'll be sitting, I'll try to walk over that way to say hello after the end of the game. Of course I won't be able to go up in the stands," said Brad.

"As soon as I get the seat locations I can call you on your cell phone. Will you be able to answer it if I call just before the game starts?" asked Linda.

"Maybe, but I'm sure I will have time to take a phone message at halftime if I can't use the phone earlier," said Brad.

"We'll walk down to the edge of the field if you think you will have time to get to us," said Linda.

"Yeah, I think I'll be able to do that," said Brad.

That was easy, thought Linda to herself. Now she had to figure out how to get Diane to wait around to meet Brad after the end of the game. She knew that would not be so easy.

"Linda, if you don't mind I might order a glass of wine with dinner," said Brad.

"Well, I don't know Brad. Are you old enough?" Linda joked.

"I'm old enough but not smart enough to know what to order. Do you have a suggestion?" asked Brad.

"Let's order a small bottle of burgundy. I'll help you out with one glass," answered Linda.

By the time dinner was served they had finished almost the whole bottle of wine and both were feeling pretty good. Linda felt comfortable enough to speak frankly about her thoughts about Professor Scott Watson.

"Brad, you wouldn't believe what Scott told me yesterday. He said he had heard almost all of yesterday's presentations before. He knew students were using copies from former students but didn't really see anything wrong with that. He said something about it is similar to letting a student use a computer to solve math problems," Linda told Brad.

"Well, he didn't think our presentation was put together by someone else. Did he?" asked Brad.

"No, as a matter of fact he complemented us, actually you, on the content of your talk. He said something about wanting to use one of your comments in a book he is planning on writing," said Linda.

"He said he is going to write a book?" asked Brad.

"Oh, I didn't tell you the best part. Scott said he is going to get a grant of over $1 million from the government that will allow him and an assistant to undertake an environmental research project. He said he is planning on taking a sabbatical leave from school at the end of next semester and travel around the world for a couple of years. His book will be about the research and will include a chapter on waste avoidance. Because of that he wants to, as he said, work closely with our team," Linda said.

Brad made a mental note to himself to talk with Jason the next day. It's possible Scott uses this story every semester to get close to one of his female students. Jason's friend that took the class last year may know if Scott told the same story to one of those students. Of course, Scott's story may be 100 percent true. In that case Scott could be trying to line Linda up to be his-live in assistant on his travels.

"That's great, but what does that mean for our team. Does Scott think he is going to lead our audit and sit in on all of our meeting?" asked Brad.

"Well, he didn't really say what his involvement will be. I guess we'll find out soon enough," said Linda.

"Tomorrow let us just ask him to tell all of us what he has in mind. It sounds like he wants us to be his gophers and carry out his instructions without any critical input from us. He can tell us what he has in mind over lunch," said Brad, sounding a little sarcastic.

"I think Jason and Kathy will welcome any help Scott will give us. I'm sure it would mean good grades for all of us, but for some reason I don't think Scott's involvement is a good idea," said Linda.

"I'm with you. It seems strange that he picked the best-looking woman in the class to discuss his ideas with," said Brad, feeling bolder now that he had finished a couple glasses of wine.

Linda tried not to show that she caught Brad's complimentary comment, but it did make her feel good for some reason.

"I guess I should be flattered that he seems to be paying so much attention to me, but I really think he just picked out the closest person to talk to," said Linda.

"Yeah, I guess you are right. How are you getting along in your other classes?" asked Brad wanting to change the subject.

"I'm only taking one other class. It is a class on library science and appears to be a repeat of a class I took twenty years ago. It is mostly a lecture class with a lot of outside reading, which I have time for. This semester I only wanted to take a couple of classes because I work one day a week on Mondays. What other classes are you taking?" asked Linda.

"I'm taking a media class, a managerial class and a real accounting type auditing class besides our environmental class. What I learn in the audit class should help us organize a good program for our environmental audit. What do you do at your Monday job?" asked Brad.

"I volunteer to help out in a bookstore at the local mall just in the afternoon. I know the owners from my church. They needed some help Monday afternoons when their other employees are scheduled off. While I'm there the owners are working in the office area in case I need any help. Before I started working there I'd stop by occasionally to buy a book or just browse around. The owners, a man and his wife, told me they were thinking of selling the business and retiring next year. In talking to them I causally mentioned that I would like to own a bookstore someday. One thing led to another, so just after my divorce earlier this year, the owners asked if I would like to work part-time to learn the business and see what it would be like to run a bookstore. So that is how I got the job," Linda told Brad.

"Now that you've worked in the store for a while, do you think you might be interested in buying their business?" asked Brad.

"I'm not so sure now. It takes a lot of time and effort to run the store, and I'd be operating the store by myself. I've also found I like the freedom of doing what I want when I want, so being tied down to a business would take that freedom away," said Linda.

"Do you think your daughter would be interested in helping you if you buy the business?" asked Brad.

"No, I'm not sure what Diane will do when she finishes college, but working in a store is definitely not what she would want to do. Her father wants her to study law, but she doesn't want to do that either. She hasn't decided on a major field of study yet," said Linda.

"Well, she still has a lot of time to decide," said Brad.

"What are you going to do after graduation?" Linda asked.

A little earlier Brad had signaled the waiter to bring another bottle of wine. He felt comfortable talking to Linda and she seemed to have opened up by discussing some personal things. Brad figured there was no reason to keep his future commitment a secret.

"I guess I didn't mention it the other night, but after I graduate I'll go back on active duty in the army as a commissioned officer," said Brad.

"But if you do that wouldn't you have to go back to Iraq or does your time over there mean you are done with the war?" asked Linda.

"Unfortunately, you are never done with the war when you are in the army. Yes, I probably would go back there or Afghanistan if the war is still going on by then," said Brad.

"Maybe by the time you graduate you'll be interested in something else," said Linda.

"No, I can't back out now. The government is paying for my education and living expenses because I signed an agreement to return to the army for at least four years. I'm not going to try to get out of that. I feel I owe something to the government for paying for my education," Brad said.

Linda had to think about Brad's comments for a time before continuing the conversation. She hadn't given it much thought but felt she should be against the war. Brad was about the first person she had ever known that was or had been in the military.

"But you can ask for duty here in the U.S., can't you?" asked Linda.

"Yeah, I could, but there is a real need for combat troops. That's what soldiers get paid to do. Besides, I've been there, so I would be able to better lead new troops," Brad answered.

"But aren't you afraid you might get killed or severely injured?" asked Linda.

Brad could see that this was a no-win conversation for him. Like most civilians Linda did not and probably did not want to see anything positive about the military. He decided to try to lighten up the conversation and see if he could get onto another subje

"Oh, the army has invested so much in me they wouldn't let me get hurt. I'd probably end up in the rear with the gear in charge of tank repairs.

If you don't end up buying the bookstore, is there anything else you would be interested in doing after graduation?" asked Brad.

"I've always wanted to travel. Maybe I could get a job as a tour guide and go to exotic places. That may seem strange since it's just the opposite of working in a bookstore," said Linda.

"I would like to be able to travel. As a matter of fact I'm planning on driving around the entire U.S. this summer," Brad said.

"That sounds like fun. I'd like to do that sometime. One of my friends and her husband are planning a tour of the New England states this fall. Then Joan and her husband may win an all-expense trip to Europe next summer. So being stuck in a bookstore doesn't sound like a lot of fun in comparison," said Linda.

"Maybe you should plan on doing something this summer while you have the chance," said Brad.

Linda had to give that suggestion some thought. She had traveled a little with Larry and Diane before Diane put a stop to that. They had been on a tour of Europe one time that was enjoyable. However, for most of the other trips they flew to a big city or a resort and stayed in a hotel while Larry was in conference. Most conferences had activities planned for spouses and family members, so there was normally not a lot of free time to do things by themselves. On a few occasions Larry had rented a cabin in the mountains for skiing trips. Linda wasn't a good skier, and Diane didn't want to learn to ski, so most of those trips Linda spent in the ski lodge while Larry skied and Diane watched TV. Listening to Brad just now she was struck by the coincidence that, like Brad, she had always wanted to get in the car and drive around the United States. Of course she didn't think she could do that by herself. Maybe she could talk Diane into going along next summer.

"You know I'd really like to do that if I could talk Diane into going along," said Linda.

"Well, if Diane doesn't want to go along you should just go by yourself. Here in the U.S. it pretty safe. You can go just about everywhere on the interstate highways. There are good motels along the way, and about every fifty miles or so, there normally is a well-populated rest area," said Brad.

"It sounds like you have traveled quite a bit. Besides traveling around the U.S. you've been to Iraq. Have you been to any other foreign countries?" asked Linda.

"We stopped in a couple of countries on the way to Iraq, but that doesn't count because I had to stay in the air terminal. I did spend several weeks in Kuwait before the war started. The army took us on a couple of tours of the Kuwait City, but we weren't allowed to wander off by ourselves.

It wasn't much different that living in a tent out in the Mojave Desert. What would you do next summer if you don't take a vacation somewhere?" asked Brad.

"Well, I'll want to spend some time with Diane before she goes back to school. Just this week something else came up. My pastor asked me if I could help out as a counselor for our church youth group. I'm not so sure I want to do that, but I feel like I have an obligation to help out. I helped out on a couple of trips that Diane took when she was in the youth group, but I don't know if I'm qualified to be the lead counselor," said Linda.

"I'm sure you could do a good job. Your pastor probably asked you because of your experience with young people in connection with Diane and her friends," said Brad.

"Yeah, maybe, I hope it's not that he wants to use me as an example of what not to do because of my divorce and because I dropped out of college to have a baby," Linda said, before realizing how much of her personal feelings she had let slip.

"No, I don't think the pastor would want to use you as a negative example. Of course, you could always get married before you agree to be a counselor unless you're having too much fun being single again," said Brad.

"That's not likely to happen. If you saw some of the men I could be having fun with you would know why I'm not planning on remarrying again, at least not in the near future. What about you? I suppose you have a lot of girlfriends. Wouldn't you like to get married and have kids someday?" asked Linda.

"Yeah, I guess I'd like to get married someday, but first I think it is important to be able to afford it. Right now I'm not seeing anyone. I haven't really had much of an opportunity to meet girls. School and football take up a lot of my time, and being new here means I don't have a bunch of friends. Besides, most of the girls I have met are like the girl that wanted to crowd in the line when we were registering. Her name is Tina Williams. She still hangs around football practice and seems to know a lot of the guys. There are a lot of girls like that. I guess you might say they are kind of like groupies," said Brad.

"If you do go back in the army, wouldn't it be very difficult to be married?" asked Linda.

Brad decided to try to explain his thoughts on that matter. He pointed out that new enlistee probably shouldn't get married. Most of these marriages are only a few months old when the service member is deployed to Iraq, Afghanistan or some other foreign country where they can't bring along their family. During this time both the service member and spouse left behind change. That would require both parties to figure out if the changes are for the better or worse after a six month, year or longer separation.

Even if the new service member remains in the United States the married couple would face significant challenges. The family income normally is quite limited. That is true even with a spousal allotment and if the spouse has a job. Usually there is a new baby within a year and that could be a blessing but probably just adds to problems facing the new couple.

On the other hand, senior enlisted and officers normally have a much easier time. First of all the financial picture is usually quite a bit better than that of new service members. The government provides either better housing for the families or higher subsistence allowance. The circle of friends is usually more mature and normally is made up of service families that face the same problems and are always willing to help each other out in difficulties. Then there is travel to interesting places. Except for combat areas, the government normally moves families to new duty stations. Quite often the family is looked upon by people in foreign countries as representatives of the United States and that should be an honor. Just like any job, life in the army is pretty much what you make of it. If you don't think it fits your lifestyle you will be miserable. If you are interested in seeing new places and learning about other cultures, military life can be very rewarding.

As Brad was talking Linda was thinking that Diane would not be at all interested in marrying someone in the military. If she were to get Brad and Linda together one of them would have to change.

"Are you planning on getting married again?" asked Brad

"Oh, I don't know, just like you I haven't met any prospects. I haven't had a date with anyone except Larry in twenty years. Actually I guess you might say I did have one date by accident. One of Larry's friends is a lawyer in the Bay Area. A couple of weeks ago he called me and said he and his wife were going to be in the area and wanted to take me to dinner. Larry and I had gone out with them several times, so I thought it would be all right. As it turned out, this guy, Bernie Mitchell, showed up at my house without his wife. He said at the last minute she decided not to accompany him on his trip. We went to dinner anyway even thought I knew I probably shouldn't have. The dinner was nice except that he kept telling me intimate things about his marriage and that his wife didn't want sex any longer. I had a hard time not letting him into my house when he brought me home. If I had known how much trouble it would be, I would have hired a cab to take me home. Besides that, Larry has given my phone number to several men, who have invited me to dinner, to go sailing, to go golfing, and some guy even wanted me to go bowling with him. Then there's a number of the married men that Larry and I know from the club and even from church that call me and ask if I need to talk to someone," Linda told Brad.

"Well, you can always send in a tape of yourself to a lonely hearts club," Brad said in jest.

"Yeah, but I'm afraid I would get the tape back with a note saying all the men that received the tape said I sounded like a pig when I laughed." Linda laughed.

Just then Linda's cell phone rang.

"That's Diane. I hope you don't mind me taking the call," said Linda as she answered the phone.

Brad could only hear Linda's comments, which were, "Hey, honey, did everything go okay today? Well, I'm sure you will do better next test. No, you didn't wake me up. I haven't gone to bed yet. No, Mark hasn't called. Have you called him yet? Why don't you call him tomorrow evening? Remember, I did tell him I'd ask you to call. All right, call me tomorrow and let me know how things are going."

"Sorry, but I asked Diane to call me every night before she goes to bed to be sure she is all right. I know she is capable of taking care of herself now, but I can't help worrying," said Linda.

"Sounds like you are a good mother. It's too bad more of the kids at college don't have parents that are as concerned as you are," said Brad.

"Her father, Larry, said I should leave her alone now that she is eighteen years old. He and his new wife, Cindy, see her almost every week end, so she is not really all by herself. I think Cindy stops by the school for lunch with Diane on occasions also," Linda said as she wondered why she was telling this to Brad.

"Do you know if Diane has a boyfriend yet?" asked Brad.

"She hasn't said anything about that. I don't think kids go steady anymore. It's like they go places in groups. I guess that is for protection against each other," said Linda, pleased to hear that Brad expressed some interest in Diane.

"It would nice to meet her next week after the game," said Brad.

"Oh, I forgot to ask Diane if she was able to get tickets to the game. I'll have to remember to ask her tomorrow when she calls," said Linda.

"You know what? I can get two tickets for you in case Diane isn't able to get any. Stanford games are always sold-out, but the visiting team is always allotted some tickets. Hardly anyone on my team wants tickets for away games. If Diane had to pay for tickets, you might as well use the ones I can get for you," said Brad.

"That would be nice if you are sure you don't have to pay for them," said Linda.

"Actually, I can probably get four tickets if you think you will want to ask someone else to the game," said Brad.

Linda quickly answered, "No, No, that won't be necessary."

By the time they finally finished dinner. The waiter came to the table and made a point of asking Linda if she was staying for dessert. She politely said yes. It was close to midnight when they finished dessert. Brad paid the bill even though Linda offered to pick up the entire tab and then at least half of the cost. Brad figured a couple of more dinners like this one and he would have to settle for a new economy van instead of a Corvette next summer. That seemed okay to him, however.

As Brad walked Linda to her car in the deserted parking lot he mentioned that they should be sure and find out how Professor Scott intended to help their environmental team. When they got to Linda's car it just seemed natural for Brad to give her a hug good-bye. The hug actually lasted for over a minute as they continued to talk. At about the same time they both became aware that the hug had gone on too long, so there was a quick release. Brad was thinking that if he had one more glass of wine he probably would have kissed her goodnight.

On the way home Linda tried to remember how much of her personal life she had discussed with Brad. She was surprised how freely she had talked during dinner now she surprised herself even more by not feeling that she had said too much. Tomorrow's environmental class should clear up some of the mystery surrounding Scott's involvement in Linda's team. Now she started thinking about how much or how little she should tell Joan about dinner when she will call her tomorrow night.

Brad was thinking how different the dinner with Linda was from dinner in Las Vegas with Kandi Kolinsky. He could hardly remember anything Kandi talked about other than she spent most of dinner talking about herself. Of course, he might have remembered more if he hadn't been thinking about what he wanted to happen after dinner. Tonight's dinner was different for a number of reasons. The original purpose of the dinner was to exchange information about school and Brad had no particular thoughts about getting together with Linda after dinner. As the evening wore on, Brad found he was genuinely interested in what Linda was talking about. The thought of maybe meeting Diane also interested him, but he didn't dwell it. By the time he got home he was thinking how he might have to punch Professor Scott in the nose if Scott started stalking Linda.

After his morning class Brad went directly to the environmental class hoping to be able to talk to the other team members before the start of the class. If Professor Scott was available they could find out what he had in mind for their team. Linda showed up several minutes after Brad. She looked really good considering she couldn't have gotten full night's sleep.

"I was hoping Jason and Kathy will show up before the start of the class so we can find out if they might know what to expect from Scott," said Brad.

"It doesn't look like they will be here soon. We may have to wait until the break to talk to Scott," said Linda.

The first half of the class consisted of a lecture by Scott, which was basically what the class should have read as their assignment. Scott's talk was more colorful and he threw in some humor to make it more interesting. Basically, Scott said the world is in a dangerous state mainly because of selfish practices by the U.S. government and big corporations. It is up to the young generation to save the planet and he will tell them how to do it.

At the break the team caught Scott before the other students had a chance to start asking him questions. Brad asked Scott to explain how he would be helping them with their research project. Scott wasn't happy to hear that question as a number of other students were listening. He asked the team to stop by his office after at the end of the class and then turned his attention to other students. He didn't say anything about buying the team lunch.

The last half of the class Scott continued his lecture this time addressing the rewards and punishment that should be put into law for good or bad environmental practices. Next week's assignment was to read more chapters from the class text book and to be prepared to discuss examples of poor environmental practices.

After class Linda led the team to Scott's office, hoping Scott was just behind them. Fifteen minutes after they got there Scott showed up. By then Jason and Kathy had left. Scott continued to stand as he talked to Linda and Brad indicating that he wanted to end their conversion as soon as possible.

"What was it you asked at the break?" Scott asked Brad and Linda.

"Last Thursday at lunch you told me you wanted to be more involved with our team and maybe lead our research. The team is concerned that we would simply be helpers for your research project and that we wouldn't be able to develop our own ideas," said Linda.

"Well, you must have misunderstood me. I simply meant that I wanted you to keep me informed on your progress," said Scott.

"Other than that what other teams are doing, how do you want us to do that?" asked Brad.

Scott hesitated before answering the question. He appeared to be thinking of changing his mind about being involved or thinking of a good way to fool the team into believing he was truly interested in helping them and not simply trying to find a way to spend a lot of time with Linda. After a few seconds he had made up his mind realizing that the team or at least Linda and Brad were probably aware of his true intentions. Scott chose to back away from his offer to provide special help for the team.

"Of course I didn't mean to imply that your team would get any special treatment. That would not be fair to the other teams. You can keep me informed by weekly progress reports starting at the end of next week. I plan on asking all the teams to do that on this Thursday's class," said Scott.

"All right, thanks for the explanation. I must have misunderstood what Linda told me about your discussion at lunch last week," said Brad.

Brad and Linda then left Scott's office and watched him walk toward the cafeteria. Brad thought about asking Linda to lunch but decided there might be a better time. Linda was thinking of asking Brad to lunch, but she also decided there may be a better time.

"Brad, you didn't misunderstand me. Scott definitely said he wanted to provide special help to our team. I guess he must have changed his mind," said Linda.

"I'm glad he did. I would rather learn on my own than have someone just give me a grade. Of course this may mean we are in for a rough time if Scott thinks we disrespected him by turning down his proposal. I'm not sure what Jason and Kathy will think of the change," said Brad.

"Let's not worry about that. I've got a feeling Jason and Kathy are going to pretty much rely on us to complete the research," said Linda.

Linda then left for home and Brad went to lunch at the football team training table.

That afternoon practice was intense since it would be the last contact practice before Saturday's game. Adding to player misery was the fact that this was one of the hottest days of the year. The temperature on the practice field was near 100 degrees. This caused a number of players to complain about the heat. Coach Buster Stewart called a break in the practice in order to put a stop to the complaints.

"If you babies can't stand the heat today, what are you going to do Saturday when it's even hotter? The heat is all in your mind, just forget about it. Lots of jobs are worked in even hotter conditions. At least nobody is shooting at you. Hey, Wilson, tell your delicate friends if it is as hot here as when you were walking around with one hundred pounds of gear in Iraq when the temperature was over 130 degrees!" yelled Buster.

"Well, Coach, I think it was hotter in Iraq. I just did the rock test to make sure. If you pick up a rock that has been in the sun here, you say, 'That's hot.' In Iraq if you pick up a rock, you scream, 'Goddamn that's hot,'" Brad answered, going along with the humor.

Brad immediately felt the eyes of his teammates turned his way. He had never told anyone about his army background. Except for the coaches and Zeke Solum he didn't think anyone else knew he had been in Iraq.

The practice finished soon after that break without anyone else complaining about the heat. Teammates then started questioning Brad right away about being in the army. By the time Brad had showered and gotten to the training table dinner several players were grouped around him asking more questions.

Brad told the group that he did not get drafted, he volunteered for enlistment. After basic and infantry training in the United States he was sent to Kuwait just before the start of the Iraq war. His job during most of the drive from the Kuwait border to Baghdad was as a .50-caliber machine gunner on top of a personal carrier. After Baghdad was captured he spent the next year and a half on patrols searching for terrorists and acting like a policeman. He then commented that the easiest way to find the terrorists was to act like a target and have them shoot at you. That way you would be allowed to fire back.

"Brad did you wounded?" asked Warren West.

"No, just some shrapnel wounds in the arms and legs. I still have some embedded in my skin, but it should all be knocked out playing football by the end of the season," said Brad.

"Did you have to fight anybody hand to hand?" asked Coach Stewart, who had joined the group.

"No, but all of us in my platoon had a number of very close firefights," Brad answered.

"What is that, I mean how that happened?" someone asked.

"Well, we had to search many houses to see if any bad guys were hiding inside. Most of the time when we had to break in a door, we just found a family of women, old men, and kids. If there were only bad guys inside, they would fire at us from a few feet away when we came in the house, so we would have to fire back. If we knew for sure that there were no civilians inside, we could fire back. Of course that didn't happen very often since it is almost impossible to be sure no civilians are in the line of fire," said Brad.

"You mean whoever shots first wins?" said someone.

"Yeah, sometimes, but we could never shoot first unless we definitely knew there were no civilians in the house. If we were sure there were no civilians inside, we threw in hand grenades after telling them to surrender, but like I said that didn't happen very often. The terrorists knew we wouldn't fire at civilians, so they would prop women and child in front of them. They started shooting when we started to come in, so we always had to hold our fire," said Brad.

"What did you do then?" Brad was asked.

"We just had to wait until our interpreter could talk the bad guys into surrendering or they got out through holes in walls into the next house. Sometimes they would yell back that they were not terrorists and they only shot at us because they thought we were Ali Baba. They called terrorists Ali Baba," said Brad.

"What did you do with any of them that you captured?" someone asked.

"We just sent them back to the base camp for questioning. After a few hours they were usually let go because we couldn't prove they were the enemy," said Brad.

"How many times did you have to search a house?" Brad was asked.

"I don't know, probably over a hundred times in a little over a year," answered Brad.

"Did it really get up to 130 degrees?" someone asked.

"Well, we were told it did. All I know is that a lot of days over there seemed hotter than it did today. Almost as bad as the heat was the sand. Every time we got out of a helicopter we were blasted with the prop wash that turned us into sand cookies sprinkled with goat turds. Of course it may be worse this Saturday," said Brad.

That seemed to slow down the questions, allowing Brad to leave for home.

CHAPTER 7

Friday morning Linda got a phone call from Joan asking her to have lunch at the club. Linda didn't think anything unusual about this request. They often would meet there Saturday mornings, but they would miss this Saturday because of the football game. Linda thought Joan just wanted to have some time away from home.

When Linda got to the club restaurant Joan was already there and was half way through a Bloody Mary.

"Hi, Joan, looks like you got an early start. I hope I'm not late," said Linda.

"You're on time. I just wanted to have a drink before you got here. You better order one for yourself," said Joan.

This was not normal for Joan, so Linda figured she had some bad news. She probably wants to tell me she can't go to the game tomorrow thought Linda.

"Okay, Joan, I'll get one of those Bloody Marys," Linda said as she signaled a waiter to come and get her order.

"I've got to tell you something, but I better wait until you have had something to drink," Joan said.

"Okay, shall we talk about the weather while we're waiting," Linda suggested sarcastically.

"Oh, I can't wait. Now remember this is not my idea. I'm against it, but Henry said you won't mind," Joan said.

"What does Henry think I won't mind?" asked Linda.

"Well, I'll give it to you straight. Henry asked Howard Douglas to go to the game with us tomorrow instead of Hannah. I said we should ask you first, but Henry said it's too late for that. Howard quickly accepted when Henry said we were going to the game with you. You do remember Howard, don't you?" Joan said.

"Oh yeah, I remember him. We met when you and Henry invited me to dinner here in the club the week after I told you about my divorce and we just happened to run into Howard who was going to dine alone. It's hard to forget a man who spits in your ear shortly after you meet him," Linda answered.

"Well, you know Howard was just trying to talk above the piano music. He has a weak voice, so he had to get close so you could hear him," Joan said.

"Apparently he also has weak eyes. Every time he started to look at me, his eyes dropped to my breasts," said Linda.

"Yeah, well, that's just because he wanted to see what your boobs looked like. All men are that way," said Joan.

"Tell me again what he does. I think you said he works for Henry," Linda said.

"Yeah, that's right. He is a lead auditor, and his wife divorced him last year. His wife took him for everything except his job," said Joan.

"What about Hannah, is she okay with being pushed aside?" asked Linda.

"Yeah, I told her there would be other games. I hope I'm right about that. Are you all right with Henry's plan?" asked Joan.

"I guess so. I really want to go to the game tomorrow. I can put up with him during the game. I just hope Henry doesn't suggest we all have dinner together after the game," Linda said.

"Thanks for going being a good sport. Remember this was not my idea," said Joan.

"I'll be okay, but I'm going to wear earmuffs. I don't care how hot it is tomorrow. Incidentally, Brad said we will be sitting in the shade by the end of the first quarter," Linda said.

"So, Linda, tell me about your dinner last Wednesday," said Joan.

"I tried to call you last night, but Hannah said Henry took you to dinner," Linda said.

"Yeah, you'll never guess where we went," said Joan.

"Well, knowing how eager Henry is for something different, I'd say you came right here to the club," said Linda.

"Oh no, we went to the La Vie En Rose. I told Henry you were going there earlier in the week and then said something like I wish somebody would invite me out to a nice dinner somewhere," said Joan.

"You didn't tell him who I went with did you?" asked Linda.

"Well, actually I did," said Joan.

"Joan, you didn't. I don't want anyone to get the wrong idea. I hope Henry doesn't mention that to anyone else," said Linda.

"Don't worry, I said your Professor Scott Watson was taking you to dinner," said Joan.

"Golly, Joan, that is almost as bad. Somehow you'll have to let Henry know that I won't be going to dinner or anywhere else with Scott," said Linda.

"Yeah, sorry I didn't know what else to say when Henry asked who was taking you to dinner. Anyway, mentioning that you were going to dinner at the La Vie En Rose got Henry to take me there," said Joan.

"You mean he just decided to take you to dinner because you told him I was being taken to dinner?" asked Linda.

"Well, not exactly, it seems that Henry just wanted to get me in a good mood before he mentioned that he invited Howard Douglas to the football game. He didn't say anything about that until I'd finished my second glass of wine. You know how I get along with wine. By that time in my confused state of mind, it seemed like a good idea," said Joan.

"Maybe Saturday night you can tell Henry that I've thrown Scott aside for Howard," said Linda.

"Henry would believe that. He thinks no one is as irresistible or exciting as an accountant." Joan laughed.

"Just don't let him tell Howard I find him irresistible and exciting," said Linda.

"Okay, now, tell me about your dinner date with Brad," said Joan.

"Look, first of all it was not a date. We simply needed to meet somewhere to decide what to do about Scott," said Linda.

"And it took you over four hours to come to a decision in a romantic French restaurant?" asked Joan.

"How do you know how long we were there?" asked Linda.

"I asked the waiter if he remembered a beautiful lady and a handsome man coming for dinner Wednesday at 8:00 p.m. He said he'd never forget the charming couple who had two bottles of wine to drink and stayed until closing at midnight," said Joan.

"Yeah, if the waiter did remember us, he probably said something like remembering a kid with his grandmother took four hours to finish a bottle of wine," said Linda.

"Linda, don't be so sensitive. Brad is quite mature looking, so the age difference is hardly noticeable," said Joan.

"If I ever go to dinner with a man again, it will be on the other side of town, and you will never hear about it," answered Linda.

"What else did you talk about? Incidentally I kept asking Henry things about his favorite subject, work, but even then could only keep him there for a couple of hours," said Joan.

"Brad did say something I didn't know. He said the government is paying for his college education because he promised to go back on active duty in the army. That means he will probably go back to Iraq if the war is still going on then," said Linda.

"Wow, that's a bummer. I guess that means nothing will come of him meeting Diane," said Joan.

"Yeah, maybe, but I'm going to try to get them to meet anyway," said Linda.

"You mean when Diane comes home for Thanksgiving?" asked Joan.

"No, remember I told you I'm going to visit Diane next week and we are going to the State and Stanford football game. Brad said he can stop by the grandstand close to where we'll be sitting after the game," said Linda.

"Then how are you just going to tell Diane that this is the guy she should marry?" asked Joan.

"I'll think of something. Look, Joan, I've got to get home. I want to make sure the gardener finishes before the pool man starts cleaning the pool," said Linda.

"Okay, we'll stop by your house a little before 11:00 a.m. tomorrow," said Joan.

Shortly after arriving home, Pastor Rogers called Linda to ask about the counselor position. It took Linda fifteen minutes to thank the pastor for the invitation to be a youth counselor but to tell him she won't be able to do that now but maybe after the first of the year. After the phone call, Linda realized the real reason she turned down Pastor Rogers was that after being around younger students at State, she didn't enjoy being around kids half her age.

Brad's Friday football practice consisted mainly of running plays scheduled for tomorrow's game. The defense did not line up opposite the offense but practiced switching alignments intended to fool the opponent's offense. Brad spent half the time at a tight end position and the other half with the defense and with special teams. After practice and dinner at the training table Warren West asked Brad to drive him to a nearby bar where Warren was to meet a mystery woman for a date.

"So Warren, who are you meeting tonight?" Brad asked as they drove to the bar.

"Well, I'm not sure. Mokie Anton told me his girlfriend wants her friend to meet a football stud. I told him I could spare some time to check her out," said Warren.

"Why not take your car in case she doesn't turn out so good and you need a quick getaway?" asked Brad.

"My car's almost out of gas, and I don't have enough money to get any more right now," answered Warren.

"How are you going to pay for drinks and anything else this evening?" asked Brad.

"I can buy two beers. From then on it's up to the babe to finance any further action," said Warren.

"How are you going to get home from the bar?" asked Brad.

"I'm planning on asking the babe to give me a ride home. I'll tell her I'll repay her in bed," answered Warren.

"What's your secondary plan if that doesn't work out?" asked Brad.

"I'll worry about that later," said Warren.

"Good luck, but if your plan on getting home doesn't work, do not, I repeat do not, call me. I'm going to bed early just like Coach Kruger told us to do," said Brad.

When they got to the bar Warren asked, or almost begged Brad to have one drink with him. Brad knew that Warren's plan was to have Brad buy him a beer before he met the mysterious woman. Brad agreed since he was curious about what Warren's arranged date would look like.

"How are you going to recognize your heavenly creature?" asked Brad as they entered the bar.

"Well, she said she would be sitting at the bar wearing a red blouse. She said she would be there by 7:00 p.m.," answered Warren.

The place was crowded and no seats were available and no woman in a red blouse at the bar. Brad had to reach between two people sitting on bar stools to place an order and to pick up the beers. Warren decided to walk around the bar to see if he might see someone else he knew. Brad looked at his watch and noted that it was about a quarter to 7:00 p.m. He decided to wait for another fifteen minutes and then leave.

"Hey, big guy, are you Warren?" asked a girl sitting on a bar stool.

Brad wondered if she was Warren's date or maybe just a scout to see what Warren looked like. The girl was wearing a green tank top with tan shorts. She had a tattoo of some sort on her upper arm that looked like somebody had been doodling on her body. He could smell her unpleasant body order, but she looked a little better than she smelled.

"No, but I know where he is. Are you waiting for him?" asked Brad.

"Sit down, big boy, so we can talk," said the girl as she slid to one side of the bar stool.

Brad decided to follow her instructions and sat awkwardly on half of the bar stool next to the girl.

"Was that dude you walked in with Warren?" asked the girl.

"That depends on if you are supposed to be wearing a red blouse," said Brad.

"The red blouse is in the car waiting for my report. If he looks all right, I'll tell her to come in and meet him," said the girl.

"Yeah, that was Warren. It doesn't matter what he looks like, he is a big spender and big time lover. You want me to get him?" asked Brad.

"Okay, I'll call the red blouse to come on in. You can get the big spender back here, and then you and I can go somewhere and get it on," said the girl as she put her arm around Brad and looked into his eyes.

She not only had body odor but also had bad breath. Brad considered taking her up on her offer but only for a few seconds. Brad figured she was a regular at the bar and was used to picking up a different boyfriend every night of the week. She smelled slightly better but not much better than an Iraqi goat, so Brad decided to decline the offer, but he wasn't sure how to do it without insulting the girl. Luckily he thought of something.

"You're not Mokie Anton's girlfriend, are you?" asked Brad.

"Yeah, I know Mokie, we get together from time to time," answered the girl.

"Well, Mokie's my friend, so I wouldn't want to cut in on him. I'll go get Warren now," said Brad, glad to get away from the girl.

Brad found Warren who was trying to hit on another girl sitting with some friends. By the time they got back to the bar stool, the girl in the red blouse had arrived. She looked and smelled better than the green tank top girl, so Brad introduced Warren and then left as quickly as possible.

On the way home Brad wondered why anyone could plan on meeting a blind date without any money. He didn't have to wonder why anyone could proposition a stranger in a bar; you have to be really hard up.

Saturday morning Linda got up early in order to straighten up the house and then get ready to meet Howard. She knew she should invite the group in for refreshments when they came to take her to the game but didn't want to prolong the visit. Perhaps just some chips and soft drinks would be enough.

Right on schedule Joan, Henry and Howard arrived. After Howard was reintroduced to Linda the group sat down for refreshments. That gave Linda an opportunity to notice Howard's attire. He was wearing nice looking blue and white checkered shorts. His green and yellow striped buttoned shirt was also nice looking, but it did not go with checkered shorts. It made Linda a little dizzy to look at him. It was apparent that all three of her guests had put on a lot of sun blocker lotion. Howard must not have had time to rub in all of the lotion as his forehead had smidges of white cream.

Fortunately everyone seemed to be anxious to start to the game, so there wasn't time for a lot of small talk. As soon as Howard got into the back seat of Henry's Lincoln Navigator beside Linda, she noticed his shoes. Howard was wearing new high top white sneakers that seemed to glow in the dark car interior. It looked like he was wearing light bulbs on his feet. It was at that time Linda noticed that Howard was wearing argyle socks. Linda couldn't help thinking that this guy needs help and that it would be so easy to straighten him out. However, she didn't want to be the one to do it.

Looking at the way Howard was dressed caused Linda to reevaluate how she looked. She was wearing tan shorts with a light blue blouse. She had white low-cut sneakers but without argyle or any other socks. Instead of a hat she had put on a sun visor that Henry said made her look like a green eye shaded accountant.

Unlike Howard, Henry wore solid color tan shorts and a solid color red polo shirt. He wore low-cut white sneakers that did not glow in the dark and white socks. Joan's outfit was similar to Linda's except that she wore a green polo shirt and a ball cap.

On the way to the game, Howard thanked Linda for the ticket and said he really liked football but hadn't had an opportunity to go to many games. Linda told Howard this was the first game she had attended for a long time and that she got the tickets from one on her classmates that is on the team. This comment caused Howard to start asking a lot of questions.

"Did your classmate say why he was giving you the tickets?" asked Howard.

"Well, we are on the same research team, and he happened to mention that he could get tickets for anyone that wanted them. The other two on the team didn't seem interested, so I asked for the four tickets," said Linda.

"That was nice of him," said Howard.

Linda wondered if Howard might be thinking she had a thing going on with a kid half her age. She felt a little more explanation was necessary, so she added, "Next week I'm going to visit my daughter, Diane, up at Stanford. Since State is playing them in a football game there, I told Diane I'd take her to the game and introduce her to this guy when the game was over. I don't know much about football, so I thought it would be a good idea if I see a game before next week."

"Oh," said Howard, who seemed to be somewhat relieved after hearing that.

"This guy's name is Brad. He wears number 54, so we should root for him," said Joan.

"What position does he play?" asked Henry.

"Well, he is on all the special teams and also plays some defensive position. This game he might also play something called tight end," said Linda.

"Yeah, I remember reading something about him in the sports page this morning. I think he regularly plays linebacker, but Coach Kruger said he might try him on offense as tight end to bolster the blocking," said Henry, who actually did know a little about the team.

They got inside the stadium a little after noon. Howard bought refreshments: he and Henry ordered beer, Joan and Linda got soft drinks, and everyone got a hotdog. Linda noticed that the cost of refreshments was almost as much as the price of four tickets.

By the time they found their seats and got settled it was almost 1:00 p.m. Henry sat on one end of the group with Joan next to him. Linda sat next to Joan and then Henry sat on the other side of Linda. Not much time was left to watch the warm ups, but Joan spotted Brad, who was participating in passing drills. Just about the time she pointed him out to the rest of the group, the warm ups ended and the teams went back into the locker room to get ready for the kickoff.

"So Linda, what have you been up to lately?" asked Howard trying to stimulate some conservation.

"Oh, not much to speak of. Since starting school I've keep petty busy studying and trying to keep track of Diane. That is hard to do since she left for school. What new with you?" Linda asked.

"Well, believe it or not I've started playing—or maybe I should say practicing golf. I've even broken 100 a couple of times. I was thinking maybe you would like to join me for a game at the club. No one there will notice if we aren't very good players," said Howard.

Linda had tried to think of a way of responding to any type of a request for a date Howard was expected to make. Before she could answer Howard, almost as planned Henry said that he and Joan would like to pair up with them. Linda was surprised Joan didn't immediately object, which probably meant she was in on the plan. This made it difficult for Linda to decline the offer.

"Yeah, maybe, that might be fun. However, it will have to wait for a couple of weeks. I'll be out of town next weekend," said Linda.

"What are you doing tomorrow?" Henry asked rather bluntly.

"Well, after church I have to meet with my environmental project team to complete an assignment for next Tuesday," Linda lied.

"Let's try for the Sunday after next. I'll call for a starting time that Wednesday when they open reservations. Can you make that day Linda?" asked Henry.

"Yeah, maybe," answered Linda in a flat tone of voice.

Just them the teams came back onto the field to start the game. Everyone in the stands stood up to cheer, which, fortunately for Linda, put an end to the golf date discussion.

As State lined up to kick off to Dudley, both Linda and Joan fixed their eyes on Brad. Once play started, the ladies lost sight of Brad in the mix of players.

"What happened to Brad, can you see if he is all right?" shouted Joan.

"Sit down and watch the game, nobody got hurt!" Henry shouted back at Joan.

Linda was a little shocked at seeing all the players bumping into each other and falling down on the field. She had seen football games on TV but never really paid much attention. It looked a lot more brutal in person she thought.

"What's your friend's number again?" asked Howard.

"It's 54, and I see him in the second line of State players," answered Linda.

Linda and Joan continued to watch for Brad while Howard tried to engage Linda in a conversation. Henry seemed to be enjoying the game, he cheered and stood up at the right times. Linda, Joan and Howard tried to follow his lead. At halftime Dudley was ahead 13 to 7. Brad had played well enough but had not done anything to distinguish himself.

"Linda, let's go to the restroom," said Joan as the half ended.

"Better hurry, halftime only lasts for about fifteen minutes," said Henry as they left.

"Well, what do you think of the game?" Joan asked Linda as they were on their way to the ladies' room.

"It's more exciting than I thought it would be. Knowing someone playing makes it more interesting. I still don't know why they start and stop so much. It's not like soccer. I remember the one year Diane played, it seemed like the soccer players just keep running around no matter who was kicking the ball," said Linda.

"I can't tell how Brad is doing. Just as soon as a play starts when he was in the game, it seems like he either knocked someone down or got knocked down," said Joan.

"Yeah, I hope that is what he's supposed to do," said Linda.

By the time they got to the ladies' room all the stalls had a long line of women ahead of them. Joan jokingly suggested they use the men's room.

After a couple of minutes they decided to come back sometime in the third quarter. As they left and were walking by the men's room they were surprised to see a couple of young girls coming out.

"Gee, I thought I was kidding about using the men's room," said Joan.

"Well, you go ahead if you are brave enough, but I'd rather just wet my pants," said Linda.

"If I were twenty years younger, I'd try it. If I go in now, I'd probably see Henry and Howard," said Joan.

Just then they saw Howard headed into the men's room.

"Maybe Howard can escort you into the restroom," said Joan.

"I know I'm going to wet my pants now," said Linda.

"Seeing Howard reminds me to ask you if he has spit in your ear yet?" said Joan.

"Not yet. Howard is a nice guy, but he keeps trying to talk to me about subjects not related to the game. I'm having enough trouble trying to figure out what is happening and to follow Brad without trying to be polite to Howard. By the way were you in on the big plan to force me to agree to a golf game with Howard?" asked Linda.

"Now don't get mad, but yes I did tell Henry that I'd try to help Howard out. This was all Henry's idea. He thinks Howard may take you out of your depression, even though I told him you are not depressed," said Joan.

"Well, I wasn't until I agreed to go to the golf game," joked Linda.

"Do you remember where our seats are?" asked Joan.

"Don't tell me you don't know. Look at the tickets," said Linda.

"Henry has all the ticket stubs. I think this is our aisle. Do you see Henry or four empty seats on the right somewhere?" asked Joan as she stood at the head of the stairway.

"No and no. Now what do we do?" asked Linda.

"I'll call Henry on my cell phone," said Joan as she started dialing.

"Do you think he brought along his cell phone?" asked Linda.

"Yeah, he always keeps it with him in case there is an accounting emergency to reconcile an account," said Joan sarcastically.

"Are you lost?" asked Henry as he answered his cell phone.

"No, I know where I am, I want to know where you're at," answered Joan.

"I can see you. Point your right arm straight ahead. Now, don't change your feet position, but move your arm slowly to the right. Stop. Now look where you are pointing," instructed Henry.

"Okay, I can see you. You can stop waving your arms now. You look like a bird trying to take off. What aisle are you on?" asked Joan.

"It's the next one to your right, genius," Henry answered.

Linda and Joan got back to their seat just before the half started. That said they would have to go again later because the restrooms were too crowded at halftime. Linda made a mental note to remember her seat location at next week at the Stanford game. Henry had resupplied the group with refreshments, which would make it difficult to stand up until the refreshments were gone.

Dudley kicked off to State to start the third quarter. For the first time Brad got a chance to play offense. The first State play was a run to Brad's side of the line, which got only about three yards. The next play was a delayed pass to Brad in the right flat. As soon as Linda saw this she jumped up spilling her soft drink and dropping her hot dog.

"Look out!" Linda yelled as if he could hear her.

The play gained the seven yards needed for a first down. As soon as the play ended Linda quickly sat down feeling a little embarrassed for showing so much excitement. Getting up by yourself and yelling was one thing, but yelling lookout was not something anyone ever yelled. No one said anything for a few seconds. Then the other three started to all speak at once.

"Is that your friend that caught the ball?" asked Howard.

"Wow Linda, you don't have to get too excited, he didn't score a touchdown did he?" said Joan.

"That's the way to go. Now let's get something started!" yelled Henry as he stood up.

Suddenly a lot of nearby fans started clapping and chanting, "Go, go, go."

"Now look what you two started." Joan laughed.

Linda felt saved from more embarrassment by Henry's action and the crowd follow-up. Still she felt she had to say something to explain her out of character action.

"I don't want that guy to get hurt and not be able to play next week. That's the only chance I'll have to have him meet Diane," said Linda.

Linda finally had to admit to herself that she might have personal feelings about Brad. She hoped Howard would believe she was only thinking of Diane. However, she felt that Henry had her figured out and even if he didn't at this time, Joan would certainly explain it to him soon enough. At any rate she was thankful for Henry taking the attention away from her.

State did score after a lengthy struggle down field taking a 14 to 13 lead. Brad was in for a few more offensive plays mostly as a blocker near the goal line during that drive. By the start of the fourth quarter Dudley had gone ahead 20 to 14. State struggled back and retook the lead 21 to 20 with less than three minutes left in the game. Linda and Joan kept their eyes glued to the field of play but managed to keep their enthusiasm under control. The trip to the restroom was temporarily forgotten.

"If State can stop them on the next few plays, we can run out the clock and finally win a game," Henry told the group.

"That should be easy, shouldn't it?" asked Joan.

"Yeah, maybe," said Henry, who was concentrating on the kickoff about to take place.

State held Dudley to only a few yards the first two plays, but then they got a first down courtesy of Warren West. A long pass was thrown to a Dudley wide receiver who was running stride to stride with Lightning Joe Resnick. Just before the pass got to that pair, Warren jumped on the back of the Dudley player causing a penalty and giving Dudley a fifteen yard gain and a first down. With only about one minute remaining in the game Dudley had reached State's thirty-five-yard line but was now facing a fourth down. A field goal would win the game for Dudley, but they needed to gain at least ten more yards for a first down and to be close enough for a field goal attempt. Time-out was called allowing Coach Kruger and his assistants to plan State's defense for the next play.

Kruger assumed Dudley would attempt a pass. So he instructed outside linebacker Mokie Anton to try an all-out rush. Brad who would be playing inside of Mokie would delay to make sure no pass receiver or runner would be coming his way and then try a delayed rush. The cornerbacks would hold their position and the free safety would help out coverage on the side vacated by Mokie and Brad.

The play started to unfold as Coach Kruger had anticipated. The Dudley quarterback took the center snap from the shotgun position. Only three receivers were sent into pass patterns with two backs staying in to block. Mokie cheated up a little before the play started probably signaling his intent to blitz. As soon as he crossed the line of scrimmage he was picked up by two blockers, the tackle and one of the remaining backs. This left a wide alley for Brad to charge through. He was coming from the left side of Dudley's line or the blind side of the right handed quarterback. Dudley's blocking back caught Brad out the corner of his eye and attempted to hit Brad with a brushing block after releasing from the block on Mokie. Sensing that the back may only try to partially block him and then drift out in the flat unnoticed for a possible dump off pass, Brad pushed the blocker hard enough to knock him backward and off his feet. This pretty much eliminated him as a receiver and allowed Brad to continue toward the quarterback who still hadn't found any of his receivers.

Dudley's quarterback was a big guy with a rifle for an arm who could easily complete a pass twenty yards down field. He may have been waiting for one of his receivers to get open deep before releasing the ball. During this time the right side of the Dudley line pinched off the State players leaving the right side of the field open for about fifteen yards before any defensive back could come up to meet any runner. The quarterback saw that opportunity and decided to run for a first down with his remaining back leading him.

By this time Brad was still a couple of yards behind the quarterback. When he saw the quarterback tuck in the ball and start to run, Brad knew he had to cut him off before he passed the original line of scrimmage, so he took an angle to meet the quarterback at that point.

Up in the stands everyone was on their feet watching the play. Linda stood on tip toes but still couldn't see much of the field. She tried jumping, but that, of course, didn't help at all. Suddenly she felt Joan grab her arm.

"Stand up on your seat like I did," Joan said.

That let Linda see Brad chasing the quarterback. Everyone was yelling, so instinctively she started yelling.

"Get him, get him!" most fans were yelling.

"Get him, Brad!" Linda screamed as loud as she could, not realizing what she was saying.

Back on the field, Brad managed to reach out and grab the quarterback's trailing left arm. This caused the quarterback to turn sideways and jerk to a stop. As he tried to pull away, his momentum helped Brad to stay on his feet so Brad could throw his full weight into the quarterback's body and slam him to the ground in a dramatic fashion.

The State fans went wild cheering. Linda through both arms straight up in the air and kept screaming.

"He's really good," she finally said to no one in particular.

"By God he's damn good. Give me five, momma!" Joan shouted.

Linda and Joan gave each other a high five hand slap as they continued to stand on their seats. Joan then glanced down at Henry who had sat down and was staring at her in almost disbelief of her excitement.

"Well, what do you think, Joanie, is this a good game or not?" Henry laughed.

"Yeah, this is even more fun than watching Lawrence Welk on TV. We have to go to the next game too," answered Joan.

Linda then felt someone behind her tap her arm. She figured she would be asked to sit down, so she stepped off the seat and turned around to apologize for blocking someone's view. Directly behind her was an older man who looked like Howard had picked out his clothes.

"Is that number 54 your son?" asked the man sitting behind Linda.

That could have been a devastating remark except that at the time Linda didn't care what anyone might think about her age. Joan once again helped her out.

"That's Brad Wilson. He is the boyfriend of Linda's daughter," said Joan.

"Oh, I'm Wendell West. My son is Warren West, number 34. Warren is Brad's teammate. They both play defense. Warren is a cornerback," said a smiling Mr. West.

"That's great," said Joan, trying to end the conversation.

"I'll have Warren tell Brad we met you," continued Mr. West.

By now Linda was sitting down and had noticed Howard, who was staring straight ahead. The crowd was still making noise, so she leaned close to Howard and instinctively placed an arm around his shoulder.

"Sorry about acting crazy, but I wanted State to stop the Dudley guy," Linda said, trying not to spit in Howard's ear.

"Yeah, that was pretty exciting, I'm glad State is going to win the game," Howard said in a flat, emotionless monotone.

"Let's get out of here and get some dinner," said Henry as the game ended with State winning 21 to 20.

"Can we wait just a couple of minutes until the crowd thins out?" asked Linda, who wanted to see if the players had time to visit with some of the fans before going to the dressing room.

"I've still got to go to the restroom. Do you want to go along?" Joan asked Linda.

"Yeah, I guess I better," answered Linda.

"What do you think of Linda?" Henry asked Howard as they waited outside of the ladies' restroom.

"She is great, but I don't think she is interested in me, although she did put her arm around me at the end of the game," answered Howard.

"Well, wait until dinner, when there won't be any distractions," said Henry, trying to make Howard feel better.

Inside the restroom Linda and Joan got in separate lines behind a few women waiting to use the stalls. When they were finally ready to leave Linda wanted to know what dinner plans Henry had in mind. Joan said they were going to eat at her house. Hannah would not only be joining them but was at this very minute fixing the dinner. Joan said after they got in the SUV she would call Hannah to make sure everything is on schedule.

On the way home Henry wanted to know what took Joan so long in the ladies' room.

"Look, it could have been worse. I made a great sacrifice to hurry up," said Joan.

"Yeah, you mean you didn't stop to brush your teeth," joked Henry.

"No, I'll tell you what I didn't do. I was going to change lines to a longer one but didn't do it just to save time," said Joan.

"Okay, I'll bite. Why did you even think of moving to a longer line?" asked Henry.

"Well, because the lady in front of me kept passing gas and I knew the stall would smell really bad by the time the lady finished her business. I was right, but it was even worse. It not only smelled bad, but the toilet didn't fully flush, and the floor was sopping wet," Joan said.

"Nice of you to tell us that, but you could have waited until we started eating dinner," said Henry sarcastically.

"Well, it's your fault for asking," said Joan.

"It sounds like you're lucky the lady didn't dump on your shoes," said Howard.

This caused muffled giggles from the others since this comment was so unexpected coming from Howard.

"Do you think Hannah has started cooking the steaks?" asked Henry trying to change the subject.

Joan called Hannah who said the food was ready. As it turned out Hannah's dinner involvement was setting up a catered spread of meat, cheese, bread and salads. No steak dinners had been planned.

"I hope you don't mind eating a deli-style dinner," said Joan as soon as they arrived at the Belsons' house.

"Just what I was hoping for. I'm not very hungry after eating those hot dogs," said Howard after thinking of something nice to say.

"I didn't think any of us would be very hungry after the game. If it's not too hot, we can sit outside on the patio by the pool. It will be easier to talk there without the TV noise," said Joan.

"Yeah, the patio will be nice at this time. While we're talking, I can barbecue steaks for anyone who wants one," said Henry, who apparently wasn't in on the dinner plan.

"So Linda, how did your friend Brad do?" Hannah asked as soon as everyone was seated at a patio table.

The question caused Linda to realize that Joan had been talking to Hannah about Brad. That didn't make Linda feel good, but maybe Joan only casually mentioned him.

"He did all right and made a big play near the end of the game," answered Linda.

"Mom said you are going to try to introduce him to Diane next week at the Stanford game," said Hannah.

"Yeah, I'll try. I thought he would make a good friend for Diane," said Linda.

"But he's a jock. Do you really think it would be a good for Diane to meet that kind of guy?" asked Hannah.

"Yes, I do," answered Linda tersely.

"All the jocks at school are stupid bullies. All they ever want to talk about is sex," Hannah persisted.

"Well, Brad is different. He's in college not high school. He can speak in complete sentences and he doesn't use that vulgar language like all your little friends use every time they come over here. Isn't that right Linda?" said Joan suddenly not wanting anyone to know she had met Brad.

"Yeah, that's what I told you. You all should meet him sometime. He doesn't act like an athletic, at least not in class," said Linda.

"If he can get us tickets to the next home game, he's all right as far as I'm concerned," said Henry, trying to lighten the conversation.

"You know you can buy tickets if you really want to go to the next game," said Joan.

"If they keep playing like they did today, I'll buy season tickets for next year," said Henry.

Linda was glad they finally got off the discussion about Brad. The rest of the dinner she tried to engage Howard in any kind of discussion. Howard was polite, but it was very evident that he realized Linda really wasn't interested in him. To his credit he didn't sulk or worse yet try to change her mind about him. When they had finished dinner, Howard waited an appropriate amount of time before announcing that he enjoyed the day but had to be going home.

Linda walked Howard to his car and thanked him for going to the game with her and the Belsons. Just before Howard got in his car Linda said she was looking forward to a golf game a week from next Sunday. For the first time since dinner a big smile appeared on Howard's face.

A little while later Linda said good-bye to the Belsons and walked home. It was still early giving her time to think about the day's activities before going to bed.

She was surprised at how emotionally drained she felt after the game. Yelling at the game was something she had not expected to do. As a matter of fact she couldn't think of the last time she had yelled at anyone or anything. She had never yelled that loud before not even when she was a kid. It was also the first time she had ever given anyone a high five hand slap as far as she could remember.

Linda waited until near midnight before going to bed to see if Diane would call. While she was waiting she considered calling Brad to congratulate him on State winning the football game but then thought that would not be such a good idea. She also thought it would be nice if Brad called her to see if she enjoyed the game, but she knew that wouldn't happen. Except for the comments by Wendell West and Hannah she enjoyed the day immensely. She felt better imagining how good it would feel to punch Wendell in the nose and to strangle Hannah, but of course she would never do that. The next week Linda will be busy getting ready for her visit to see Diane.

After the game Saturday night Brad declined an offer to have pizza and beer with a few of the players. He wanted a steak instead and realized most of the players would rather go to the local pizza parlor to meet girls and act like heroes to the other customers. After dinner he went back to his room at the transit quarters hoping to relax and study. For some reason he didn't feel like calling Megan Albers or trying to pick up some other girl.

Instead he thought of calling Linda to see if she enjoyed the game. He had to admit to himself that he enjoyed being with her and enjoyed their conversations. However, he convinced himself that his feeling were not romantic or sexual in any way. Then again she did have a great body. By the time he got home he had decided calling Linda that night might not be a good idea. He could call her Sunday afternoon to discuss the environmental class assignment.

When Brad got back to the transit quarters he saw Doug Foley talking to the duty clerk.

"Hey, Wilson, you're just the guy I need to see," said Doug as Brad can into the office area.

Doug is an army sergeant assigned to transit hotel as a clerk. He checks people into the quarters and does other administrative tasks. Brad had thought that for the last few days he had been away at a training seminar.

"How was your training seminar? Were you able to round up any female troopers to spend some free nights at your hotel?" Brad joked.

"No, I didn't meet anyone new. Can you give me a lift to the airport? I have to be there before 10:00 p.m.," asked Doug.

"Yeah, maybe. If you are meeting someone there, how are you going to get back here?" asked Brad.

"My girlfriend, Rosie Hammond, is going to pick me up. I told her I'd arrive on flight 47 at 10:30 p.m.," said Doug.

"Why don't I just drive you home since you are already here?" asked Brad.

At this point Doug decided he needed to explain his great plan. It seems earlier in the week an old girlfriend, Kathy Jones, came to town for a couple of days. Doug wanted to spend time with her, so he asked for three days' leave from his army duties. He then told Rosie that he had to go to an army clerical seminar in Denver and that someone would take him to the airport from work. Kathy dropped Doug off at the transit hotel earlier that afternoon before leaving town. As planned Doug told his Rosie he would be arriving home on a 10:30 p.m. flight from Denver and would call her to pick him up when he got off the plane. Now he wants Brad to take him to the airport so he can leave his travel bag on the baggage claim carousel with a used claim form he picked out of the trash earlier in the week. His plan is to be standing by the carousel where he told Rosie to meet him. That way it will look like he just got off the plane, which should keep her from suspecting anything.

"Isn't that a little bit dishonest?" asked Brad.

"Yeah, actually it is a lot dishonest. Can you give me a ride over there?" asked Doug.

"Okay, but I'm not going to be there when your friend shows up," said Brad.

By the time Brad got back to his room he didn't feel like studying. He could do that in the morning and then have something to talk to Linda about if he called her later in the day.

CHAPTER 8

Sunday morning Linda got up early planning on going to church. She felt it would be a good idea to let Pastor Rogers she was still a good church member. But before she left for church Joan called.

"So Linda I just called to apologize for Hannah's remarks about jocks yesterday. I hope you didn't pay any attention to her," said Joan.

"No, I'm okay, I think Hannah was just trying to warn me about maybe not knowing enough about Brad," said Linda.

"Speaking of him, did you invite him over last night to go skinny dipping in your pool?"

"Golly Joan, I never thought of doing that. I guess I could do that today if you promise not to watch us from your window."

"Not watch from my window? Are you serious? I'd get Henry's moon telescope to get a good look."

"Well, I'm going to church this morning, so that will have to wait."

"I think everything turned out all right yesterday, don't you? I think Howard enjoyed being with you, and I know Henry and I enjoyed the game," Joan continued.

"Yes, I had a good time. Howard was a good sport. I'm sure he didn't enjoy the game any more than I'm going to enjoy playing golf with him a couple of weeks from now. You know I haven't played for almost a year," said Linda.

"Maybe you and I can go out to a driving range and practice hitting the ball before the big game."

"Yeah, that would be a good idea. I really need some practice."

"By the way, are you really having your team over today to go over your environmental assignment?" asked Joan.

"No, but don't tell Henry. I just didn't want to play golf today," said Linda.

"Well, you could still invite Brad over. If you do I can come over for a couple of hours while Henry and Howard are on the golf course."

"You know we are supposed to give an update on our audit plan Tuesday and as far as I know we do not have a plan and if we do I don't know who will give the update. I really should call all the team members to make sure somebody is ready for Tuesday."

"Yeah, well, call Brad first and invite him over. If you two can come up with something you won't need the other two."

"I think we can handle everything by phone. Joan, I know you are kidding when talking about Brad, but I hope you don't think I have any serious thoughts about having him as a boyfriend for myself," Linda said.

"No, no, I don't. I just am having fun dreaming. I've had the seven-year itch for over fifteen years now, so I like to think what it would be like to have sex with a young stud. I know it will never happen to me, but you've got a chance to take advantage of an opportunity of a lifetime," said Joan.

"Look, Joan, I have to finish getting ready for church. I'll talk to you tomorrow about finding time to practice our golf swings," Linda said, ending their phone conversation.

Linda did make it to church on time. After the services a number of women did talk to her briefly. Linda realized she may be imagining it, but it seemed to her that all the women were shielding their husbands from her. Almost none of the men had anything to say to her except Pastor Rogers, of course.

"Glad to see you this morning. Remember the counselor position is still open if you change your mind," Rogers said when Linda stopped to compliment him on his sermon.

"Maybe after the first of the year," Linda replied.

Brad got up at the usual time and went to a nearby coffee shop for breakfast. He then did his laundry at the transit quarters. After that he ironed the shirts and pants that he just washed. The next couple of hours were spent studying for school. Shortly after noon he felt it might be a good time to call the members of the environmental team to discuss the assignment for Tuesday's class. He decided to call Linda first.

"Hi, Linda this is Brad Wilson," Brad said when Linda answered.

"Yes, Brad, I was thinking of calling you. I wanted to congratulate you on winning the game yesterday. Joan and her husband Henry went with me. Joan's daughter was supposed to, but she had to attend a friend's birthday party," said Linda when she answered the phone, conveniently not mentioning Howard.

"Well, I didn't exactly win the game by myself, but I'm glad we won, and I'm glad you enjoyed the game."

I was also about to call Kathy and Jason to find out what we should do for class Tuesday," said Linda, changing the subject.

"Well, that's why I'm calling. I put together a summary of our progress and I thought I could compare what I have with what you and the others have. I also have some examples of bad environmental practices by some business that Scott asked us to talk about."

"Brad, I haven't come up with anything yet," admitted Linda.

"Have you heard from the other two?" asked Brad.

"No, would it be all right with you if I just call Jason and Kathy and tell them you can give the update?"

"Yeah, that sounds like a good idea. Let me know if they have any ideas," said Brad.

After talking to Brad, Linda called both Jason and Kathy and left messages on their cell phones. As expected she didn't hear back from either of them.

Monday morning Linda made arrangements for her trip to see Diane. She booked a Friday flight to San Jose instead of San Francisco thinking it was closer to Palo Alto where Stanford is located. She planned on getting to Diane's apartment in the late afternoon and then having an early leisurely dinner with her. Saturday after the game Linda wanted Diane to meet Brad and hoped that she would go along with her plan.

That afternoon Malcolm Edwards dropped by the store and was able to engage Linda in a discussion. Linda was actually happy to talk to Malcolm and was surprised to hear herself talking about how much she enjoyed the football game. In the past Malcolm had done most of the talking, but he turned out to be a good listener and seemed to be interested in what she had to say. Now that Linda didn't have to think about what she should do if Malcolm asked her for a date she felt free to talk about herself.

Linda also made another major decision. She told the Cushmans she was reluctantly unable to continue volunteering at the bookstore due to school requirements. The fact that she lied about school taking up too much of her time bothered her, but she felt she couldn't say she wanted more time to spend with a boyfriend,

For the first time Brad was happy to watch the game films at practice Monday. Coach Kruger was obviously pleased with the result and talked about how they could upset Stanford this coming Saturday. He said a few new plays would be used and one of them turned out to involve Brad as a tight end.

Monday night when Brad got back to the transit facility he was immediately surrounded by several transit staff members. Brad was asked to go over the play near the end of the game when he tackled the Dudley quarterback. A win by State rekindled some enthusiasm for the football team by the group. Brad suddenly had become somewhat of a hero for saving State from losing another game.

Tuesday morning Brad and Linda got to the environmental class early. As usual Jason and Kathy showed up just before class began, which didn't allow time to compare notes. Brad gave the status report for Team 1 and also listed several examples of poor environmental practices by businesses. Brad said the examples represented input from the entire team.

"I'd like to talk to teams one and six for a few minutes before you leave. Everyone else is excused," Scott announced at end of the class.

Scott had ended the class about a half an hour early so he would have time to talk to the two groups.

"Two members of Team 6 have dropped the class, which needs to be addressed. I have an idea that I'd like to discuss with all of you to see if this would work. Very simply I'd like to reassign you Jason and you Kathy to Team 6, which has the same research subject as yours. I think Team 1 is a little further along and perhaps better organized than Team 6. Jason and Kathy can help Team 6 catch up, and I will help Team 1 if they seem to be getting behind. How does that sound?" asked Scott.

No one spoke for a few minutes. Then Brad indicated it would be fine with him if everyone else agreed. One by one, the other students said that would also be all right with them.

"Well then, consider it done. I also want to let you all know I appreciate your cooperation," said Scott.

With that the session broke up. Jason and Kathy seemed to be happy to be with a couple they could more closely relate to. Brad and Linda decided to discuss the change further after leaving the others.

"That was unexpected. What do you think he has in mind for us?" Linda asked Brad.

"Oh, I don't know, but if we keep up on the assignments and Scott likes what we come up with, he may not need to get involved with us at all," said Brad.

"Yeah, let's try to do that. I promise I'll be more help from now on. I think we should insist that if he wants to work with us that we are both involved at the same time."

"I agree," said Brad happy that Linda apparently didn't want to get personally involved with Scott.

Wednesday and Thursday were uneventful for both Brad and Linda. At class Thursday Brad gave Linda two tickets to the Stanford/State football game. He said he would try to find them after the game as he headed toward the locker room.

Friday was a busy day for Linda. She took a morning flight to San Jose arriving just after noon. By the time she rented a car and got to Diane's apartment it was after 2:00 p.m. The weekend went downhill from there for her. It started with Wellesley Goldstone letting Linda into Diane's apartment.

"Hi, Linda. Diane told me you would be visiting this weekend," said Wellesley.

Linda hadn't been told about Wellesley and wondered why he was in Diane's apartment. She took an instant dislike to him. Although she realized it might be old fashioned, she thought he should address her as Mrs. Wallace.

"Who might you be, young man?" asked Linda trying to not act too surprised.

"Oh, I'm Wellesley," he said, offering no other explanation of why he answered the door.

With that Diane appeared holding a cell phone to her ear.

"Hi, Mom, I see you've met Wellesley," Diane said as she ended her phone conversation.

Linda started to say something nice to Wellesley but then thought some more. She wanted to spend a quiet dinner with Diane and didn't want this yahoo butting in. Even though she knew Diane would not like it Linda decided to act as if Wellesley wasn't there.

"Diane, you're looking good. I brought some of the things you asked for, they are in the car," said Linda hoping Wellesley would offer to get them for Diane.

Linda and Diane continued with some small talk when it became apparent that Wellesley was not going to offer to help her get Diane's packages from the car. Wellesley tried to interpose himself in the conversation, but Linda completely ignored him and Diane didn't seem to mind.

"Diane, how about showing me around the campus? I'd like to see where your classes are located. We can then have an early dinner," Linda said during a lull in the conversation.

"Okay, Mom, let me change clothes," answered Diane.

As soon as Diane disappeared to change clothes, Linda looked directly at Wellesley and spoke to him for the first time since she came in the door.

"Wellesley, it's time for you to go home. I haven't seen Diane for over a month and I want to talk to her about some personal matters," Linda said.

"Yeah, okay, I'll say good-bye to Diane and see you tomorrow," answered Wellesley.

Linda hadn't expected to see Wellesley again and was irritated that he was going to be a problem.

"I'll say good-bye to Diane for you so you can leave now," said Linda.

Wellesley wasn't sure what to do, so Linda opened the door for him.

"Diane, I've got to be going, so I'll call you later," Wellesley finally called out to Diane as he left.

"Okay, Lee, I'll talk to you later," answered Diane from her bedroom using Wellesley's nickname.

Linda thought it strange that Diane didn't seem to mind Wellesley leaving. However, she was happy he was gone and was amazed at how assertive she had been.

As Linda and Diana walked around the campus it became clear that Diane was not doing well with her studies. Linda tried to offer some encouragement, but Diane still seemed depressed about her poor studies.

"You know, Mom, Wellesley helps me a lot with my homework. If it wasn't for him I'd probably fail history," Diane said.

"I was wondering what the deal is with Wellesley. Is he your steady boyfriend?" asked Linda.

"Well, kind of. We spend a lot of time together, you know studying, but he's not sleeping with me or anything like that," lied Diane.

"I'm glad to hear that. I hope you don't mind me chasing him away this afternoon, but I wanted to spend some time with you. By the way, were you able to get tickets to the football game?"

"No, Wellesley said we can get them at the stadium tomorrow."

"Well, I got tickets from State. I hope you don't mind sitting with the State crowd."

"Did you get three tickets? I told Wellesley he could go to the game with us," asked Diane.

"No, I only have two tickets. Wellesley can get his own ticket at the stadium tomorrow," said Linda.

"But, Mom, how is he going to sit with us?" asked a visibly upset Diane.

"Well, he will just have to wait until after the game. Maybe we can invite him to dinner with us tomorrow," said Linda.

"Yeah, that's a good idea," said Diane feeling somewhat better.

At dinner that evening Diane talked a lot about how much help Cindy has been. From the conversation Linda could tell that Cindy was spending a lot of time on campus and it soon became apparent why Cindy was doing that. Linda was amazed that Diane didn't seem to care how much time Cindy spent flirting with some of the boys at the university. Linda also realized that Diane was becoming even closer to Cindy and further away from her. Even Wellesley seemed to be more important to Diane than her. Linda was beginning to feel depressed.

"Diane you know next Thursday is my birthday. I'll be thirty-seven years old. Can you believe that?" asked Linda trying to have Diane focus on her.

"Wow, Mom, some of my professors aren't even that old," said Diane, making Linda feel even worse.

It was still early when Linda and Diane got back to Diane's apartment. Linda suggested they go over some of Diane's homework to see if she could help. The first thing Diane wanted to do, however, was to call Wellesley.

"Hey, Lee, my love, guess what, Mom invited you to have dinner with us after the game tomorrow," Diane said when Wellesley answered her phone call.

Linda could only hear what Diane was saying, but it was clear that Wellesley was not happy with not being able to sit with them at the game. After several minutes of back and forth chatter Diane told Wellesley to hold on for a minute.

"Mom, Wellesley says he has a friend that will sell us three tickets so we can all sit together. It will cost us a little extra of course," Diane said to Linda.

That comment caused Linda's dislike for Wellesley to intensify. Certainly he knew she wanted to spend private time with Diane, but apparently he was too selfish to care about that. Besides asking her to buy tickets in addition to what she had, asking her to pay above face value for the tickets was really over the top. Linda knew it would be more difficult to get Diane to meet Brad if Wellesley were around. Thinking fast she came up with the following reason to decline Wellesley's offer.

"I told some friends that will be at the game that I would look them up, so I don't want to change seats. Maybe Wellesley can meet us after the game and we can go to dinner from there," suggested Linda.

"Mom says we have to use her tickets. I'll let you know where we can meet after the game," Diane told Wellesley.

Diane felt it necessary to show her displeasure by pouting the next couple of hours and then going to bed early. Linda fixed a bed for herself on the couch but was too upset to go to bed until after midnight. Despite that she still got up an hour before Diane the next morning.

"Oh, Diane, I was going to fix breakfast, but you don't have any food except snacks and soft drinks. What do you normally do for breakfast?" Linda asked when Diane finally got up.

"Cindy usually comes down here on Saturday and we have brunch in the school cafeteria," said Diane.

"Okay, let's go over there now before it's time to leave for the game."

"I'm not very hungry couldn't we just get something to bring home?"

Linda sensed that Diane didn't want to be seen with her in the cafeteria. This was an unexpected shock to Linda, but she decided to not let it bother her. By the time they got some food and finished eating it was time to walk to the stadium for the start of the game.

Their stadium seats were located in the end zone that was close to the exit the players would use when leaving the field. As the teams were going through pregame practices, Linda tried to find Brad. When she spotted him she turned to Diane intending to point him out to her. Diane, however, was talking on her cell phone to Cindy.

Later after the teams had returned to the dressing rooms for final game preparations, Linda called Brad's cell phone. As expected he didn't answer, but Linda left a message telling Brad the aisle she and Diane were close to. She said they would be able to come down to the end of the stands to meet Brad at the end of the game.

"Who were you calling, Mom?" asked Diane.

"One of the State players is in one of my classes. He said he would like to meet you, so I left a message on his cell phone telling him we could come down to the end of the stands after the game," Linda answered.

"That gives me an idea. I'm going to call Wellesley and give him our seat numbers. That way when the game begins, he can come over here and sit in one of the empty seats."

"Can't you wait until after the game to see Wellesley? After all we are going to have dinner with him tonight,"

Diane called Wellesley anyway. He hadn't planned on buying a ticket to the game, but Diane explained to him that he could buy the cheapest student ticket and then sit in an unsold seat near where she and Linda were sitting.

During the game Linda tried to keep her composure. She didn't stand up and yell when Brad or the State team made a good play, but she was intent on watching the game. During the first half she hardly said anything to Diane who didn't seem to notice as she spent most of the time texting or talking on her cell phone.

"Diane, let's go to the restrooms now before the half ends," said Linda.

"Okay, then we can get something to eat. Wellesley said he still hasn't gotten into the stadium yet," said Diane.

By the time Linda and Diane got back to their seats the third quarter had started. A few minutes later Wellesley appeared.

"Hey, hey, hey, look who's here," said Wellesley as a way of letting Diane and Linda know he found them.

"Hey, Lee, we've been looking for you. Mom, can you change seats with me so I can sit on the aisle. Lee can sit on the steps," Diane said, obviously happy to see Wellesley.

It was only a few minutes later when an usher told Wellesley he couldn't sit on the steps and that he would have to find a seat of his own.

"Come on, Diane, let's get something to eat," said Wellesley as he got up from the steps.

"Mom, I need some money," Diane said to Linda as she started to leave with Wellesley.

Linda considered telling Diane to have the jerk pay for the food but caved in and gave Diane twenty dollars. Even though she had just had something to eat Linda asked Diane to bring her back a soft drink. She hoped that would cause them to return within a reasonable amount of time.

It was over thirty minutes before Diane and Wellesley returned. While they were gone Linda concentrated on the game. Stanford was obviously the better team; they looked a lot bigger than the State players and had a 21 to 7 lead at the start of the fourth quarter. Brad had only played on defense and special team plays. He was in on a lot of tackles but had not done anything spectacular.

When State went on offense at the start of the fourth quarter, Brad was sent in as a tight end on offense. State started a time consuming drive that finally ended in a touchdown closing the score to within seven points of Stanford after the extra point. Brad caught two short passes and dropped two that probably should have been caught during the drive.

Diane and Wellesley returned before State scored, which allowed Linda to point out Brad. Neither Diane nor Wellesley who was sitting on the steps again, seemed impressed. Linda noticed an empty seat two rows down and suggested Wellesley sit there before the usher asked him to leave again.

The game ended after Stanford made a field goal, making the final score 24 to 14. Linda immediately grabbed Diane by the arm and more or less pulled her down the aisle to where she hoped to meet Brad. Diane mildly objected, asking if it was really necessary to meet this guy.

Wellesley joined Linda and Diane at the end of the aisle as Linda tried to pick Brad out of the group of players slowly coming their way.

After a short time Brad separated from the other players and headed straight to Linda.

Brad greeted Linda by saying that he was glad she was able to attend the game but was sorry State lost the game.

"Brad, this is my daughter, Diane. She is a student here at Stanford," Linda said, completely ignoring Wellesley.

"Hello, Diane, I guess you enjoyed the game since Stanford won," said Brad.

Before Diane could answer, a big Stanford player grabbed Brad by the arm, causing him to take a couple of steps sideways.

"Good game 54, nobody has gotten by me as much as you did today," said the Stanford player.

"You guys are good. Maybe we can offer more competition next year," answered Brad.

"Next year I'll be playing on Sundays," the player said, indicating he hoped he would be playing for a professional team.

As the Stanford player trotted away, someone called out, "Hey, Cal State."

Brad looked up just in time to see one of the Stanford fans throw beer from a cup at him. Most of the beer fell short, but some splashed on Linda's leg. The fan and a few of his friends laughed and started walking toward the exit.

Right after that Wellesley said "I guess we really whipped your ass today."

Brad's mood changed markedly after the beer was thrown at him, so his reaction to Wellesley's comment caused him to react without much forethought. Brad stepped directly in front of Wellesley and pulled him by the shirt so their heads bumped. Fortunately for Wellesley Brad had taken off his helmet.

"What do you mean, we? You weren't on field, were you? Stanford is a highly rated Division I-A team that won by only 10 points on their home field. That is not an ass whipping," Brad loudly told Wellesley.

After Brad let go of Wellesley no one spoke for a few seconds until Brad said it was time for him to go to the locker room. As he was leaving Brad said he was sorry some beer splashed on Linda. He then said if the fans caused any trouble for them as they left that maybe the big guy, pointed to Wellesley, can scare them away.

At a later time Brad felt he had to explain to Linda that the only reason Stanford didn't run up the score was because Coach Kruger was a good friend of the Stanford coach. As far as the Stanford team was concerned they probably thought the State game was no more than a practice. They ran only conservative plays so that they wouldn't give away new plays they would want to use against better teams. Substitutes played most to the second half for Stanford.

Linda was disappointed that Diane didn't say one word to Brad. However, she was amused at the way Brad interacted with Wellesley.

Wellesley was quiet for a change as they walked to a nearby restaurant for dinner. Once they were seated Wellesley started talking about how he was going to sue Brad and State for assaulting him. After a few minutes of listening to him, Linda spoke up and told Wellesley to grow up and forget it.

"Wellesley, why don't you start acting like a man instead of a wimp? If you wanted to say anything, you should have spoken up at the time. It's too late to do anything now," Linda lectured Wellesley.

Linda was surprised at what she had just said. She expected Diane to immediately take Wellesley's part and defend him, but neither Wellesley nor Diane said anything for several minutes. Linda broke the silence by asking what Diane was going to order for dinner. Almost no conversation took place for the rest of the dinner. All three seemed anxious to finish the meal and leave.

When they got back to Diane's apartment Linda positioned herself between Wellesley and Diane. She then said good-bye to Wellesley hoping he would take the hint and leave. Wellesley hesitated a short time hoping Diane would invite him in, instead Diane simply said she would call the next day.

Linda hoped that she and Diane could have an informative mother-and-daughter discussion, but Diane wasn't interested in talking. Nevertheless, even with short indirect answers from Diane, Linda understood that Diane was not happy at Stanford. Unlike high school Diane was not the most popular girl in campus. In fact she had only a few friends. It also became quite clear that Diane was a spoiled, daddy's girl that until now had always gotten her way. Even worse Linda was shocked to realize that Diane was not doing well in school. Her A+ grades in high school didn't produce the knowledge to comprehend college courses.

In the morning Linda got up early again and straightened things up in the apartment before Diane got up. Diane announced she wasn't hungry and didn't want any breakfast. Linda sensed Diane didn't want to be seen with her and would probably get something to eat later in the day. Since Diane wasn't interested in talking to her, Linda decided to leave for the airport a little early. Before leaving she reminded Diane of her birthday hoping Diane would remember to call or send her a card.

After Linda left Diane called Cindy to tell her what a terrible time she had when her mother visited. She said Linda was very rude to Wellesley but that Wellesley understood that Linda was too old to relate to younger people. Diane said she had to meet some jerk football player that assaulted Wellesley.

Cindy said she felt sorry that Diane's weekend was spoiled. Then she wanted to know more about the football player that assaulted Wellesley and why she had to meet him. Diane explained that the jerk was in Linda's class at school and for some reason she thought Diane would like to meet him. Cindy then said she would visit Diane at school Monday afternoon.

On the plane ride home from the football game Brad sat next to Warren West who wanted Brad to talk about his experiences in Iraq. Warren wanted to know what it felt like just before going out on a mission. Brad didn't want to discuss that and tried to get Warren to talk about something else but then decided it best to just answers the question and hope that ended the conversation,

"Well, I suppose everyone feels differently. One way to explain it is to think how you feel while you're waiting in the tunnel before taking the field to start a football game. You know you or another player may get seriously hurt, but you hope it doesn't happen to you. The difference is that in Iraq you know some of the guys you're with may get killed. In football when you take the field how would you feel if you knew that during the game several fans would be periodically shooting at you with rifles and that you were expected to continue playing knowing no one in the stadium would do anything to stop the shots?" Brad answered.

That kept Warren quiet for a while then he had another question.

"Weren't afraid you were going to get killed?"

"Yeah, but everyone has that fear just like some people are afraid to fly. I just figured that if it happened, it happened," said Brad.

"Well, I suppose that if you believe in life after death, it makes it easier. I don't believe that, so it's harder for me to not be afraid. I don't know how anyone could believe there is a god and that there is life after death," said Warren.

This irritated Brad, so he thought he should give a complete but concise answer to Warren.

"Look I am a Christian, so I do believe in life after death. That doesn't mean I necessarily believe or understand everything in the Bible. As an example I don't think there are two old guys sitting up in the sky watching what everyone is doing all the time. If there are, I don't think they would say things like, 'Hey look, Dad, there is Brad Wilson. Let's freeze his mind for a couple of seconds and make him look stupid,'" said Brad.

With that Brad stopped talking for a couple of seconds while he stared off into space.

"It seems I lost my train of thought, but I remember now. As I was saying I know lot of people are nonbelievers and they may be right. That doesn't bother me as long as they don't make fun of me. But here is the deal. At the end of life if the unbelievers are correct there is no consequence. On the other hand if I'm right I'll go to heaven and the nonbelievers will go somewhere else that's not so nice. As far as I'm concerned being a nonbeliever is an unreasonable risk to take especially since in order to achieve everlasting life is to simply be a true believer."

That put an end to Warren's questions while he pondered what Brad had just said.

That would have given Brad a chance to get some sleep except Coach Cutis wanted to talk to him at the rear of the plane. The other coaches sat in front, but Curtis had a habit of asking defensive players to sit in an empty seat next to him so he could review their play with them. The players said it was like sitting in a hot seat. Fortunately Curtis only wanted to compliment Brad on his play that day and then to discuss some other things.

"Brad, you do know Coach Kruger isn't going to compliment you no matter how well you play. As a matter of fact you are on his shit list. Do you know why?" asked Curtis.

"Maybe because Kruger is crazy?" answered Brad.

"That's true, but besides that, there is another reason. Let's just say it's because of Bud Helvig. It seems Kruger recruited Bud three years ago from some junior college in Texas. Bud was one hell of an athletic. He's playing professional football now, but back then he was almost unknown. Bud couldn't get into any of the big schools because of academic short comings. In other words he was dumb or actually dumber than shit. Except for football, that is. It was like some gifted people that have extraordinary ability in one special area but ordinary or less than ordinary ability in other areas. Anyway Bud seemed to be able to know what plays would be run by opponents and he was always able to blow up the plays. He was almost a one man defense. However, his academic record was as bad as his football skills were good. Kruger somehow kept him eligible. Nobody knows for sure, but everyone figures Kruger has someone take tests for Bud and also bribed professors to give Bud passing grades. Then there were other problems. Off field Bud was a gentle giant halfwit most of the time. Unfortunately he also had a tendency to get into bar fights. He sent several men to the hospital with broken bones. Kruger always tried to cover for Bud, but that didn't always work. Eventually the NCAA investigated. The NCAA found multiple infractions of rules involving multiple players, coaches, and facility members. The result was heavy penalties including reduced scholarships, reduced schedule, and lost bowl participation for two years with five years' probation after that."

"What does that have to do with me?"

"It seems Kruger is looking for a linebacker with Bud's ability. With Bud playing Kruger could concentrate on offense, which is his special love. Since no one will ever be as good as Bud he thinks all linebackers are not trying hard enough. Kruger knows you are the best of the current linebackers, so he feels if he continues to pick on you that somehow you will magically become Bud Helvig."

"Well, that is not going to happen, but I appreciate your explanation."

"Yeah, well, I'll let you know why I'm talking to you if you promise to keep this conversation secret. To be truthful there is something in it for me."

"Okay, I can keep quiet."

"It's almost a certainly that Kruger will be gone after this season. It's well-known that Kruger has been applying for coaching jobs all over the country. It's also well-known that no school wants anything to do with him. It's not so much that he is a dishonest cheat, but the big mark against him is that he got caught. This year the school is prepared to fire him. The school would have fired him two years ago but couldn't afford the termination payment in his contract. At this time it appears the school is in a better position to negotiate a reduced payment by threatening legal action against him. Anyway this means we have a chance to return to powerhouse football starting next season. But to start that, we need you, Zeke, and a few other players to return along with several new high-quality players. To get new recruits we need to offer then scholarships. That's where you come in. You're not on a scholarship now. If you need it, I can arrange one for you, but I'd rather use the available scholarships for new recruits. Someone told me the government is paying your tuition and living expenses. Is that right?"

"Yes, that's correct."

"So you're able to return next year without a scholarship from State? I know some walk-on players get student loans until they qualify for a scholarship, but that's not the case with you, is it?"

"I'll be okay without a scholarship and I am planning on playing football next year."

"Good, that's what I wanted to hear. I should point out a number of good qualities Kruger has before you get the idea he is all bad. Kruger did help Bud get a professional football tryout. That's worked out well for Bud. The infractions that Kruger was guilty of are things most coached do at one time or another. It's just that Kruger overdid it and got caught. His cheating was so blatant that the NCAA couldn't ignore it. When he's away from football I understand he is a really nice guy."

"Look, Kruger really doesn't bother me as long as he doesn't follow through with his threats to throw me off the team. In the army new recruits are always being yelled at by sergeants and the sergeants are always being yelled at by officers except when in combat. I do appreciate the talk and I will not repeat anything you've said."

Brad then went back to his seat just as the plane started landing. Fortunately there was no time for Warren West to ask about the Curtis talk.

CHAPTER 9

The football team didn't get back from the Stanford game until 11:30 p.m. Brad had a few beers with some teammates, so he didn't get to bed until after 3:00 a.m. It was almost 10:00 a.m. Sunday morning by the time Brad got up. He briefly considered going to the campus church but quickly discarded that idea. Brad hadn't been to church since he left Iraq, but he didn't feel comfortable going to church by himself. Instead he decided to spend the rest of the day studying for lack of anything else to do.

Several times Brad stopped studying to think about the Stanford game and about meeting Diane. Even though Diane had not said a word to him, Brad instantly decided he had no interest in ever seeing her again. However, he was pleased that Linda did attend the game and looked forward to seeing her in class Tuesday or maybe before. He decided to call her and then decided to not call. There was no real reason to call except, perhaps, to talk about the game.

By the time Linda got home late Sunday afternoon she was extremely depressed. Diane was not doing well in school, her only school friend seemed to be a bozo, and worse of all Diane was spending too much time with Cindy.

Linda didn't know where to turn for help coping with these issues. Her problems were too embarrassing to discuss with Joan. Linda thought of calling Larry. That would give her an opportunity to casually mention Cindy's real reason for spending so much time visiting Diane at school. That thought was quickly dropped as not the right thing to do. Linda then thought she would be able to talk about her concerns if Diane would call to wish her a happy birthday later in the week as she had promised to do. Around 8:30 p.m. Linda took a sleeping pill and went to bed.

Linda woke up even more depressed. When Joan called the next morning, as Linda knew she would, Linda suggested they go shopping thinking that take her mind off her troubles and at the same time would not allow Joan to ask too many questions about the Stanford trip. That worked well until they stopped for lunch at a mall deli.

With only a little prodding from Joan, Linda couldn't help but tell all the details about the Stanford trip, including her realization of how immature Diane revealed herself to be. Joan's supporting comments did nothing to make Linda feel better. Talking to Joan brought back painful memories that sent Linda into even deeper depreciation. Maybe going class the next day would get her in a better frame of mind.

Tuesday morning Linda got up early. She decided to wear some of the new clothes she had bought. She put on a very neat and business like suit that would make her stand out even more from the way other girls dressed, but by this time she was through trying to blend in with the younger crowd. Linda was anxious to get to the classroom and arrived almost ten minutes before the time class was scheduled to begin. She hoped Brad would be early. Just as she hoped, Brad sat down beside her a few minutes before class was scheduled to begin. By this time they had established seating arrangements as the two end seats in the front row of the classroom. As usual Scott Watson was about five minutes late for class, which gave Linda and Brad time to talk.

"Well, hello there, good-looking, you look pretty sharp this morning," said Brad, thinking to himself that she even smelled good.

"It was nice seeing you at the game Saturday and thanks for introducing me to Diane," continued Brad.

Hearing the complement caused a warm glow came over Linda temporarily easing her depression.

"Diane said she was sorry there was no time to talk, but maybe she could see you when she comes home for Thanksgiving," Linda lied.

"Yeah, that would be great," Brad also lied as he really wasn't interested in seeing Diane again since he knew he could never get to first base with her.

"How is Diane getting along with her studies and social life?" Brad continued.

Linda knew this question was coming but had not prepared herself to answer. As she started to talk she almost burst out in tears.

"She is doing all right, but I told her she should spend more time studying."

Brad sensed this was not the case from the emotional response.

"After class let's get some coffee in the Student Union. I'd like to explain why we lost the game Saturday," Brad said, correctly thinking Linda would want to discuss more about Diane but not at this time.

Scott opened the class with the following announcement; at class next Tuesday all teams will announce the business you will be auditing and present your audit program to the class. Scott passed out a list of business' that would agree to an environmental audit and discussed things to consider during the audit. That only took about twenty minutes. Scott then dismissed the class said the teams should spend the next week working on the assignment and would not need to come to this week's Thursday class.

"Linda, I'd like to talk to you and Brad for a few minutes," Scott said as Linda and Brad started to leave.

I really don't want to talk to Scott, thought Linda, but she knew she had no choice but to do so.

"You and Brad are obviously more mature than other teams, so I'd like you to be the first to give your presentation next Tuesday. That way it should be an incentive for the other teams to do their best in their presentation. As I had promised, I can spend some time with you, say tomorrow, around 4:00 p.m. I'll be home getting ready for my weekend trip, so maybe we can meet at my apartment. It is close to the campus," Scott continued.

Linda spoke first to tell Scott that Brad wouldn't be able to meet at that time because of football practice. Just as Linda knew he would, Scott said that since that was the only time he could be available that maybe just Linda could meet with him and, of course, fill Brad in later.

Linda recognized Scott's offer as a thinly veiled attempt to get her alone with him. She was not interested in forming a personal relationship with Scott and felt obligated to firmly let him know.

"No, that is not a good idea. Brad and I work pretty well together, so I think we can come up with a good plan, but thanks for the offer," Linda said as she looked directly at Scott.

Brad was surprised but pleased to hear Linda's response. He was also surprised that the thought of Linda and Scott getting together bothered him. After all it really was none of his business if Linda found Scott interesting and would like to start a relationship with him. He and Linda certainly did not have a personal relationship although, for the first time, he felt that would not be such a bad idea.

Brad and Linda then went to the Student Union. Brad pointed out that Stanford could have scored 100 points against State Saturday but didn't mainly because the two coaches were good friends. Brad went on to say that playing against a team of Stanford's caliber was actually good for State. He then said he hoped Linda's visit with Diane went well. This opened the door for Linda to talk about how she thought she was losing her daughter to Larry's new wife. Without realizing it she described in details how she felt about Wellesley and Cindy. Somewhere in her comments she said something about tomorrow being her birthday and that Diane would probably not call to wish her a happy birthday. As she talked it became apparent to Brad that Linda was feeling depressed.

"Look, here is the deal. Since we won't have to go to Scott's class Thursday we can stay up late and celebrate your birthday at the La Vie En Rose restaurant. It will be my treat since I made a little money at a job. Since it's your birthday I'll pick you up at your house so you won't have to drive," said Brad.

Linda hadn't expected that and wasn't sure what to say. After a few seconds she agreed to dinner. By then it was almost noon, so Linda went home and Brad went to team lunch room.

Time seemed to drag by until Wednesday night. Linda realized she was eagerly waiting to see Brad again. Finally at 7:30 p.m. Brad arrived at her house.

"Brad, let's take my car if you don't mind driving it," said Linda.

That's a really good idea thought Brad who liked the idea of driving a late model BMW. Before they started Linda had to describe a few of the car features. First she had to explain that you just needed to push the start button to start the car. The car key could remain in Linda's purse. Then she explained the six different ways the driver's seat could be adjusted. Once Brad had the adjustment he liked, he pushed another button for the car to remember the setting in case he ever drove the car again.

The arrived at the restaurant around 8:00 p.m. and were seated immediately in a secluded section. The restaurant was not crowded, but there were several diners who were seated far enough away so their conversation could not be heard.

This time instead of wine Brad ordered a gin martini. Linda decided to try the same drink. Over the next three hours they each would have two more martinis. Each drink seemed to relax Linda more and more, so she was able to talk in detail about her concerns over Diane.

Just before 9:00 p.m. Linda's phone rang. Thinking it may be Diane, she checked the caller identification.

"It's just a nuance call. One of Larry's old friends, Bernie Mitchel, is probably calling to invite me to dinner. I made the mistake of going to dinner with him one time after the divorce and that will definitely be the last time," Linda told Brad.

Linda felt compelled to tell the rest of the story. It's seems Larry and Bernie went to law school together. Over the past several years Bernie and his wife, Lisa, had socialized with Larry and Linda frequently even though the Mitchells lived in the San Francisco area. Linda liked Lisa but not Bernie, who liked to tell off color jokes and make suggestive remarks to Linda.

"I have an idea if you want to put a stop to his calls. Why not invite him to your house. When he gets there I'll beat him severely about the head and shoulders and tell him if he ever calls you again I'll break his neck," said Brad.

Linda couldn't help but laugh at the thought of that happening. She then had a thought of her own.

"Brad, suppose I do invite Bernie to dinner at my house tomorrow, could you be there also?" asked Linda.

"Sure, you really want me to break some of his bones?"

"No, not that, you shouldn't have to touch him. I have a plan to stop Bernie from any further contact with me. After dinner I'll tell him I talked to his wife who was surprised to hear he was having dinner at my house. If Bernie gets ugly after that maybe you can escort him out the door."

"Okay, you want to call him back. Wait first you'd better listen to his message to see why he is calling."

"Okay, I'll turn on the speakerphone so you can here."

"Hey, Linda, good news. I'm here in LA on business and have a free night tomorrow, so I'd like to take you to dinner. It's important I talk to you about a new venture I'm starting that could involve you. Hope to hear from you tonight," Bernie said.

"When you call back be sure and sound interested in his new venture," suggested Brad.

"Hi, Bernie, I was surprised to hear from you. What are you doing in LA?" Linda asked Bernie over the phone.

"It's a really big deal Linda. I discussed this with Larry and he is all for it. It's too complex to discuss on the phone. That's why we could discuss my plan over dinner. I'll be interested in your thoughts and maybe your help. I can pick you up at your place at 7:00 p.m. We can have dinner at your favorite restaurant of maybe my hotel's steakhouse," Bernie answered.

"Look why not have dinner at my house where we can talk in private. I can fix some steaks if that's okay with you."

It's unfortunate Linda and Brad could see Bernie's reaction to the invitation to have dinner at Linda's. Bernie couldn't believe his good luck. He had anticipated having to come up with a good story to get into Linda's house after dinner, but now he figured Linda would be receptive to his advances. He couldn't speak for a couple of seconds as his face froze in a glassy eyed stare thinking about great it would be to get Linda in bed.

Finally Bernie was able to say in a high-pitched voice, "That's a great idea. I'll be there at 8:00 p.m. with your favorite wine. See you tomorrow, I can hardly wait."

"He really got excited when you suggested having dinner at your house. He'll probably have wet dreams tonight," said Brad.

"Yeah, he did sound happy," Linda said although she wasn't sure what wet dreams were.

"Are you really going to fix dinner tomorrow?" asked Brad.

"Sure I assume you'll be ready for a steak dinner by tomorrow night."

"Two hours from now I'll be ready for a four-course dinner. I'll try to get to your house around 7:00 p.m."

Brad and Linda continued talking and drinking for another hour before finishing dessert. Brad suggested they have a glass of Grand Marnier to top off the evening.

The drinks were served in snifter glass, which caused Linda to ask why such a small amount of liquor was served in that size glass. Brad just said because it allows the liquor to breathe, which improves the taste. He was just repeating something he'd heard someone say once hoping it made sense.

On the way back home Linda had trouble staying awake and wondered if Brad was also having that trouble.

"I'd better make you a cup of coffee before you try to drive back to your place," Linda told Brad.

"Okay, that's a good idea," Brad answered hoping this may lead to something better than coffee.

Over coffee Brad commented on how much he liked the house and how big it was. He asked Linda if she planned on continuing to live there now that her divorce was final.

"Well, you know I'm not sure what I'll do with the house eventually. Right now I have no plans to move. My parents want to stay here for a few weeks after they sell their house in Chicago early next year. After they find a new house here in California or Arizona, I'll know better what Diane's plans are. If she wishes to live with her dad, I may want to move to a smaller place. Then again I like living here and having a lot of space. I shouldn't have any trouble maintaining the place. Maintenance people take care of house cleaning, landscaping, and the swimming pool. It's also nice for Diane to have her own room and to also have an extra bedroom for guests, that is, if I ever have any," said Linda.

"Well, you might have a guest tonight if I get any sleeper," Brad said, sensing an opening to stay overnight.

Brad was a little surprised at how much he desired Linda. Before he had always thought of her as a big sister, but that wasn't the case now. His mind was racing trying to think of a way to see if Linda would accept his advances.

Linda also took note of Brad's comment. Like Brad until now she hadn't had any thoughts of becoming intimate with him. But her feelings had changed tonight, almost like having a switch thrown by an unknown hand. Linda also remembered some of the things Joan had said about taking advantage of an opportunity for sex before it's too late. The problem is that having sex or not is not as easy as deciding to change clothes. What if she lets Brad know what she wants, but he isn't interested.

"I might like to take a short nap if you don't mind. I can sleep on the davenport in the family room if you think you can trust me," Brad finally said.

"Yeah, would you like to spend the night here?"

Brad almost couldn't believe what he heard, but he didn't hesitate in answering yes three times. He also nodded his head so rapidly it made Linda laugh.

You don't need to sleep on the davenport, you can use the bed in the room upstairs," Linda said.

Brad was pretty sure Linda was referring to a spare bedroom but was hoping just by chance she meant he could sleep with her in her bed.

After washing the dishes and putting them away Linda gave Brad a big hug and thanked him for taking her to dinner.

"Well, I enjoyed dinner too. Of course the drinks helped," said Brad.

"You know Brad you never asked me how old I am. I think I'd better tell you."

"I'm guessing you are not fifty years old yet. Am I close?"

"I'm thirty-seven years old today. Does that surprise you?"

"You look to me like a twenty-one-year-old movie star. Do you want to know how old I am?"

"You're twenty-five. I figured it out from some of the things you've told me about yourself."

"All the time I thought I was being discreet about my youth."

While they were talking they continued to hug each other. Linda was no longer sleepy but, even so, she was ready for bed. Now was the time to let Brad know her feelings somehow.

"Let's go upstairs while I can still walk."

Brad agreed not knowing what Linda had in mind. When they reached the top of the stairs Brad decided this was the time to find out what Linda would agree to. Without saying anything he just followed Linda into her bedroom. So far, so good he thought.

Linda decided she would be okay with Brad sleeping with her even though she didn't want to think about having sex. Maybe Brad would just want to go to sleep. She decided she would let him take the lead.

"I'm going to change in the bathroom. It'll take me several minutes," Linda said.

Brad wasn't sure what he should do while he waited. He could get undressed and jump into the bed, but that didn't seem right. He wondered if he should turn on the TV in the room to pass the time until Linda was ready. He knew that was not a good idea either, so he just walked around the room with his hands in his pockets.

When Linda came out of the bathroom she was wearing a flannel nightgown that came up to her neck. Brad figured that was a bad sign, but that changed for the better when Linda spoke.

"There is a condom in the bathroom," Linda said without looking at him.

The bathroom was quite large. There were two sinks with a wide and long real marble top. There were a lot of small bottles and tubes containing cosmetics spread across the top. A large marble sunken bathtub and separate shower with a marble seat were on the other side of the room from the sinks. The toilet was enclosed in a small room at the end of the room. A small auxiliary walk in closet was also at the end of the room beside the toilet room. Clothes could be hung on one side with room on the floor for a shoe rack. Drawers were on the other side wall leaving room underneath for two large dirty clothes hampers. That's where Linda must have put her clothes except for her shoes, which were neatly placed on the shoe rack. Brad neatly stacked his clothes in one corner of the sink but placed his shoes on the closet shoe rack next to Linda's shoes.

When he got into bed he found Linda lying on her back at attention with arms to her side looking straight up at the ceiling. Her body was stiff as a board as though she was expecting physical torture. It was almost comical, but Brad knew better than to laugh. Instead he tried to think of something to relax her.

"It's been a long time since I've had sex with anyone, but I think I can remember what to do. Before we start aren't you supposed to be upside down?" Brad jokingly asked.

"You know I haven't had sex with anyone but Larry since we were married. Even that stopped last year when we separated," Linda said, ignoring Brad's attempt at humor.

"I understand. You do what you want to do and if I can't stand it I'll just scream."

That seemed to somewhat relax Linda. The next problem was how to get her nightgown off since she hadn't made a move to do so herself. Brad was able to roll Linda on top of him so he could pull up on the nightgown. With great difficulty, since Linda continued to tightly hug him, he finally did succeed. Brad found she had a great body, especially for a thirty-seven-year-old lady, thought Brad.

Linda was not a screamer but a gentle moaner. The tone of moans changed pitch depending on what Brad was doing giving him some idea of what she liked or didn't like. Thinking about it later he couldn't help but laugh, but at this time he concentrated on the business at hand.

When finished both were sweating and panting for breath. After a few minutes Linda said she was going to take a shower. Without being asked Brad followed her all the way into the shower. By this time Linda seemed to have lost her inhibitions and seemed to enjoy freely participating in some serious groping. When they got back in bed Linda had her nightgown on indicating sex was over for the night.

Instead of going to sleep Linda wanted to talk some more. This was to become her routine after sex as Brad was to find out. At a later time when Brad commented on her desire to talk in bed before going to sleep Linda said she didn't know why she felt the need to do so since she had never done that with Larry.

"Were you able to have sex very often in Iraq?" Linda asked.

Brad felt it odd that both Linda and Kandi waited until after sex to ask that question.

"You mean besides with animals?" joked Brad.

"You are kidding aren't you?"

"Yes, I was joking. There weren't a lot of American women in Iraq. The army women almost immediately hooked up with officers, senior enlisted men, or a steady boyfriend. Those that didn't made it known they wanted no part of cohabitation. Then of course there were the Iraqi women. The army prohibited fraternization with them. The Iraq government would punish any woman suspected of being overly nice to American servicemen. In addition the Iraqi men would kill women for dishonoring their family. I really don't know how the Iraqi women felt because there was never an opportunity to talk to them. The younger women were always with their husband, father or brother when in public at least in the villages. Anyway most of the women I saw were overly heavy with some face hair and they all smelled like goats. That said no one was about to take a chance with a woman wearing a burqa."

Linda then wanted to again explain why she was an inexperienced lover. She wanted to know if Brad was satisfied. Of course he said yes at least until morning. Considering they had talked for almost three hours over dinner Brad wondered how she could come up with so much more to talk about. Finally Linda decided to stop talking and go to sleep. Both slept soundly until almost 9:00 a.m., which meant he would miss his morning auditing class.

Linda got up to fixed breakfast and then went back to bed after Brad left. About half an hour later Joan called.

"So Linda I noticed a strange car in your driveway this morning. Did you have an early morning visitor?" asked Joan.

Linda knew Joan figured out what she and Brad were up to last night, so she figured she should give a brief sanitized version of the big event hoping that would satisfy Joan.

"You know Brad and I probably had too much to drink last night, so by the time we got home we were both very sleepy. I didn't want Brad to get a drunk-driving ticket or get into an accident, so I told him he could stay overnight in the guest room. We didn't get up until about an hour ago," Linda said.

"I can believe the first part, but you lost me when you said Brad could use the guest room. Knowing Brad, if you did say that I'm sure he had another idea. So how about giving me the details?"

"You know I'm not a kiss and tell person, so you'll just have to use your imagination."

"Okay, do you want to go to the mall this morning? I need to get new clothes for winter."

Linda and Joan did shop for a couple of hours and then took a coffee break. At that time Linda couldn't help but tell Joan a few details about the previous night. She said she shouldn't have ordered three martinis and a Grand Marnier because that lowered her inhibitions. In other words that is really why she agreed to sex later that night. Linda didn't go into detail except to say that she enjoyed the sex and thought Brad was thoughtful and funny.

Joan didn't press for more details but did wonder what Linda thought was funny. It sounded a little kinky

"Joan I have to tell you I'm having dinner with one of Larry's friend, Bernie Mitchell, tonight. Bernie called last night asking me to have dinner at his hotel, but I invited him to have dinner at my house instead," Linda said.

"My, my, you're really acting outside the box now. Suddenly having two lovers is a big change from a loving stay-at-home, no-fun housewife. Does Brad know about this?" asked Joan.

"Yeah, Brad knows, I've also invited him to dinner."

"Wow, you've really moved into the big leagues. Having two lovers together sounds like a professional. I know it's been a long times since you've had sex with anyone other than Larry, but don't you think you should go a little slower?" Joan said before Linda could explain the dinner plan.

"Let me explain. You know by mistake I agreed to have dinner with Bernie at a restaurant earlier this year. I told you how much trouble I had stopping him from getting in my house when he brought me home. Anyway Bernie called when we were having dinner and left a message. I didn't take the call when I saw it was Bernie calling. I explained the Bernie situation to Brad saying Bernie probably is calling to ask me to dinner. Brad suggested I call Bernie back and invite him to dinner at my house so Brad could be there to punch Bernie in the nose."

"Great idea. Can I come over and watch the excitement? Be sure to take pictures."

"There really won't be a physical fight. Instead before Bernie leaves I'll tell him not to call me again or I will have the big football guy beat him up. I'm sure Bernie will get the message, he is such a wimp."

"What time is Bernie going to get to your place, and what time will Brad be there?"

"Bernie is due at 8:00 p.m. but Brad will show up around 7:00 p.m. That will give us time for a couple of drinks before Bernie gets there."

On the way back to his room Brad relived last night's sex in his mind several times. He was hoping there would be many more sexy nights with Linda but knew he should go slowly. He thought Linda enjoyed the sex as much as he did but would somehow like to find out if she was expecting something different.

When Brad got back to the transit facility the duty clerk, Doug Foley wanted to talk to him.

"We missed you last night Wilson. Was that a one night stand of something serious?" asked Foley.

Brad didn't think his activity was not something he wanted to discuss with Foley, so he tried to end the conversation with a short answer.

"Well, you never know. If I get lucky I'll miss your bed check again tonight," Brad answered.

"So how about setting me up with one of those college girls. I could teach them some tricks I learned in Japan."

"What about your other two girlfriends? Is either one of those up for a trade to me for a broad minded college girl?"

"Yep, you can have either one for a couple of nights."

"Let me think about it. I'll see you tomorrow."

Brad wasn't sure how much of what Foley said was in jest, but regardless he didn't intend to follow through on anything that was discussed. He couldn't help thinking that if it wasn't for Linda he might have been interested in Foley's suggestion.

CHAPTER 10

Football practice Thursday was mostly uneventful. A large part of the time Brad spent thinking, actually daydreaming, about helping Linda fend off Bernie Mitchell that evening. As soon as the practice ended, Brad hurried to get cleaned up and dressed. He wanted to get to Linda's well before 7:00 p.m. when Bernie was scheduled to arrive. He put on a blue long-sleeve shirt and tan Dockers trousers. He wore his best black dress shoes. As he left the locker room he heard the expected catcalls from teammates.

"Hey, Brad, you're looking pretty sharp, got a hot date tonight?"

"Who's the babe, is it Bonnie flat chest?"

"Watch out for Dirty Donna, she's a screamer and can bust your eardrums, I know for a fact."

As soon as Brad arrived a little before 7:00 p.m., Linda made a gin martini complete with shaved ice and two olives. "You might want to drink this before Bernie gets here," said Linda. She was wearing tan knee length tan shorts, a pink blouse and low heeled sandals. Linda wore her hair in a ponytail, something she hadn't done for a long time.

Brad offered one olive to Linda and then ate the other one as he thanked her for the drink. He then started the patio gas grill. While they worked together getting ready for dinner, Linda felt obligated to provide more information about Bernie.

Larry and Bernie met at Stanford Law School. They maintained contacts with each other as they both become successful attorneys. Linda and Larry had gotten together with Bernie and his wife, Lisa, many times over the past several years. The two couples had much in common except that the Mitchells didn't have any children. Linda liked Lisa and got along well with her but disliked Bernie's pretentious attitude. Several times she mentioned to Larry that she felt uncomfortable with Bernie's many sexual innuendos and many aggressive bear hugs whenever an opportunity arose. Larry said that was just Bernie's way of trying to be funny and that he was friendly to everyone. Linda didn't appreciate Bernie's humor or bear hugs. When Larry decided to take over his father's law practice, Bernie who lived in the San Francisco area helped Larry get established with the local legal community.

Linda was pretty sure Bernie knew of Larry's intimate relationship with Cindy before she did. She was also pretty sure Bernie had many out of marriage sexual relationships of his own. Shortly after Larry announced the divorce, Lisa called to try to comfort Linda. Then after the divorce was final Bernie started calling Linda to offer to help her get through the emotional trauma of a divorce. During the phone calls he always mentioned that he traveled to Los Angeles once every month for business. This is only the second time she took him up on his offer to meet.

Bernie was fifteen minutes late, which was normal for him. However, it was obvious he was eagerly looking forward to a quiet private dinner at Linda's home.

Brad answered the door and saw about what he had expected. Bernie was a little shorter and a little heavier than him. He was dressed in an expensive blue business suit. He had some flowers in his right hand and a wine bottle in the other hand. Bernie had a nicely trimmed mustache just above a big toothy smile that immediately disappeared when he saw Brad.

"Hello, Bernie, I'm Brad Wilson," Brad said as he took the flowers from Bernie and shook hands with him.

"Oh, Bernie, you've met Brad. He and I are in the same Environmental class at school. We've been working on a presentation together, so I asked him to join us for dinner. I hope you don't mind," said Linda

For the first time Bernie spoke, "I have some flowers and wine for you Linda."

Bernie quickly recovered from his initial shock of seeing Brad and decided to take control of the situation by attempting to give Linda a big hug. It didn't turn out as well as he had expected. Brad had given Linda the flowers, which she held high on her chest as Bernie approached her. Even though he crushed the flowers, Bernie wasn't able to put much of a squeeze on Linda because he was still holding the wine bottle. His attempt to plant a kiss on Linda's lips didn't go well either. Linda turned her head causing Bernie to kiss the hair over her ear. Linda gently pushed away from Bernie and suggested they go out to the patio.

Bernie's mind was racing, as he assessed the situation. He didn't think Brad was Linda's lover, so Linda probably just invited Brad to dinner to protect her from him. Bernie was half wrong and half right. Just in case, Bernie decided he should marginalize Brad by pointing out how young and intellectually shallow he is while stressing the age difference between him and Linda.

"So Linda, I understand you had a birthday yesterday. How does it feel to hit the big thirty-seven?" asked Bernie as he looked directly at Brad to see his reaction.

Bernie was disappointed to not see any reaction by Brad.

Linda kept busy setting something to snack on at the patio table. She pretended to ignore the birthday comment. However, she wondered how Bernie knew of her birthday and age. It upset her to think Larry must have told him.

Bernie then turned his attention to Brad and spoke to him for the first time.

"What's your major at school, young man?"

In Bernie's mind he had just scored two major points, letting Brad know how old Linda is and letting Linda know that Brad was a lot younger than her. Bernie really wasn't interested in Brad's answer. The question was asked to point out to Linda how unprepared young people are for taking on responsibilities.

Brad did answer that he was pursuing a degree in Business Administration with a field of concentration in management. Bernie was surprised that Brad didn't say he hadn't decided on a major, so Bernie decided to try again.

"Really, that's nice, what do you hope to manage?" Bernie asked sarcastically.

This guy is really an arrogant asshole though Brad.

After a second or two Brad collected his thoughts and answered, "After graduation I hope to return to an earlier job and manage people."

Linda put a temporary stop to the grilling by asking if Bernie wanted to let go of the wine, which he apparently didn't realize he was still holding. Linda took the wine bottle and started indoors toward the kitchen, Bernie followed.

"Whoa, I see someone has been drinking on the job. I hope you aren't becoming an afternoon lush. A divorce is traumatic, but you don't have to turn to alcohol for comfort. It looks like I got to you just in time," said Bernie as he spied an empty tall stem martini glass on the kitchen counter.

Brad indicated he drank the martini, which caused Bernie to turn his attention to him.

"Well, I wouldn't have thought of you as liking martinis. What is your favorite vodka?"

"It was a gin martini," answered Brad

"Bernie, why don't you take off your coat and tie? You'd be more comfortable," said Linda.

"Thanks, I think I will," answered Bernie.

Bernie did take off his coat and tie then looked at Brad perhaps thinking Brad would hang them up for him. The two of them stared at each other for a couple of seconds before Brad said Bernie could hang his coat and tie in a closet by the front door.

Linda said they could start cooking their own steaks, so the group went back out on the patio. Bernie had hoped to spend some time talking to Linda before dinner discussing a secret plan of his that involved her. He decided he would casually bring up the subject at dinner and then after dinner ask Linda to discuss his plan privately with him. He hoped Brad would the take the opportunity to leave.

Brad put his steak on the grill first since he wanted it medium well. Linda who wanted a medium cooked steak was next and Bernie who loudly announced he liked his meat blood red was last to start cooking his steak. While they waited for the steaks to cook, Bernie keep talking to Linda and didn't say a word to Brad even as Linda tried to bring him into the discussion. Brad did direct a few comments toward Bernie, which were totally ignored. By chance all three steaks were done about the same time. They all then sat down at the dining room table that Linda had set up earlier. Linda had Brad sitting at the head of the table. She and Bernie sat on opposite of the table.

Conversation at dinner was cordial, but it was obvious that Bernie and Brad would never be best friends. Linda kept feeding Bernie questions about himself, which allowed him to talk almost nonstop. He seemed pleased that they were drinking the wine he had brought and managed to mention twice at different times that the wine was a special brand, implying high cost, that was his favorite. Linda and Brad managed to have quick side conversations while Bernie kept talking. Brad quickly lost interest in what Bernie was saying and instead started thinking about sleeping with Linda later that night. For the first time Brad realized Linda had become more than a friend and that he had a strong physical desire to be with her. The way she looked with a ponytail, almost like a teenager, stimulated him even more.

About half way through dinner Bernie suddenly stopped talking about himself and asked Brad what plans he had once he finished college. Brad indicated he would go back on active duty with the army.

"Go back in the army?" The answer surprised Bernie. "If you've already served in the army, why would you want to sign up again?" asked Bernie.

"I've signed an agreement to do that in order for the army to pay for my college education," answered Brad.

"Well, there are lots of ways to get out of that. When you get your degree come and see me. I'll be able to void any contract you may have signed without any trouble."

Brad had formed an unfavorable impression of Bernie starting with Linda's description of him. Seeing Bernie in person added to Brad's dislike of him. The statement Bernie just made verified Brad's thought that Bernie was totally devoid of character. Brad wondered how anyone could so cavalierly suggest that contracts don't have to be honored. In essence Bernie said that Brad could take full advantage of the government's offer and then fail to comply with his part of the contract. In Bernie's defense, many other individuals that learned of the contract also suggested that Brad try to get out of his commitment after the government finished paying for this education. Whether or not it was true, Brad always got the impression that no one could understand why anyone would want to join the army. Even worse was that most people had totally forgotten about 9/11 and didn't know that their country was fighting a war.

"Nice of you to offer, but I actually want to honor my commitment."

"But if you go back in the army, they may send you to Iraq or Afghanistan. You haven't been over there yet have you?"

"Yea, actually I spent three years in Iraq."

At this point Bernie seemed genuinely interested in hearing more about Brad's time in Iraq. Brad on the other hand was not interesting in talking about it especially to Bernie and tried to discourage questions with short answers. However, through a series of questions Brad indicated he was heavily involved in combat or combat situations most of the time but that except for several shrapnel wounds in his arms and legs he did not suffer any serious injuries.

Finally as dessert was served, Bernie made his planned announcement. He mentioned that he was thinking about running for a state representative position in his home district and that he may open a field office in the Los Angeles area. He went on to explain that even though no one not living in his district could vote for him, a Los Angeles office would allow local members of his party to get to know him. Those individuals could contribute to his campaign and also influence party members in Bernie's district to vote for him. Both Linda and Brad said he should go forward with this. However, Linda did not show the wild enthusiasm Bernie had hoped.

While they were finishing dessert, Linda went to the kitchen to get some fresh coffee. This was the opportunity Bernie has waited for. He put his hand on Brad's wrist and said he wanted to talk to Linda about a confidential matter and asked Brad to let them talk in private for a few minutes. With that Bernie quickly walked to the kitchen and stood closely beside Linda who was just pouring coffee into a serving pot.

"Linda, I want to talk privately to you about a confidential matter. If I open an office here, I want you to be my office manager. There wouldn't really be much to do, but I'd need someone I could trust," said Bernie.

What Berne didn't say was that Linda would make a nice companion at social and dinner meetings. That would make others think Bernie had bagged a hot babe for out of marriage fun. That would be something that would surely favorably impress the political crowd.

Linda turned to look at Bernie and with a steady low voice said she would never work for him and that he should not ask her again. Bernie sensed Linda's dramatic mood change but decided to press the issue anyway.

"Look there is more I need to tell you about my offer. Why don't you send the Boy Scout home so we can talk about this in more detail? We're adults, so we don't need a kid hanging around. You can trust me," Bernie said as a big grin came across his face.

"I know I can trust you. That's what I told Lisa," said Linda.

"Lisa, when did you tell her that?

"I called her to say I was sorry she wouldn't be coming to dinner. I must have called her shortly after you had talked to her this afternoon. She said you told her you were going to a basketball game tonight and that you would call her from the airport tomorrow morning. I told her to not worry because Brad would join us for dinner and that he would not leave before you did."

"Well, you know, Lisa wouldn't understand why I wanted to have dinner with you this evening."

"Well, she knows perfectly well now."

"Look, Linda, let's stop playing games. You know why you invited me to dinner here at your house instead of a restaurant. Don't think I missed those long wishful looks you've given me so many times in the past. Now that you're divorced, we don't need to pretend anymore. We need each other, I know it, and you know it."

As he was talking, Bernie grabbed Linda's right arm, turning her to face him. He placed his right arm as though he was about to hug her. Bernie was becoming more aggressive and his voice had risen to a high level. Linda was shocked at the aggressiveness of Bernie and was about to pull away when she was even more shocked at what happened next.

Brad had walked unnoticed up behind Bernie. Brad pushed his left hand under Bernie's right armpit pushing his arm and shoulder high enough to cause Bernie to stand on his tiptoes. At the same time he pulled Bernie away from Linda and swung him around so that Brad was now between Bernie and Linda.

"You're leaving right now," Brad said as he started pushing Bernie backward toward the front door. Brad had used this same procedure many times on Iraq prisoners or suspects, so it wasn't hard to get Bernie to comply.

"All right, you can let go of me now. You know what you're doing is considered abuse," Bernie said in a high-pitched voice.

Brad paid no attention to what Bernie was saying but kept walking him toward the closet so Bernie could get his coat and tie. Once Bernie had his coat and tie he was walked to his car and pushed inside. Brad didn't let go until Bernie was sitting sideways in the driver seat of his rented car.

"Tell Linda I'll call her and you'll also be hearing from me," Bernie said trying to use his best lawyer voice.

"You are not going to call, write, e-mail, or try to contact Linda in any way ever again," Brad answered. He didn't have to mention that is what is best for Bernie and also for Linda.

Bernie took his time putting on his coat in the car before leaving. Brad waited outside until he finally drove away.

Linda and Brad had talked about how to get Bernie to leave, but having Brad walk him out the door in the manner he did was not exactly what they had in mind. Linda hadn't anticipated Bernie's complete loss of composure, so she agreed Brad's action was exactly correct considering the circumstances. What to do after Bernie left was also discussed earlier.

As soon as Bernie was out the door Linda executed her part of the post Bernie plan. She called Lisa Marshall.

"Hi, Lisa. Well, Bernie just left, and it's not even 10:00 p.m. yet. I wanted to let you know how the dinner went before Bernie had time to make up a story," Linda said when Lisa answered the phone.

Linda then went on to say everything went well until Bernie wanted to discuss his confidential plan with her in private. Linda then went on to describe how Brad walked Bernie out the door. Lisa thought that was just what Bernie deserved. Lisa also said Linda was lucky to get the football guy to help her out.

A short time later Brad executed phase two of the post Bernie plan. Thinking that Bernie would park his car a little way from the house to see if Brad would leave within a reasonable period of time, Brad did get in his car and drive away. After driving for about fifteen minutes Brad drove back to Linda's house.

Brad told Linda he hadn't noticed Bernie's car, and Linda said Bernie had not called, so maybe they were overreacting. Linda said she now felt silly about asking Brad to do the drive around, but said she hoped Brad understood. Brad did understand but also did feel it silly.

When they were almost finished cleaning up and putting the dishes away they stopped to have another cup of coffee and a piece of cake. That gave them time to talk. Without realizing it Linda had become comfortable talking about personal issues with Brad.

"Bernie will tell his wife and probably Larry about tonight's dinner," said Linda. A smile came over her face as she wondered how he will describe his departure. Brad then described tonight's event from Bernie's point of view as he would tell his wife.

"I want to tell you about the weird situation with Linda Wallace. Larry asked me to call her when I was in LA to see how she was getting along. Well, when I called she sounded kind of funny on the phone and asked me if I could have dinner with her at her place that night. I assumed something must be wrong, so I agreed to dinner even though I had to cancel plans for a basketball game I was going to attend with some clients. I felt Linda must be having some kind of difficulty.

"When I got to her house, this big football player was there. Linda said she and the guy had been working on a school project together. She then made some excuse about asking the football guy to stay for dinner, but I'm pretty sure the guy just invited himself and that Linda wanted me there to be sure the guy didn't cause any trouble. I told Linda I'd stay until after the big guy went home. You know I work out every week, so I'm in pretty good shape. I knew I could handle the guy if necessary.

"Thinking about the future I wanted the big guy to know that I'd always be available to protect Linda. That is why I make up this stupid story about getting ready to open an office in LA and have Linda be the office manager. I'm pretty sure the big guy was dumb enough to believe me, but I'm a little concerned that Linda may have thought I was serious. You know, it's really a good thing that I called."

About this time Bernie was in fact talking to his wife on the phone. His comments to Lisa were almost verbatim what Brad suggested. Unfortunately for Bernie, he didn't consider that Linda discussed with Lisa the real facts leading up to the dinner. The next day Lisa called Linda to say that Bernie will not call Linda again, ever.

By then it was nearly 10:00 p.m., so they decided to go to bed. Even though this was only the second time they had slept together, it seemed quite natural and as if they had been together many times. Linda was relaxed when they got in bed and did not lie down at attention as she did the first time. Passionate sex started almost immediately. They were both breathing heavily when they finally finished, so it was a few seconds before they spoke.

Linda wanted to know what Brad thought of Bernie. Brad said Bernie was about what he expected based upon Linda's description. He wondered if Bernie really thought they would believe this story about wanting to open an office in Los Angeles or even running for a local state representative. As Linda suggested, Bernie would probably give his version of the dinner to Larry. Because of Bernie's description, Brad didn't think Larry would believe that he and Linda were lovers or even close friends. This is pretty much what Linda wanted to hear although she didn't say that to Brad.

Brad continued saying that there was a couple of things Bernie said that he really didn't like. For some reason Brad felt like talking about how he felt when Bernie said he didn't think he could ever be in the military.

A lot of people liked to say that when they found out that Brad had been in the army. Almost all probably meant that as a compliment, but Brad sometimes interpreted it differently. The comment seemed to imply the person making the comment was too smart to join the army. Conversely anyone who joins the army must be ignorant.

Brad felt he joined the army as an enlisted man but didn't feel he was an ignorant half-wit willing to blindly follow order because he didn't have the mental capacity to think for himself. The military doesn't want that kind of person.

In basic training the troops learn combat tactics, the purpose of the training and why it was important. They learn to do things because they trust and depended upon each other. Most appreciate being part of a group that has clear cut objectives and a plan on how to accomplish the objective in an efficient and effective manner. Contrary to what is often found in civilian life, soldiers feel they can depend upon fellow soldiers to do whatever had to be done.

Most Hollywood movies about the military erroneously or maybe intentionally stereotype all military personnel into two distinct groups. One group includes all senior enlisted personnel who are portrayed as psychopathic ignorant sadists and all upper grade officers who are portrayed as being ignorant self-centered and arrogant interested only in personal aggrandizement. The other group, the heroes, they are always the new enlistee or junior officers who are so much smarter than the rest of their group that they don't have to follow orders. They know the military and war are not necessary. If someone attacks Americans it is because we have done something wrong or made them feel bad. So all we have to do is to talk nice to them and apologize for anything that we may have done to offend them. Of course we must forgive them for destroying U.S. property, killing innocent civilians and cutting off heads of captured Americans because we deserved it. Then we should give them lots of money and put them on permanent foreign aid.

Bernie said something else that Brad took exception to. Bernie said Brad didn't have to honor his commitment to the government and return to the army. He said that he could easily have Brad's contract with the army voided and seemed to think that Brad would like that. Brad found it hard to believe that not only Bernie, but many others thought it all right to back out of an agreement after accepting agreement benefits. Regardless of how others thought, Brad had enough character to know it would be wrong to not honor the contract and stiff the government for the cost of his education and living expenses for two years. Something else that set Brad apart from most people is the fact that he actually felt it a duty and honor to serve in the military. The terrible things about war he saw in Iraq only strengthened his belief that the United States is correct in trying to eliminate state sponsored oppression as well as working to keep that type oppression from taking hold in the United States.

Brad suddenly realized he was saying more than he had intended. He felt Linda would not understand or agree with his thoughts, after all why should he think she was different from most other people?

"Of course, I could be wrong. I really don't feel that way about most people just guys like Bernie," Brad said, trying to backtrack on some things he just said.

After Brad finished talking, Linda was silent for a few seconds. She tried to process Brad's line of thinking. No one in Linda's family had been in the military. No one in Larry's family had been in the military. Linda couldn't think of anyone she knew other than Brad that had been in the military.

She had been too young to know much about Gulf War I. Because it was such a short war and the facts that the United States won without committing any atrocities the national media pretty much ignored the war as soon as it ended. Vietnam was different. Linda learned in school that the Vietnamese war was wrong and that the United States lost the war. The fifty thousand troops that died fighting the war should never have gone there. The real heroes of that war were the wimps that went to Canada to avoid serving in the military, and the superheroes were the people that bombed government buildings even though they killed several innocent people. Because that is what she had been taught in school, she did have a negative feeling about the military in general but not about individual soldiers.

"Wow, you really have strong feelings about how you think most people view the military," Linda finally said.

"Yeah, but I promise to not talk about it again. For some reason I just resented Bernie's comments. It would have been best if I said nothing and just punched his lights out," Brad responded, trying to lighten the discussion.

"Yeah, I would have like that," joked Linda.

With that they both agreed that they should try to get some sleep before it was time to get up.

During breakfast they rehashed talk about last night's dinner and then discussed their day's activity. Linda had to chuckle when she described the way Bernie looked when Brad walked him out the door. Linda said she would spend most of the day studying. She promised to complete the Environmental Auditing assignment and asked if Brad could stop by Monday to go over what she came up with. Of course Brad eagerly agreed, hoping that Linda would invite him to stay overnight with her.

Linda then took the opportunity to tell Brad about Sunday's golf date with Howard. She was careful to explain that the date was set up by Joan and Henry thinking she needed to meet a nice man. Henry of course assumed all accountants are nice men and would make great mates. Linda said the Belsons didn't know of her relationship with Brad and thought she would appreciate meeting someone to date. She went on to say that even though Howard was a nice man, she had absolutely no interest in continuing to see him.

The quick breakfast turned into almost an hour of lively talk. Both of them found it easy to talk freely and express their inner thoughts. Neither of them mentioned Brad's last night military comments or last night's sex.

While Brad was at football practice Linda did complete the class assignment, which didn't require much effort. The class was asked to be prepared to discuss how their project will benefit society. In essence, it simply amounted to citing text book material. Linda did take care to craft a smooth talk as she was sure Scott Watson would call on her. It was almost certain that only a couple of teams would be prepared to talk in class, so Scott needed to call on some team that actually was prepared to stimulate some discussion, and he knew he could count on Linda and Brad.

After finishing the school assignment Linda called Joan to see if she would be interested in going shopping that afternoon but also because Linda wanted to talk about last night's events. Joan said she had to help Henry entertain some business clients that afternoon and evening. However, she did have a few minutes to find out about what happen at the dinner that Linda had designed to blindside Bernie.

Linda gave a detailed account of the evening. When she started telling about Bernie being escorted out the door she couldn't help but get the giggles. Joan then asked what she really wanted to hear, did Brad stay all night. Linda didn't want to talk about that detail, so she simply said Brad did stay overnight, and she got up early to fix breakfast. Without thinking too much about it, Linda casually mentioned that she didn't have time to comb her hair or put on makeup before going downstairs and that she only had time to put on a nightgown. That comment seemed to excite Joan.

"You put on a nightgown? Why did you do that? I don't think Brad would have minded if you just walked around buck naked," asked Joan.

"I couldn't do that. It would be much too embarrassing. Besides, the sight of my body would probably make Brad lose his appetite."

"I'm not so sure about that. I think it would make him think of eating something else."

Linda could feel her face flush with embarrassment, so she quickly changed subjects.

"Will Hannah be able to go with us to the football game tomorrow?"

"Yes, she reluctantly agreed. I told her we would be sitting in the students section, so she is probably fantasying about hooking up with one of the college boys.

"Saturday night Brad invited me to have dinner at Tony's Pizza right after the football game. Most of the team will be there with their girlfriends. Brad convinced me no one will say anything about our age difference. I decided this would be a good opportunity to see if I could fit in with his crowd," Linda said.

"You haven't forgotten about golf with Howard Douglas Sunday morning have you?"

"Oh golly, it's a good thing you reminded me. I almost forgot probably because I really don't want to see poor Howard."

"Where are you going to stash Brad when we pick you up Sunday morning?"

"Brad won't be spending the night here. You know I have to have a break now and then. Actually I told him about my golf date with Howard this morning, I think he understood that you forced me into the date. I'm sure Brad will allow me one last fling with a wild accountant."

"Okay, tomorrow come over about 11:00 a.m. We'll try to get to the game early so you can see your boy warm up before the game. Will you be coming back with us?"

"Yes, I'll come home, change clothes, and then drive myself back to Tony's. That will give Brad time to clean up after the game and get to

Tony's. I'll call him when I get there so he can meet me outside. That way we can enter the restaurant together."

The Greenbrier game was almost a walk over for State. It seems the team had gained considerable confidence after the Stanford game and won easily 21 to 0. Even so the Belsons enjoyed the game. Linda kept her composure during most of the time and only stood on her seat two different times. She was also careful to not shout for Brad to watch out.

By the time Linda got to Tony's it was around 6:00 p.m. Loud music and loud laughter could be heard as soon as she reached the parking lot making her wonder if it was really a good idea to show up.

Brad brought Linda to a table he had been sharing with two other couples. A waitress was just clearing the remains of three large pizzas and three pitchers of beer when they arrived. Replacements for the food and beer were on the way. By previous agreement each couple would contribute $50 for the pizza and beer. When the money ran out everyone was on their own.

"This is my friend Linda. We're teammates on an environmental project. Linda, this is Zeke, Sally, Matt, and Nancy," Brad said, introducing the group.

Sally and Nancy were not even close to the girls' names, but no one seemed to mind. As it turned out Zeke and Matt had just met the girls and were thinking only of a one night hookup. They might have though the same thing about Linda but didn't say so. The talk immediately turned to the day's football game. As they were talking many people had comments for the group as they passed by.

"So are you with the old guy here?" one of the men asked Linda

"Yeah, I'm here to see he doesn't go wild again like he usually does after a game," Linda answered.

"I'm known as the old guy because I'm the oldest player on the team," Brad explained,

That made Linda feel a little better as it was an indication that the age difference between her and Brad didn't seem too great.

A waitress came back to see if anything else was needed by the group. Thinking Tony's was a typical Italian restaurant said she would like a glass of house red wine. This caused funny looks from the group and from the waitress. It was the first time anyone had ordered wine in the past year.

Later everyone got up to dance. This was the first time Linda and Brad had danced together. Linda felt a little self-conscious since she hadn't danced in a long time and wasn't sure long she could last. She did make it until the band took a break hoping Brad wouldn't ask her to dance again. He didn't, but another of Brad's friend did. After the band started while

Brad and Zeke were engaged in an important football talk a young man said Brad wouldn't mind and probably wouldn't even miss her.

Fifteen minutes later Linda told Brad she was ready to go home. While walking her to her car Brad asked what she thought of Tony's. Linda said she was glad to meet some of Brad's teammates. She had a good time dancing and promised to not order wine again if she ever came back to Tony's.

Sunday Linda skipped church so she could get ready for the big golf game. Promptly at noon Henry, Joan and Howard arrived. They had reservations for a 1:00 p.m. starting time at the club golf course, so the group had agreed everyone should get their own breakfast and skip lunch. They would all have an early evening dinner together at the club after finishing golf. Even so Linda served cookies and lemonade for the group before they headed off to the golf course.

Linda noticed that Howard's attire had improved from what he had worn to the football game. He wore tan shorts, a pullover solid blue color polo shirt, golf shoes and white cotton socks. Still something seemed odd about Howard's appearance. It took Linda a couple of minutes to realize Howard was wearing a green sun visor and sunglasses, which he didn't bother to take off in the house.

Henry was dressed similar to Howard except for the visor and sunglasses. Joan was dressed to Linda. Both wore white knee length shorts, solid colored buttoned short sleeve shirts tucked into their shorts, and golf shoes without socks.

Once they got on the course it became evident that Howard had sharpened his game. He seemed to know what club to use and could speak in golf terms. Without being overbearing he offered good advice to the other three. It took almost three hours to play only nine holes due to slow play by the women. No one seemed to mind, however, even when two different groups wanted to play through.

During the play in addition to offering golf advice, Howard did manage to talk a little bit about himself and to find out a little bit about Linda. It seems Howard's life had not been easy. He was raised by his mother and never had any real father figure associations. He had to work his way through college at a state university but made good grades. Howard was very smart as far as analytical and conceptual skills were concerned. It was his social skills that were lacking. He married his first girlfriend, who was five years younger than him. It took him several years, but he had been able to work his way up to a principal position at Henry's accounting firm. Just when things seemed to be going well, his wife left him for a younger man. Howard didn't say so, but it was evident that he not taken the divorce well.

Linda couldn't help but feel sympathy for Howard but not so much that she would want to date him again. Later she mentioned to Joan that she thought Howard was a very smart nice man. Joan suggested maybe Howard would be a good find for Diane. This caused them both to laugh at the comment and get the giggles when they thought of how the two would get along together.

The group spent almost three hours over dinner and later refreshments on the club patio. Howard and Henry both had some accounting jokes that actually were funny. Everyone was able to express their thoughts on a wide range of subjects, including movies and TV shows, politics, religion, and to a limited extent even sport

When Henry drove the group back to his house, Linda got out to walk to her house next door. Howard got into his car to drive to his place but not before giving Linda a big hug. Linda thought about giving Howard a kiss on the cheek but did not.

About 9:00 p.m. Linda called Brad to let him know about the day's activity. Brad said he had an uneventful day working out and watching football games on TV. After football practice Monday Brad did come to Linda's to go over the environmental assignment ant to spend the night.

CHAPTER 11

Later the next week Linda called Joan to invite her to dinner that Sunday.

"Sunday after Henry leaves for New York City maybe you and Hannah would like have dinner at my place.

"Thanks, but I promised Hannah I'd take her to some R rated movie she wants to see and Sunday is the only time I'm willing to take her. Instead why don't you have dinner with us tomorrow evening? Henry hasn't seen you since we played golf with Howard Douglas."

"Okay, I think I can fit it in my busy schedule."

"Busy schedule, you're not kidding me I know Brad's football game is out of town this Saturday. Dinner will be around 6:00 p.m., but stop by a little earlier so we can talk."

"Okay, see you around 5:00 p.m. Saturday."

Friday In the afternoon Linda did go shopping by herself. The next evening she would be having dinner at the Belsons, so she decided to buy a small gift for Hannah Belson. Linda decided on a hairbrush, comb, and mirror set, hoping it would be something Hannah didn't have. Linda remembered Diane seemed to enjoy getting a similar set when she was Hannah's age. On an impulse Linda decided to buy a gift for Brad. A polo shirt with an American flag on the pocket caught her eye. She hesitated for a couple of seconds trying to decide if a shirt would be too intimate for someone who is only a friend. Then for the first time she admitted to herself, considering the fact that she has sex with him more than once, that Brad was more than just a friend. She then bought an extra-large shirt.

Earlier in the week the football team met at noon for the trip to Colorado. The coaches wanted to have time for the team to walk the playing field before checking into the hotel. The coaches walked ahead of the team pointing potentially troubling parts of the playing field. A high or a low spot, a hole, a spot with no grass, and certain other things. Brad couldn't help thinking there was no way anyone could remember all the things being pointed out especially in the heat of the game. About the only thing the team got out of the walkover is that the grass was short and the ground was hard. There would be time before the game to practice plays and review the game plan.

The team then checked into a nearby hotel. An hour or so later they had dinner in a private dining room and then assembled in a conference room to discuss the game plan once again.

By then it was close to 10:00 p.m., so the team was sent to their rooms with instructions to not come out until morning breakfast.

Brad was assigned a room with Warren West, which would make it difficult to talk to Linda on the phone. However, he decided to call anyway and then he decided to not call. Then he remembered his phone was off, so he turned it on to see if he had any messages, from Linda. There were no messages, so he put the phone down and started to get ready for bed. Just then Linda did call.

Linda and Brad talked for almost half an hour about almost nothing. Linda wanted to know if there was any trouble on the trip, what the weather was like in Colorado and if Brad was ready for the game. Brad asked how Linda spent the day, what she had planned for Saturday, and if she finished the school project. Even though there was nothing of substance in the conversation, Brad felt really good after talking to Linda. The conversation ended by Brad saying he would stop by Linda's house about 5:00 p.m. Sunday. They both wished each other well, but neither one told the other that they loved them. That would come later.

Brad had a hard time falling asleep. He should have been thinking of tomorrow's game, but instead he was thinking of Linda. It dawned on him that this was the first time that he had a real girlfriend even if she was twelve years older than him. He finally fell asleep with a big grin on his face.

Linda woke up Saturday morning feeling mildly depressed. She probably would have been more depressed if it wasn't for Joan inviting her to dinner that night. Linda had no real plans until dinner and no one to talk to. Brad was busy with football, and Diane didn't want to talk on the weekend. For the first time she suddenly realized that she didn't have any friends except the Belsons and Brad. The friends she and Larry use to socialize with had all dried up. Even the phone calls from husbands of friends suggesting that she could always count on them for help had stopped. Worse yet it was becoming more clear each week that she was losing her daughter to the bimbo, Cindy.

Linda decided to pass the time by reading a new book. As soon as she started reading she found her mind wandering, so she couldn't concentrate on the book. Linda gave up on the book and started thinking about her situation and what the future would bring. She realized she had become closer and closer to Brad. Would their friendship continue after the end of the school semester? What would happen if he dumped her? There wasn't any indication this would happen, but then again she didn't see being dumped by Larry

Linda started evaluating her situation with Brad. He said he wasn't interested in the girls that hung around football players. However, since he had become known as a stud football player, a lot of different girls stopped by to talk to Brad at the campus restaurant. Linda knew that because she frequently met Brad for breakfast at the restaurant before class. She wondered why Brad didn't seem interested in any of these girls or if he was and just didn't let her know.

Linda became more uncomfortable as she continued to evaluate her relationship with Brad. She decided she must know Brads feelings toward her then she would know how she felt about him. She quickly realized that didn't make sense. She knew she had strong feelings for Brad, at least for the near future. She didn't want to think of the age difference and what the situation would be ten year from now, so she didn't think about it. Still she felt she should find out what Brad had in mind for them over the next several months. She didn't want to just ask him, which may scare him off. Then again maybe that would be better than thinking their relationship would continue to grow and be blindsided once again.

Her thoughts didn't make her feel any better, so she decided to go somewhere, but where? She could go to the club. There were always things to do there. It was a nice enough day for a swim in the club pool. She might see someone she knew there and invite them to the club brunch. If see didn't meet anyone she could just have brunch by herself. She finally decided to go to an early movie, any movie, at a local shopping center. As she was buying a movie ticket she realized that this was probably the first time in her life that she would be going to a movie by herself.

The football game was going State's way in Colorado. Brad was now a fixture as a starting linebacker but was also often used on offense as a tight end. The team was anxious for a win and began to smell victory after the first quarter. State scored one touchdown and would have scored again if quarterback Zeke Solum hadn't fumbled a handoff deep in Colorado territory

Brad was playing very aggressively. He had one quarterback sack and had knocked down a couple of passes, Brad enjoyed playing football. He felt he needed some physical contact that he had missed since leaving Iraq. Late in the third quarter, however, he had some misfortune. While chasing an opponent Brad stepped into a small hole causing him to fall and miss a sure tackle. Brad wasn't hurt, but he was embarrassed and immediately realized that the coaches had pointed out that very hole during the previous night's walkover. Brad assumed he'd hear about not being aware of the hole Monday when the team reviewed the game film, and it would turn out to be a correct assumption. Despite Brad's blunder, State won the game by a score of 28 to 7.

On the plane ride home some of the guys wanted to stop by Tony's Pizza for a few beers and pizza if the plane arrived on time. Brad knew most of the team was not old enough to drink beer legally, but the older guys could buy beer for the younger ones. Brad agreed to join the group realizing the main reason he was invited was to be the primary beer purchaser. He figured that there wouldn't be much more than an hour to spend before closing.

The gang did get to Tony's in time to have a few beers before closing. Big surprise, about a dozen college girls were at the cafe waiting for someone, anyone, to buy them a drink. Most of the guys headed for girls they knew, leaving Brad and Warren West to pick out a small table for themselves. Almost immediately two girls sat down uninvited at their table. Both girls were good-looking; both wore skin tight pants and blouses with low-cut necklines. It seems the girls had their own game plan.

Instead of taking an interest in the girls, Brad's thought turned to Linda. For some reason by being at Tony's he felt like he was cheating on her. Brad soon wished he had gone straight back to his place and skipped Tony's. He made a mental note to never stop here again after any games. Later Brad would think that maybe fate caused him to agree to stop at Tony's. It might have been to test him to see if he remains true to Linda. If so, Brad feels he passed the test.

Brad bought beer and pizza for the four of them game. Brad was surprised that no names were exchanged. Apparently the girls knew Brad and Warren and didn't think they needed to introduce themselves. The girls first asked questions about the game, but soon the talk turned personal, mainly about Brad. This made Brad uncomfortable since he wasn't interested in developing a relationship with either girl. He tried to discourage questions with short or one word answers and also tried to bring Warren into the conversation. Warren did make a lot of comments but was mainly ignored by the girls. Just before the last call for drinks the talk became blunter. One of the girls asked Brad if he ever had a double, two girls for fun. This made Brad a little uncomfortable, so he told the girls it was nice talking to them, but he had to leave. As he was leaving, he said to Warren that maybe he could drive the girls home and maybe score a double. Warren's face exploded in a big grin, and the girls both giggled. Brad thought his comment wouldn't be taken seriously, but then again maybe it would.

On the way home Brad briefly thought about a missed opportunity with the girls. A couple of weeks ago he would have jumped at the invitation, but now it was different. Brad then decided it was good that he didn't take the girls up on their offer. He told himself that he probably would have ended up with a double dose of herpes.

Linda's movie ended a little before 2:00 p.m. She had to fight the urge to immediately go see the Belsons but knew that would not be a good idea. She then thought of seeing another movie just to kill time and occupy her mind so she wouldn't continue to analyze her relationship with Brad. Instead she went home took a long bath and tried out several clothing combinations before selection a combination she felt would be appropriate for dinner By then she only had an hour to kill before leaving for the Belsons. Linda spent most of the hour wrapping the gifts for Hannah's and Brad.

Finally, 5:00 p.m. arrived, so Linda prepared to walk over to the Belsons. She didn't want it to appear that she was anxious to get there, so she decided to be fashionably late. Therefore she didn't get to the Belsons until 5:05 p.m. Linda gave Hannah her gift and made some small talk with Henry and Joan as Hannah tore into the gift. After a few minutes, Joan asked Linda to help her with a few things in the kitchen. Joan wanted to talk to Linda almost as much as Linda wanted to talk to her.

As they were going to the kitchen Joan told Linda that Henry had finished reviewing the financial effect of Larry's proposal to swap his half interest in the house for Linda's half interest in Larry's business profits. Linda had turned to Henry for help when Larry suggested the swap.

However, as soon as they were out of hearing range for Henry and Hannah, the talk quickly turned to Linda's romance, as Joan put it. Joan wanted to know how serious the affair was and how long would the affair last. Linda desperately wanted some advice on if she should continue to pursue the affair or if she should act like an adult and look for someone her age for romance.

Joan turned out to be the perfect medicine for Linda's depression. Joan said there was nothing wrong with a thirty-seven-year-old woman having a romance with a twenty-five-year-old man, provided they were both single.

Joan said she sensed Linda was reluctant to introduce Brad to her friends or even be seen with Brad but that she should get over that. Most friends would understand and those that didn't may not really be friends. Joan went on that even if the affair only lasted a couple of months there is nothing wrong in enjoying it while it lasts.

Linda voiced her concerns with Joan. What if Brad has a different undesirable side or what if he dumps her without any warning? What will Diane and her parents think when they learn that Brad is on twenty-five years old. What if she can't continue to satisfy Brad sexually, or what if she just loses interest.

Joan said it best to discuss the situation with Diane first. That would be better than telling Larry and have him or worse yet have Cindy tell Diane. When you talk to Diane don't say you've found the love of your life and you are thinking of marriage. Just say recently you've become romantically involved with a younger man and you are not sure how long it may last.

Linda felt this was good advice. She thought to herself that she should call Diane tomorrow and pretty much say what Joan suggested. Linda figured Bernie would tell Larry about Brad being at dinner. She knew that Larry would suspect something more was going on with her and Brad, so it might be a good idea to also let him know tomorrow.

About that time Hannah came into the kitchen. She thanked Linda for the present and said she could really use the gift. Hannah then started helping with dinner preparations.

Linda really appreciated being asked to dinner at the Belsons. Being around others and enjoying talking to them keep Linda from feeling so lonely. The talk centered around Hannah's school activities and Henry's trip to NYC.

Hannah was a member of the school choir and was planning on trying out for the school swim team. That would mean spending many hours practicing at the school pool and at the club pool. Joan, of course, would have to accompany Hannah at the club pool, which would take a lot of time in the late afternoon and over the weekend. Linda immediately thought to herself that maybe she could volunteer to give Joan a break now and then by taking Hannah to the club pool. That would give Linda something useful to do.

In response to questions Henry talked about all the fun things to do in NYC. Of course, he pointed out because he would be in meetings most of the time that he would not be able to do much else while there. As he was talking Linda thought it would be so much fun to spend a few days in NYC, taking in the sights, going to a Broadway play, eating at famous restaurants and of course shopping. Linda then started day dreaming of a trip to NYC over the Christmas holidays. She knew Diane would be spending the holidays with Larry and Cindy at Lake Tahoe, so Linda thought maybe she could talk Brad into going with her.

Linda had been to NYC once before in connection with one of Larry's business trips. Larry, Diane, and Linda arrived in NYC late one Saturday afternoon in February 1999. That evening they all attended a Broadway play, which Linda really enjoyed but which Diane didn't. The next day, Sunday, Larry wanted to register for the business conference and then set up his PowerPoint program for a class he would give in breakout sessions the next couple of days. Because that would take most of the day, Linda and Diane decided to take an all-day bus tour of the city. That was not a pleasant experience. About half an hour into the tour, Diane, who was eleven years old at the time, announced that she was bored and wanted to go back to the hotel. To make matters worse, the day was quite cold and the bus was not heated. The California winter coats Linda and Diane had did little to keep out the cold. Linda stuck it out for almost four hours but then gave in to Diane's constant complaining. They left the tour, caught a cab back to the hotel and spent the rest of the day watching TV in their hotel room. The next morning Linda and Diane boarded a plane home to California. Larry would return home a few days later after the conference ended.

After dinner Linda and Hannah helped Joan clean up and wash the dishes. Linda and Joan didn't have any time to discuss personal matters. When they finished Henry asked if he could talk to Linda about Larry's swap proposal.

Linda was grateful for Henry's help in this matter especially since Henry was not charging for his professional advice. Henry had explained that if he were to charge Linda it would have to go through his company and the hourly rate would be about $440 per hour. Linda knew Henry would provide her free advice as a friend even if he was an independent contractor.

Linda and Henry met in the room Henry used as a private office. As he always did when they were discussing this issue, Henry assured Linda that he did not discuss any of the details with Joan or anyone else except Larry. Henry then went on to review the situation. Part of the divorce agreement split both the house and Larry's business profits fifty-fifty between Larry and Linda. Larry was now proposing that he give up his interest in the house if Linda would give up her interest in his business profits. Henry pointed out that the current value of the house was greater than the annual business profits. Since Larry had only recently opened the business, the amortization of start-up costs would probably eat up all business profits for the next few years. However, in a few years the business could reasonably expect to be highly profitable. So Linda should weigh a number of things before making a decision. The best purely economic decision would be to not agree to the swap even if it meant risking not having the business show a profit within a reasonable period of time. However, taking full control of the house would avoid future dealings with Larry over the use of the house. Henry said Larry was planning on calling Linda tomorrow to see if she would agree with his proposal.

Linda thanked Henry for his review and went home around 8:30 p.m. She decided to not call or text Brad since she would see him the next day. She also decided to not call Diane since Diane had made it known she didn't want Linda to call on the weekend since Diane normally would be with Larry and Cindy. Linda did decide to go to church Sunday morning, however, even though she would go by herself.

After church Linda had time to think over Larry's proposal in light of what she had heard from Henry. She made up her mind to agree to Larry's proposal.

Brad got up midmorning Sunday. He decided to exercise at the team gym for an hour or so mainly just for something to do. Brad looked for Warren when he got to the gym. A number of other team members were already working out, but Warren was not among them. Brad joined in on the discussion about the Colorado game and preparations for the upcoming Idaho game. A couple of the guys wanted to know if he made out with the two girl team. Brady said Warren beat him out, so he had to go home alone. No one believed Warren could beat out Brad or anyone else for that matter. A number of comments were made about Brad stepping in a hole and missing a tackle. Brad knew his teammates were just kidding him, but he also know Coach Kruger would not see anything funny about missing a tackle that could have been avoided if Brad had paid attention during the walkover.

Brad ate a late breakfast/early lunch and then spent a couple hours studying for his classes. By then it was close to three o'clock. Brad wished he had told Linda he would get to her house at that time or maybe even eight o'clock that morning. Finally it was time to start for Linda's.

When Linda met Brad at the door she gave him a big hug. Brad was wondering if he should kiss her but decided not too since he didn't want to make the Bernie mistake. Linda asked Brad to tell her about the game. Brad gave her the highlights but did not mention falling on his face and missing a tackle. The game highlights might be on the local TV sports news, but Brad didn't mention it since he feared it would show him completely whiffing a tackle.

Linda went over the environmental audit assignment, which took about five minutes. Linda assumed Brad would be staying for dinner, so she said it was time to finish preparations. Brad also assumed he be staying for dinner, so he followed her into the kitchen. Both of their assumptions were correct. When Linda left for the kitchen, she remembered Brad's gift. After unwrapping the shirt, Brad thanked her with a kiss. Linda thought the shirt was worth it.

At dinner Linda mentioned that Larry may call her sometime that evening. She said if Larry did call it would not last long since Larry only wanted an answer about a proposed change in their divorce settlement. Then she added that it would be all right if Brad listened in. Linda realized that sounded somewhat awkward, but she hoped Brad got the message that she and Larry had not remained close.

Larry didn't call that evening and it is probably good that he didn't. By 8:00 p.m. Linda and Brad were having a good time wrestling each other and rolling around on the floor. At dinner they had finished the rest of Bernie's wine and one more whole bottle. They then started playing a simple card game Brad knew. Each player puts a dollar in pile. Then each player would simultaneously turn over cards tossing them to either side of another player. As soon as a joker card is turned over everyone that sees it can grab the money. Of course this leads to a lot of physical contact among the players.

At some point Brad found himself on top of Linda. Both of them stopped and looked at each other for a few seconds. Brad thought that would be a good time to kiss Linda, so he did. Linda responded with affection.

"Well, I hope you don't think I'm trying to take advantage of you simply because I had you pinned to the ground," Brad said trying to make light of the kiss.

"I was not pinned. I was just about to roll you over and bite your nose off," answered Linda.

"Oh yeah, I will admit you're pretty tough, but my nose is way too big for you to bite it."

"Oh yeah, well, you must know that I have a big mouth."

"Oh yeah, well, I'll fix that," Brad said as he kissed Linda again.

"Brad, I think it's time to go upstairs." Linda laughed.

With that they did go upstairs and to bed. Sex was really good and satisfying to both. Neither of them was sleepy, so they talked for the next hour or more. Linda first wanted to explain the swap proposal. That led to a short history of her marriage. Linda then confessed that she hadn't told Larry or Diane about Brad. Brad said he would follow her lead, but it was all right with him if Linda told everyone she knew about their relationship. However, Brad didn't mention that he also had not told any of his friends about their relationship. That caused Brad to realize that he really didn't have any friends other than Linda. He knew and got along with his team members but didn't consider any of them close friends.

Brad talked about being lucky to meet Linda and how he enjoyed being with her more than any other girl he had ever known. Brad surprised himself by opening up so much to Linda. That wasn't his nature. Normally he was guarded when talking about himself and never liked to divulge much personal information.

Many of the questions Linda had about their relationship were answered to her liking. Brad almost felt comfortable enough talk to Linda about moving in with her but didn't think it was time for that yet. Besides he was not sure he really would want to move in with Linda, at least not now.

Brad woke up early and couldn't go back to sleep, so he got up around 5:30 a.m. By the time he finished shaving with a razor left by Larry and taking a shower, Linda was awake. She said if Brad would start some coffee she would come downstairs and make breakfast in a few minutes.

When Linda finished taking a shower and fixing her face, at least to some degree, she put on a very sheer nightgown. As soon as she saw herself in the mirror she realized the gown was almost transparent and showed so much of her body that if caused her face to turn red with embarrassment. Linda quickly changed into a heaver and much more modest gown. She took a couple of seconds to think about it before deciding to not put a bathrobe over the gown. She had put on a bathrobe last time Brad stayed overnight, something she neglected to mention to Joan.

When Linda came into the kitchen she looked at Brad to see if he noticed that this time she did not have on a bathrobe. By the look on Brads face she could see that Brad definitely did notice. As if planned they hugged and kissed. Linda then got busy cooking bacon and eggs.

Brad left a little after 8:00 a.m. and headed directly to school. On the way he thought again about moving in with Linda. That would be nice for many reasons but not so nice for others. They each had long-standing habits, likes, and dislikes, so it would be hard for either of them to change in any way to accommodate the other. The other big obstacle was money. Brad already felt uncomfortable having Linda fix so many dinners. If he did move in he felt he would have to pay some kind of rent. That would be a problem since he didn't currently pay rent and he really couldn't afford to spend even an extra couple hundred dollars a month. Besides seeing her everyday would cause him to spend even more money on daily activities. Brad wouldn't have minded that except that he didn't have that much money. Of course Brad realized that Linda may not have the remote interest in having Brad move in with her. That caused him to quickly forget about the idea of living with Linda, but his thoughts made him realize that if he didn't pay his fair share he would be no better than a gigolo.

After Brad left Linda didn't go back to bed but did finish dressing. She figured Joan would call soon, so she decided to watch TV. As she was watching the morning news her thoughts turned to Joan's suggestion about telling Diane and other about her new romance. She hadn't talked to Diane since the previous Thursday, so tonight would be a good time to tell her. She could call Larry late in the afternoon and mention her romance after talking about the swap. She figured Larry wouldn't have time to talk to Cindy until evening, which would give Linda time to call Diane before Cindy did.

Joan did call as expected. For the past several years since Henry started his monthly trips to NYC Joan and Linda had Monday lunch together, normally at the club.

"Can you make lunch today or are you and the big guy still in bed," asked Joan

"I've been up since 6:00 a.m. and am now ready for lunch. We can go to the club in my car unless you want to walk," said Linda.

"Let's take your car. I'll come over there about 11:30 a.m. if that's okay."

"That's a deal. Did you get Henry to the airport on time yesterday?"

"Yeah, after almost missing his plane last month we were at an hour earlier than normal. Now to get down to what I want to hear, what did you do with Brad last night and this morning?"

"Oh, nothing much. We went over the school assignment, ate dinner, drank a lot of wine, played a fun card game on the floor went to bed and had sex."

"Sounds like a dull evening just like us old married folks except for the sex. Maybe you can tell me why you had to play the card game on the floor."

"You'll have to use your imagination, but I will say the card game was a lot of fun."

"Just tell me this, were you able to keep most of your clothes on?"

"Look before I forget it, please thank Henry for his advice on Larry's swap proposal," Linda said as she purposely changed the subject.

They talked for a few more minutes but still had things to talk about when they met for lunch.

About an hour later Larry did call Linda.

"Hello, Linda. I'm calling to ask if you've made a decision on my swap proposal?" said Larry as Linda answered the phone.

"Yes, I've decided. Henry Belson explained the financial aspects to me. He said it probably would be best in the long run if I kept half of your business profits," Linda replied, hesitating for a couple of seconds, and then continued.

"However, I'm willing to go along with the swap just to make you happy."

"It's not just me, Linda. This transaction will benefit both of us. For what it's worth, I think you are getting the best of the deal."

"Yeah, right. Fax me the papers and I'll have my attorney look them over. You and he can work out any differences."

"As you know your attorney, Jason Clark, and I have already worked out the details. I assume you are still using Clark."

"Yes, Clark is still my man and I still want him to look at the copy I sigh."

"I'll have your official copy delivered to Clark tomorrow. I'll ask him to have them delivered directly to you on Wednesday assuming he signs off on them. You'll have to be home to sign when they are delivered to your house. Also, your signature must be witnessed by a notary public."

"Okay, I can do that."

"Look, Cindy and I are going to be in Los Angeles this coming weekend. Maybe we can meet you at the club so you sign my copy of the agreement. Cindy is a notary, so she can witness both of our signatures. Also I'll need to tender my resignation from the club, and I'd like to show Cindy the place while I'm still a member."

"All right I'll buy dinner and make reservations for 7:00 p.m. if that works for you."

"Yes, that would be nice. Since there will be two of us and only one of you I can pay for dinner. That would be the last time I'll be able to buy anything there."

A couple of things quickly flashed through Linda' mind before she answered. One positive thing she could say about Larry was that he was not a petty cheapskate. She also realized this was a great opportunity to tell Larry about Brad.

"If you bring Cindy I'd like to bring a friend. I'll ask him to show up about 7:15 p.m. so we'll have time to finish the personal transactions. We can split the dinner cost."

"Is your friend the jock that Bernie Marshall told me had dinner with you two?"

"Yes, that's right. I'd like you to meet him. I think he would be a good find for Diane."

Linda surprised herself with the last comment about Brad being a good find for Diane. She hadn't intended to say that. The comment must have just popped out of her mind since until Saturday she had been planning on telling that to Larry. It was too late to back down now even if it meant a delay in telling Diane about Brad for another week or so.

"Why do you think Diane would be interested in a jock?"

"Why don't you ask the bimbo what she thinks?"

"Let's not call Cindy a bimbo. You'll just have to get used to the fact that Cindy is now my wife."

"All right I won't call Cindy a bimbo if you stop calling my friend a jock."

"I will if you don't mind giving me your friend's name."

"His name is Brad and he is a nice young man."

"Are you sure he wouldn't be a better match for you?"

"Brad is young enough to be our son and I'm not that desperate yet."

"All right, Cindy and I will meet you Saturday at the club around 7:00 p.m., and your friend can join us around 7:15 p.m."

Linda was glad to finally agree on the swap. However, she was upset with herself about not telling Larry that she was romantically involved with Brad. She was pretty sure Larry would quickly figure that out at dinner. If he didn't Cindy would certainly explain it to him. She would still have time to call Diane Sunday morning before Larry and Cindy got back home. Since Larry and Cindy would still be in Los Angeles Sunday morning Diane would not be with them and therefore shouldn't mind taking her call.

When Joan arrived Linda complemented her on her outfit. Joan was wearing a blue pull over blouse with a kind of sailor bib on the back. She had white pants with low heeled sandals. Linda was wearing a green blouse, tan knee length shorts and low heeled sandals. At the club they decided to sit outside for lunch. The day was one of those rare October days when Southern California was blessed with a warm gentle Santa Ana breeze blowing in from the east.

Linda asked Joan if she and Hannah enjoyed the movie they had gone to yesterday evening. When Joan started describing the movie Linda almost wished she hadn't asked.

"You wouldn't believe all the crazy action that took place in the movie. If there was a plot I never figured it out. It seems the hero is being chased by a whole bunch of bad people including an incredibly beautiful blonde that is only wearing half of her clothes. Early in the movie three bad guys beat up on the hero. For about five minutes they hit the hero with a pipe kick him in the head when he falls down and choke him. Suddenly the hero regains his power. In the next ten seconds the hero throws one bad guy over the side of the building, I forgot to tell you that for some reason the fight takes place on the roof of a high rise building. The hero then kills another bad guy by hitting him in the back of his head with the pipe after causing him to bend over by kicking him in the balls. The third guy is choked to death by the hero.

"The hero then goes to his girlfriend's house where he is not too beat up to engage in sex. All we see is the hero and his girlfriend in bed under the covers. The dialogue here is really great consisting almost entirely of oh, oh, baby, baby, yeah, yeah. Just what you and Brad probably said last night.

"Then there is an even less believable scene. The hero is pushed out of a helicopter but somehow manages to grab onto one of helicopter landing struts. As he is hanging on with one hand, a bad guy starts stomping in his hand. Suddenly the hero is able to grab the bad guy's leg and, with gorilla strength, yank him out of the helicopter. For some reason the bad guy is not able to grab hold of the strut. Then the hero flips himself back into the helicopter, which is being piloted by the beautiful blonde. I don't know what happened after that because at that point I fell asleep," Joan finally finished saying.

"Sounds great, what was the name of the movie?" asked Linda.

"I have no idea, but I know it should have been titled, Unbelievable Stupid, Garbage."

"I think I saw a similar movie some time ago only in my movie the hero shoots four bad guys with a pistol. The bad guys are all shooting at him with machine guns, but of course they never hit him."

"My movie must be a sequel to your movie."

"What did Hannah think of your movie?"

"Some of her friends told her it was a really good movie, so Hannah loved it. She thinks she knew the movie plot. She knew who the actors were and thought they delivered their lines perfectly, she thought the action scenes were believable and thought the dialogue was cool."

Linda and Joan talked until about 2:00 p.m. After Linda got home the loneliness crept in again. She would like to talk to Brad but knew he would be starting football practice shortly. Linda hoped Brad would call her later that night so she could invite him to the Saturday dinner. Until then Linda realized that she was alone and didn't have anything of importance to do the rest of the evening. She started thinking that it would be nice if Brad would come home to her house every night.

Brad's day went quickly. He did pay attention in his classes and felt he was actually learning something. Like every Monday the team watched the film of the East Colorado game at the start of practice. The coaches continually pointed out player errors and on a few occasions gave credit to someone, usually the quarterback for a good play. Brad knew he would be cited for falling down and missing a tackle. Coach Kruger did the honors. Kruger seemed to enjoy calling out Brad more than anyone else on the team. After the film ended the team went out on the field for some drills. On Mondays there was very limited physical contact, so the players didn't wear pads. All during practice Brad had to listen to players telling him to watch out for imaginary holes, tall grass, little rocks and bare spots.

After practice and dinner Brad did call Linda. Brad really didn't have any reason to call except that he felt like talking to Linda. On the other hand Linda had a couple of issues she wanted to talk to Brad about.

"Brad, this coming Saturday I'm having dinner at the club with my ex-husband Larry and his new wife Cindy. I'd like you to join us if you can make it after Saturday's game. I'll need some moral support. Also if you join us I'm sure that would keep Cindy from making snide remarks about me," Linda said in one long sentence.

"Sure I'd be happy to be there. This time it will be my treat. Of course if we eat at the club you will have to charge the dinner, but I'll reimburse you," Brad answered.

"It seems like everyone, but Cindy is offering to pay for the dinner. Larry offered to pick up the tab, so let's let him."

"What is the occasion for dinner?"

"Larry wants me to sign some papers authorizing a minor change in our divorce agreement. My attorney and Henry Belson both assured that the change benefits me more than Larry."

"What time should we get to the club?" Brad asked assuming he would drive Linda to the club.

"Brad, I'm sorry to have to ask you to go along with a little deception again, but this will be the last time. I still haven't told Larry you are more than just a friend. I want to tell Diane before Cindy does and I'll be able to do that Sunday morning. I'll then call Larry and tell him. It's important that I be the one to tell both Diane and Larry directly. If we tell Larry and Cindy Saturday or before Cindy will certainly call Diane before I can. I also don't want to tell Diane before Saturday or she will tell Cindy who will tell Larry."

"That makes sense to me. I can meet you at the club."

"Thanks Brad. We can get together at my place after dinner if you would like."

"Yep, I'd like that. I'll also be interested in meeting Larry."

"Can you meet us around 7:15 p.m. at the club? Larry and I'll get there a little early to sign some papers."

"That should give enough time to get to the club after the game. Also if Cindy starts to give you a bad time I'll put a gag on her like I use to do to some bad guys in Iraq."

"That would be all right with me. Actually it might be best if you just gauge her before she says anything."

Linda and Brad continued their conversation for several more minutes talking about different subjects. Brad didn't ask to stay overnight with Linda but was planning on asking her when they met for breakfast at the school cafeteria

Brad and Linda meet the next morning. Linda spent several minutes explaining once again why she hadn't told Larry or Diane about their relationship. That didn't bother Brad, but he wasn't sure anyone would believe he and Linda were just good friends. He also felt guilty trying to act as though they were.

Remembering that he hadn't repaid Linda for the dinners he had at her house, Brad asked if she could join him for dinner at the French restaurant. Brad figured he wouldn't be missed at the training table and his budget would allow him to splurge. Lind quickly accepted but said she would rather fix dinner at her house. Brad then quickly accepted

At the Environmental class, as expected, Linda was the first person Scott Watson called on to discuss the assignment. Linda gave an excellent talk, which caused Scott to complement her. Then Scott asked Brad if he had anything to add perhaps trying to embarrass him and make it look like Linda was the brains of their team. Brad actually was able to discuss some additional points. However, he did not receive a complement from Scott.

By this time a pattern had developed for Brad and Linda. They would meet at the school cafeteria for breakfast. On Tuesdays and Thursdays before their different 8:00 a.m. classes. They would get together again at for the Environmental class. Brad would stay overnight at Linda's Tuesday, Thursday and Sunday night. Sunday they would go to a matinee movie or play. Brad would pay for the Sunday events and often bring drinks or dessert to dinner, which allowed him to feel he was making some financial contribution to the relationship.

The rest of the week went quickly and suddenly it was Saturday.

CHAPTER 12

Home game days always followed the same routine for the football team. Any players needing medical attention or needing extra time to be taped were required to be at the stadium no later than 10:00 a.m. All other players had to be at the stadium an hour later. Players were not allowed on the field until 11:30 a.m. That would allow up to an hour and forty five minutes to warm up and practice plays. The team would then go back to the locker room for about twenty minutes and then return to the field five minutes before the scheduled 1:10 p.m. kickoff.

When Brad got to the stadium just before 10:00 a.m. he found out he would have to play a lot at the tight end position because Tommy Foster, the starting tight end, was having trouble with cramps. That would be in addition to playing full time defense and all special teams. That caused Brad to spend a lot of time practicing with the offense units and more time usual practicing catching passes before the start of the game. The extra practice paid off as Brad ended up playing on almost all plays that day. The extra effort by Brad would be felt later that night.

State got off to a good start and by halftime was leading by a score of 21 to 7. Then midway through the third quarter Brad suffered an injury that was not serious enough for him to leave the game, but never the less, would require medical attention. It seems as he was getting up after a play when someone stepped on his left hand. Within a few minutes the hand began to swell. That should have been looked at when Brad would come off the field when the team on offense had to go on defense. Because Brad was playing both offense and defense he didn't have time to have his hand looked at during the change of possession. By the end of the game the back of his hand looked like there was a balloon under his skin.

X-rays of the hand showed tendon strains but no breaks. The team trainer then decided to puncher the hand to let out some blood and pus that had built up. A bandage was put on the hand and then an ice pack was wrapped around it. The trainer told Brad that after he took a shower and got dressed the trainer would put a cast on the hand. Brad wasn't sure it made sense to take a hot shower with an ice pack on his hand, but doctor's orders were orders.

Brad reported back to the trainer after getting dressed with difficulty. The cast was actually an elbow length cotton glove with the tip of the fingers missing. A wire brace was placed on top of the glove separating the fingers and holding them in place. This didn't allow Brad to bend his fingers or wrist. Since Brad was planning on going straight to the club, he dressed in a suit and tie. Fortunately a couple of his teammates helped him button his shirt and pull his left coat sleeve down to his wrist. The trainer tied Brad's tie.

By then it was close to 6:00 p.m. so Brad took off for the club. On the way his hand started to throb and became very painful. He decided to take two of the pain pills the trainer had given him with the warning that the pills would make him sleepy. Brad arrived at the club about fifteen minutes early, so he took the pills, hoping he could stay awake at dinner. By the time he went inside he was tired, sore, and very irritable, not the best way to present a good appearance.

The Belson family—Joan, Henry, and Hannah—had attended the game with Linda. Lately Hannah had expressed an interest in football perhaps because she knew someone that was friends with one of the football jocks. During the game Hannah pointed out Brad's play several times and seemed to be almost as interested in watching him as Linda was. Joan thought Hannah's interest was rather odd since Hannah had always had a low opinion of jocks as she called football players.

Joan was also interested in watching Brad primarily because he was the only player she knew. Henry on the other hand was interested in the entire game. He was happy to support the local team. Henry's business had season tickets to the cities' two big university powerhouse football games, but Henry seldom used the tickets himself. After a few years of following those teams he had lost interest mainly because so many of the players had criminal records and were of such low character he couldn't relate to them.

On the way home from the game, Linda said she would be having dinner with Larry and Cindy at the club that night but that maybe the Belsons could come over to her house Sunday evening for dinner. She also casually mentioned that Brad would be at her house Sunday afternoon to study for their environmental class. She said if the Belsons could make dinner she would also invite Brad. Henry said that would be nice and that he would like to meet Brad. Hannah said noting, but Linda noticed a big smile on her face.

When Linda got home she took a bath and spent the next half hour trying to decide what clothes to wear. She didn't think it would be a good idea to wear a sexy dress that showed a lot of cleavage. She also didn't want to look too formal, so she selected a light blue dress that would allow her to wear a number of jewelry pieces. At the last minute Linda realized she hadn't had her hair done for almost a week, but it was too late to do anything about it now. Still that bothered her for the rest of the evening.

Linda arrived at the club several minutes before 7:00 p.m. Linda asked the hostess, who knew her, to be seated at a table in a dark part of the room. The table had two chairs on one side and bench type seating on the other side with the back and right side against walls. Linda purposely sat on the bench side and slid to the right corner. This would require Brad to sit beside her and cause Larry and Cindy to sit in the chairs on the other side of the table.

Larry and Cindy arrived right on time. Linda could tell Cindy didn't like the table location or the seating arrangement, but she did not say anything. Score one for our side thought Linda. Cindy was dressed provocatively, of course. Her hair looked like it had been done that day. For that matter so had Larry's hair.

After cordial greetings Larry asked Linda to sign the agreement papers, which she did. Cindy then took her notary stamp, which was the self-ink type, and notarized both sets of papers. Cindy said she would log the transactions in her notary book when she got home.

While they were waiting for Brad Larry ordered a bottle of wine after spending a several seconds looking over the wine list.

"So Linda, Larry said you invited a big jock to join us tonight, what's his name again?" asked Cindy.

"His name is Brad Wilson and that looks like him coming toward us right now," answered Linda.

Both Cindy and Larry turned sideways to look for Brad as he approached from their left. The hostess who was leading Brad to the table was about six inches shorter than Brad causing him to look even bigger than he was. Just before Brad got to the table Cindy turned toward Linda, gave her a wink and whispered that Brad was a real stud.

"Brad this is Cindy Wallace and my ex-husband Larry Wallace. Cindy and Larry, Brad is in one of my classes at school," said Linda.

"Hello, Cindy," said Brad as he looked directly at her.

He then walked behind Cindy's chair to shake hands with Larry instead of reaching over the table. Another score for our side thought Linda realizing this would impress Larry. To his credit, Larry stood up to shake hands.

"It's nice to meet you Larry," said Brad as he gave Larry a firm but not bone-crushing handshake.

No one spoke for a few seconds as Brad sat down. However, Linda noticed that Cindy had a star struck look on her face. Linda thought she knew what Cindy was thinking and it was X rated. One more score for our side thought Linda.

Brad immediately noticed that Cindy's boobs looked like they were about to fall out of her dress. For some reason the words of an old song came to mind, something about being so nice to come home too. Brad also noticed that Larry was dressed appropriately in a dark business suit. Just then the waiter delivered the bottle of wine. While the waiter was uncorking the wine Larry asked if he would like a glass of wine or if he preferred a beer.

"I'd like a gin martini, straight up with two olives," Brad said as he looked at the waiter.

"Boy, you really know how to order a drink," said Cindy causing Larry to wince.

That silly remark just gave more points to our side thought Linda.

"Cindy, Linda said you saw a musical at the Music Center this afternoon. Have you ever been there before?" asked Brad.

"No, this was my first time. I'd like to go again sometime. Of course I think the San Francisco Opera House is nicer," answered Cindy, obviously trying to impress Brad.

By this time Larry had completed his wine-tasting procedure, which Cindy missed, and poured glasses for Cindy, Linda, and himself. Larry said he would propose a toast to their health as soon as Brad's drink was served. Larry made the comment as a suggestion that no one take a drink of wine until Brad's had a drink. Cindy didn't get the hint and took a big drink of the wine. She then announced that the wine was really good. More points for our side thought Linda.

When Brad's drink arrived he placed one olive on Linda's bread plate and the other one on his bread plate. Immediately both Cindy and Larry seemed to realize that Brad and Linda were better friends than they were letting on. Larry did propose a toast after which everyone was silent for a few seconds as they tried to gather their thoughts.

Finally Linda said she and the Belsons had seen the football that afternoon. She congratulated Brad on the teams win. She said Henry Belson thought Brad played a good game.

Dinner was ordered and while waiting to be served the group engaged in polite conversation. Larry offered bread to everyone. Brad reached for the bread with his right hand. Up until then he had keep his left hand out of sight below the table. Without thinking Brad started to use his left hand to pick up a butter knife. The sight of Brad's cast startled everyone, which caused Brad to apologize for not mentioning that he had hurt his hand earlier that day.

Cindy was the first to speak, "Brad, what happened to your hand?"

"Someone stepped on it during the football game today. It's not as bad as it looks. No bones were broken, so the cast should come off in a couple of days," answered Brad.

"Will you be able to play in next week's game?" asked Linda.

"Luckily for me, next week is a bye week. I'll be ready for the following week though," answered Brad.

At that time dinner was served. Cindy ordered lobster and steak cooked rare, the most expensive item on the menu. Linda ordered a salmon dish. Larry and Brad both ordered filet minion steaks both medium well. As soon as Brad tried to pick up the steak knife he realized he would never be able to cut his steak. He was looking for the waiter to ask that his steak be cut in the kitchen when Cindy suddenly pulled Brad's plate close to her as she picked up Brad's steak knife.

"Let me give you a little help," Cindy said as she started cutting the steak.

Larry and Linda glanced at each other but said nothing.

"Nice of you to help, Cindy. I was thinking I might have to eat the steak like we do at the team dinners," said Brad causing the others to smile.

Eventually Brad was asked the question he knew would be asked. He decided to give a direct complete answer instead of having details drag out over several minutes.

"Brad what are you planning to do after college," asked Larry.

"I'll go back on active duty with the army. I made a commitment to do that since the army is paying for my college education," answered Brad.

"But if you do that, won't you have to go to Iraq, or have you already served time there?"

"Yes and yes, I've already been to Iraq and if the war is still going on two years from now, I'll probably go back."

"You know I can probably get you out of that commitment if you give me a call after you graduate."

At this time Cindy decided to jump in the conversation.

"Brad, when you were in Iraq, did you have to shoot your gun?" asked Cindy.

By this time the medicine effect seemed to start taking hold. Not the pain relieving part but the part that made Brad sleepy. Until now he had been able to ignore the pain in his hand, but it suddenly started to bother him.

"Did I have to shoot a gun? Yes, I fired machine guns and my M16 rifle. That is what I was paid to do," answered Brad.

"Did you hit anything?" Cindy asked.

"Oh yeah, I hit buildings, vehicles, trees, goats, and a camel," said Brad, trying to keep the conversation from becoming too serious.

"You killed a camel, why did you do that?" Cindy asked.

"I didn't kill a camel it was already dead when I hit it."

"Well, why did you shot a dead camel?"

"I wasn't trying to hit the camel. I was shooting at some bad guys that were hiding behind it and were firing at me."

"Did you hit them?"

"Yes, I did," said Brad as he looked directly into Cindy's eyes.

This caused a lull in the conversation, so Brad tried to get off the subject.

"Cindy, you seem to be interested in what happened in Iraq. If you really want to know you can find out firsthand. Just join the army. I sure they would be happy to see you and you would have all your questions answered," said Brad.

"Oh, I could never join the army," said Cindy.

With that, Linda instinctively grabbed Brad's arm. She could tell by the tone of his voice that he was getting irritated and she obviously didn't want Brad to give his rehearsed response to this comment.

"Brad, would you like another martini?" she asked.

"Yeah, that might be a good idea," Brad said after picking up his martini glass to be sure it was empty.

Brad immediately knew he shouldn't have ordered another drink, but it was too late now. However, he didn't have to drink the martini after it was served. Instead he made another mistake and did finish off the martini. He would soon regret doing that.

"I think I'd like to try one of those. Can you order one for me just like yours?" Cindy asked Brad.

After that remark Linda stopped counting points. It had to be plain to Larry that her find in Brad was much better than his find in Cindy.

"Do you think you can handle it after the wine?" asked Larry speaking for the first time in a while. It was unusual for him to not be heavily involved in any conversation where he was present.

"Yeah, I'm a big girl now," answered Cindy as she flashed a big grin at Brad.

"Two Bombay Sapphire gin martinis, straight up with olives shaken but not stirred," Brad ordered when the waiter appeared.

Brad sensed that the waiter seemed to be getting ready to ask if both drinks were for him.

"One for me and one for the blond kid," Brad said as a rebuttal to Cindy's remark about being a big girl.

A while later when they all had finished dinner, including dessert and coffee, Linda took the opportunity to excuse herself to go to the ladies' room. Cindy decided to follow.

When they were in the ladies' room Cindy had a lot to say about Brad.

"Larry said you thought Brad would be a good find for Diane. He's way too much for her. You should take my advice and hookup with him yourself," Cindy said to Linda.

"Brad is young enough to be my son, so there is no danger of that happening," lied Linda.

Anyone but Cindy could tell Linda was lying. Linda's eyes opened wide and her voice reached a high pitch.

"Well, if you're still thinking of having Diane meet Brad, why don't you send him up to see Larry sometime. Larry and I could arrange for the four of us to get together so Diane and Brad could get to know each other. I know Diane would really have fun showing Brad around the campus."

"I was thinking Diane could meet Brad when she comes home for Thanksgiving. You know they actually did get to see each other right after the Stanford football game. Brad said Diane was very pretty."

"Yeah, Diane told me you wanted her to meet some jock after the game. She really didn't have a chance to talk to him. I'm sure she would like him better if he wasn't wearing a football uniform."

"Well, the football season will be over by Thanksgiving, so Brad won't be in uniform next time they meet."

"Look Linda you and I both know Brad is way too mature for Diane. I'm serious about you taking advantage of the opportunity to have a real live sexy affair before you are too old. Brad couldn't stop staring at my boobs tonight, so I know what he wants. Has he ever tried to poke you?"

"Poke me, do you mean with his finger?"

"No, silly, I mean poke you between your legs with his thing. That's the way kids at school are describing casual sex now days. If you give him a couple more drinks you could have an all-nighter."

"Thanks for your advice, but I'll keep looking for someone closer to my age."

"I hope you don't mind me flirting with Brad. It's harmless. I like to do that because it makes Larry a little jealous. That will make him better in bed tonight I think Brad likes me flirting with him too."

Linda's opinion of Cindy couldn't get any lower, but still Linda was shocked after listening to her the last few minutes. Linda didn't want to hear anything more from Cindy, so she said they should be getting back to Larry and Brad.

On the way back to the table Linda started wondering if anyone had poked Diane or more realistically how many guys have poker her. She also wondered how many girls Brad had poked and how many he was still poking. Cindy's comments and her thoughts caused her face to turn red with embarrassment.

While they were gone, Larry and Brad had a somewhat testy discussion.

"Brad, what made you quit school to go in the army?" Larry asked.

"I joined the army in 2001 just after the country was attacked on September 11. It seemed to be the right thing to do," said Brad.

"Yes, but you could have waited until you finished college if you only had two more years."

By this time Brad was not feeling well. His hand was throbbing, he was having trouble staying awake and now Larry had just implied that he was stupid for joining the army. So Brad decided to forcefully respond to Larry's question.

"For Christ sakes, Larry, three thousand people had just been killed by some assholes attacking our country and more attacks were being planning I didn't think it would be a good idea to wait two more years hoping the next attacks wouldn't get me. As I said I thought it was the right thing to do at the time. After spending three years in Iraq I still believe I made a good decision. I'll tell you something else, being in combat and being involved in firefights is a lot more exciting than sitting in a classroom or even playing football. I'm always amazed at why most of you people couldn't care less about the importance of national defense.

"Well, I didn't mean to imply it was wrong to join the army."

"Yeah, I know you didn't. It's just that when people find out I was in the army the first thing they do is to ask why I would do something so stupid. Look, let me apologize for my comments, sometimes I get carried away."

Neither Larry nor Brad spoke for a few seconds until Brad tried to change the subject with a comment.

"I wonder if the girls have decided to leave and stick us with the bill," said Brad.

"It's beginning to look that way," responded Larry.

"If they don't get back soon I may just take a nap. The pain medicine I took earlier and the martinis are making me sleepy."

"Here they come now."

Larry picked up the tab, and they started to leave.

"Linda, do you mind if Cindy and I stop by your house for a couple of minutes. I'd like to pick up something I might have left while I'm looking maybe you can show Cindy the house," Larry asked.

Linda glanced at Brad before answering. Since she had invited him to spend the night, she was sure Brad would realize it wouldn't be a good idea for him to go directly to her place, but she still wanted him to spend the night. Somehow she had to let Brad know.

"Sure, that will be all right, but I don't know how you plan on carrying out your wine collection," Linda finally answered.

"Yeah, I didn't forget, but if you don't mind I'll have to arrange for a service to ship them to me. I'll try schedule that soon."

Larry and Linda both had valet parking while Brad had parked his car in the lot. That would give Linda an opportunity to get Brad alone for a couple of minutes.

"Brad, did you remember to bring Scott Watson's critique of our environmental project presentation with you today? If it's in your car maybe I can borrow it. I'd like to review it tomorrow," Linda asked.

"Sure I'll get it for you," answered Brad even though he knew there was no critique.

"I'll go with you to your car I know you are not feeling well and are anxious to leave."

Once outside everyone repeated the usual pleasantries when saying good buys. After Brad and Larry shook hands Cindy gave Brad a big hug and whispered in his ear that she would like to see him again. Brad didn't know if he should hug Linda or not. Brad had purposely not paid much attention to Linda during dinner as Linda had requested. Brad decided he wanted to hug Linda anyway, so he did.

Then as Brad and Linda walked toward Brad's car, Linda asked Brad if wouldn't mind waiting a while before coming to her place. She said she would call Brad as soon as Larry and Cindy left, which she said wouldn't be too long. That was fine with Brad it would allow him to take a cat nap in his car while he waited for Linda's call. It would be a full hour and a half before Linda called.

Larry and Cindy arrived at Linda's house a little before her. As soon as they all were in the house, Linda started a downstairs tour of the house for Cindy. Larry said he thought he had left some things in the room he had used as an office, so he started looking around there. Fortunately, he did not go upstairs. Otherwise he might have found a number of Brad's personal items in the bathroom.

The tour and Larry's search only took a few minutes, so Linda felt obligated to offer to make some coffee, hoping they would decline. They did not. Even worse when they finished coffee Larry wanted to show Cindy his cellar wine collection. That wasn't just a matter of having Cindy take a one minute peak at the collection. Larry went into a length lecture on wine including an explanation of why he had the special wine room constructed just to preserve his valuable collection. Fortunately, Larry didn't notice the one bottle Linda has used the first time Brad had dinner at her house. As soon as they left, Linda called Brad.

Linda apologized over and over again for asking Brad to wait in his car when he arrived. She said there was some fresh coffee that might make him feel better. The talked for a while, but it was evident that Brad really wasn't feeling very well. So around 10:00 p.m. they decided to go to bed. Brad feel asleep almost immediately, sex would and did have to wait until morning.

Brad was almost back to normal by breakfast time. His hand still bothered him, but when talking to Linda he was able to ignore the pain. Linda and Brad both wanted to talk about the dinner. First Linda asked what Brad felt about Larry and Cindy.

"Well, Cindy, like you, is very beautiful and has a great body. Almost as good as you. She seems very friendly. Unfortunately, she has the mind of someone stuck in the third grade," said Brad.

Linda tried not to laugh but couldn't help herself.

"Brad I have to ask you something about what Cindy said. I'm almost too embarrassed to say this, but she said all the kids at school are referring to casual sex as poking someone or being poked. Have you heard anyone use that term?"

"No, the guys I know use more graphic terms. Cindy must be talking about kids in middle school.

"Okay, now what did you think of Larry?"

"You may not like this, but I was favorable impressed with Larry. He presented a professional appearance and he demonstrated considerable restraint by not slapping Cindy around when she made those silly comments. Actually, I feei a little sorry for him. By now I think he knows he made a monumental mistake in leaving you and marrying Cindy. He is going to suffer for his mistake for many years to come," Brad said.

Without saying it Brad figured that Larry's marriage to Cindy would not last another year. Brad also figured that Larry would then want to reunite with Linda. If that happened and he and Linda were still involved with each other what would Linda do? Brad decided to address that issue at a later time.

Brad's comments caused Linda to feel obligated to tell him about her marriage to Larry. It was a happy marriage for the most part. Larry certainly was a good provider. Linda didn't have to work after the first two years and had just about everything she wanted. Still she always thought something was missing. There was never much time to do things as a family. Larry's work kept him away from home a lot. Even in the evenings and weekends Larry always had to spend some time on business matters.

Larry was always able to find time for Diane, however. There were a number of trips to Disneyland, and the beach weather permitting. He also took her other places where children were welcome, often without Linda. Besides buying lots of presents, he often read bedtime stories to Diane when she was young. Teaching Diane life necessaries and administrating discipline was left to Linda. Naturally this resulted in Diane becoming a Daddy's girl. Worse yet as her affection for her dad grew, her respect for Linda pretty much disappeared.

Linda wasn't sure when Larry began seeing other women. She suspected it had gone on for some time before she began to notice. Once she confirmed the living arrangement Larry and Cindy had in San Francisco she demanded a divorce. That seemed to surprise Larry so much that he offered to stop seeing Cindy. Linda wasn't receptive to that idea. Larry had gone too far, and their relationship could never be repaired. After seeing Larry today, she was certain she made the right decision in asking for a divorce.

"Before I forget Linda, I want to give you credit for fast thinking in coming up with the story about wanting to review our project critique I wasn't sure what I should do when Larry asked to stop by your house. If you hadn't been able to talk to me I thought I'd just take a nap in my car for an hour or so and then call you to see if the coast was clear to stop by your place. It's funny that that is just the way things turned out. Incidentally, I really needed an hour of sleep," Brad said.

"I felt so bad for you, sleeping in your car, but I thought it better to not have you stop by when the two love birds were here. I'll call Diane later this morning to let her know about us. Just as soon as I finish talking to her I'll try to get a hold of Larry hopefully before Diane calls him. As of right now I'm done asking you to play like you don't know me," Linda said.

Brad and Linda continued to talk for another hour or so until it was close 9:30 a.m. Linda then decided it was time to call Diane. Brad said he would be watching the football pregame and then football games on

Linda knew she would have to make this call sometime. She had practiced how to tell Diane many times, still she was worried that the call would not go well. Linda was right the call did not go well.

"Hi, Mom," Diane said as she answered Linda's call.

"Hi, Diane, I'm glad I caught you at home," Linda said

"Yeah, I was about to go out."

"Well, I won't keep you on the phone long, but I wanted to tell you I had dinner with Larry and Cindy last night,"

"Yeah, I know. Cindy said you brought some jock with you. Is that the same jerk you wanted me to meet at the Stanford game?"

Hearing that, Linda had to fight hard to keep her composure. Cindy's call to Diane destroyed the way Linda had wanted to lead up to explaining her relationship with Brad. Referring to Brad as a jock was bad enough, but calling him a jerk when she had only seen him one time for less than three minutes was stupid, immature, and just mean. Linda had to depart from her intended script and would have to explain her relationship with Brad somewhat less poetically than originally intended.

"Diane my friend's name is Brad Wilson. Please don't refer to him as a jock or jerk. We've been seeing each for some time now. He is younger than me, so I don't know how much longer our relationship will last."

"Mom, have you gone crazy? That guy is my age. How can you stand to be seen in public with a kid years younger than you?"

"Well, I have an answer for you. I have no problem with the fact that Brad is younger than me. It doesn't seem to bother you that your father not only is seen with but married someone fifteen years younger than him. If that doesn't bother you had better not have a problem with my relationship with Brad."

"Dad's situation is different. You are not sleeping with him are you?"

"Yes, as a matter of fact I am and have been for over a month. Your father and I are no longer married, so there is nothing wrong with having an intimate relationship with anyone I choose."

"What's wrong is that your friend is a young stud according to Cindy. I don't want to meet this guy, and I don't want to hear any more about him."

"That is an unbelievably immature attitude. I'm not asking you to approve. I just thought you should know about Brad and me. When you get to be an adult I think you will understand."

"I am an adult and I never will understand. I don't want to hear from you again until you stop seeing the jerk."

With that Diane hung up on Linda. Surprisingly that didn't seem to bother Linda. She had done her duty, so to speak and now she wanted to call Larry. She assumed Diane would not be going out but would be calling Cindy instead at that very minute.

"That didn't go very well," Linda said to Brad as she was calling Larry.

"Sorry to hear that. Maybe we can talk about it if you like when you finish talking to Larry," answered Brad.

"Hello, Linda," said Larry as he answered the phone.

"I need to bring you up-to-date on a phone call I just had with Diane," said Linda.

"Yeah, I think Diane just called Cindy, did something happen,"

"Nothing really happened. I just told Diane about my relationship with Brad, so as I said I'd like to let you know before Diane finished talking to Cindy."

"Cindy just said you and Brad are having an affair. What is that all about?"

"It's about an intimate relationship I'm having with Brad. I'm sure Cindy figured it out and must have told Diane last night. I was waiting to tell you until I could talk to Diane. I wanted to be the one to tell you, not Diane and especially not Cindy."

"Are you talking about the kid we had dinner with last night? You cannot be serious that guy must be years younger than you."

"I am serious and a twelve-year age difference is a lot better than a fifteen-year difference in age like the difference in your age and Cindy's."

"Have you given any thought to how this will affect Diane? I mean your lover is about the same age as Diane's boyfriends."

"Look I know what you are implying, but Brad and I have already discussed Diane. She is nowhere mature enough for Brad to be interested in her. Besides that, she is self-centered and manipulative. In other words, she sometimes acts like she is still in grade school instead of college. Besides, she has already told me she thinks he's a jerk."

Larry thought to himself that Linda didn't know how men think. In most men's minds, a great, or even a near great, female body always trumps a great mind. However, he didn't mention that because he knew Linda would think that is why he got involved with Cindy. Even if that were true he didn't think Linda would understand.

"We need to discuss this further before Diane visits you. This is not the time, however. I'll call you some night later this week."

"That's great. If I'm not busy, I'll take the call."

"You want to set a time to talk?"

"Call any evening after 7:00 p.m. except Thursday."

"All right, I'll try to call Tuesday or Wednesday."

Linda felt relieved after the phone calls. She still needed to discuss the situation with her parents, but there was no hurry to do that. Neither Larry nor Diane was apt to contact them, or so she thought. It would be difficult having anyone from the church congregation or her dwindling circle of friends meet Brad for the first time, but she felt she could handle that. Brad had taken her to a number of after-school events, so she was pretty sure everyone at school knew they were a pair. Brad said he had no qualms about having all of his friends and acquaintances know she was his lover. Her only concern was how long it would take for Diane to lose her attitude.

"So I take it the phone calls could have been better," Brad said as Linda sat down beside him on the sofa.

"Well, it could have been worse, but not by much. I'll tell you about it later, but first would you like me to make you some popcorn," answered Linda.

"Yes, I would. Why don't you make some for yourself while you are at it," Brad said, hoping an attempted humor would make Linda feel better.

Soon Linda had made enough popcorn for both of them to go along with a couple of soft drinks.

"Who's winning?" asked Linda

"My favorite team," Brad answered, realizing that Linda didn't know one team from another.

"Is your hand still hurting? If so, you can always go to the emergency care place?"

"It's getting better. Tomorrow I'll see the team trainer before class. He'll probably take off this silly cast."

"Well, don't rush it. By the way, I'm not complaining, but your hand felt like ping-pong paddle against my back last night."

"Really, well, maybe tonight I'll go a little lower and give you a couple of whacks."

"Oh, I almost forgot to tell you I've invited the Belson family to dinner. You met Joan once, but I don't think you've met Joan's husband Henry or her daughter Hannah."

"I remember Joan and it would be nice to meet the rest of the family."

"Henry is a CPA who enjoys football. Hannah is fourteen years old and is interested in meeting you so she can tell her friends at school that she knows a star football player."

"Well, I don't know about being a star, but as I said I'd be happy to meet Hannah and Henry."

Linda fixed a light lunch just after noon. Brad continued to watch football on TV while Linda started getting ready for dinner. Brad offered to help and was assigned the task of setting the table during halftime of the game he was watching. Linda wanted Brad to sit at the head of the table, Henry on his left and Joan next to Henry. Linda would sit to Brad's right and Hannah next to Linda.

About 2:00 p.m. Linda's mother called. As so many times in the past they spent the first few minutes talking about the weather first in Chicago and then Los Angeles, then they each asked about the others health and finally they talked about Diane's activities.

Then Linda's mom brought the subject of moving to California. It seems Linda's father had retired late last year and by now had pretty much severed his business ties in Chicago. It seems they now planned on visiting Linda after the first of the year so they could spend time looking for a nice place to move to. Linda said they could stay at her house. She had an extra bedroom and had been looking forward to their visit.

Now that Brad was in the picture she wasn't sure how to let her parents know about him. She had only casually mentioned to Brad that her parents may want to visit. Brad, in essence, said he would not spend any nights with Linda during the parents visit if that is what Linda wanted. Linda said that wouldn't be necessary because she would notify her parents of her relationship with Brad. While talking to her mother, Linda kept busy in the kitchen, so Brad didn't hear what Linda was saying. After the call ended, Linda told Brad they just talked about the same things they always talk about.

The Belsons arrived at 5:00 p.m. Brad shook hands with Henry. He said he remembered Joan and gave her a hug. Brad wasn't sure how to greet Hannah. He knew it wouldn't be a good idea to hug her and shaking hands didn't seem right either. Instead he asked what grade she was in at school.

Brad found the Belsons easy to talk with. They were friendly and it was obvious they were all very intelligent including Hannah considering her age. The first conversation topic was Brad's hand. Brad's explanation of his injury led the conversation to football.

Henry thanked Brad for the tickets to yesterday's game and said everyone was happy State won. Henry seemed to be quite knowledgeable about football. He apparently followed State, as well as other college and professional teams. Somewhere in the conversation Brad asked Henry if he had played football in high school or college. Henry said he hadn't played since high school where he was a 165-pound center. The center position is not considered a skilled or glamorous position like quarterback or wide receiver. However, it does require the ability to first concentrate on centering the ball and then carrying out a blocking assignment. Brad figured Henry was able to compensate for his lack of weight with intelligent play. Brad decided Henry was a good guy.

Hannah had a chance to talk about being in the choir and about trying out for the swim team. Brad pointed out being on a sports team requires a commitment to spend a lot of time practicing. Hannah said she could do that and that her mom would take her to the pool at the clubhouse every weekend. A pained expression came over Joan's face as she nodded affirmatively. Hannah did decline to sing a solo saying she was only part of the choir.

At dinner Brad asked Henry if he enjoyed having to go to NYC every month. Henry said he didn't mind it was just part of his job. On the flight there and again on the flight back home he was able to finish a lot of business required reading. He only wished he had more time to spend doing tourist things like sightseeing.

Joan mentioned that at least once a year she and Hannah accompanied Henry usually in a summer month when Hannah was out of school. They would spend a few days in the city and then drive to nearby attractions including a lot of historical sites. Hannah was able to learn a lot about the history of the country and a lot about geography as well as local customs.

As she listened to Joan, Linda came up with what she thought would be a great idea. Maybe she could talk Brad into going to New York City with her over the Christmas holidays. Diane had already said she would be spending the holidays with Larry and Cindy skiing in Colorado. She decided to bring up the subject later that night.

Brad mentioned he was taking accounting and auditing classes at school. He said his older brother, who is a certified public accountant in Kansas City, Missouri, suggested he study accounting. It would also come in handy for a second career. Henry said his firm has done business with a local air force facility, so he knows the military does have accounting positions. He thought Brad may want to try to get into that field when he goes back on active duty.

That started Linda thinking. It would be great if Brad does get one of those assignments. As far as she knew there were no accountants running around battlefields. She would talk to Brad about making accounting his major so he would qualify for what would be a safe office position. Then she realized that in her mind she was already thinking of a long term commitment with Brad. She wondered if he was thinking along the same lines. That would be another topic to discuss with Brad but not tonight.

The Belsons left before 9:00 p.m. Brad and Linda quickly cleaned and put away the dinner dishes. They spent the next hour talking before going to bed. Before Linda could tell about her plan to visit New York City, Brad surprised her with a plan of his own. He suggested they spend the Thanksgiving weekend in Las Vegas at his expense. Brad had been practicing his personal austerity program in order to save some money. By now he figured he had enough savings to pay for a hotel room, food gas to get there and maybe a dinner show. Linda would have to be on her own for gambling.

Linda thought she would really like that. She had only been to Las Vegas one time and only for two days. But then she remembered Diane was scheduled to visit that weekend. This was the first time Linda would have to decide between Brad and Diane and she realized this was going to be a continuing problem. Taking Diane with them to Las Vegas was out of the question. Diane would take all the fun out of the trip just like she always did on trips. A few days ago Linda would have immediately declined Brad's offer, but this time she thought maybe something could be worked out. Unknown to her a solution to her dilemma was in the works.

CHAPTER 13

Monday morning Brad had his hand looked at by the football team trainer. The makeshift cast was removed for closer examination and then replaced. X-rays indicated the injury was healing, but it would take a few more days before it would be safe to remove the cast permanently. Since no football game was scheduled that week Brad hand would have time to heal before the final game of the season against South State the following week.

Tuesday morning Brad and Linda met for breakfast in the school cafeteria. Linda told Brad that she had several ideas about how Diane's visit could be rescheduled so they could go to Las Vegas Thanksgiving weekend. Her plans depended on Diane staying with Larry and Cindy that weekend. If so, then maybe Diane could visit her a weekend before or after Thanksgiving. An alternative would be for Linda to visit Diane some weekend before or after Thanksgiving.

Linda then told Brad she would like to treat him to a few days in NYC over the Christmas holidays. She knew Brad showed interest in the Belsons talk about their visits there.

Brad immediately accepted Linda's offer with the provision that he bear half the costs. Linda knew even half of the costs of a NYC trip would be way too much for Brad. Sometime soon she and Brad would have to reach an understanding on finances. She was not only willing but would prefer to pick up costs for almost all their activities together. In blunt terms, she could afford things that Brad could not. She would rather do things than not do them because Brad couldn't afford them. That, of course, would be difficult to get Brad to agree to. However, this wasn't the time to argue about costs. She would just make plane, hotel and show reservations and pay the costs herself. Brad could share incidental costs for such things as fast food.

Up north in the San Francisco Bay Area another conversation was going on. Larry and Cindy were continuing a conversation that started Sunday after Linda had talked to Diane and Larry.

"Larry, you can't let Diane visit Linda as long as she is involved with that guy, Brad. It just wouldn't be right," Cindy yelled.

"All right, just calm down. We've already been over this. As part of the divorce I gave custody of Diane to Linda until Diane turned eighteen. Now we have joint custody. Neither I nor Diane can deny Linda from seeing Diane," answered Larry.

"But Diane is not with Linda now. Linda gave up the $2,000 a month award for taking care of Diane. That was part of your divorce since you are paying for her education. Isn't that the same as giving up her right to see Diane?"

"No, not according to the law."

"But Linda doesn't know that. Why not just keep Diane up here and let Linda fight to get her back. Diane told me she doesn't want to see Linda again until that guy isn't around."

"Look, Diane isn't scheduled to visit Linda until Thanksgiving week. I'm pretty sure Linda won't object if Diane accompanies us to Hawaii instead. Maybe by Christmas Linda will have come to her senses and given up on Brad."

Cindy had to stop and think for a minute or so. Larry's suggestion presented her with a no-win proposition. Up to then she hadn't thought of what Diane would do over Thanksgiving if she didn't visit Linda. By now Cindy was getting tired of being Diane's best friend and was looking forward to being along with Larry in Hawaii. Still the best way of getting Linda to stop seeing Brad, which is what Cindy wanted most, would be to make Linda choose between Brad and Diane. Cindy had delusions of somehow hooking up with Brad herself once Linda was out of the picture. Cindy finally decided there was almost no chance of Linda breaking up with Brad before Thanksgiving even if Diane refused to visit her then.

"Well then, let's take Diane with us to Hawaii," Cindy finally said.

"All right, maybe you can text Diane, and I'll call Linda tonight to let her know," Larry responded.

Diane knew she didn't want to visit Linda as long as Brad was around, but she wasn't sure she wanted to go to Hawaii either. She spent a week on the big island of Hawaii a few years ago with Larry and Linda. They stayed in a five-star hotel right on the beach. That was nice for about two days and then she got bored. It might be different this time since Cindy said they would be spending at least two days on the main island of Oahu.

She decided she could stand going to Hawaii if it would make her mom decide to stop seeing Brad.

Larry did call Linda that night. He was surprised at how quickly Linda agreed to let Diane choose Hawaii over her. Linda did say she would try to get up there to see Diane sometime in the next couple of weeks.

Brad was staying overnight, so Linda gave him the good news. Their trip to Las Vegas was on for Thanksgiving weekend. They were both happy with those arrangements.

Both Larry and Cindy were not so happy. They would have preferred to not bring Diane along with them to Hawaii. Diane was also not so happy. She really didn't want to go to Hawaii, but in her mind it was better than visiting her mom and Brad. In essence the three of them had decided that in order to keep Linda from being happy, they would agree to make themselves miserable

Thursday night Linda called Diane, who chose to not take the call even though she was home. Linda left a message saying she understood that Larry would be taking her to Hawaii Thanksgiving week. Linda said she would like to come up there alone the first weekend of November to see how she was getting along. Linda finished the message by asking Diane to let her know if that would be all right with her. Linda felt it odd that she had to ask permission from her daughter to see her.

Diane didn't get back to Linda until the following Tuesday morning. She called when she knew Linda would be in class and wouldn't be able to take the call. Diane left a message saying the first weekend of November should be all right for Linda to visit, but she would have to confirm it the week before. Diane's juvenile action didn't seem to bother Linda. She was still reeling from a fun weekend

The following Friday, two of Brad's army buddies from Iraq, Bill Carson and John Murdy, showed up at the transit facility where Brad lived when he wasn't spending the night with Linda. The two would be staying at the transit facility until they could get government transportation to their next duty station, Korea. They knew Brad was living there while going to school, so they tried to find him. The transit facility duty clerk told the pair that Brad was probably at football practice. The clerk gave Brad's phone number to them and said they would probably have to leave a message.

Brad didn't get the message until after practice a little after 6:30 p.m. He immediately got in contact with them. After briefly bringing each other up-to-date on their activities they decided to meet at the Time Out bar, where Bill and John were, and then go to a nice restaurant for dinner. Brad decided that would be better than eating at the team training table.

On the way to the bar Brad called Linda to see if she would like to join them for dinner. It took a while to convince her that she would enjoy meeting his friends. Brad asked to Linda meet them at one of the best restaurants in the area at 7:30 p.m. Linda knew the restaurant and called for reservations at 8:00 p.m. since there wasn't enough time for her to get made up and to the restaurant any earlier.

After Brad got to the Time Out about fifteen minutes were spent renewing their friendship. Brad then got the pair in his car and headed for the restaurant. On the way, he mentioned that he had invited his date for the night, who was a little older than him. Referring to Linda as his date for the night was standard army talk for a girlfriend. John wanted to know why Brad hadn't ordered a couple of girls for him and Bill. Brad said they didn't have to buy them dinner since they could always pick up a couple of girls from the groupies hanging around the gym.

Linda got to the restaurant before the others, who as she correctly suspected, would be late. She heard the guys coming before she saw them and immediately wondered if she had made a mistake in showing up. As soon as introductions were made and Linda could see the guys weren't drunk out of their minds she felt a lot better. She felt even better when Brad gave her a big hug.

Bill and John had been on thirty days' leave—"leave" is an army term for vacation—during the past month, so most of the talk at dinner was about what they had done during that time. No one mentioned Iraq. The guys would talk about that after Linda went home. Neither did Bill or John mention Linda's age at dinner. That would also be discussed with Brad later.

Bill talked about visiting his family in western Pennsylvania. All of his high school friends had married or left the area, so he spent the first couple of days just relaxing at his parents' house. Most of remaining time was spent drinking at the local bars trying to meet women. He did have some success. As previously planned, he spent the last couple of days with John in Las Vegas

John had a similar story. He spent a few days visiting his parents in a suburb of Minneapolis. He also visited his two older married sisters who lived in the area with their families. All of the family members were pleased to see him, but it was evident that he didn't have much in common with them anymore. Like Bill he spent a lot of time in local bars trying to meet women. Like Bill he had some success.

Brad and Linda's interest perked up when the discussion turned to Las Vegas. Linda mentioned that they were planning on visiting the city in a few weeks.

"Linda, the main thing you will have to do is to make sure Brad doesn't stop by one of the so-called gentlemen's clubs. I won't tell you how I know this, but it can cost $25 for a glass of beer. Of course I will admit they do have some really great entertainment," said John.

"Did Bill tell you that?" joked Linda.

"No, no, it wasn't me. I couldn't even get into one of those places. The doorman looked at me and said I wouldn't be able to afford it. The guy actually did me a favor by not letting me in," said Bill.

"You don't have to worry about me. I have a plan to win big at the crap table," Brad chipped in.

"Well, Brad, when you win the big bucks you might think of taking Linda to a couple of shows," said John.

"Did either of you see any of the shows?" asked Linda.

"You mean besides the show that the drunks put on along the Strip?" joked Bill.

"No, neither of us had time to see a show. We were too busy losing money gambling," said John.

"Did you really lose a lot gambling?" asked Linda.

"No, mainly because we didn't have much to lose. However, John almost did win a lot until he made a big mistake. Tell them about it, John," said Bill.

"Yeah, well, here is the sad story. I bought in at the crap table for $200. For over an hour I won a little and lost a little. Then suddenly some guy started rolling numbers. This went on for maybe a dozen or more rolls. I keep pressing my winnings, so pretty soon I had money spread all over the table. In other words I had large place bets on all the numbers along with a number of proposition bets. When I realized that I knew it was time to go down on the place bets and take my winnings. However, I decided to wait for one more roll of the dice, big mistake. The shooter rolled a 7, which wiped out all my place bet winnings. It gets worse. I still had a couple of hundred dollars, so I decided to start over. This time I wouldn't be greedy, I'd quit as soon as I doubled my money. Guess what in a matter of minutes I lost all the money I started with. Of course it was kind of exciting for a couple of hours," said John.

The group continued to talk for about an hour after finishing dinner. Before they left the restaurant they agreed to stop by Linda's house about noon the next day for lunch. In the afternoon they would tour the city. Brad and Linda offered to be tour guides. Linda enjoyed the talk and seemed to fit in nicely with the men. Brad joked that the guys were going to try and find a cheap gentlemen's club. With that comment Linda gave Brad a hug and said she was going home.

Brad thought about going to Tony's Pizza but decided to stop there the next night. That way Linda would be there to protect Brad from the local groupies. Instead of Tony's, Brad directed the group back to the Time Out bar.

The bar featured classical country and western music Friday and Saturday nights. For some reason not many college kids went there. Middle-aged working-class people frequented the bar for the most part. Several single women were there when the guys arrived.

After ordering bottles of beer, Bill and John both found girls to dance with. Brad concentrated on drinking. During a band break Bill and John sat down with Brad and announced that all of the good-looking dancing girls had already hooked up with someone. That gave the trio time to talk about their time in Iraq.

Both Bill and John had joined the army two years before Brad. They both had served in Afghanistan in 2002 and were then deployed to Iraq in 2004 where they were assigned the same company as Brad. By that time Bagdad had been taken, so the army's mission had changed to searching out small groups of insurgents. Because they weren't all in the same platoon, they didn't get to know each other until several months later. That happened during a fierce firefight that occurred when the entire company was trying to clear the bad guys from a small town.

As the fighting progressed through a cemetery Brad found himself using a large headstone for protection when Bill and then John moved in beside him. In between firing the three exchanged names. Each of them wanted someone to know what happened to them if they got killed.

Back at Time Out, the talk soon turned to Brad's school activities and then to Linda. Bill and John wanted to know if Brad really was a big football star and if he had beautiful girls trying to make it with him all the time. Brad said he was just one member of the team and that all the beautiful girls already had boyfriends. They then wanted to know how he knew Linda.

Brad explained how he and Linda met and why they were attracted to each other.

"So Brad it sounds like you grabbed onto the first girl you met at school. Did you notice that she might be a little older than you?" asked John.

"Yeah, that's the way I like my women, experienced and desperate," answered Brad.

"That's not a problem as far as I'm concerned. Last night the woman I was with was a little older than me," said Bill.

"A little older than you. Your friend's false teeth were older than you," said John.

"Yeah, well, at least my friend was more mature than your girl who looked and acted like a twelve-year-old," Bill responded.

"It sounds like you met up with a mother-daughter team," Brad said.

"No, no it was nothing like that. The old lady was a schoolteacher, and the younger one was one of her students," joked John.

About that time Bill focused in on two girls sitting across the room from them. He decided to ask one of them to dance and started toward them. He was feeling the effects of drinking many beers and seemed to have a little trouble walking. He was walking slowly but raising his legs several inches higher than needed with each step as if he was walking through deep snow.

As he watched Bill, John told Brad he thought Bill was a little drunk. He then started to take a drink from his beer bottle but missed his mouth and spilled beer all over his left shoulder.

"So you think Bill may be a little drunk. Of course you are stead as a rock," Brad said.

"Yeah, well, I shouldn't have tried to drink with my bad left arm," said John.

"What's wrong with your arm?"

"I don't know yet. I'll tell you when I find out."

For some reason that seemed to make sense to Brad.

By this time Bill had come within two feet of the girls table. They were sitting in a booth with the table in front of them. As Bill leaned forward to ask for a dance, he put his hand on the table accidently pushing it into the girls and trapping them against the back of the booth.

Bill then said something that sounded like inviting one or maybe both of the girls to dance. Both girls declined the invitation. When he got back to his table he told Brad and John that the girls said he could go dance with himself or do something like that.

About that time the bar waitress asked the group if they wanted to order another round of drinks.

"None for me. I'm the designated driver," Bill said as he sat down in slow motion.

With that the guys decided it was time to leave. Brad said to the designated driver that if he felt he could drive, he should follow Brad back to the transit facility.

Saturday morning Brad called Linda to make sure she was still willing to act as tour guide for his two friends. Linda said she was up to it and offered to use her car, the big BMW.

As they were eating lunch Bill mentioned that this was the first time in years that anyone had invited him to dinner in a real house. John said he couldn't remember the last time anyone had invited him to dinner. They said they always ate out while on leave or not in army mess halls.

"When is the last time you had a home cooked dinner, Brad?" Bill asked.

"Why, I think it was the night before last," answered Brad.

"I mean before you met Linda, smarty."

"I really don't know, probably when I was in high school and living at home."

Linda found that hard to believe. It wasn't that she didn't believe them but that she thought everyone ate most meals at home.

About that time everyone decided it was time to start the tour. This was the first time both Bill and John had been to Los Angeles. Because of that Linda had mapped out a number of landmarks for the guys to see. They could stop anywhere along the tour. Linda was interested in stopping at Century City, The Farmer's Market, and Rodeo Drive because she liked to shop at those locations. The guys weren't interested in shopping, but they were interested in the expensively dressed women that were shopping at those locations.

Late in the afternoon they stopped at the Music Center in downtown LA. Linda thought this might be an opportunity to see if Brad might be interested in going to a show there from time to time. As they were walking in front of one of the theaters two women dressed with head scarfs and ankle length dress came toward them.

Thinking they may be Iraqi, Bill greeted them using the Arabic Mesopotamian dialect language. The women seemed to understand and answered in what may have been the same language. Bill then attempted to introduce himself as Yousef Ali Bill and John as Haboob El Johnnie. This caused the women to giggle while pulling their scarfs over their mouths. By then two men had approached and took positions in front of the women.

"How do you know Arabic?" one of the men asked in perfect English.

"We learned a few words while in Iraq. I thought you might be Iraqi, so I thought I'd see if you could understand me," Bill answered.

"We're originally from Iran, but we know a little of that form or Arabic. Your pronunciation is pretty good. Do you know any more phrases?"

"No, just thought I'd just try the one I thought I knew. It was nice to meet you."

Bill then started to walk past the Iranians and motioned with his head for his group to follow. After they were out of earshot, he mentioned the worst thing he could have done was to make the men think he was making a pass at the women.

"Yeah, it they thought that they might have tried slit our throats," said John.

"Just keep walking and don't look back," Brad said trying to scare Linda.

It worked as Linda immediately suggested they go to the car. Brad then explained that he was only kidding and that the Iranian group probably appreciated someone trying to speak their language.

"I've had enough excitement for today. Let's head off to Tony's," said Linda.

The tour and the group headed to Tony's Pizza. Brad and Linda were anxious to get something to eat while Bill and John were anxious to meet some college girls.

Tony's always gets busy late in the afternoon on Saturdays especially during the football season. Even though State did not play that day, the usual crowd showed up. Tony's didn't accept reservations. However, Brad was able to get them to save a table for his party. He said he was bringing some big spenders. That and the fact that Brad would draw a crowd by himself convinced the management to hold a table for them.

A number of Brad's teammates were there along with the usual groupie girls. As soon as they sat down Zeke Solum came over behind Brad and put his hands on his shoulders

"Let me see your hand, Brad. I want to be sure you'll be ready for next Saturday," Zeke said.

"The hand is better and bigger than it's ever been. See it's almost twice the size of my other hand," Brad answered as he held up his swollen hand.

"Linda you better make sure he doesn't do anything with his hand that shouldn't do," Solum said as he looked at Bill and John realizing he didn't know them.

Brad spoke first, "This guy is Yousef and the other guy is Haboob. They're a couple of army buddies. Zeke is our quarterback and team leader,"

"Hey, did you guys know Brad in Iraq?" asked Zeke.

"Yeah, we saved his life many times over there. Sometimes I think it was a mistake. My name is really John," joked John.

"I glad you guys all make it back. Do you think you will have to go back there?"

"Not for at least two years. Tomorrow we're leaving for Korea,"

"Well, good luck."

"Brad, the coach put in a couple of plays for you at tight end this week. We'll need to practice them starting Monday.

"I'm raring to go," Brad said.

Linda added, "I'll make sure he keeps his hands in his pocket when he's around me."

A number of other men and women stopped by to say something to Brad as they ate dinner. Linda was recognized as Brad's girl, which impressed her. Bill and John were impressed by the girls that stopped by.

By the time they finished eating the band had started. Linda was surprised by one of Brad's friend asking her to dance. She glanced at Brad who shook his head affirmatively. Brad told the friend to bring Linda back in one piece.

When Linda left, Brad waved at one of the girls he knew and motioned for her to come to his table.

"Hey, Brad, you want to dance?" asked the girl, Alice, when she reached Brad's table.

"I can't dance now. I'm supposed to guard Linda's purse while she out there having a good time with some stranger. Speaking of strangers, how about asking one of these strange guys to dance? They are friends of mine from out of town and they don't know anyone here yet. One of them is Bill and the other one is John, take your pick," Brad answered.

"You didn't tell me which is which. She looked at the closer of the two. Are you John?" Alice asked

"Yeah, that's me," said John as he started to get up.

"I'll dance with Bill," Alice then said.

"Thanks, Sally," Brad said.

"My name is Alice."

"Yeah, I knew it was something like that."

Brad then got another girl to dance with John just before the band stopped playing. Linda then returned to their table, but John and Bill chose to sit down with the girls. That gave Brad and Linda a few minutes to talk.

"Do you think the guys enjoyed the tour today," asked Linda.

"I think they enjoyed being with us," answered Brad.

"It's too bad they have to go to Korea. Will they be in any danger there?"

"I don't think so, as long as the North Koreans don't do something stupid. Unfortunately the North Koreans have a habit of doing stupid things."

"Well, it looks like they have made some friends. We may not see them again before we leave. Do you think they get can back to their rooms all right?"

"Yeah, they will be all right. They can always call a taxi if they can't talk one of the girls into driving them home. It looks like they are both busy telling exaggerated war stories to their new friends."

Linda looked to where Bill was sitting. He was saying something she couldn't hear, but he was waving his arms and smiling. John was doing about the same thing at a different table.

"We can leave pretty soon but not before I get to dance with you," Brad said to Linda.

"I don't know Brad, I've already danced once and that's a big effort for an old lady," joked Linda.

"We'll both feel like teenagers once we start dancing. I'll put your purse in the car trunk before the band starts up again," said Brad.

After a while the band did start up again. Brad and Linda danced for one song after another until the band took their next break. By then it was time for them to go home.

Before leaving they made sure Bill and John had made arrangements to get back to their rooms. They said good-bye quickly without getting emotional and left without looking back. Linda thought that a little cold, but Brad said Bill and John understood that is the best way for everyone.

Normally Brad wouldn't be staying overnight Saturday with Linda, but this Saturday like last Saturday was different this week because there was no football game and last week because of the dinner with Larry and Cindy. Because of that Linda wondered what she should do about attending church the next morning. She wanted to go because she hadn't been the previous week. If she did go to church this might be a good time to have Brad accompany her.

On the way home Linda asked Brad what he thought of going to church with her. Brad had left his one and only suit at Linda's after the dinner last week so he would have something appropriate to wear. After thinking about it, Brad told Linda he would like to do so if it wouldn't embarrass Linda.

Shortly after the got home they went to bed. Linda was worn out she hadn't danced that much in a long time, if ever. However, she was not too tired for sex. Sunday morning they got up early and got ready for church. Linda was a little antsy about showing off Brad, so she thought it best if they attend the first service where she would see, or be seen, by fewer people she knew.

Brad was also a little apprehensive about going to church. He hadn't been to church for a long time and wasn't sure what to expect. Fortunately, services started just after they arrived, so introductions to Linda's friends would have to wait.

After services as is the custom, Reverend Rogers greeted the congregation as they filed out of the church. Since Brad and Linda were seated near the back, they were one of the first to see the reverend. Linda was hoping they could then quickly leave. That didn't happen.

"We enjoyed your sermon this morning reverend. I'd like you to meet my friend Brad Wilson," Linda said.

"Nice to see you today, Linda, and nice to meet you, Brad. I hope you both will continue to join us every Sunday," the reverend said.

Normally Linda would wait to talk to other church members, but today she was ready to leave. Just then however, Rogers called out to Linda and asked her to introduce Brad to the couple talking to him. Fortunately Linda could remember the name of the couple.

Brad I'd like you to meet, Jim and Mandy Hall. My friend is Brad Wilson," said Linda.

"Pleased to meet you both," Brad said as he shook Jim's hand.

"It's nice to see you today. We missed you last week. Brad, are you a friend of Diane?" commented Mandy.

"I'm a friend of Linda. We are in the same class at school," Brad answered.

It seems the Halls wanted to talk some more, but Linda said they wanted to get to an early brunch at the club and started to leave.

They didn't make it very far until a number of friends wanted to talk to Linda and to meet Brad. It seems the whisper express had passed along the word that Linda Wallace was seeing a younger man. A lot of friends just had to see for themselves.

A small crowd soon formed around them. Slowly the crowd split into two groups, the women around Linda and the men around Brad. Linda was asked how she was getting along, how Diane was getting along, if she had talked to Larry recently and then, what everyone really wanted to know, how she met Brad.

Some of the men recognized Brad as a member of the State football team. The Saturday paper's local section had an article about the team. The article mentioned that Brad was an Iraq veteran and that he would be going back on active duty after graduation.

Brad was surprised by the knowledgeable questions asked about the team. Several questions were asked about Coach Krueger. They wanted to know if he would be fired after next week's game. If he wasn't fired would he be able to recruit some top notch players like he did in his first years at State.

As soon as they could Brad and Linda broke away from the crowd. They arrived at the club shortly after they started serving brunch, so the place was not crowded. Linda wanted to sit outside in far corner of the patio hoping no one would stop by to talk to them.

"Well, what did you think of church?" Linda asked.

"I liked the sermon. The church building was nicely designed and the people we met all seemed very nice," Brad answered.

"Yes, but weren't you surprised at how interested in you everyone was?"

"Maybe everyone was just glad to see you. It seems you have a lot of church friends."

Linda was wondering what the church women were thinking about her. She was pretty sure not many people would say much to her, but she was sure there would be plenty of talk among them. She was pleased that Reverent Rogers didn't react negatively

It wasn't long before people started stopping by their table. Pretty much the same questions were asked as were asked by the people at church. Brad picked up the fact that two different people asked if Brad thought Coach Kruger would be fired. Perhaps they knew something he didn't know.

Linda and Brad decided to stay home that afternoon. Linda was expecting a call from her mother, Ethel Dowling, who did call shortly after 1:00 p.m. This would have been a good time to tell her parents about her involvement with a younger man, but she didn't take advantage of the opportunity. Instead she and he mother spent the first few minutes asking and answering the usual questions.

Ethel then gave Linda an update on their long range plans. Now that Linda's dad, Ralph, was retired they still planned on selling their house in Chicago and moving to California or Arizona. They had decided on putting their house on sale after the first of the year. Before they moved they wanted to spend some time looking for a place live. They would take Linda up on her offer to let them stay at her house as long it took to get settled in a new home. Before the phone conversation finished, Ethel again asked Linda to spend the Christmas holidays with them in Chicago. Linda lied and said she wanted to spend time alone with Diane during the holidays. By this time Linda knew that Diane would be with Larry and Cindy and that she planned on being with Brad in New York.

After the phone call Linda thought about her parents' situation. She wanted to wait until after the first of the year to talk to them about Brad. She knew her parents would send a Christmas present and card to Diane. She was also sure Diane would not get around to thanking them for several weeks, so Diane would not be likely to tell the parents about Brad before Linda could talk to them.

"Brad, my parents want to stay here a few weeks after the first of the year. I want to wait until we get back from New York before telling them you'll also be staying here when they arrive," Linda.

"On the way back from New York why don't we just stop by Chicago and surprise them?" asked Brad.

That caused Linda to laugh as she thought how much of a shock that would be to her mother.

"I can just see Mom if we did that. She would have a heart attack. Sometime I'll tell you about her. She is a wonderful mother, but she isn't living in the real world as far as current social norms are concerned. In time you two would be the best of friends, but it would take time."

"Maybe if I grew a mustache and dyed my hair gray it would ease her shock."

"You'll be just fine just the way you are."

"What will your dad's reaction be?"

"Dad's will be okay. That doesn't mean he won't be surprised, but he can handle it a lot better than Mom."

Linda felt compelled to tell Brad a little about her mom.

"Mom helped Dad get through school and started in his law practice by working in the bookstore at the University of Chicago. That's where Dad got his law degree. By the time I was born, Mom didn't have to work anymore. Because of that and the fact that I'm an only child, she always had time for me. I confided in Mom about everything, and she was always there to give me direction. Unfortunately it made it difficult for me to make independent decisions. To some extent I let Mom do my thinking. It wasn't until I got to college that I realized how little I knew about life. Mom never got around to telling me much about boys. Anyway she still thinks she should be consulted on any major decisions I make. I'm sure she still feels the need to protect me and wouldn't initially understand our situation," Linda told Brad.

"Sounds like a nice lady that still feels the need to protect you. If you can make some popcorn, I'll rub your back," Brad said, trying to get off the subject of Linda's mother.

The rest of afternoon and evening was spent watching football on TV and eating popcorn.

CHAPTER 14

Monday morning Brad left Linda's early as he needed to stop by his room before class. The duty sergeant told him Bill and John left for Korea Sunday morning. He said they got back to their rooms just in time to put on their uniforms, pack up and make it to the airport bus. He added both told him they had a good time Saturday night. Brad wondered who they had a good time with.

Brad hadn't studied at all over the weekend, so he felt unprepared for all of that week's classes. Linda could help him out with the environment assignment, but he would have to somehow catch up on reading and problem assignments for his other classes. This was not a good week to spend a lot of time studying, however. Football practice would be longer than normal and more physical. Saturday's game against rival South State was a must win from the coaches points of view. A win was critically important for Coach Kruger. It might save his job. A win would also help recruit future players for whoever would be coaching.

Before football practice that afternoon, Coach Kruger gave an emotional talk.

"Men, we've got a great opportunity to start State's football program back to a NCAA Division I level. A win Saturday will avoid another losing season. A win should get us off NCAA sanctions and allow us to go back to full schedule for next season. We will be able to schedule some powerhouse teams, which will draw attention to State. That will help to attract top notch players and create more local fan interest. Game attendance will improve creating more revenue for the school.

"South State is a very good team. They have only lost one game so far this season. They beat us badly last year and they think they can do it again this year. Well, I think you've evolved into a team good enough to beat South State. I've seen you progress from a bunch of no buddies to a cohesive confident team.

"For Saturday's game the coaches and I are adding a number of new plays. Plays that South State hasn't seen and doesn't know we have. Play calling will be aggressive and we will take risks when the situation dictates it. I know all of you will give 110 percent Saturday. If you do I'm sure we will win," Kruger said, concluding his speech.

At practice new plays were put in for all three phases of the game— offense, defense, and special teams. Brad was scheduled to play on all three teams, so there would be a lot to learn in the next few days. To make matters worse the coaches stressed that it was important for players to learn the new plays for their role even though there was no assurance any of the new plays would be used in the game.

The new defense plays were relatively simple for Brad. His only involvement would basically be, in a given situation, to blitz the quarterback abandoning his normal assignment. Brad had often rushed quarterbacks and even had a few sacks but had never run a full blitz. This was a gamble that Brad would tackle or distract the quarterback before a pass could be completed to the player Brad normally would have covered. Brad thought that would be a great play for someone as fast as Superman. Since he didn't think he was quite that fast he hoped the play would never be called.

One new offense play would only be called when Brad was playing the tight end position. Brad was scheduled to alternate playing that position with Tommy Foster and would only come into the game when State's offense was within South State's twenty-yard line. Brad was seen as a better blocker than Tommy. The new play called for Brad to fake blocking the defensive tackle enticing the defensive end to rush the quarterback instead of bumping Brad at the line of scrimmage to keep him from catching a pass. The great plan then was for a lob pass to be thrown to Brad who, according to plan, would bull his way into the end zone for a touchdown.

Two new plays were installed for special teams. Brad's assignment on these plays would be the most difficult for him. One of the plays would involve a new surprise onside kick. The intent was to have the ball bounce and roll for ten yards in the center of the field. Brad's assignment was to somehow run past the ball and block one of the giant defensive players so the kicker could cover the ball.

The second new special team play was designed for receiving South State punts or kickoffs. The plan was a simple reverse but had never been used by State. Derrick Washington would catch the ball and start running to his left. After a few steps he would hand the ball to Lightning Joe Resnick who was doubling back running toward him. Resnick would then run to the right of the field. Brad's assignment would be to stay on the right side of the field so he could block players coming across the field after Resnick started his way. Brad figured that by the time Resnick got to his side of the field there would be eleven players for him to block. That's only if Washington caught the ball, he wasn't tackled before he could hand off to Washington, and Resnick didn't muff the handoff.

At the end of practice Coach Kruger wanted all the players to pledge not to talk about the new plays to anyone. He threatened to kick anyone caught talking about the new plays to anyone off the team. Considering that this would be the last game of the season and the fact that Kruger probably would be fired, the threat didn't carry much weight.

Brad knew the new plays were not trick plays. Almost every team except State had the plays in their playbook. Coach Kruger probably figured this team didn't have the talent to run the plays before this game. It may be a good sign that Kruger now has confidence in the team. Then again, maybe the coach is just desperate and thinks the team can't win without something different.

Most of the players felt they could beat South State without any new plays. They felt they could out muscle and out fineness their opponent. Learning new plays for the first time late in the season would only be a distraction. Every member of the team hoped that they wouldn't have to use any of the new plays during the game. A lot of jokes were made in the dressing room, but no one said anything more once they left for dinner at the training table.

It was close to 8:00 p.m. when Brad called Linda. He briefly explained that the team had to practice extra hard because of the importance of Saturday's game but did not say anything about new plays. He then said he may have to depend on her to give a status report on their environment project at the class. Linda actually had been able to study over the weekend, so she said she would be ready. Brad said he missed seeing Linda that day and that he was looking forward to morning breakfast.

Tuesday at breakfast Brad asked Linda what she had done the previous day.

"Joan called early and wanted to know what I thought of Bill and John. I told her they were nice boys and didn't cause any trouble. Except for the afternoon tour, I'm sure they had a good time. I also said I danced more than I had in years," Linda said.

"We probably should have asked Joan and Henry to join us at the Tony's Pizza," said Brad.

"You know I think they would have enjoyed it. I would have loved to see Henry dance."

"I'll bet you could have outlasted him on the dance floor."

"I don't know about that. I told Joan I was so tired when we got home that we went to bed right away. I shouldn't tell you this, but Joan asked how many times we had sex that night."

"You didn't tell her, did you?"

"I told her I didn't know for sure. I said I passed out after three times, so I don't know how many times you had sex with me when I was unconscious."

"I hope she realizes you were just joking and that I'm not that kind of monster."

"Yes, she knows. I think Joan likes to fantasize about what it would be like to be with a stranger."

"Do you thing she would ever cheat on Henry if an opportunity comes along?"

"No, never, she loves Henry too much. She just likes to let her imagination run wild."

"What about Henry? He must have many opportunities when he goes to New York."

"Besides Joan and Hannah the only other love of Henry's life is numbers. I think he would get more excited looking at spreadsheets than naked women. Of course, I didn't think Larry would have girlfriends either."

"I tend to agree with you about Henry. From what little I know about them I can see that Henry and Larry have vastly different personalities."

"It's almost time for our first classes. I'll see you at our environmental class. This afternoon I'm going to play like I'm studying in the library, but I'll really be looking for another innocent young man to grab a hold of. I think I'm pretty good at that seeing how easy I captured you."

"I'm not worried. I put the word out that if anyone comes near you, I'll beat them severely about the head and shoulders."

Brad and Linda did meet at the environmental class. Scott Watson lectured most of the time, so Brad wasn't asked to report on his and Linda's project. However, Scott did make an unexpected announcement. The entire class was invited to an environmental party at his condo the Thursday evening before Thanksgiving. Scott said the students would be graded upon the environmental way they acted and the condition they left the area in when they left. None of the students had any idea what that meant. Someone asked it students would be graded down if they didn't attend the party. Scott said absolutely unless they had a valid excuse such as a broken neck.

Linda's calendar was quickly filling up. This Saturday there would be the South State football game. Monday she and Brad were going to a Halloween party at the club; Friday she would start a weekend trip to see Diane. Later in November there would be the Watson party and then the Las Vegas trip. She needed some help planning for all these events. So she asked Joan to lunch at the club. Linda decided she really didn't want to see if someone would hit on her at the library.

Over lunch the first plan had to do with the Halloween party. Joan and Henry would be there. They already had arranged for Hannah to spend the night at one of her girlfriends home. The party wouldn't start until 8:00 p.m. Costumes were optional. Unless Linda could get Brad to wear either his football or army uniform they would not be wearing costumes. Joan said Henry would be dressed as an accountant, that way he wouldn't have to change clothes when he came home from the office. They had reservations and would be sitting at a table for eight. That meant they would share a table with two other couples that they may not know.

Linda then talked about her plan to visit Diane. She believed she could convince Larry and Cindy to not have Diane visit them that weekend. She was right about that. Both Larry and Cindy were getting tired of having Diane spend so much time with them. Linda liked Joan's advice about telling Diane that she and Brad would be in Las Vegas Thanksgiving weekend. Joan thought that would be a bad idea. Why take a chance that Diane would change her mind and opt for Las Vegas over Hawaii. Linda would make plane and hotel reservations for the Diane trip tomorrow. Linda didn't want to spend another night trying to sleep on Diane's sofa.

Linda then mentioned the Scott Watson pre-Thanksgiving party.

"Joan, what does acting environmentally mean to you?" asked Linda.

"Well, I think it means to take a dump or a whiz outside instead of the bathroom," answered Joan.

"I'm sure fertilizing and watering the grass outside would be environmentally friendly. It would also save water by not having to flush the toilet. Even so, I'll use the toilet. I just hope Scott doesn't want us to reuse toilet paper."

"Oh, that would be so gross. Of course you never know about environmentalist a lot of them are just plain goofy."

"Brad said some guy brought a barrel, so Scott could use it to catch rainwater at one of Scott's parties. Another girl wore a disposable paper dress and underwear. That was great until one of the guys lit the dress on fire."

"To be serious, remember to recycle cans and bottles. If you bring anything be sure to and bring it in a reusable bag."

"Yeah, everyone will think of that. Maybe I can come up with something unique."

The two ladies spent the next hour or more talking about New York City. Joan was able to recommend many things to do and see, weather permitting. Unfortunately Joan had no ideas about hotels.

Linda still had to make reservations for the Las Vegas trip. She would discuss that with Brad later.

That afternoon at practice the bulk of the time was spent learning the new plays. Since each phase of the game, offense, defense and special teams, practiced separately, Brad was constantly being shifted between the three groups. This of course made it impossible for him to properly practice any of the new plays. All the players and coaches except Coach Kruger felt that was a waste of practice time. The time would have been better spent practicing plays that definitely would be used in the game.

Brad didn't get to Linda's until a little after 8:00 p.m. As usual Linda had coffee and dessert ready for when Brad arrived. Linda was ready for a snack since she had finished dinner a couple of hours ago. Brad, of course, was always ready for something to eat even though he had just finished a big meal. Linda wanted to talk about the Las Vegas and New York trips. Brad wanted to go to bed right away, not necessary because he was tired. They talked for over an hour before going to bed and then they talked some more.

For the November Las Vegas trip Linda wanted to drive there Wednesday the twenty-third and return Sunday the twenty-seventh. They would mean they would be in heavy, almost bumper to bumper, traffic all the way to and from Las Vegas. Linda had researched the shows that they may want to see. She said once they decided on the show then, she would make reservations at that hotel. Brad said any show that had naked dancing girls and loud music would be all right with him.

The December New York trip would take more time to plan. At this point they were thinking of flying there Friday the twenty-third and returning Monday January the second. They decided the next day would not be too early to make plane, hotel and show reservations. Over the next couple of weeks it would be fun to plan other activities while there.

Brad agreed with all the suggestions even though he knew he would never be able to pick up even half of the cost of either trip. He knew he couldn't continue to let Linda pay his way whenever they were together. The longer he stayed with Linda the bigger this issue would be come. Brad knew he would never be able to match Linda's budget. He also knew Linda would not want to forgo spending money on him since that would mean missing out on many fun opportunities. For the first time Brad gave some serious thought to a long term relationship with Linda. If Linda stayed with him once he went back on active duty he wondered if she could adept to military life. Brad also let himself think of what live would be like if he married Linda. The first big problem would be that Linda would lose her alimony. That would mean they would have to greatly scale back their lifestyle. At this point Brad decided to see how things worked out over the next few months before thinking much more about long term relationships.

Talking about the trips seemed to energize Linda more than normal in bed that night. Later they talked some more, this time about the Halloween and Scott parties.

"Joan and I feel it is not necessary to wear costumes to the Halloween party. Only a few people did so last year. I'm not sure what the entertainment will be, but it will probably involve audience participation. Think you can handle that?" said Linda.

"Anything but karaoke singing will be all right with me," answered Brad.

"You know, I've never heard you sing. I think it would be fun to do a karaoke number together."

"You're on your own for that. Or better yet you and Joan could sing something like Ghost Riders in the Sky."

"I've never heard that song, is it a good one?"

"Yeah, it's a cowboy legend. Part of the words are yippy i o, yippy i a. I'm sure you can do that."

"Let me hear you sing it."

"All right I'll sing the song first. Then let's do it together."

With that they began singing and howling the yippy words like a couple of wolfs. Brad's singing caused Linda to started laughing. He told if she didn't like his singing she could practice the song with Joan tomorrow. Linda thought that funny and got the giggles, which, of course, led to another round of sex.

Wednesday at football practice more time was spent on the new plays. Unfortunately for Brad another complication arose when practicing the one new offense play for him. It seems the local TV station wanted to interview one player from State and one player from South State Thursday night. Coach Kruger wanted Zeke Solum to represent Cal State. To be sure Zeke knew what to say and what not to say Krueger yanked Zeke from football practice to practice the TV interview in Krueger's office. The TV practice took almost an hour, which seemed strange since the interview for two players would take less than five minutes of air time.

This meant that Alan Porter would play quarterback and would lob the pass to Brad. Alan was the second string quarterback and would play if Zeke were injured. Alan's specialty was to throw long passes, not short lobs. The first time the play was run with Alan, the defensive coach ordered the defender to rush full speed. This caused Alan to throw Brad a quick bullet pass instead of a lob. Brad first touched the pass with his left hand, which hadn't completely healed, causing immediate pain. The play was run again, but this time the defender was told to stay with Brad and to not let Brad make the catch. Alan again threw a bullet, but this time Brad caught the ball with his right hand only. Still, by the end of practice Brad's left hand had swollen up again making it hard for him to bend his fingers. Brad decided to not mention the swelling to the trainer since he didn't want to wear a cast again.

Thursday at breakfast Linda noticed Brad's hand seemed to be swollen. He said it would not be a problem by game time Saturday. Linda wasn't so sure about that and to be truthful Brad wasn't so sure either, time would tell.

Changing the subject Brad asked if she and Joan had been able to practice the song. Linda said Joan preferred to only sing the yippy words. Linda then said that she had been able to make all the reservations for the trip to see Diane and the Las Vegas trip. She had plane and show reservations in New York but hadn't decided on a hotel yet. Brad wasn't much help on picking a hotel other than suggesting a midtown Manhattan location. A number of hotels came to mind, but Brad didn't want to recommend only hotels that he might be able to afford. He also didn't want to recommend a costly hotel since he knew Linda would be picking up the cost. The relationship with Linda was great, but this pointed out to Brad that finances had to be discussed with Linda in the not too distant future.

Part way through football practice that afternoon Zeke severely sprained his ankle. He wouldn't be able to put pressure on the ankle at least for a day. That meant he may not be able to play Saturday in the biggest game of the year for State. It also meant Zeke wouldn't be able to participate in that evenings TV interview. Coach Kruger didn't want South State to know his starting quarterback probably wouldn't be able to play at full speed, if at all Saturday. Kruger also knew cancelling the interview would let South State know something was wrong. Because of this he cut practice short so he could meet with the other coaches to pick someone else for the interview. The meeting didn't go well.

"All right, here is the situation. Zeke will be on crutches tonight and tomorrow, but he should be able to play Saturday. Tomorrow we'll get Porter up to speed in case he has to replace Zeke Saturday. Now about the TV interview, I want someone else to be there. Who do you think is best qualified to represent us without sounding stupid? I want someone that can speak English in complete sentences," Kruger said.

"Anybody but West," Coach Harrison commented.

"Not anybody. I said I want someone that can speak in complete sentences and that looks presentable but still looks like a football player. No short, skinny goofy-looking guys," Kruger shouted.

"How about Wilson?" asked Coach Alvey.

"I don't want him. Coach Curtis, go out there and bring back someone that is wearing a shirt with a collar and shoes, shoes and socks."

"How about Michael Paul?" asked Coach Alvey.

"No, we can't' send him. They'll think we're sending two guys, Mike and Paul."

"Coach, this is the only guy I could find wearing real shoes," said Coach Curtis as he pulled Brad into the office.

"All right, Wilson, you're going to be on TV in about an hour. Zeke can't make it, so you have to fill in for him. Just give short answers to the questions and, this is important, look mean. We'll call the station and tell them Zeke has to study for exams, so we're sending you instead. Do not say anything about our new plays. Have you got that?"

Brad was told the TV station wanted him at the studio by 7:15 p.m. Coach Kruger told him to be there no later than 7:00 p.m. He wanted to make sure he got there before the player from South State. None of the coaches would be there because they hated each other and would probably start shouting and then start fighting. Brad got the address and directions to the studio from Coach Alvey and started on his way. He figured he could barely make it there by 7:00 p.m. if ran through all red lights and averaged fifty miles an hour on city streets. On the way he practiced looking mean. He also had time to call Linda to tell her to watch him on TV.

Back in the coaches' room, Curtis called the TV station. After several minutes of waiting and being transferred he was able to talk to someone about the interview. They wanted a brief biography of Brad similar to what they had for Zeke. About all Curtis could think of to say was that Brad played linebacker and special teams. When pressed for more information, Curtis said Brad had spent the past three years killing assholes in Iraq for the army.

Brad knew that the TV station was the smallest in the Los Angeles area. They didn't have a large audience, so they often ran stories no other station would cover. The big TV stations each had a weekly half hour programs for the head coaches of the two big local college teams. Tonight would be the only time all year when any player or coach from either State or South State would be on live TV. Brad wanted to make good impression for the school but also for Linda.

Some guy named Steve met Brad at the TV station main gate. He got in the car and directed Brad to a parking area and then led Brad to a small waiting room inside the station. He told Brad that Dixie Duffy would conduct the interview, which should start about 8:10 p.m. As soon as she finished her news segment she would met Brad and get him ready. Brad was told to help himself to the huge buffet in the room. Since he hadn't had time to eat, Brad did help himself to a large portion of food. By now it was about 7:20 p.m. and the South State player still hadn't shown up.

"Hi, Brad, I'm Dixie. I understand you were in the army in Iraq," said Dixie Duffy as she entered the room.

Dixie was a very beautiful blonde dressed expensively in a solid red colored dress with a high neckline. She appeared to be about thirty years old and about five feet eight inches tall.

Brad thought it odd that Dixie's first question was about his army experience as they shook hands.

"Yes, that's right. But I'm studying at State now," Brad answered trying to get off the army subject.

"First, I want to thank you for your service. I'd hope to talk to you and the South State player at the same time, but the South State guy, Bishop Anderson, is having trouble finding the station," said Dixie.

Dixie then went over the questions she would ask on air. She wanted to know if there was anything she shouldn't ask about and said Brad didn't have to answer a question if didn't feel it important to do so. Bishop still hadn't arrived, so Dixie started asking about Brad's service in Iraq. At the same time a makeup person was working on Brad to get him ready for the camera.

About ten minutes later Bishop made his grand appearance.

"Hey, hey, how you doing. I'm Bishop," Bishop said to Dixie as he headed for the buffet.

Bishop Anderson looked the part of an offense tackle. He was about six feet tall and looked like he weighed at least 280 pounds. He was wearing a ball hat backward, a tee shirt with number 76, nylon shorts that came down to midcalf, and sandals without socks. He had what appeared to be the start of a goatee and tattoo's on both arms and legs. Considering the way Bishop looked, Brad figured the TV people knew it wouldn't do any good to put makeup on him.

"Bishop I'm Dixie, I'll be interviewing you and Brad. I need to go over a couple of things quickly because I have to go back on the air in five minutes," said Dixie.

"That's okay, I'm ready. I've given lots of interviews, so that won't be a problem."

"Look, I'm going to have to leave, but Steve will be here shortly. He will bring you to meet me on camera when it's time. I'll shake hands and introduce you first, Bishop then you Brad. Any questions before I go?"

"Not for me. I'm always ready."

Brad shook his head no.

"So you're the State guy," Bishop said to Brad as he continued to eat with his hands.

"Yeah, nice to meet you Bishop," Brad responded.

"Yeah, well, it won't be so nice when we meet Saturday. I understand you're a linebacker. I'll probably have to flatten you a few times, nothing personal. Hey, what did you think of Dixie? I'd really like to hump her. Maybe I'll give her a call next week."

Bishop continued to talk about Dixie for several more seconds using more and more crude descriptions of what he would like to do with her. Then suddenly he turned his attention to Brad.

"You know you're going to lose big time Saturday. You guys aren't even in our league. I know a lot of your guys. I went to school with some of them. They couldn't even make the high school team. You'll probably get knocked out in the first quarter, the early first quarter."

Bishop's comments about the game really didn't bother Brad. There is always trash talk in games. Brad heard some terrible treats and curses from Iraqi prisoners that were much worse than what was just said and the Iraqis meant what they were saying. What did bother Brad were the comments Bishop had made about Dixie. Not that he thought Bishop would follow through with his comments but that he would think those things and even worse talk about the thoughts out loud to a stranger. Brad also wondered why South State would send Bishop as a representative of their school.

Steve suddenly came into the room putting a stop to Bishop's meaningless talk.

"Okay, we're about ready, remember this is live TV. No four-letter words, no swearing, and no name calling—in other words, no trash talk. Leave that for the game," Steve told Brad and Bishop.

Dixie opened the program by explaining the importance of the game to the two teams and that this was a long-standing rivalry. She then called Bishop into the camera range. Bishop half walked half skipped out to meet Dixie. Instead of shaking hands Bishop gave Dixie a high five hand slap. He then stood backward to his chair and hopped on it instead of sitting down normally.

Now it was Brad's turn to be introduced. As he approached Dixie he noticed she had her right arm up expecting a high five slap. Instead Brad reached up to take Dixie's hand, pulled it down to waste level and then shook hands. He sat down in his chair in the normal manner.

Let's start with you, Bishop. I understand you are an offensive tackle number 76. Tell us a little about how it is to mix it up with the big guys," Dixie said.

"Well, you know, that's where the real action is, like a war. I've been a starter for all four years, and I've had plenty of brutal fights. I've been noticed by a lot of National Football League scouts, so I think I've got a pretty good chance of playing professional football next year. But my number is 79," said Bishop.

"Your shirt has number 76, shouldn't it be 79?

"Why?" said Bishop apparently not understanding the connection.

"Who do you think is going to win Saturday's game?" Dixie continued.

That set Bishop off on his practiced trash talk, almost word for word what he had earlier said to Brad. He did add a couple of new comments however. He said South State knew all about Cal State's new trick plays and that they wouldn't work. He then said he had flattened so many opposing players that he is now called the pancake man. It was apparent he would have used up all of the time if Dixie hadn't stopped him.

"Hold on, Pancake, let's let Brad get in here. Brad you're a linebacker who also plays on special teams and sometimes as a tight end on offense. Who do you think will win Saturday?" Dixie asked Brad as she tried to stifle a laugh.

"I believe we have a good chance to surprise everyone and win the game. We've been improving every week, and we've had a good week of practice, so we should be at the top of our game," Brad answered.

"Bishop mentioned that sometimes it's almost like a war during the game. I believe you spent three years in Iraq and have been in actual combat. Do you think it will be that bad Saturday?"

"Well, I hope not. As bad as it gets Saturday I'm pretty sure all of us will come out alive."

"Don't count on it soldier boy. We'll show you what a war is really like," Bishop interrupted.

Dixie gave Brad a look of disbelief but didn't acknowledge Bishops comment otherwise. She continued asking Brad questions and Bishop continued interrupting with childish comments.

At the conclusion of the interview, Brad thanked Dixie for inviting Pancake and himself to appear on live TV. When he called Bishop Pancake he and Dixie couldn't help but to start giggling.

Bishop noticed this and asked what was so funny.

"You don't understand, Pancake. We're not laughing," Brad said as he and Dixie continued laughing.

"Well, actually we are laughing, but we are not laughing at you," said Dixie as she continued to laugh.

"To be truthful, Pancake, I'm laughing because I think it is funny that anyone not in grade school would like to be called pancake," said Brad.

As Bishop walked off the stage he gave Brad the finger and mouthed some very bad words.

As soon as she was off camera Dixie asked Brad if he could talk to her for a few minutes before he left. When they got to the waiting room, Dixie mentioned that the station may want to do a human interest story about him. That is the very last thing Brad wanted, so he tried to explain that there really wasn't much of interest concerning him. Nevertheless, Dixie said asked for his phone number and said they would get back to him in a few weeks.

By the time Brad left the station it was after 9:00 p.m. Brad turned on his phone and saw that he had half a dozen missed calls. He immediately returned the most important one, the call from Linda.

"So Linda did you see the interview on TV?" Brad asked when Linda answered his call.

"Yeah, you were great. How about that other guy. Was he for real or did they just ask for a clown to make the interview more entertaining?" Linda asked.

"He's the best South State had to offer. I hope you didn't believe any of his trash talk."

"Once he said the game would be more of a war than what you went through, he lost all creditability."

"Look, I'll be a little late getting home tonight. Dixie and I are going to have a few drinks at her house."

There was complete silence on Linda's end of the conversation for several seconds before Brad spoke again.

"Okay, let me tell you the truth. I'm on my home now and should be there in five minutes. Dixie and some TV guy wanted to talk to me after the interview for a couple of minutes, so I was late getting out of there. I'll tell you what we talked about when I get home."

Because of Linda's reaction to his earlier attempt at humor, he realized he shouldn't try to joke about having other girlfriends.

"Well, if you don't get here soon, I'm calling Pancake to invite him to have a couple of drinks with me."

"I'm at the gate now and starting up the hill to your place, so hold on a few more minutes."

"Okay, the door will be unlocked for the next three minutes only. Hope you can make it in time."

Not only was the door unlocked, but Linda was standing in the open doorway when Brad arrived. She greeted Brad with a kiss and hug.

As soon as they got inside, Brad listened to his phone messages. Coach Kruger shouted something about Brad telling Bishop the team's new plays. Kruger said he wanted Brad in his office at 7:00 a.m. and reminded Brad that anyone talking about the new plays would be dismissed from the team. Brad knew he hadn't said anything about new plays, but he also knew he would never be able to convince Kruger. He also didn't think he would be dismissed, but he would just have to wait until morning to find out.

Linda wanted to know what Dixie had to say to Brad after the interview. Brad told her but indicated that he didn't think anything would come of it. Linda thought it would be a good story and that Brad should let Dixie know he would be available to participate in such a story.

Just then Brad got a phone call from Coach Curtis.

"I watched your interview tonight. Did you tell the South State guy about the new plays?" asked Curtis.

"No. I'm not sure anyone said anything to him. He probably was just guessing because they probably have practiced some new plays. I think he was just trying to get a reaction from me," answered Brad.

"All right, tomorrow morning, I'll be at your meeting with Kruger. Loren Bailey, the school athletic director, will also be there. I just talked to him, and he assured me you will not be dismissed from the team.

"There is something else I want to talk to you about. You need to keep this to yourself and not tell anyone else. If you do tell anyone I'll deny ever saying anything. There will be a news announcement Monday morning. Either Coach Kruger will announce he is resigning or Director Bailey will announce that Kruger has been fired. It's up to Kruger to determine which announcement is made. The school president has approved of the changes. Bailey will discuss this with Kruger Sunday. I know about this because I'll be introduced as the interim coach. As a courtesy to Kruger and to avoid distractions to the team before Saturday's game, this has to be kept secret. Are you with me on that?"

"Yes, I'll not say anything to anyone. I'm not totally surprised about Kruger leaving, but I heard he has one more year on his contract. Congratulations on your promotion, I'm sure they'll make you the regular head coach before next season."

"Yeah, I hope so too. The reason I've been named interim coach is because the school can't afford a big-name coach. They can't even afford to pay to search for a coach until the end of next year. Kruger's contract calls for him to be paid at least half his annual salary if he is fired. Anyway, I'm telling you this because I want you to know Kruger cannot kick you off the team. In addition I want to make sure you will be back next year and that you will work with me and the other coaches this spring to get ready for next season,"

"Sure, I'm planning on playing one more year and would be happy to help out anyway I can."

"Yeah, well, you're not on a football scholarship. I can offer you one if you need it, but I'd like to use it for another new guy. We only have a limited number of scholarships as you know and I need all of them for new talent. By the way who's paying for your education?"

"The army is paying my school costs and living expenses because I signed a contract to go back on active duty when I graduate,"

"Geese, Brad why did you do that. You've already served your time. If you go back in they'll probably send you back to Iraq,"

"Yeah, well, that's just what I want. I really like shooting big guns," Brad said sarcastically as he became irritated with the comment.

When the phone call ended Linda wanted to know what the coach wanted.

"Kruger was mad that Bishop said something about State having new plays for the game. Kruger thinks I told Bishop before the interview. Coach Alvey said to not worry about it," Brad answered.

Brad did not say anything about the pending changes in coaches.

Linda then said Joan had already called. Joan said Brad looked cool and collected during the TV interview. Joan also mentioned that she had overheard Hannah talking to one of her friends on the phone earlier in the evening. Hannah told her friend to be sure and watch the interview to see the guy she had dinner with last Sunday. Joan said all the Belsons were looking forward to attending the game Saturday with Linda.

"You know I think Hannah has her eye on you Brad," Linda said.

"I think she just wants to show off to her friends that she knows some football player. I wonder if Hannah's friend thought she had dinner with Pancake," said Brad making Linda laugh.

Later after they went to bed and had sex, Linda wanted to talk about Monday's Halloween party and her weekend trip to see Diane. It seems Brad and Linda had fallen into a set routine. Brad would spend the night with Linda three times a week. After sex they would spend an hour of more talking. Linda enjoyed these bedtime talks. She seemed to feel freer to talk about personal matters in that environment. Having Brad stay overnight only three times a week allowed Linda time to be alone and relax the other nights.

Brad on the other hand would have liked to spend every night with Linda. The only problem for Brad was his financial concerns. He still felt uncomfortable letting Linda pick up almost all of the expenses when they were together. Brad did not know how to resolve the problem. The only ways he would be able to match Linda's wealth would be to win millions of dollars in a lottery or marry Linda and have her income reduced to his. Neither option seemed possible in the foreseeable future.

Linda hadn't been able to find out what couples would be sharing their table at the Halloween party. She thought it would be nice if she knew the other people, but then she would feel uncomfortable being so much younger than Brad. On the other hand if she didn't know the other couples, it might be difficult talking to them, but she might not feel so uncomfortable with the age difference. Brad said he would not feel uncomfortable meeting new people even if they questioned the age difference.

The trip to visit Diane was a bigger concern for Linda. She dreaded having to call Larry to remind him that she would be taking care of Diane the next weekend. Normally she would have waited to hear from Diane, allowing her to visit; however, she was worried that Diane wouldn't call as promised. Linda was determined to visit and would call Diane Thursday if she hadn't heard from her by then. Linda scheduled a flight to San Jose arriving a little before noon. Her plan was to check into a hotel near Diane's apartment and then get to Diane's in the late afternoon. There would be time for a mother-daughter talk after dinner. Saturday they could go shopping or anything else that Diane may want to do. The biggest concern would be getting rid of Diane's friend, Wellesley Goldstone, or anyone else wanted to spend time with Diane that weekend.

For a brief moment Linda wondered if it would be a good idea to have Brad accompany her. She quickly discarded that idea since she knew Diane would resent it. Besides Linda wanted time alone with Diane. Still Linda knew that sometime soon she would have to clearly explain her relationship with Brad to Diane. Linda was slowly beginning to realize what a spoiled daughter she had. By this time she was about to fall asleep and Brad was already snoring.

In the morning Brad got up before Linda. Before leaving he stopped by the bed to say good-bye. Linda took this opportunity to ask Brad a question she had wanted to ask ever since watching the TV interview.

"Brad what did you think of the TV lady, Dixie?"

"She was very nice. She acted very professionally and did not ask any surprise questions."

"Do you think she really wants to do a story on you or do you think she just wants to see you again?"

"Well, if she does want to see me again, she's out of luck. I prefer brunettes. She may want to see the South State guy though. He said he was thinking about calling her for a date."

That caused Linda to laugh. She had heard the answer she wanted to hear.

Friday morning Coach Curtis and Director Bailey were already in Coach Kruger's office when Brad arrive at 7:00 a.m. Kruger seemed about ready to explode, but that was normal.

"Good morning, gentlemen," Brad said as he entered the office.

Director Bailey introduced himself but did not indicate why he was there.

"Did you tell the South State guy we were installing new plays for Saturday's game?" Kruger asked Brad not wasting any time.

"No," Brad answered.

"Well, do you know how the guy knew about our plays?"

Brad repeated what he had told Alvey last night. After that no one said anything for a few seconds. Bailey thanked Brad for coming and said he could leave. Kruger continued to stare at Brad as he left but said nothing.

Normally on Friday mornings Brad would work out in the gym and then study some before lunch and afternoon practice. This morning he has the team trainer look at his hand, which was still bothering him somewhat. The trainer would tape a pad on the back of Brad's hand before Saturday's game.

The trainer was also working on Zeke Solum. Zeke was not on crutches but did have a big boot like protection on his lower leg.

"So Zeke, are you a go for tomorrow?" asked Brad.

"Yeah, I'll be okay by morning. Of course during the game I'll have to stand like a statue waiting to be flattened since I won't be able to run or even step forward," Zeke answered partly in jest.

"That sounds great Zeke. Hope you have time to practice getting knocked down."

The afternoon practice was a no pads walk through. Kruger wanted to practice the new plays again even though the plays were simple enough to be learned in the in the first practice. Zeke didn't practice, so Alan Porter took over at quarterback.

Brad noticed that Kruger and Curtis were not talking to each other. Normally Curtis, as offense coach, would call all offense plays while Kruger watched. This time Kruger was running the offense while Curtis watched. Brad figured Kruger was upset with Curtis for asking Director Bailey to attend his meeting, to not let him dismiss Brad from the team.

That night the team watched a movie together after dinner. The movie was another thriller where the hero was able to do unbelievable things in order to save the world from total destruction. When the movie was over Kruger wanted all the players to go home and get a good night's rest. That's just what Brad did after talking to Linda for over an hour.

CHAPTER 15

The weather Saturday was perfect for football. The sun was shining and the temperature would be in the low seventies. Brad arrived at the stadium around 10:00 a.m. Zeke and some other players were already there. Zeke had his foot in a cold water tub trying to reduce swelling before being wrapped.

The trainer placed a sponge like pad on Brad's hand and then wrapped it tightly. He said he would change the bandage and give Brad a shot at halftime if needed. Once out on the field to warm up, Brad looked at his hand. He noticed that he could bend his fingers only about half way. He knew he would not be able to grab and hold on to anyone, so he would have to figure out a way to compensate in order to be able to tackle anyone.

Linda had time to clean the house and do some grocery shopping before getting ready to go to the game. She knew Brad would not be staying at her house that night. He said he would be expected to join team members at Tony's to celebrate the season, whether they won or lost that day. Linda was invited to join them but declined. She figured it wouldn't be much fun if they lost and it would be too much fun it they won. Brad said after eating pizza and drinking beer for a couple of hours, he wouldn't be much good the rest of the evening, so he would go straight back to his room.

The Belsons wanted to leave for the game a little early. Henry figured that since attendance would be almost double what it normally would be, he wanted to get a parking spot close to the stadium before they were all gone. As they were walking to the stadium, they heard a few comments about Brad being on TV. Linda wondered how anyone knew they knew Brad until she noticed that Hannah was wearing a jersey with number 54, Brad's number.

"I like Hannah's jersey. Where did she get it?" Linda asked Joan.

"The college bookstore sells those jerseys. Hannah and I stopped by yesterday after school. Now Linda I'm sorry to have to tell you this, but I think Hannah has a crush on Brad and is trying to steal him away from you," Joan answered.

"Oh no, I don't need any competition especially from someone younger than me," Linda said feeling comfortable in joking about her age for the first time.

This was the fourth game Linda and the Belsons were attending, so they had become friendly with Warren West's father, who sat behind them, and some others in the surrounding seats. Because they were early they had time to spend time talking to others. That caused a few more comments about Brad performing well on TV. For some reason that made Linda feel important, just because she was a friend of a football player.

At the start of the game State received the opening kickoff. Zeke limped onto the field to start the offense. The first two plays were quick handoffs to the running back gaining only a few yards. Zeke dropped back to pass on the third down was thrown to the ground before he could get the pass off. It was obvious that Zeke would not be able to move fast enough to get out of the way of pass rushes or to operate the majority of running plays.

It gets worse for State. On the fourth down punt by State, Brad was one of the first defenders to reach the South State punt returner. He was able to get his left hand on the return man but could not grab a hold. This allowed the return to go another ten yards before other State defenders could tackle him. South State then proceeded to march down field with short runs and short passes. They scored near the end of the first quarter. The only positive aspect for State was that it took almost a full quarter of the game to score.

For some reason Zeke was sent back out to start the second offensive series for State. Predictably State could not make a first down and had to punt the ball back to South State.

By this time Brad had ripped the bandage off his hand so he would be better able to tackle. South State apparently realized Zeke would not be effective for State, so they continued to use routine plays using uptime while advancing the ball.

State's had a good defense and was able to keep South State from scoring again during the remainder of the half. Brad noticed Bishop Anderson was playing well and was also keeping up trash talk. On a few occasions Bishop was supposed to block Brad but without much success.

At halftime, Coach Kruger finally gave up on Zeke and said Alan Porter would replace him at quarterback. Kruger also said South State would get the ball to start the third quarter and would most likely continue their pattern of running on first down, passing on second down and then doing what they needed to do to get a first down.

"We are going to get back in this game right away. On South State's second play they will probably call a pass. I'm going to call the new blitz play. Wilson, you've got to make the play and knock their quarterback down. Do you understand that?" shouted Kruger.

Brad did understand. The play was called and it worked almost perfectly. Brad lined up a couple of steps behind the defensive end on the right of State's defense. The South State left offensive tackle, in this case Bishop Anderson, was first responsible for blocking the defense end, which he did. That left Brad free to blitz into South State's backfield and to somehow get by the running back, which blocked on most pass plays. This time the back had to attack the State middle linebacker, which was blitzing up the middle of the line, leaving Brad unblocked. Brad hit the quarterback hard enough to jar the football loose, which was recovered by State on the South State ten-yard line.

Brad started to run off the field as the offense came onto the field, but he was waved back. Alan Porter came up beside Brad and said the words new play for Brad to hear without looking at him. In the huddle Alan did call the new pass play to Brad. The play worked just like planned. Brad caught the lob pass and was able to get into the end zone for a score.

Most of the rest of the game was a defensive struggle. Finally midway through the fourth quarter Alan completed one of his specialties, a long pass downfield. This put State in position to kick a field goal, which they did. The game ended with State winning 10 to 7.

On the way home Linda called Brad on the Belson's car speakerphone. They knew Brad wouldn't be able to answer the call, so they all left a message congratulating him on a good game. Linda asked him to call later that night.

"Your guy played a good game today. I was surprised to see him catch the touchdown pass," Henry said to Linda.

"You know I didn't even know it was Brad until you told me," Joan said.

"Yeah, Brad said he might have a few plays on offense, but he didn't tell me he was going to score a touchdown," said Linda.

"Is he coming to your house for dinner tomorrow?" Hannah surprised everyone by asking.

"Well, he is coming over tomorrow afternoon, but he will be taking me out to dinner. If you would like you can come over and congratulate him on playing a good game," Linda said to Hannah.

"I was just wondering. Some of the boys at school think the coach may get fired. Do you think Brad knows," Hannah asked.

"I've got an idea why don't you all come over about 1:00 p.m. for a mini brunch. I've got cheese, crackers, wine, milk, coffee and angel's food cake. Brad can tell Hannah what he knows about the coach and the rest of us can plan for the Halloween party," said Linda.

"You know, I'd like to find out what the story is with Coach Kruger. The refreshments sound good. Have you got any cigars?" asked Henry.

"Sorry, Henry, I smoked the last cigar last night. However, if you can find a smoke shop, maybe Joan can go in and buy us a couple boxes," said Linda.

"Yeah, Joanie. Think you can do that," said Henry.

"Oh no, I remember the last time Henry smoked a cigar. Remember, Henry, you gave out candy and cigars when Hannah was born and decided to smoke one yourself," said Joan.

"Hannah, you were almost a fatherless baby and would have been if your dad hadn't put out that smelly cigar," Joan continued.

"Golly, Dad, I didn't know you smoked," Hannah said.

"Yeah, well, I guess your mom didn't tell you about that and the two of us riding around on my motorcycle either," said Henry.

"Mom, you really didn't ride on a motorcycle, did you?" asked Hannah.

"Yeah, I did. Your dad use to give me rides whenever I got up enough courage," answered Joan.

"Dad wasn't that dangerous?" Hannah asked.

"Yes, but it was inexpensive, and I didn't have much money at the time. Sometimes it's all right to take reasonable risks," said Henry.

"I never worried about your dad riding a motorcycle because he never went over thirty miles an hour," Joan said.

"Well yeah, that's right when I was giving you a ride. You always dragged your feet and kept shouting to slow down. Remember the first time I gave you a ride, as soon as I started the engine, before we moved an inch you told me I'm going too fast," Henry said to Joan.

"I didn't say that. I said don't go too fast meaning after you get started. Let's talk about that later," Joan said as they arrived at Linda's house.

Once inside her house, Linda began to feel lonely. She wished she had accepted the offer to help the team celebrate at Tony's. Then she decided that wouldn't have been a good idea. She wasn't a big beer drinker and remembered the commotion she caused the first time she was there and ordered a glass of wine. She realized how much she missed having Brad to talk to.

The thought of Henry and Joan on a motorcycle made Linda smile. They just didn't fit the mold of bikers. Tomorrow she would ask if they had any pictures.

Brad called a little before 10:00 p.m.

"So Brad, I think you were great in the game today. Did the coaches or team give you any award for scoring a touchdown?" asked Linda.

"No, everyone contributed to the win. We all celebrated as a team. I wish you would have joined us. A lot of the guys wanted to know how come you there," Brad said.

"I'll bet they just wanted someone to dance with that they could keep up with. Are you having a good time?"

"Yeah, I did have a good time. I'm home now getting ready to go to bed. I knew it was time to leave Tony's when I noticed I was blowing bubbles out of my nose. I did want to ask you if you would like me to go to church with you tomorrow morning."

"That would be nice. Do you think you could make the early service? I need to stop at the grocery again to pick up some things I missed today."

"Sure, I did leave my suit with you didn't I?"

"Yes, it's still here. I need to tell you, even though we are going out to dinner tomorrow night, I've invited the Belsons to stop by at 1:00 p.m. for a mini brunch. It seems Hannah and Henry want to know if Coach Kruger is going to be fired."

"That's all right with me, although I wouldn't be able to say anything about Kruger even if I knew."

"You know I think Hannah just used that as an excuse to see you again. Joan said she thinks Hannah gets social points with some of the boys at school if they think she knows a real football player."

"It will be nice to see the Belsons, they are all very nice. I'm going to hit the hay now so I can get up early tomorrow."

"Okay. Good night. Brad, I love you."

"Yeah, me too. I mean I love you too Linda. See you in the morning."

Neither Brad nor Linda was able to go to sleep for some time after going to bed. Linda wondered why she told Brad she loved him, she hadn't planned on it. She couldn't remember the last time she said she loved Larry, but she knew it was a long time ago. She couldn't even remember the first time she said she loved Larry. Brad's response worried her. She wondered if he meant it when he said he loved her or was he just being nice. It would have been better if Brad had said it first. Well, at least he got her name right.

Brad was also thinking about Linda's comment. He couldn't remember anyone ever telling him they loved him, not even his parents. He knew his response was not right, so he knew he had to somehow correct the false impression he gave that he was just saying some words. Then he had what he thought would be a good idea, so he got up and called Linda.

"Hello, Linda. Look I know this sounds silly, but I just called to say I really love you. I don't think I've ever said that to anyone before," Brad said.

"I'm glad you called. I was a little worried you were just being polite earlier," said Linda.

"No, no I really meant then, but I just had trouble saying it. Tomorrow I can show you how much I love you, maybe before church."

"Okay, I'll probably still be in bed when you get here."

"Just what I wanted to hear. I'll try to get there around 6:00 a.m."

After the phone call they both were able to get a good night's sleep.

Brad and Linda make it to the early church service and did spend a few minutes talking to some of the other church members. Linda thought it might just be her imagination, but it seemed there were more people at the early service than last week. She wondered if some new members came just to see Brad. After that they stopped at the local grocery store. While shopping Linda ran into some friends that she hadn't seen for a while. She introduced Brad as her friend rather than a classmate from school as she always had before. Brad was beginning to feel this is way it is like to be married. He enjoyed the feeling. Linda paid for the groceries

Brad had time to watch football on TV after helping Linda get ready for the Belsons who did arrive around 1:00 p.m. The talk soon turned to the State game. Henry asked why Zeke played the entire first half considering that he was so immobile. Brad explained that the backup quarterback, Alan Porter was inexperienced and also had never played a full game. Because of that and the fact that State's defense didn't allow any more scores, Kruger wanted to wait until the second half to insert Porter. Brad found it strange that he was actually defending Kruger, who he knew didn't like him or actually hated him.

Hannah then spoke up and asked if Kruger was going to be fired. Brad repeated what he had said to Linda about not being able to say anything that he might know. However, he did say Kruger wanted to talk to all the players Monday afternoon about how to keep in shape during the off season. As soon as he said that he realized that gave the false impression that Kruger would not be fired. That in turn would probably lead to Hannah calling her friends that evening to tell them she knew Kruger would not be fired. Of course that would cause her to lose all creditability with her friends and make her not trust Brad.

As soon as he could get back into the conversation he said he needed to clear up his earlier comment. He said even though Kruger said he wanted to talk to the players Monday, he may get fired today or later in the week. It's best to just say you don't know if anyone asks you.

That made matters worse. It meant he all but broke his promise to Coach Curtis to not say anything to anyone about Kruger's position.

Henry and Brad talked more about football and then about accounting. Henry said he could help Brad with his auditing class if needed. The other three talked about shopping and some recent movies.

The Belsons knew Brad and Linda were going out to dinner, so they left about 3:00 p.m. after Joan and Hannah helped Linda put away the uneaten food and wash the dishes. The local TV station did show a few State plays from Saturday's game including Brad's two great plays.

About that time Joan called to let them know who the other two couples would be seated at their Halloween party table. The couples would be Wayne and Donna Smith and Larry and Betty Fellers. Both Linda and Joan knew them slightly. All of them were a little older than Linda.

Brad and Linda had dinner at La Vie En Rose. Both felt more comfortable this time and were able to talk freely about several subjects. Linda seemed excited about the Las Vegas and New York City trips but was somewhat apprehensive about the Diane trip.

Brad suggested Linda and Diane drive town to Monterey and Carmel on Saturday. Linda thought that would be a great idea since neither she nor Diane had ever been there. That would keep Diane captured during the two-hour drive down and two-hour drive back, so they could have an uninterrupted conversation.

It wasn't until they finished eating and were having after dinner drinks, wine for Linda and Cognac for Brad, that Brad apologized for making a joke about going to Dixie's place after the TV interview.

"You know, I thought I was making a joke when I told you I was invited to Dixie's place. I now understand it wasn't a good idea," said Brad.

"It's all right now, but I will confess when you said that it did bother me for some reason. I guess I'm afraid of losing you," said Linda.

"You don't have to worry. I have no plans on going out with anyone else. I'll also be careful to not make silly jokes."

As they were talking, their hands met across the table naturally without being planned. Just before they left they kissed across the table.

Linda couldn't help thinking how different this dinner was from the first time at the restaurant. That time she tried to act as an older sister to Brad. Whenever the waiter came to the table she was sure to make some comment about how nice it would be for Brad meets Diane.

Brad also was aware of the difference between this dinner and the last one at this restaurant. It was so easy this time to act natural instead of trying to act cool. Holding hands would not have happened the first time. However, it made him feel good this time even if his left hand was still quite sensitive and painful.

Monday morning Brad stopped by the gym to get some things from his locker. He also wanted to see if Kruger was there and if he would say anything about a talk with Athletic Director Loren Bailey. Kruger was not in his office, but Coach Curtis was.

"Wilson, come in here and close the door," Curtis said to Brad.

"Good morning, Coach, you seem right at home in this office. I hope you're able to stay here for a long time," Brad said as he sat down.

"Bailey had me attend the meeting with Kruger yesterday morning. It didn't go well. I'm not going to get into details, but Kruger yelled and screamed something about suing the University and wanting a check for his remaining salary immediately. He then left without signing a letter of resignation so he will be fired. I'm telling you this because at this afternoon's meeting I want you to make a little speech about let's not dwell on this but instead think about getting ready for next season. Think you can do that?"

"Sure, I'll be ready to say something by then," Brad answered.

Brad initially had no idea of what or why Curtis wanted him to say something. Later he realized Curtis wanted Brad to ask the team to support him. Curtis knew that a number of returning players had been recruited by Kruger and may not like the idea of Curtis replacing Kruger.

By the time Brad got to the school cafeteria for breakfast a couple of teammates had told him of Kruger's departure. No one mentioned that Curtis would replace Kruger, so Brad decided to also not mention it. Brad did call Linda to let her know the word was out so she could tell Hannah if it wasn't too late. The rest of the day passed quickly until 3:00 p.m. when the team met.

Coach Curtis gave a short talk simply saying that Kruger was gone and he would be the interim coach. He then gave information and instructions for the team to keep in shape until spring training. He said Brad wanted to talk to the players, indicating that it was Brad's idea to address the group.

Brad had prepared what was intended to be a short talk. He started commentating about the winning season. He thanked the coaching staff, including Kruger, for their patience in working with the players. Brad asked the team to show their appreciation for the seniors with some shout outs about catching on with some NFL team. At this point he mentioned the importance of supporting Coach Curtis so that he could be made the permanent head coach. He then intended to talk about the importance of staying in shape for spring practice and getting ready for next season.

However, more thoughts came into his mind instead he unintentionally turned his talk into a mini motivational speech.

"You know I think the season ended just when we were reaching our peak. I can't wait until next season. It looks like we will get off NCAA sanctions, so we may have a full twelve-game schedule. You players that will be back have the size, skill and motivation to win every game next year including the Stanford game. One thing that may be missing is the mental toughness that's required to do your best every game. It's easy to slow down at times because if we lose a game no one dies," Brad said.

The session ended quietly. It didn't take Brad long to clean out his locker and leave. He stopped by his room to change into some business casual clothes and then headed to Linda's.

Linda spent part of the day planning for the weekend trip to visit Diane. She still hadn't heard from her or called Larry yet, but she planned on calling both tomorrow night. During the day Linda also did the weekly wash. This caused her to wonder if she should ask Brad if would like to use her washer and dryer. This would be a big step in their relationship. In essence this would be an invitation to start moving his clothes to her house. The next big step would be to just move in for good. Linda wasn't sure she was ready for that yet, although she wasn't necessarily against having Brad live there.

About that time Brad arrived. He would be staying overnight that night and also the next night, so this time he did bring a change of clothes. Linda decided to wait until Tuesday night to see if Brad would need to use the washer and dryer.

Linda said Joan found out what the program would be for to night's Halloween party. Since most of the guests will be middle-aged, only a few will wear costumes. Instead there will be audience participation in a couple of games.

Before dinner there will be a 'bob for apples' game. One couple from each table will be volunteered to compete against other couples to see who can eat an apple off a string dangling from the ceiling. After dinner a group of professional actors will create a murder scene. Suddenly the lights will go off and a gunshot will be heard. When the lights come back on, someone will have been shot and the audience will have half an hour to figure who committed the murder. Prizes will be awarded winners and runner ups for each game.

Brad and Linda both thought that will be fun, but neither wanted to volunteer for the 'bob for apples' game. Little did they know that their table guests would volunteer them for that game.

Henry Belson drove the four to the club a little before 8:00 p.m. By then most of the guests had arrived and were socializing before being seated.

Linda found the two couples that would be sharing their table and introduced Brad to them. This time she said Brad was her good friend. Both of the men had thinning hair that was beginning to show some gray. Both of the women appeared to have had their hair done earlier in the day. All four wore glasses, and all appeared to be slightly overweight. The men wore sport coats without ties. The women wore dresses, high-heeled shoes, and stockings. Their clothes looked to be of good quality.

Brad noticed that everyone there seemed to be appropriately dressed. No ball caps worn backward, no tank tops, no shorts, no sandals, no baggy pants, and no sunglasses. This was quite different from the way the kids dressed at Tony's.

The group found their assigned table and assigned seating arrangements. Men and women alternated chairs, so Linda sat to Brad's right, and Donna Smith sat to his left. Henry sat between Linda and Joan. Larry Fellers sat on Joan's right. Betty Fellers and Wayne Smith rounded out the table. Both couples seemed surprised at the age difference between Brad and Linda but did not mention it.

As soon as everyone was seated, the host announced the first game and asked for volunteers. Almost in unison six people at their table volunteered Brad and Linda. They didn't even have a change to protest. Each couple lined up on a stage by a dangling apple after having the host loosely tie their hands behind them. As soon as the game began each couple working as a team tried to bite enough off their apple so that it would fall off the string.

Their apple was lower than Brad's chin but higher than Linda's mouth. This meant Brad had to bend over to try to bite the apple, and he caused Linda have to look up to get to the apple. Linda got to the apple just before Brad but couldn't get her teeth into it. This caused the apple to slide sideways and caused Brad to bump into Linda almost biting her nose. After they composed themselves, Brad suggested Linda wait until he could bite and hold the apple with his teeth. She then could take bites out of the apple while Brad held it steady. That seemed like a good idea. Of course it didn't work exactly as planned. Almost every time Linda got a bite of the apple, she pulled it out of Brad's grip. This caused them to have to restart their plan several times. However, in a short time together they ate enough of the apple to cause it to fall to the floor. Unfortunately one couple had finished before them, but they did get the consolation prize, two caramel-covered apples. The winning couple got four caramel-covered apples.

When they got back to their table, they were congratulated on working so well as a team. Both Brad and Linda had to check themselves over for bruises or missing teeth. After that they both agreed to donate their apples to their table mates saying they didn't want to see another apple for a long time.

Betty, Donna and Joan couldn't wait to show Linda and Brad pictures taken of them during the game. As expected the pictures, to say the least, were not very flattering but were funny. During the game they didn't realize how many times their faces touched, but the pictures clearly showed that. Linda immediately begged the three ladies to delete the pictures then later asked for copies when she realized the pictures were not going to be deleted.

The game, probably as intended, stimulated conversation among table members and made for a more relaxed atmosphere. Because everyone except Brad knew each other, the group spent several minutes bringing each other up on individual activities. The Fellers and Smiths talked about their sons and daughters accomplishments. It seems the three boy and two girl children were all in their late twenties, had advanced degrees, and worked as highly paid professionals. This made Brad feel inferior until he realized none of those kids had ever been in do-or-die combat as he had on numerous occasions over three years.

By the time dinner was served the talk got around to Brad. As Brad expected the usual comments were made about not having to honor his contract to go back on activity duty after he graduated. This time Brad didn't make his feelings known deciding to not throw cold water on a congenial conversation. The fact that Linda patted his thigh helped him make that decision.

As dessert was being served the club host described the next game. On the stage behind a curtain a group of actors had set up a family style living room. A short play would be performed ending in one of the actors being killed.

The audience was provided with preprinted note pads describing the actor's part. At the end of the play the audience would be asked to determine who the killer was. The first table coming up with the correct answer along with written logic in determining their response would be the winners.

As the play unfolded a number of clues were given for reasons players would want to kill another player including:

> A wealthy man who wanted to get rid of his wife and marry his mistress

A jealous wife who hated her husband for being unfaithful

A disrespectful son who wanted to take over his father's business

A mentally disturbed daughter who thought people were trying to kill her

An underpaid butler who was recently turned down for a pay raise

An unappreciated maid who was tired of people taking advantage of her

The audience wasn't told who would be killed. Just before the end of the play the lights went out, the curtain was dropped and a shot was heard. After the lights came back on and the curtain was raised, the audience could see that the wealthy man had been shot dead.

"I think it was the crazy daughter," said Larry.

"She wasn't crazy. She was mentally disturbed," said Betty.

"What's the difference?"

"Well, you can be very smart and still be mentally disturbed."

"You mean like your mother?"

"Maybe it was the jealous wife," offered Wayne.

"Why do you think that?" asked Donna.

"Well, women are always saying they want to kill their husbands. How many times have I heard that from you?"

"Yes, but I've never done it, yet."

Henry spoke up at this time to remind the group they needed to review the facts to prove who the killer was. He suggested they start by listing the clues they have. Henry showed the group a simple stickman drawing of where the actors were before and after the shot was fired.

"I could see through the curtain that the muzzle flash came the right side of the room," said Brad.

"Well, that should eliminate the crazy daughter and the unappreciated maid who were on the opposite side of the room and victim," said Henry.

"According to Henry's sketch, the only person that changed places after the shot was the butler. Maybe that means he is the killer," said Wayne.

"No, it doesn't. Maybe the butler just moved to turn on the lights," said Joan.

"We don't know why the lights went off. There were several lamps in the room. No one could have turned them all off or all on simultaneously," said Linda.

"I guess we are to assume someone pushed the circuit breaker even though we don't know where that is supposed to be," said Henry.

"I remember seeing a moving light just after the gunshot. Maybe that explains why the butler moved. He might have been using his cell phone light to find the circuit breaker," said Brad.

"If that's the case, the butler is ruled out," said Henry.

"That leaves only the jealous wife and disrespectful son," said Linda.

"I still think it's the jealous wife. Did you notice that she didn't seem upset when she saw that her husband had been shot?" said Wayne.

"Just because she's not sorry he's dead doesn't mean she killed him," said Donna.

"Before the lights went out the wife was sitting facing the audience, the son was seated to the left of the audience facing our right, and the wealthy guy has just started to walk to our right. If the wife had shot him he would have fallen toward us, but he fell facedown with his head to our right. Doesn't that mean that the son has to be the killer," asked Henry.

After a brief pause everyone in the group agreed with Henry, so they presented their findings to the host. To their surprise they were the first group to submit their answer.

After review the judge said the group missed a few clues, but they had enough facts correct to reach the correct conclusion, the murder was committed by the son. The prize was a good one. A free dinner for two at the club for all four couples.

The group lingered for almost another hour engaging in social talk before getting ready to leave. The men shook hands and hugged the women, which was awkward enough to look like a scene from a *Three Stooges* movie. As Wayne was shaking hands with Brad he quietly mentioned that Linda was a nice lady and that he hoped Brad would treat her right. In essence Wayne implied that Brad might just be a gigolo after Linda's money. Although he didn't feel that way he realized that is the first impression people would have when they see him with Linda. The only way to destroy that train of thought would be to let time prove that assumption wrong.

On the way home Joan promised to send Linda pictures of the 'bob for apples' game. Brad congratulated Henry for taking control of the murder game discussion and getting the facts together for a correct answer.

As soon as they were home Linda wanted to know what Brad thought of the Fellers and Smiths. Brad said they all were very nice and they all seemed to like Linda.

"Well, I'm glad you liked them. Incidentally, I hope you treat me right as Wayne ordered," Linda said indicating she had overheard Wayne's comment to Brad.

"Yeah, you'll be all right as long as you do as I say immediately," joked Brad.

"I was worried that you might get the wrong idea about Wayne. I'm sure he was just trying to be nice although it would have been better if he had just said something about just watching over me."

"His comment was well intended, so I didn't take any offense to it. Do you see them often at the club or gym?"

"No. Actually I hadn't seen any of them since my divorce. Someone must have filled them in on my status since they didn't ask any questions about why I was with you instead of Larry."

"Yeah, they didn't look too surprised to see me. It just goes to show that you can't keep any secrets from your friends."

The next afternoon Linda would finish plans for the trip to see Diane. In the evening she would call Larry and Diane to make sure they remembered she would be visiting. She also made a mental note to herself to talk to Brad about using the washer and dryer.

CHAPTER 16

Tuesday morning Brad and Linda had breakfast at home and then drove to school separately. They got together for the environmental class, which turned out to be an hour and a half lecture by Scott Watson. The class let out a little early, but before they could leave Scott wanted to talk to Linda. Since they were going to have lunch together Brad stayed with Linda as Scott talked to her.

"Linda, I thought you might want to earn a few extra credits. Actually I need some help getting ready for the environmental party at my place later this month. It won't require much of your time. How about if I buy us lunch so we can discuss it more then?" said Scott as he completely ignored Brad.

Twice a year Scott would choose one of his female students to help with the preparations for his class parties. It was well-known by other staff members and most students, except for the individual approached by Scott, that his real intentions were to convince the girl to have sex with him. This class Scott was concentrating on Linda. She was a couple of years younger than him. She had a great body, dressed appropriately, and could carry on an intelligent conversation. In summary she had class. That was something missing from his earlier conquests. By this time he was tiring of mindless talk from younger girls; however, he still liked the sex. Scott was thinking Linda would make a good long time partner.

Linda knew what Scott's real agenda was, mainly to first get friendly and personal with her hoping sex would soon follow. She also wondered how she could get extra credit for the class when Scott had already assured her of an A grade. She figured just declining his offer at this time would only lead to more suggestions in the future. So she decided to try to show Scott that her interests were with Brad not him.

"Brad and I were going to have lunch together, so if you care to buy both of us lunch, we can talk about both of us helping you," Linda replied.

Scott was not expecting that response. He figured his charm and power to provide a passing grade would intimidate her into accepting his offer. He knew if he backed off his offer it would confirm his real intentions. Because of that he said, of course Brad was welcome, trying to pretend that it really didn't matter to him.

The three of them went through the school cafeteria food line with Scott leading Linda following then Brad. Scott paid for the three lunches. Brad, as usual, was hungry, but he was careful to not order the most expensive items or dessert. Linda ordered a salad as did Scott.

When they found a table, Scott found he hadn't given much thought to what help he needed from Linda. Instead he had planned ways to get Linda to talk about herself so he could figure out the best way to seduce her. At that time he still didn't considered Brad a hindrance to his plans for Linda or even any competition. Thinking quickly, he revised his plan to first talk about help for the party while at the same time somehow marginalizing Brad.

"So Linda, in the past I've had one of the students help me plan and prepare the food for the party. We've tried several things in the past, but we've found it is difficult to get healthy food that tastes good to a young crowd. We can't serve alcohol and, of course, drugs are off limits. So I thought you could give me some ideas about what would appeal to the younger crowd," Scott said.

"Brad would probably know what the younger crowd likes more than I would, but I assume that by healthy food you are thinking about vegetarian food, cheese, crackers, yogurt, and things like that," answered Linda.

"Yeah, that's about right, but can you think of anything else kids your daughter's age would like. I mean other than alcohol and drugs," said Scott trying to inject some humor.

Linda wondered how Scott knew she had a daughter. She had never mentioned it to him. She figured Scott had been researching her personal life and she didn't appreciate it. Her first reaction would be to ask how he knew she had a daughter but then decided to stay on the subject in order to finish the discussion as soon as possible.

"What do you think, Brad?" asked Linda.

"Maybe we could bring some vegetarian pizza. I understand all kinds of nuts are good unless you are allergic to them. That's about all I can think of. I personally would like steak and potatoes," said Brad.

"Well, Linda, perhaps you can put together a list of food items. Then you and I can discuss it over lunch after Thursday's class. At that time I'd like to get your thoughts on the program and entertainment I'm planning," Scott said, making it known he wasn't inviting Brad to lunch.

"Why don't you just give me a list of what you're planning so I'll be ready to discuss it," said Linda

"Well, I don't have it with me right now. If you can stop by my office after my next class, I'd like to give it to you there," Scott said with a big smile.

Both Linda and Brad caught the cute, juvenile comment about wanting to give it to her there.

"Linda doesn't have any class this afternoon, but I do. If you really want us to review it, you can give me the list after your next class. I'm staying with Linda tonight, so she and I can look over your list, and we can discuss it at lunch next Thursday if you wish," Brad said, surprising both Linda and Scott.

After a long pause, Scott said that would be all right. He then said since everyone was finished eating, he would be getting back to his class. Before class, Scott stopped by his office to think over what just transpired. He realized he had underestimated Brad and Linda's relationship. He hadn't thought Linda would let Brad sleep with her, but now he knew that was only wishful thinking.

Scott's ego made him think he could convince Linda to drop Brad and take up with him. Ignoring Brad didn't work, so he would have to point out to Linda that his intellect was far superior to Brad's and that Brad's youth made them look ridiculous together. At that point, Scott started thinking about how nice it would be to have someone as sophisticated as her attend social functions with him. He had only rarely taken any of the college girls anywhere other than movies and private dinners.

Brad and Linda made it a point of kissing good-bye even though Scott had left. Linda went home and Brad went to his first afternoon class. There really wasn't any class for Brad. Instead he had committed to a two-hour workout in the gym every weekday in order to keep in shape for football.

A couple hours later Brad did stop by Scott's office. He was given a hastily handwritten note outlining the party agenda. Scott decided this would be a good time to find out more about Brad for use in attacking his character in the future.

"So, Brad, I understand you're a pretty good football player. Are you on a scholarship?" asked Scott.

"No, the government is paying my school costs and living expenses. I signed a contract to go back on active duty as a commissioned officer when I graduate," Brad answered. He thought it best if he just gave Scott the information instead of having Scott tease it out of him with a series of questions.

"Really, you mean you've been in the army? Does that mean you've been to Iraq?"

"Yes, that's right."

"Surely the army will send you back there or some other awful place once you get your degree. Have you thought of getting a football scholarship and voiding the army contract?"

Those comments were pretty much what Brad had expected to hear. At least Scott suggested letting someone other than the government pay for the rest of Brad's education.

The answer made Scott think that maybe Brad was more mature then he first thought. He knew Brad always seemed prepared in class, but he attributed that to Linda's guidance. This would make it more difficult to entice Linda away from Brad, but he was determined to try. This would be an interesting challenge. Maybe a direct approach would work since his real intentions must be known by now.

"Are you and Linda going to take some of the same classes next semester?" asked Scott.

"We haven't decided yet. First we want to pass your environmental class," answered Brad.

"Well, neither of you need to worry about that. I've never flunked anyone yet. I don't think anyone ever got less that an A, but of course that could change."

"We're looking forward to your party. It sounds like it might be a lot of fun."

"I hope so. You might get bored with a lot of the juvenile stuff that interest the younger generation. I am serious about getting some help putting this show on. Linda and your help would be appreciated."

"Yeah, we'd be happy to help."

"You and Linda seem to get along pretty well. Are you going to stay together next semester?"

"Yes."

That pretty much finished Scott's probing of Brad's background.

That afternoon Linda continued planning for her weekend trip. The air, hotel, and car reservations were completed. By using the internet, she was able to plot a driving trip from the Palo Alto area to Monterey. That should take up most of Saturday and give Linda a lot of time to talk with Diane. Now she concentrated on what she wanted to talk about with Diane and how best to go about it.

First Linda would want to know how Diane is getting along in school. She would encourage Diane to talk about her school friends and especially about Wellesley Goldstone. Next she would ask how Diane was getting along with Cindy and Larry. That should lead to the Thanksgiving trip to Hawaii and the Christmas trip to Lake Tahoe discussion. She would then mention that her parents would be visiting for a few weeks after the first of the year and that Diane should plan on spending a weekend at home to see her grandparents. Finally she would want to talk about Brad even though she had no idea of how to discuss their relationship with Diane.

That was a great plan, but as we all know, things rarely go according to plan. What Linda hadn't considered was what Diane would want to talk about.

Brad got home around 4:00 p.m., which was a couple hours earlier than when he had football practice. Linda went over her trip plan, then wanted to know what Brad had planned for the weekend. He said he would be busy all weekend studying and working out. He promised to not spend any time at Tony's.

It wasn't until they were eating dinner that Linda remembered Scott's list. The list contained the usual party activity, mainly eating, drinking and mingling. Other than asking each attendee to briefly state what they did during the week to improve or maintain the economy there was no program.

"What new activities do you think we could suggest to Scott?" asked Linda.

"Well, we could suggest the apple bob game," said Brad.

"We'd better not suggest that, the kids would knock each other out. I've got an idea let's tell Scott his agenda is perfect."

"Okay, maybe we think of something in the next couple of days."

By then it was time for Linda to call Larry and Diane. The call to Larry was short. Larry said Diane was getting along well and that she was expecting Linda Friday afternoon. The call to Diane was also short but disappointing.

"Hi, Mom, I was going to call Thursday," said Diane as she answered Linda's call.

"Diane, I'm looking forward to seeing you. It's been almost two months since I was up there," Linda answered, ignoring Diane's greeting.

After a few seconds of silence

"I should get your place around 4:00 p.m. so we'll have some time to talk before dinner. We'll go to your favorite restaurant in the area. Can you make reservations for us?"

"If you want to eat somewhere around here, we might as well just go to the local coffee shop," answered Diane.

"Sure, that would be all right. Have you gained any weight?"

"No, I've actually lost a few pounds. Cindy had me on a special diet she knows about. I feel great,"

Linda didn't want to get into a long discussion over the phone, but Diane's comments distressed her. She wondered if Diane was mocking her when she indicated a coffee shop would be good enough for her. The most upsetting comment had to do with Diane's weight loss. Diane had never been overweight. Cindy, who knew nothing about everything, should not be giving Diane any suggestions about diets. Linda would have to somehow get Diane to stop taking directions from Cindy.

The next couple of days passed quickly. By Thursday Brad and Linda had not thought of anything else to add to Scott's party plan and told him so. They did volunteer to bring all the food and drinks since Scott said he would reimburse them for the cost. Scott's offer to buy lunch was politely declined.

Friday Brad drove Linda to the airport. Then he found he didn't really have anything to do for the rest of the day. He actually didn't have any plans until Sunday afternoon when he would pick Linda up at the airport. By afternoon he had to resist the urge to call Linda. They had agreed that Linda would not call him until late Friday unless something went wrong. By then he realized how much he missed being with Linda.

Linda's flight was non-eventful. She arrived on time, got her rental car and started for Diane's house. She was a little early, so she spent some time driving around the area where Diane lived to see if she could find a nice restaurant. There were several in the area, so she stopped to make 6:00 p.m. reservations at a restaurant she liked.

Linda gave Diane a big hug when she got to her apartment. A quick look around the place showed that it seemed to be clean but a little messy. Wellesley Goldstone was nowhere to be seen. However, he had left signs that he had been there earlier, an empty Coke can and a cigarette butt in an ashtray, probably marijuana. After non-emotional greetings there were several seconds of awkward silence. Linda had hoped Diane would ask her about the trip, her welfare or anything. Instead Diane said nothing and did not offer any refreshments. However, there was a lot Linda wanted to say, but she wanted to avoid upsetting Diane and getting into arguments. Because of that she chose what she hoped would be a noncombative subject to discuss.

"Let me know how things are going at school. Are you keeping up with your studies?" asked Linda.

"Yeah, no problem only I don't know why I have to take the English and math classes. Almost everyone in my English class is from a foreign country and some of them can't even speak English. We spend so much time on basis reading we don't have any time for anything else. The math class is just as bad. Most of the students are dumb jocks that can't even add or subtract properly. I don't know why Dad didn't get me out of taking these classes. They are both a waste of time," answered Diane.

"Sorry to hear that, but you're almost through the semester. How about your history and social science classes?"

"They are okay, but I don't know why I have to study ancient history. I like the social science class. We discuss current issues like why minorities are still being oppressed and why the U.S. is always starting wars."

"Are you getting good grades?"

"Colleges don't give out grades before the end of the semester anymore. If anyone is getting behind the instructor will work with them one on one."

"What are you studying in history?"

"Oh, I don't know something about wars between England and France. They were always fighting each other in the past you know."

"Have you thought about the classes you need to take next semester?"

"Yeah, there are two required courses I have to take and then Cindy said I should take another social studies course and a course in women power."

The two continued to talk for about another hour. As they were talking Linda almost, without thinking, casually begin straightening up little things around the apartment. One look into the bedroom stopped her from continuing the tidying up. The bedroom was a mess with clothes, both Diane's and Wellesley's, spread around the room and on the floor. By then it was close to 5:30 p.m. so Linda decided it was time for Diane to start getting ready for dinner.

"Diane, I haven't had lunch and I'm starving. Let's go to dinner right now," Linda said.

"Yeah, okay, let me a couple of minutes," Diane answered.

It took a full fifteen minutes before Diane was ready to leave. Linda wondered what she did during that time since she hadn't changed clothes or brushed her hair. Fortunately the restaurant was close by, so they were able to make the 6:00 p.m. reservation time.

Linda had planned on finding out more about Cindy's influence on Diane at dinner. Before they left the apartment Diane must have mentioned Cindy a dozen times. Linda learned that Cindy normally would visit Diane at least one day a week at school. They would have lunch at the school cafeteria and then Cindy would wait in the cafeteria until Diane finished her afternoon classes around 3:00 p.m. What bothered Linda was that Cindy was able to get a couple of students to date Diane, but apparently none of the men followed up on the dates.

As soon as they were seated, Diane immediately wanted to talk about Linda's relationship with Brad. Linda had hoped to save that subject for the long drive to Monterey. She certainly didn't want to discuss the relationship in a public restaurant, but she had no choice.

"Mom, I want to know if you are still seeing that stupid jock," Diane almost shouted.

The timing of the comment couldn't have been worse. The waiter had just arrived at the table to get drink orders. Linda wanted coffee and Diane asked for a soft drink.

"Yes, I'm still seeing Brad. He is on the football team, but please be polite and refer to him by name instead of calling him a jock. Brad is very mature and has had many traumatic life threatening encounters that I hope you will never have to experience. He is not stupid and you are very mistaken if you really think that considering the fact that you have never held a conversation with him," answered Linda.

"Well, he can't be too smart if he quit college to go in the army after we started a war. How can you stand to be seen with someone half your age?"

"Are you saying it is stupid to be patriotic and who told you we started a war."

"Oh, Mom, you're so dumb. All the professors at school know we're at fault for the 911 attack. If you were going to a real university instead of some four-year junior college, you would learn how our country has been mistreating the Middle East countries for hundreds of years. No wonder they hate us. We're killing innocent women and children every day over there just so we can occupy some foreign country."

Once again Diane's timing matched the arrival of the waiter, who was there to take dinner orders. Diane predictably acted like a spoiled child and said she wasn't hungry but did want another soft drink. Linda hadn't had time to look at the dinner menu but ordered a Cobb salad and a bowl of soup.

Linda wanted to get off the world political subject and back to her relationship with Brad. She figured since the subject was opened she wanted to finish it that evening.

"You asked how I can stand to be seen with Brad. Yes, it's true he is twelve years younger than me and when we first started going places together I was a little embarrassed. However, I've gotten over that. By the way did you ever ask your father how he could stand being seen with a girl over twenty years younger than him?" Linda asked.

"That's different. It's not unusual for men to date younger women. Besides, Dad knew what he was doing," Diane said.

"Yes, you are right, it is considered all right for a man to date a younger woman, but that's not the case for a woman dating a younger man. However, there should not be any difference. You said you want to take a women power course next semester. Don't you think you'll learn that women should not be treated any differently from men? In other words, I'm pretty sure your professor will tell you there is nothing wrong with a woman dating a younger man."

"It's different because everyone knows the younger men are just money grabbers only interested in getting money from women. Isn't it true that you pay for everything when you are with that guy?"

"Yes, that's right because I can afford it just like your father pays for everything when he is with Cindy and even for things Cindy spends when he is not with her."

"That's different. Dad and Cindy are married."

"Larry was spending lots of money on Cindy for over a year before they were married. Apparently you don't think that was wrong. For your information I don't buy Brad expensive gifts, or any gifts for that matter. He pays his own way when we are not together and he does pay for a number of our expenses when we are together. That is a lot different from the way your father spent money on Cindy while he and I were still married. As you said I'm sure he knew what he was doing."

"Yes, but they were intending to get married. You can't be thinking of marrying that guy. I'll never speak to you again if that happens."

Diane's voice was high pitched and loud enough to be heard several tables away. Linda realized Diane was getting agitated. Whenever Diane had faced adversity she always backed down or ran away. She couldn't go to her bedroom now, but she could go to the car. Because of that Linda tried to tone down the rhetoric.

"You don't have to worry about that. I'm just enjoying my independence and catching up on many things I missed out on when I was younger. I hope you don't mind my having some personal enjoyment for once."

This seemed to quiet Diane for several seconds. Perhaps she had never considered her mother's feelings but instead thought only of herself. Maybe it wouldn't be so bad if the relationship didn't last much longer.

"Tell me you're not going to bed with him. That would be awful. Remember how many times you told me sex before marriage is wrong. If you are having sex with that guy I don't want you to ever preach to me again about doing the right thing."

"Diane I'm just thinking about your welfare. I don't want you to make the same mistake I made at your age. Do you understand why I'm concerned about you?"

"Yeah, I understand. You're sorry you got pregnant because you never wanted me to be born. Too bad you didn't get an abortion. I'm sure that would have made you happy."

"That's not true and you know it. I've always loved you Diane. What I meant was that it would have been better for you if your father and I had waited a couple of years before having you. If we had you wouldn't have had to live with your grandparents for the first year of your life. That is the most important time when mothers need to be with their babies. I'm so sorry we missed out on the natural bonding that should have taken place during that time."

"So why did you give me to Grandma Wallace?"

Linda didn't know how to answer that question. The truth was that Larry's parents threatened to take legal custody of Diane if she didn't voluntarily give them custody. First of all Diane probably wouldn't believe that. Also if she told Diane the truth it would destroy the fragile relationship Linda maintained with Larry's parents. That's not something Linda wanted.

"Larry and all four of your grandparents all convinced me it would best for you if Larry's parents took care of you during the week. You don't remember, but you stayed with your father and me on the weekends. After the first year, against the advice of Larry and all your grandparents I quite school to take care of you. I've never regretted that."

"All right, Mom, I know you care for me. I just don't understand why you are against me having a good time with my boyfriend. Nowadays girls don't have to get pregnant and don't have to have an abortion. I know how to practice safe sex. If you and that guy can sleep together, why can't I sleep with my friend Wellesley or anyone else I want?"

Once again Linda was at a loss of words. She knew Diane would eventually ask that question and she knew it would take hours and hours to provide an explanation to Diane. This was not the time to go into a lengthy discussion. That would come later in the year.

"I just don't want you to get hurt. If you don't know now you will when you get a little older. Sex is always better when you care about your partner."

"Oh, how would you know, Mother? Remember you told me you've never had sex with anyone other than Dad. As least not before you met that guy you've been seeing."

Linda decided to give up on the subject and talk about something else.

"Tomorrow I was thinking we might enjoy driving down to Monterey and Carmel. Does that sound like a good idea?"

"That's such a long way for a drive. Tomorrow I should study and get ready for next week's classes."

Even before Diane answered Linda realized she had phrased the thought in the form of a question giving Diane a way to decline the invitation. She was able to recover by making up a story to cause Diane to want to go on the trip.

"Well, when I talked to Larry this week, he suggested you and I look at some property in the area. Cindy mentioned that that would be a nice area for weekends away from the city and also a good investment as property values are down now."

"Okay, Mom, maybe Dad would be interested in buying some property there."

Linda found it hard to believe how easy it was to change Diane's mind simply by mentioning Cindy. If necessary she could use that ploy many times in the future if needed to persuade to do something that she otherwise would not want to do.

When they got back to the apartment Linda was surprised to see Wellesley there. It was still early; however, Wellesley appeared be dressed for bed in either pajamas or his underwear. Wellesley greeted Linda by first name and then asked Diane where she had been.

Linda realized that Diane wanted to shock her by having her boyfriend stay overnight at her apartment. She figured Diane had taken so long to get ready for dinner because she had been talking to Wellesley on the phone. With Wellesley there talking to Diane about any personal matter was out of the question. So even though it was only a little after 8:30 p.m., Linda went back to her hotel.

At the hotel Linda tried to watch TV while thinking over the earlier conversation with Diane and also planning for the Monterey trip. She had told Diane they should get an early start around 9:00 a.m. Now she tried to figure out how to get out of pretending to look for real estate in the Monterey area. Her only hope would be that Diane would forget her mentioning it, but that was a long shot. About the only positive thing that came out of their discussion was that Diane now referred to Brad as that guy instead of that stupid jerk/jock.

As promised, Linda called Brad to let him know how things were going with her. They talked for over an hour, which made Linda feel good.

Saturday Linda got to Diane's apartment right at 9:00 a.m. Wellesley again greeted her by calling her by her first name. He was still wearing his pajamas/underwear attire.

"Mom, I asked Lee, as she called Wellesley, to come with us today. He said he could drive," said Diane.

That was not going to happen there was no way she would sit in the back seat of her rental car while her daughter and boyfriend carried on a conversation without involving her. Linda immediately and forcedly told Lee to get dressed and leave. He will not be going with them today. Lee hesitated for a few seconds until Diane told him she would call him that afternoon.

Diane, for some reason, didn't say anything more about having Lee come with them. She did seem to want to talk as they started on the trip.

"Do you how to get there. I understand it will take about two hours," asked Diane.

"Yeah, that sounds right. I looked at a map, so I think I can get there. As soon as we get out of the heavy traffic we'll stop for breakfast," Linda said.

"That's a good idea. I'm hungry this morning for some reason."

"You're probably hungry because you didn't eat last night, or did you have a late-night snack."

"No, I went to bed early. I told Lee I was really tired, so he slept on the sofa."

After driving a few miles they found themselves in the city of Morgan Hill where they stopped at a local restaurant for breakfast.

"How are you and Lee getting along?" Linda asked.

"Oh, he's okay. Actually Cindy says he's pretty much of a dork. He helps me with some of my classes, so it's nice to have him around. Next semester I don't think I'll need his help," Diane answered.

"I assume you are having sex with him."

"No, not real sex. We just fool around a lot, but I won't let him poke me."

The comment about being poked was another indication of how much influence Cindy had over Diane. Linda wanted to know more about Diane's sexual activity but was almost too embarrassed to ask. Then again maybe it would be better if she didn't hear any more about it. She decided to change the subject.

"So you seem to be getting along well with Cindy. Does she visit you often?" asked Linda.

"Oh yeah, she likes to meet me for lunch at the school cafeteria at least once a week, and then most weekends I'll spend time with her and Dad at their place. Cindy knows a lot about kids my age. She is really smart," said Diane.

"Is she able to help with your homework?"

"Well, she's not too good in math, but she told me about a lot of books that I should read to find out more about life."

"Is that how she met Lee, I mean at lunch."

"No, I usually don't see Lee until after school. Cindy met Lee one night at my apartment when she stayed overnight with me. Cindy has done that a couple of times when Dad had to go on a business trip. That's why Cindy thinks Lee is a dork. He tried to kiss her once when I was in the kitchen. Cindy just laughed at him, which kept him quiet the rest of the evening."

Diane went on to say that Cindy had introduced her to a couple of different guys she had met at the cafeteria. Neither of the guys asked her out for a second date since she wouldn't have sex with them. They still stopped by to talk to Cindy at the cafeteria however.

Something else Diane said seemed rather odd. One Sunday afternoon after dropping off Larry at the airport for an out of town trip, Cindy stopped by to see Diane. She said she would like to spend the night at the apartment. However, about midnight Cindy got up, took a shower, got dressed and left. She told Diane that she wanted to drive home before she got stuck in heavy morning traffic. That didn't make sense to Linda. Why not get a couple more hours sleep and leave at 4:00 a.m. and why couldn't she wait until she got home before taking a shower.

That caused Linda to start fantasizing about why Cindy did what she did. Maybe she wanted to meet one of the guys she knew from school for an early morning tryst. That seemed as unlikely as a plot in a B movie, so Linda gave up the thought. Still she wondered what Larry felt about Cindy spending so much time visiting Diane at school. She also wondered if Larry had any idea of the negative influence Cindy was having on Diane.

When they got back on the road the conversation turned to what to do in Monterey. Although the sun was shining a cool breeze was blowing, which made it necessary to wear a sweater or light jacket. That meant spending time getting sun on the beach would be out of the question. Shopping in some of the quaint stores in Carmel would take up most to their time. Then there was the Monterey Bay Aquarium to see in Monterey. If they needed to spend more time in the area they could always look at some real estate.

The drive from Palo Alto took them south on Highway 101. To get to Monterey then needed to take State Route 156 to State Route 1. The road narrowed to one lane each direction when they turned onto State Route 156. This caused Linda to concentrate more on driving. The weather also changed. The sun disappeared as low clouds moved in from the coast.

No one spoke for several minutes before Diane announced that she didn't think it a good idea to continue. She said it would be too cold to spend much time outdoors and she didn't feel like shopping. Linda kept driving saying since they were almost there they should at least drive around to see some of the historical areas. Diane didn't speak again until they reached Monterey.

Linda parked the car on Cannery Row, intending to visit some of the historical buildings. That was the setting for a couple of famous novels by John Steinbeck that Diane would probably study in future English classes. Diane announced she didn't want to go any of those old buildings. Linda then mentioned that the aquarium is a well-known attraction, so Diane might learn something she could use in one of her college courses. Diane said she wouldn't be studying to be a fisherman, so she would wait in the car. Linda tried to reason with her by pointing out that there were a number of young men walking in the area and it may not be safe in the car. As a last effort to get Diane to get in the aquarium, she said Diane could use the restroom inside and then wait in the lounge.

After spending an hour or so wondering around the aquarium it was time to go. That time of year it gets dark by 5:00 p.m. and Linda wanted to start back before them. Even so she thought they would have time to stop by Carmel for a short time and still get on the road before dark. Linda found Diane in the lounge area talking to a couple of young men.

"Oh, Mom, these guys were telling me about Monterey and Carmel. They said we should visit here when the weather is better," said Diane.

"Hello, I hope my daughter hasn't kept you from walking around the place," Linda said to the two men.

"No, we were just leaving when we saw a lady in distress. Diane didn't have the right change for the vending machine, so we helped her out," one of the men answered.

"Do you both live here?"

"Yes, at least for a while. We are both going to army language school," answered one of the men.

"They are studying Arabic and are going to be spies," Diane blurted out.

"Well, that's not exactly correct. We don't know for sure what the army will do with us when we finish here," the other man answered.

"I've got a friend who just came back from Iraq. Do you think you will have to go there?" asked Linda.

"We've both had one tour of duty there. If we go back at least we'll be able to talk to some of the locals. Do you know what outfit your friend was with in Iraq?"

"All I know is that he was with the infantry and saw a lot of combat."

"Well, he's lucky to get back alive. Has he got all of his arms and legs?"

Linda and the two men continued the conversation for a few more minutes. Diane didn't seem to have anything to contribute. As they were leaving the men said good-bye to Diane and told Linda they wished the best for her friend.

As soon as they got in the car Diane started berating Linda for flirting with the men.

"Mom, how could you keep talking to those guys? They were half your age just like that guy you like at home," said Diane.

It was obvious Diane was jealous of the fact that her mother could draw attention of the guys away from her. As usual when things didn't go her way, Diane decided to act out the silent treatment and pretty much stopped talking all the way back to her apartment.

Linda did want to see Carmel herself and hoped Diane would change her mind, so they stopped there for about an hour. Diane remained in the car not even wanting to get something to eat or to use the restroom. By the time they started back to Palo Alto, it was almost nighttime. Linda drove carefully but not too slowly all the way back home. It was only around 7:00 p.m. when they reached the apartment. Surprisingly Lee was not there to greet them. Diane went immediately to her room saying she was tired from the trip and had a headache, so she was going to bed early. Linda decided it best if she just went back to her hotel room. As she left she said she would stop by around 9:00 a.m. in the morning with something to eat for breakfast.

Before she went to sleep Linda thought over the activities over the last two days. The trip was not as pleasant as she had hoped. Diane still seemed to upset with her. Diane felt Linda was at fault for the divorce and thought it terrible that Linda was seeing Brad. Worse of all Cindy seemed to have replaced her as Diane's mother. For the first time Linda realized that Diane had turned out to be a naive selfish brat. Fortunately that could change over time.

The next morning Diane was up and talking but not saying much. After about an hour it was time for Linda to leave to catch her plane home. She said she hoped Diane would enjoy Hawaii and asked her to call from there to let her know how she was getting along.

At the airport Linda called Brad to let him know her plane would be on time and thanked him for volunteering to meet her when she arrived.

CHAPTER 17

With Linda away Brad spent most of the weekend at the transit facility. Saturday and Sunday after working out, he spent a few hours studying and then watched football on TV. He was really looking forward to Sunday afternoon when he would meet Linda at the airport. He would be staying with Linda overnight.

On the way home from the airport Linda wanted to talk about how she and Diane got along. She said the trip was not enjoyable since Diane acted immaturely most of the time either sulking or refusing to talk. Linda also mentioned that Diane still hasn't accepted the idea that she and Brad are in a relationship. Linda did not mention her talk with Diane about sex. Brad commented on his dull weekend and then tried to console Linda for feeling bad about her visit.

Over dinner Linda mentioned her conversation with the two soldiers who were studying at the government language school.

"Language school is pretty hard to get into. You have to take a special test and then you have to pass an extensive background check in order to get a security clearance. You know the navy runs a postgraduate school in Monterey also, so most weekends and evenings there are a lot of young men and women walking around the downtown area. I'm surprised Diane didn't want to walk around and mingle with the crowd," said Brad.

"Well, you know she might have if she had known that before she decided to act like I was holding her against her will. Why don't you apply for the language school when you go back on active duty?" Linda said.

"I might just do that, but I'm pretty sure my first assignment will be back to the infantry. The army needs people with combat experience even if the war has wound down by the time I get my degree. After one more tour I might apply for the school."

"You know they said something that sounded really bad. I assume they were joking, but they asked if you still had all of your arms and legs. Did you ever have one of those roadside bombs explode by you?"

"Yeah, that happens to almost everyone at one time or another. You just have to be lucky to escape major injuries. Of course almost everyone gets hit with shrapnel."

Brad wanted to get off the Iraq experience subject, so he asked how Linda liked Monterey and Carmel. Linda thought Carmel was great and would have liked to have time to visit more of the antique shops. She would like to visit the area again when the weather was better. They agreed they may spend a weekend there sometime in the late spring. Without planning to do so, they each had let the other one know that they were thinking about continuing relationship.

Shortly after dinner Joan called to be brought up-to-date on the weekend trip. She also wanted to know if Linda and Brad could join her and Henry for dinner at the club Thursday or Friday. They could use their winning dinner tickets.

While Linda and Joan were talking Brad got an unexpected call from a friend he knew from junior college.

Roger Reid and Brad paled around together while they were going to school but hadn't seen each other in over three years. The last Brad had heard from Roger he knew he had finished college and gotten married. On the phone Roger said he was in the Los Angeles area for a consulting assignment that would last until Wednesday. They agreed to get together Monday night at Roger's hotel.

When Linda had finished talking to Joan, Brad told her about the call from Roger. Brad said he met Roger when the both played linebacker on the junior college football team. They had somewhat keep in contact over the past three years. Brad said Roger in the past was pretty wild and had a gutter mouth. Brad thought it might be better if he checked Roger out to see if he would be suitable to meet Linda. Linda agreed and actually was looking forward to some time by herself Monday.

Roger's hotel was in Newport Beach, which took Brad over an hour to reach because of heavy traffic. Even so it was still early when Brad arrived at the hotel. Roger was already in the hotel bar talking to a couple of women. After Roger greeted Brad and introducing the women as consulting clients, Roger and Brad moved to a booth. The two women excused themselves and left the bar.

Brad asked Roger how he was getting along. That might have been a mistake because Roger that caused Roger to tell a long story about an old surgical procedure.

"I guess I never told you about my big operation have I?" asked Roger.

"No, you mean you went under the knife and survived? Did you have a football injury?"

"No, it was something entirely different. Let me tell you about it in case this ever happens to you.

"One summer morning before enrolling in Kansas University when I was taking a shower I noticed a big bulge in the groin area. No, not that bulge, this was something new. I watched it the next couple of days and noticed that it seemed to get bigger when I leaned one way but disappeared when I leaned the other way. Anyway I figured I'd better find out what was wrong.

"Luckily I had insurance with the company I was working for that summer. I called a recommended doctor for an appointment, but of course it wasn't that simple. They wanted to know why I needed to see a doctor, so I told them I think I had an enlarged prostate, not knowing where the prostate is located in the body, or maybe a big cancer lump. I was given an appointment two weeks away. The appointment was for 10:00 a.m., but I was told to get there fifteen minutes early to fill out some forms.

"The big day arrived and I did get there early. It took me almost an hour to fill out all the forms. Besides asking for the usual personal information I had to tell my life's story. Then there were the embarrassing questions. Among other things, they wanted to know if I ever used drugs and if so how often. They wanted to know if I cry or throw up a lot. They wanted to know everything about me except how long was my cock. The lady at the desk found several questions I hadn't answered and a couple where my answers were not complete. Anyway they hadn't called me to see a doctor yet, so I was glad I wasn't told to be there an hour early.

"After finally completing the forms I asked the guy sitting next to me if his appointment was also for 10:00 a.m. It turns out his appointment was for 9:30 a.m. Shortly after that he was taken into the exam room. It wasn't until 11:15 a.m. before I got to an exam room. Instead of a doctor a nurse took my vital signs saying the doctor would see me soon. The doctor did show up half an hour later.

"The doctor wanted to know what was wrong with me, so I told him about the lump. He told me to drop my pants so he could see what I was complaining about. Fortunately he had closed the door to the exam room. It took him about two seconds to tell me I had a hernia and ask if I wanted to have it fixed. That seemed like a silly question, but I found out later that some men just get a special belt called a trust to hold the hernia in. I said I wanted it fixed right away, so the doctor recommended me to a hernia specialist. The doctor said I might as well have all blood work, a urine sample, and X-rays taken then so the specialist wouldn't have to have it done at this place. It was close to 1:00 p.m. before I left the place. So I spent about three hours at the office but only talked to a doctor for less than five minutes.

"At the specialist's office I went through the same routine—fill out forms, see the doctor for about five minutes, and then have all the lab work done again. My surgery was scheduled two weeks away at an outpatient facility. That meant they would cut me open in the morning put some kind of padding inside me sew me up and let me go home. They made a big deal about having someone drive me to the facility and drive me home. They made it clear I would be in no condition to drive myself.

"The day of the operation I drove myself to the facility at 6:00 a.m. and parked in a remote area of the parking lot far from the building. After the operation I had arranged for a friend at work to pick me up at the facility door and then drive me to my car in the parking lot. I would drive myself home.

"Once again I had to fill out paperwork and have all the lab work done for the third time. About an hour after I got there a middle-aged nurse took me to a curtained off cubical and told me to take off all my clothes except for my socks. She gave me one of those backless hospital gowns to put on. Just after I got the gown on the nurse came back told me to lie on the bed and then gave me an injection that made me sleepy. A short time later they wheeled me into the operating room. An IV was set up and I saw some black liquid going into my arm. What I thought was a few seconds later but was really about two hours later after the operation I woke up back in the cubical I noticed the nurse had both arm under my gown. She had a big grin on her face, so I thought she must be playing with my balls. As it turned out she was just putting my underwear back on me. However, I wondered why it took her almost a minute to do that and why she thought she had to do that.

"I was told to stay in bed until I felt able to get up and finish getting dressed. I almost immediately got dressed because I had to take a whiz. When I got in the bathroom I noticed that my entire groin area was black and blue. My cock was so wrinkled up it took me several seconds to straighten it out and get it back in working order. That convinced me that the nurse had spent the past two hours massaging my private parts. That didn't bother me too much except that I missed out on all the fun.

"After I left the bathroom I was given some crackers and a small plastic bottle of grape juice. The crackers tasted like cardboard and immediately sucked all the moisture out of my mouth including the juice I had tried to drink. The cracker started forming into a ball, so I spit it out. It bounced on the floor like a hard golf ball. About that time my friend showed up to get me out of there. As planned he just drove me to my car in the far part of the parking lot.

"On the way home I stopped to get a hamburger and soft drink. Just like the cracker, the hamburger tasted like cardboard and started sucking the moisture from my mouth before I could spit it out. I felt a little bloated but otherwise all right. I figured that was because of the padding they put in me, so I was wondering if I would feel that way the rest of my life. The doctor told me to take one of the big pain pills they gave when I got home and every four hours after that if needed. Even though I wasn't in any pain I did take one pill, which soon made me sleepy. It was about noon, so I decided to take a short nap.

"Later that afternoon I got a call from the nurse. She said she just wanted to see if I was still alive. I told her I was doing okay and that I had taken on of the pain pills. The nurse told me not to take the pills if I didn't need too because they could cause constipation. As soon as I heard that I made a mental note to throw the pills away as soon as I got up. After the call ended I decided to get up because I had to take another whiz.

"When I got up to a forty five degree angle, I felt so much pain at my side that I froze. I immediately looked around to see if I could reach the pain pills. I didn't care if I wouldn't be able to take a dump for another two months. Unfortunately the pills were out of sight. After a few seconds I thought about lying back down and wetting the bed. Then I realized it would hurt just as much going back down as it would to continue to get up. As you know I have a really low tolerance for pain. However, I did get up and managed to get to the bathroom. If I stood up and didn't move I didn't feel any pain, but I still thought I needed another pill. As it turned out the pill didn't do much to stop the pain, but it did make me sleepy. I wasn't about to lie down at least for the next few days, so I thought maybe I could sleep standing up if I leaned in the corner of the room. Of course that didn't work, so I tried to lie down without bending my hips. That didn't work out very well either.

"Well, to finish my long story, since I wasn't supposed to do any heavy lifting for two weeks, the company let me work in the office those weeks. That really worked out well as it led to a regular office job where I learned about the inventory program. So sometimes good fortune comes from unexpected actions."

After ordering drinks, Roger said he got a job in Kansas City, Missouri with an information systems management firm after graduating from Kansas University. The next couple of days he would be helping a company install a new computer program.

"Last time you called me you were heading back to the States from Iraq. So what have you been doing since you left the army?" Roger asked.

"I've gone back to school at Cal State to finish my last two years. I hope to get a degree in another year," answered Brad

"You're not married, are you?"

"No, but I've met a very nice lady that I might marry someday."

"I thought you might have looked up good old Mary Ann Black?"

"No, I haven't heard from her since I left school. I thought you were interested in her."

"Well, I was for a while. After you left, I took her out a couple of times, but I didn't get anywhere with her, at least not with my cock. I did get this handful of cum one night though."

As he made that comment Roger took a close look at the palm of his right hand. He then corrected himself saying actually it was my left hand. He then put his left palm close to his nose so he could smell it and said, "Yeah, this is the one." About that time Roger suggested they move to the hotel steakhouse for dinner. Roger charged the drinks and tip to his room and told Brad that the dinner was on him. Over dinner and another round of drinks Roger continued talking about what he had done the past few years.

"Well, as you know, I enrolled in Kansas University intending to play football. The coaches told me they couldn't offer me a football scholarship, but instead they filled out an application for a student loan for me. All I had to do was sign the form, which I did. Incidentally I still owe about $50,000 on the loan for two years of school. Then they wanted to redshirt me so I could learn the system and then play for two years. This would mean I'd have to spend another year at school. Anyway I agreed but found out that all redshirt players are used as a hamburger squad. You know what that means. We were basically movable dummies for full practice scrimmages. The second year I did get moved up to being eligible to play in games but only got into a grand total of three games for the entire season. I got even with them though by graduating and not coming back for another season," Roger explained.

"So when did you get married?" Brad asked.

"That's another long story and it's a really sad one. You remember Ashley Johnson, well, that's who I married."

"Yeah, you send me an invitation to the wedding by e-mail. Unfortunately, my captain didn't understand how important to you it was for me to be there, so I couldn't make it. You did get the present I sent, an authentic burqa for Ashley, didn't you?"

"I really could have used something like that starting the second day of our marriage."

"You know in the Middle East sometimes women are required to wear burqa for wedding dresses. Can you imagine having a marriage arranged for you and not meeting or being able to see your wife until after the ceremony?"

"I can just imagine how women are chosen for marriage. It must be like a livestock auction. This girl is highly desirable, she had two arms, two legs and only one nose."

"You know recently because of the conflicts going on over there, you might not be kidding about having to certify that a prospective bride does have all her limbs. It would also be nice to know if the girl has been surgically altered to destroy her sexual pleasure."

"Yeah, I've heard that a lot of the men don't seem to care. Most probably would prefer a girl like that to goats. Notice I said most men, some of those guys really love their goats at least until they slit their throats and eat them."

"It's really not that bad, but women's rights groups are nonexistent in most Middle East countries. Can you imagine a twelve-year old girl being told she has to marry some thirty-five-year-old man that has never taken a bath or a shower in his life."

"Let's get back to Ashley. I can tell you for a fact that she had all the right parts in the right places and the all worked the way they were supposed to work except maybe her brain."

"Okay, I remember you first started going with her in high school but then lost track of her until she showed up at KU."

"Yeah, in high school we were hitting it off pretty good until she introduced me to her parents. That was a real disaster. That happened just after graduation, and I was so embarrassed I stopped seeing Ashley and left town to attend our good old junior college."

"So what happened when you met the parents?"

"Well, like I said it's a long sad story. It was a Sunday when Ashley invited me out to the family farm. By this time, Ashley and I were in a pretty serious relationship, so I wanted to make a good impression. Even though it was July, I decided to wear my one and only suit, which was wool. By the time we got to the farm, I was already sweating like a hog. When Mrs. Johnson greeted us at the door, I was hoping she would ask me to take my coat off. She did not. I wasn't sure if I should ask if it would be all right to take off my coat or maybe just do it. Instead I did nothing.

"Mr. Johnson introduced himself when we entered the family room or what they called the parlor. I thought maybe he would say I could take my coat off. He did not. He also didn't say I could call him by his first name. Ashley and I sat down on the sofa. Mrs. Johnson sat an easy chair angled toward the sofa. Mr. Johnson sat in a big over padded recliner angled toward the sofa from the other side of the room. A big wood burning fireplace was directly across from the sofa. Fortunately it was not lit. The sofa material felt like high grade sandpaper immediately causing my butt to itch.

"Ashley had told me dinner would be served at 6:00 p.m., so we would have almost two hours to talk. Mr. Johnson started the conversation by asking me a series of questions, such as where are you going to college, what do you want to do when you finish college, what do your parents do, do you have any brothers or sisters, and several more questions. This was worse than a job interview. Fortunately the questions were the soft ball type, which were easy to answer. It wasn't like he was asking me to explain macroeconomic. While I was being questions I kept thinking about how much my butt itched. I was able to get some relief by slightly moving my behind thinking no one would notice. Later Ashley would tell me that I not only kept jerking my body, but I was also making funny faces. Ashley and her mother tried to stop the interrogation by making related comments to help me give the right answers.

"Finally Mrs. Johnson served some cookies and ice tea, which pretty much ended Mr. Johnson's questions. When I reached for my glass of ice tea, which was on a glass coffee table in front of the sofa, it was necessary to slide forward scratching my butt for one brief second. That really felt good. In the next minute and a half I must have reached for the ice tea and put it back a dozen times. When I finished the ice tea I started on the cookies. By then the parents were talking about Ashley and some cute things she had done as a child. I was having trouble keeping up with the conversation because I couldn't stop thinking about how much my butt itched. Without realizing it whenever I got some relief from the itching I broke out in a big smile. Ashley would later tell me everyone noticed I was smiling and nodding my head at times that had nothing to do with what was being discussed. It gets worse.

"Mrs. Johnson got up saying she would get another pitcher of ice tea. At the same time I reached for the last cookie. In trying to bear down and drag my butt across the sofa seat to provide short time relief to my itching butt, I made a sound like a short fart. For an instance everyone froze. No one said anything and no one looked at me, but it was obvious everyone heard it. So now what should I do. I wanted to yell out look that wasn't a fart, but that didn't seem like a good idea. What I did do was even more stupid. I thought I could say something to Ashley that the Johnsons wouldn't hear as they were talking to each. So I asked Ashley if she heard that, meaning the fart sound. Ashley answered by asking heard what. I then said I don't know I didn't hear it either. Once again that caused a few seconds of awkward silence.

"In order to break the silence I asked Mr. Johnson a question about the farming business. With that he offered to show me around the place. That is something I really didn't want to do. I was still had not taken off my suit coat and I was wearing my best dress shoes. So I didn't want to walk around outside in dirt and pig shit. Regardless of that I agreed to take the tour. I though getting off the sofa would end my butt from itching. Unfortunately it did not. However, I did get up enough nerve to ask if anyone would mind if I took off my coat and tie.

"The barn yard tour wasn't that bad. I got to meet the family, cows, horses, pigs and chickens. Most of the animals ignored us except for a little chicken that kept following us. I learned a lot about tractors and combines, of course I'll never use that information. I'll admit the Johnsons farm was about as clean as a farm can be and Mr. Johnson was very knowledgeable as far as crops were concerned. By the time we finished the tour, dinner was almost ready.

"As soon as we got back in the house Mr. Johnson guided me to the bathroom door and told me to take my time because dinner wouldn't be ready for another fifteen minutes or so. It was obvious the bathroom had been prepared for me. The women must have used it while I was getting the barnyard tour. The whole room was smelled of fresh roses. I know because a can of fresh roses room spray was strategically placed right over the toilet. I'm sure the Johnsons thought I needed to take a dump and they were worried I would smell up the place. I didn't need to take a dump, but I did take about ten minutes scratching my butt. I didn't know how I could swing it, but there was no way I was going to sit on the sofa again. Everyone looked at me when I came out of the bathroom. They all seemed to be hoping I wouldn't fart again. At least they didn't ask me to use the outhouse instead of the inside bathroom. Nothing unusual happened during dinner except that everyone seemed to be eating as fast as they could and no one was talking.

"It was several days later before I got up enough nerve to call Ashley. Our relationship had cooled, so I told her I was leaving town. The junior college had set me up for a job in a warehouse loading and unloading furniture. I worked there the rest of the summer and then took a leave of absence until after the football season. I didn't see Ashley again until a couple of years later when I ran into her at a KU party."

"I was sorry to hear your marriage didn't work out. Do you still maintain contact with Ashley?" asked Brad.

"You mean besides sending her alimony checks?" answered Roger.

"Well, I thought you might give it another try. I understand over have of divorced people try to patch up differences and start over again."

"No chance of that. My only hope is that Ashley marries some other dummy so I can stop paying alimony. By the way, Brad, you and Ashley would make a good pair. As I said she has a great body and rich parents. How about giving her a call."

"Sorry Roger, I've lined up a good deal right here in town."

"Oh, that reminds me. Remember those two women I was talking to when you arrived. Well, they're going to meet us in the bar at 8:00 p.m. The both have rooms here, so if you play your cards right, your girl may invite you upstairs. I get the one in the green dress. I'll tell you something, the blue dress wanted to check you out before agreeing to come to the bar tonight. You don't have to worry, I could tell by the look she gave you that she will show."

"I can stay for one drink only then I'm heading straight home, alone. I'm on a short leash, so I don't have much time. I'm leaving after one drink or at 8:30 p.m., whichever comes first."

The women did show up a little ahead of time. After introductions they all squeezed into a small booth. The woman in the blue dress seemed to be in her early twenties. She was very nice looking and dressed well. It didn't take long before she mentioned that she was married, but that her husband had not accompanied her on this business trip. She pressed her body close to Brad as she slowly sipped her drink. It felt better than scratching an itchy butt. Brad was sorely tempted as described by what the Bible says, but he continued to resist. Early on he had announced that he would be leaving shortly, but he was still there at 9:00 p.m. Fortunately Roger wanted to order another round of drinks, which presented Brad with a good excuse to leave, which he did.

On the way back to his room Brad considered how easy it would have been to stay overnight with the woman in the blue dress. The fact that he didn't made him realize how close he had become to Linda. While thinking this he got an urge to call Linda to let her know he was on his way back to his place alone.

"So Linda you missed on a funny but sad story tonight. My old friend Roger hasn't changed much in the last three years, he is still a good story teller," Brad said as Linda answered the phone.

"I'm glad you had a good time. Will you be seeing him again? From what you say about him it would be interesting to meet him. Remember we're having dinner with the Belsons Thursday at the club."

"Yeah, I told him I wanted him to meet you. I'll try to get him to meet us at Tony's Wednesday night if that's all right with you. Roger would fit right in with the college crowd."

"Don't you think we should treat him to dinner at a nicer restaurant?"

"Roger won't mind Tony's. He will probably want to stay there after we leave."

After the call ended Linda wondered if Brad had told Roger about their age difference. By this time she wasn't too worried about it but hoped Roger wouldn't be surprised.

Late in the afternoon Tuesday Brad called Roger to confirm dinner Wednesday. That gave him an opportunity to let Roger know Linda was a little older than him.

"So, Roger, my friend, Linda is a little older than me, but she still has most of her teeth and can still get around without a walker," Brad said.

"That's all right with me. I can get to Tony's around 6:00 p.m. My seminar finishes tomorrow at noon, but then I have to pack up and check out of the hotel. That will only leave me an hour or so to say good-bye to my friend with the green dress."

When they all met at Tony's, Linda asked Roger about his job, which started him talking for a long time.

After high school graduation the junior college that Roger planned to attend arrange a summer job for him working in a furniture store warehouse. The school athletic department worked with local business to provide jobs to student athletics. The jobs were intended to keep the students in shape over the summer and to provide some spending money to supplement athletic scholarships. Roger continued to work part time at the job after the football season ended. The part time job continued until he graduated with a business degree from Kansas University. During that time Roger was able to advance from a warehouse floor laborer to an office staff member directing the store inventory. That provided him with an opportunity to learn a new computer application for an inventory system. By working with the computer people that were helping with the inventory program Roger was able to master the application. After graduating from KU he was hired by the computer company to market and help install the inventory application to new businesses.

"Just think of what might different our lives would have been if Brad had been hired at the furniture store instead of me. You would have missed out on all the fun of going to Iraq," said Roger.

"Boy, I really missed out. Maybe in my next life I'll be luckier," Brad answered.

Although he didn't mention it Brad was happy the way things turned out. He figured that if he had married instead of enlisting in the army he might have made the same mistakes Roger made. He was certain Linda had no bad habits and felt fortunate to have hooked up with her.

While listening to Roger's story Linda was thinking along the same lines. Maybe it wasn't too late for Brad to get a degree in information systems and become a highly paid consultant. She then realized she was assuming she and Brad would stay together after he got his degree. She also realized that she was thinking it would be better if Brad didn't go back on active duty with the army.

"Roger, are you married?" asked Linda.

"No, so I'm available in case you get tired of America's hero," answered Roger.

"Well, Brad doesn't have to worry for a while. Sorry, about my question I didn't mean to pry into your private life."

"That's all right. It might be interesting to talk about why my wife and I divorced. It's a long story, but I'll keep it short. My wife had a terrible secret that I didn't find out about until after we married. It had nothing to do with sex. As a matter of fact both of us agreed sex was the best part of the marriage.

"Ashley's parents gave us a very nice wedding including a honeymoon to Mexico. They even helped us with a down payment on a new house in Kansas City. The trouble started when we moved in. Before we were married, I never visited Ashley's room. She lived with another girl in a women-only school dorm, so we always got together at my place.

"Starting from the first day at our new house, it should have been apparent that Ashley was a packrat. Of course I thought it was just a temporary thing, but it got worse. We had decided that Ashley would take care of our finances since she hadn't been able to find a job after graduation and would have the time to do so. For the first several months, I deposited my paycheck in our checking account. Ashley put together a budget, which I never saw. Ashley allowed me to get a small allowance every payday. If I spent more than my allowance, I either had not spend any more money on myself or beg Ashley for more money. Actually that wasn't so bad. I stopped drinking, at least during the day, and I ate lunch at the company cafeteria. Most weekends and some week nights, we ate at nice restaurants. Ashley paid for those dinners.

"The big trouble started after a few months when I came home to find the electricity off in our house. This seemed strange since we had set up automatic payments from the checking account. Ashley said we would have to wait until my payday, four days away, before she would have money to pay the electric bill, including late and reconnect charges along with a deposit. Of course I wanted to know why we didn't have enough money to pay the bill. Ashley said it was because I didn't make enough money.

"The real story as I soon discovered was that Ashley was spending lavishly on personal items mostly for clothes. She had over a dozen dresses and a dozen shoes most of which she had never worn. It seems that if she saw a dress she liked she would buy three different colors of the same dress. She even bought me a number of shirts and pants but neglected to tell me. By this time, I stopped ignoring the mess she was creating around the house. It seems she never threw anything away. Paper sacks, empty cans, and bottles were in every room. There was even unwrapped partially eaten food in the refrigerator. I'm sure there would have been dirty dishes in the sink if I hadn't been told it was my job to wash all the dishes. It gets worse.

"After looking into our finances, I found we owed all utilities and had about $20,000 of credit card debt. I told Ashley I was going to open up a new bank account in my name only to deposit my paychecks and that I was cancelling all of our credit cards. In addition, our roles would be reversed as far as far as finances are concerned. That's when Ashley said I didn't love her and she was going home to her parents. The end result is that I lost Ashley, the house, the car, and all the new clothes Ashley had bought for me. I also got stuck for all the bills including half of Ashley's student loan not to mention alimony. So that's my sad story, of course that's my side of the story. I don't know what Ashley would tell you, but I'd really be interested to hear how she would rationalize her actions. Incidentally Brad, have you ever been to Linda's house?"

"Yeah, I checked her out and other than having 250 pairs of shoes she's almost normal," said Brad.

"Well then, Linda, have you ever been inside Brad's room?" Roger asked.

"You know I never have. I've always wondered what he's hiding there. Guess I better stop by sometime, Brad," said Linda.

"I'd really like to have you over, but unfortunately as I've said many times, the government won't allow nonmilitary people inside the transit facilities because of top secret activities that go on there," Brad joked.

Roger's story about his divorce started Linda thinking about what if Brad had some mysterious secrets. Linda had never asked Brad if he had any student loans or other debt that she would be partially responsible for if they married. Joan had also warned her about the possibility that Brad may have suffered from posttraumatic stress disorder. Linda decided that it may be time to find out more about Brad. She decided to have a serious talk with Brad after she got up enough nerve to ask him if he wanted to use her washer and dryer. Then she had another idea. She would encourage Brad to move some of his clothes to her house to see if he was neat or sloppy about his personal items. By this time, Brad was spending four or five nights at her house, so it just made sense that he should leave some of his belongings there.

Brad, on the other hand, didn't give much thought about Linda having some dark secrets. He was as naive as Roger had been before his marriage.

After finishing dinner, Roger said he was going to head back to the airport for his flight back to Kansas City. Unfortunately for him, he didn't have time to meet any of the college girls in the restaurant. However, before they left the restaurant, Linda excused herself to go to the restroom. That gave Roger an opportunity to tell Brad what he thought of Linda.

"Brad, you sure picked out a winner in Linda. She looks good, smells good, dresses very well and, best of all, she has class. By that I mean she knows how to talk to people making them feel comfortable. So that said, I'd like to buy her from you. I'd give you all the money I have or will ever make. Is that a deal?" asked Roger.

"Seriously, do you really think she is so nice?" asked Brad.

"Yeah, she impressed me as being very nice. To be truthful, I did notice that she was a little older than you when I first saw her, but I quickly forgot about it. Are you thinking about staying with her after graduation?"

"Yeah, I'm thinking about it, but that's a long way away. It also depends on what she wants. I hope it doesn't come down to having to choose between her and the army."

"Well, that will be your decision. If it were me, I'd stick with the babe."

On the way home, Brad asked if Linda would like to stop by his room, just to make sure it wasn't a mess. Linda passed on that suggestion saying she wanted a rain check for some time in the future.

Linda did say she felt sorry for Roger because of him losing everything in the divorce. Brad agreed it was unfortunate but said Roger seemed to have recovered nicely. She then asked Brad if he ever felt bad about not following Roger's path instead of joining the army.

"No, I never have had second thoughts about joining the army when I did. It's hard to explain, but I felt I did the right thing and I'm very proud of what the U.S. accomplished in Iraq. I can't believe I would feel better designing new computerized applications," said Brad.

Linda decided to change the subject. This wasn't the time to get into a serious and complicated political discussion about if it was a mistake for the United States to attack Iraq. However, she knew that that subject would have to come up again.

"You know I was just thinking since you've been spending most nights with me, maybe you should move some of your clothes into one of my closets. That way you wouldn't have to stop by your room before going to class on weekdays. You should even use my washer and dryer so you don't have to go to the laundromat," said Linda.

"Actually, I was about to suggest the same thing. If it doesn't cause you any problems, I would like to leave some things at your place. The timing is just right. November is one of the months that I do laundry."

"Tell me you're joking and that you do your laundry more than once a month."

"Okay, I really don't let my laundry pile up several months. However, I don't have much laundry. I take most of my clothes to the cleaners. That way I don't have much to iron."

Linda felt good about resolving the laundry issue, now she had to think about how to learn a little more about Brad without asking direct questions.

Thursday's environmental class only lasted an hour. Scott said he wanted give the students time to plan for his Saturday party. However, he did ask Linda and Brad to stay for a while to go over the list of food and other items they had agreed to bring to the party. The party wouldn't start until 7:00 p.m. but Linda and Brad promised to get there by 6:00 p.m. to help set up the food and decorations.

That was a very busy week for Linda. After taking a couple of days to recover from the Diane trip there was the Roger Reid dinner tonight's dinner at the club and then Scott Watson's Saturday party. Next would be church services Sunday morning and then Sunday evening the church party. She couldn't remember a time that so many unrelated social events had occurred in a single week.

While they were getting ready for dinner Linda told Brad he could use the closet, the dresser and the bathroom medicine cabinet that had been Larry's. She also thought it a good idea to let Brad know her schedule and to let him know about the maintenance work around the house that be happening.

Most Sunday mornings there was church services. Monday was housecleaning. Three ladies would spend about three hours from about 9:00 a.m. to noon at the house. Tuesday and Thursday there were school classes. Wednesdays the landscape crew took care of the yard and patio during the day and there was grocery shopping in the afternoon. Every other Friday was hair salon day. Alternate Saturday mornings were spent working out with Joan at the club.

The house was at the crown of a cul-de-sac facing north. The houses on the sides were angled northeast and northwest, so the side windows of the houses did not match up. The master bedroom was upstairs on the east side. Diane's bedroom was next on the south side, followed by a bathroom and then a guest room. On the far west side was a second master type bedroom also with private bath. That room would be used by Linda's parents when they visited. The stairs ended on the west side closest to the second master bedroom.

Downstairs as you came in the front door the living room was on the right followed by the dining room. The stirs were in the middle of the entry hall angling to the left. The family room was on the left followed by a small breakfast nook. The kitchen was on the south side between the nook and dining room. North of the family room behind a door was the laundry room, which also served as a pass through to the garage. The garage could house three vehicles. Currently the BMW and Diane's Ford Focus used two of the spaces. The remainder of the garage space was used for storage.

If Brad moved in with Linda there would still be room for the Dowlings and Linda to live there also even though it would be quite awkward.

CHAPTER 18

Thursday night by design the Belsons, Linda, and Brad got to the club before the other couples because Joan wanted to make an announcement. Henry was going to get an award from his company for outstanding accomplishments during the past year. The award included a two week vacation in Europe. Joan went on to say that they wouldn't be able to take the trip until next summer, which was the least busy time of the year for Henry's business. Waiting until the summer would also allow Hannah to accompany them.

Brad proposed a toast to congratulate Henry when drinks were served. Joan then asked Henry to explain what he did to deserve the award. Henry seemed a little embarrassed by the request, but he did give a brief explanation.

"Well, to be truthful, it seems the annual award is more of less passed around between all regional partners. I hadn't won before, so the executive partners probably figured it was my turn. Basically the award is for exceeding regional annual goals and objectives. The Partnership' fiscal year ended September 30, so the results weren't compiled until last month," Henry explained.

Henry by nature was a soft spoken humble man. He was smart enough to qualify for scholarships to get through undergraduate and graduate school along with some part time teaching when he was in graduate school. He and Joan met when she was working part time in the school bookstore to help pay for her education. The bookstore didn't pay very much, but by working there she got a 50 percent reduction on tuition and school supplies.

After he received his MBA degree, Henry was hired by one of the biggest CPA firms in the United States. For the first two years, Henry worked long hours at relatively low pay to qualify for his CPA certificate.

During that time he was required to travel quite a bit around the eastern part of the country. Joan often joined him when she could get time off work. Henry stayed with the firm and over a number of years and was able to able to advance to a partner level in charge of the western region. By that time, Hannah had arrived. Joan no longer had to help support the family finances by working and was able to become a stay-at-home mom, something she enjoyed.

As Henry and Joan were discussing their life, Linda started comparing it to her life. For the most part she had led an idyllic sheltered life. Her father had arranged for her to skip kindergarten and start grade school at the first grade level. Because she possessed a quick mind she was able to keep up with her classmates. She even graduated from high school with honors and started college just before her eighteenth birthday. At first her mother had visited her every month at her apartment close to the Stanford campus. That year Christmas was spent in Chicago. Linda wanted to get ready to resume classes the first week of January, so she returned to her apartment alone a few days before New Year's Eve. That turned out to be a major turning point in her live.

Linda was surprised to see several of her girlfriends at the school library where she was doing researching for one of her classes. The friends invited her to a New Year's party at a fraternity house that they would be attending. Linda thought that would be fun hoping a boy she had dated a few times would be there. His name was Larry Wallace. She had planned on leaving just after midnight.

Things started to go downhill as soon as she arrived at the party with two of her girlfriends. They were told there was a $10 charge for the party. Just then three men appeared who offered to pay for the girls to get in. Larry was one of the men. The girls should have realized that, in essence, the men were buying them for the evening, but they choose to ignore the danger.

At this point Linda forced those thoughts out of her mind. It was very painful remembering how Larry seduced her. She had never talked to anyone about that night, not even her mother. For some reason, however, she knew she would eventually talk about it to Brad.

About that time the Fellers and Smiths arrived. After exchanging greetings they spent of the evening talking about club activities, current events and other general subjects. Dinner was over before 10:00 p.m. The Belsons picked up Hannah from her friend's house on the way home. After that Brad and Linda were just glad to get home and go to bed early, which they did do.

Without planning to do so, Linda and Brad had developed a bedtime pattern. After a little foreplay if they were to have sex they would then spend up to an hour or more talking. It seems they both had many things to talk about. For an instant Linda considered talking about how she got pregnant. However, she let the opportunity pass by.

Friday Brad and Linda tried to think of something to bring or do at Scott's party the next night. They decided to have the students participate in an ice breaker game. As each person arrived Scott would paste a sticky note with the name of a cartoon character on their back. They were told to not tell anyone what name was on anyone else's back. When the game began everyone was asked to find out what name was on their own back by asking questions that could only be answered yes or no by other students. The real object of the game was to get students to talk to each other, so only one question could be asked of any one individual. The first person figuring out the correct name on their back would win the grand prize, a bunch of bananas. Scott would be the judge.

The only other thing they could think of was to bring some natural fruits and nuts from the local environmental store. As it turned out none of the other students had any environmental related ideas either. They must have realized that the environmental theme was only a ploy to get the students to have a partly at his house.

As promised, Brad and Linda did get to Scott's house an hour before the other students. That gave them plenty of time to set up the food and explain the game to Scott who liked the idea. Enough sticky notes had been prepared for all party attendees. Most Disney cartoon characters were represented on the notes along with a number of other characters.

Several minutes were spent trying to decide appropriate character names for students. Brad thought Hansel and Gretel would be good stickers for Jason Olson and Kathy Dugan. Scott said he had the perfect students for the Mortimer Snerd and Pinocchio stickers. Scott couldn't help but laugh thinking about names he would assign to other students. Brad was assigned Superman, and Linda got Wonder Woman by Scott. Although they would play the game, they would not try to win.

The game as intended did create a lot of interaction. Scott got uncontrollable giggles when the student with the Mortimer Snerd sticker mistakenly asked if he was Prince Charming. One of the students asked Brad if his character was alive. Brad said all characters were fictional or cartoon characters, so all were dead. The student was allowed to ask another question, so he asked what year his character died. Brad simply answered yes as he reverted to the rules.

Surprisingly the game lasted almost an hour before someone finally figured the correct name on their back. The rest of the night was spent dancing after the food was gone. Scott made a rule that after the first dance everyone had to dance the next four dances with four different partners. Linda was worried that no one would want to dance with her, but she was mistaken. When the second dance started a boy yelled out he wanted to dance with Wonder Woman. Although it took until the fourth dance, Scott finally got his chance with Linda. Of course all the girls wanted to dance with Superman.

For the rest of the semester many students were stuck with their sticker note names. Even Scott played along often calling students by sticker names. Unfortunately he couldn't help but laugh the one time he called on Mortimer Snerd.

On the way home Linda said she really enjoyed talking to the students and thought all of them were very nice. Beside Scott she said she danced with Red Rider and Elmer Fudd. Even Scott was a gentleman the entire evening. Brad said he didn't get close to the girls he danced with, so he wondered how Linda knew the names of her dancing partners. Knowing he was teasing her Linda punched him in arm.

They were in bed before 11:00 p.m. because Sunday would be a busy day. Church in the morning, football games on TV for Brad, and then the church party that evening.

The next morning they discussed that night's party.

"You know I have an assignment to bring some kind of salad for twenty-five people," Linda said.

"Assigned? Who made that assignment?" asked Brad.

"This is a potluck party, so all couples are asked to bring one dinner course. I got salad. Because there are expected to be about two hundred attendees, every couple is asked to bring a certain amount of food for one dinner course. Eight of us will each bring enough for twenty-five people to cover the two hundred guests expected."

"Wait a minute if the other ninety-two couples each bring enough food for twenty-five people that would be enough for over two thousand guests."

"No, this has already been figured out in the past. Not everyone brings enough for twenty-five guests. There are forty people bringing only enough main course food for five. That's because the unit cost of say steak is so much more than that salad. The dessert, drinks, and supplies will be divided up among the remaining fifty-two couples. Based on history of past events it's assumed all two hundred guests will have two drinks and two desserts apiece. Got it?"

"Yeah, that makes sense. Somebody must have spent a lot time figuring this out."

"We've been doing this several years and it always seems to work out. By the way the other half of each couple, that means you, Brad, have some duties. Someone has to arrange food on the buffet line, set the tables, and, best of all, clean up after dinner."

"Nice of you to warn me. I'll remember to bring an apron. Do the cleanup guys get to eat the leftover food?"

"The leftover food is taken home by some of the guests, so you better eat as much as you can before they stop serving."

"Who is bringing the Champagne, wine and beer?"

"This is a church-sponsored event, so there will not be any alcohol, so don't plan on bringing your own bottle of spirits."

"Okay, I'll just have to get soused before we get there."

"You'll enjoy the party without getting drunk. You know some of the people that will attend and everyone is always very nice. Of course the hugger will be there. That is the one person I'd rather not be around."

"The hugger? You mean some guy goes around hugging people?"

"Yeah, he's also called the groper. The guy is only a little over five feet tall, so when he hugs women, he rests his head on their bosom. One hug is bad enough, but he wants to hug everyone good-bye as the party ends. The last time he hugged me, I noticed his hands over my rear end."

"Does this guy go around hugging people Sundays at church?"

"Not anymore. Pastor Rogers finally had a talk with him and pointed out that not everyone wants to be hugged. The story I heard was that the guy talked for about an hour explaining hugging has therapeutic value and that he's doing favors by hugging and that everyone benefits even if they don't know it. Despite that Pastor Rogers said if he continues to hug people at church he would be arrested."

"So why will he be allowed to hug people at the party?"

"The hugger maintains the party is not the same as a church service and no one has complained to him."

"If he tries to hug me I will. Not only that. I'll choke him out if he tries it with you."

Linda wasn't sure if Brad was serious, so she quickly asked him to promise to not do that.

Sunday they attended the early church service. After the service most everyone talked about the church party later that day. It made Brad think of how high school kids acted getting ready for a prom. He mentioned this to Linda on the way back to Linda's place.

"Well, you know, Brad, even though most of the people have known each other for years, they don't socialize much outside of Sunday church services. A couple of years ago, the congregation was over a thousand, but it's down to under five hundred now. We haven't been able to attract new members as the older ones die and other members move away. It seems the younger generations have become less religious and more secular. Pretty soon you and I may be the only ones left," Linda said.

Brad thought to himself Pastor Williams and other church members were so nice to him thinking maybe he would become a church member. Brad felt somewhat like a fish that had been hooked and was being slowly reeled in. Like a fisherman, the pastor didn't want to try and yank him into membership and risk driving him away instead. Brad also didn't miss Linda's comment about continuing to be together.

"Yeah, it's kind of sad that religion means so little to the younger generation," Brad said.

They stopped at a grocery store to pick up the readymade salad Linda had ordered along with about a dozen bottles of different type salad dressing. Linda would bring a couple of combination spoon/fork utensils for serving the salad to the partly. By 4:00 p.m. they left for the party. Dinner was scheduled to be served at 6:00 p.m., which would allow two hours to set up the buffet serving line and then socialize with other guests.

Brad spent most of the first hour helping arrange the food. As one of the younger members he willing assumed the role of moving heavy objects into place. The task went quickly since everyone bringing food arrived on time and it seems like everyone, but Brad knew how to arrange the food.

Brad found Linda with a small group who happened to be discussing politics. Someone said they thought the United States should leave Iraq and never go back.

"Would you serve in Iraq if the draft started again," someone asked Brad. Many of the members knew Brad played football for Cal State, but neither he nor Linda had mentioned that he had served in the army in Iraq.

Linda answered for him, "Brad already served in Iraq for two tours of duty, so he may not have to go back."

"Actually, I wouldn't mind going back to finish our task over there if it's still going on when I finish college," Brad said.

For several seconds no one said anything until the hugger showed up. Brad was intially glad to see him since it ended an awkward silence. That thought changed quickly as everyone started getting hugged.

"Someone new. I haven't met you before. I guess you know I'm a hugger, so I'll have to give you a big hug," said the man.

"Well, I'm not a hugger," said Brad as he put his hand on the hugger's chest holding him at arms length.

"Well, it's still early. I'll get you later," said the man as he sauntered off toward another group.

The group Brad had been talking too had quickly separated in order to get away from the hugger. Linda was talking to a couple Brad recognized, so he joined them. They were discussing a movie that neither Brad nor Linda had seen. The couple took about five minutes describing the movie and then it was time to start lining up at the buffet food line.

The party was pretty much over by 9:00 p.m. Brad has just finished washing the salad utensils when he caught a quick movement out of the corner of his eye. The sixth sense he had developed in Iraq caused him to turn around quickly. It was just in time to see the hugger approaching with his arms wide open.

"I told you I get you sometime tonight," the hugger said as he lunged forward.

Brad was able to use his left arm to stop the pending hug. This time Brad grabbed the top of the hugger's shirt with his fist. He yanked upward until his fist was under the hugger's chin causing the hugger to stand on tip toes. Brad then put his face within six inches of the hugger and looked him directly in the eye.

"If you touch me, you little pervert, I'll break your neck. It's time you go home. You're going to walk directly out the door behind you when I let go. If you stop, I'll be right behind you, so I can pick you up and throw you out the door," Brad said in a low voice.

That worked. The hugger left without even saying bye to anyone. Fortunately no one had seen or heard that encounter. Brad had been careful to speak softly and to not use any profanity in a church environment. However, he was surprised or actually shocked at how quickly his mood had changed to being overly aggressive. Maybe he was experiencing post dramatic stress. Possibly he hadn't felt that before because he had been able to release any anger that might have built up by playing football. Brad really wasn't that mad at the hugger, so he knew he acted much too strongly.

On the way home Brad did mention that he had confronted the hugger but did not go into details. However, he did tell Linda he had remembered his promise to her to not kill the guy.

Tuesday at school Linda asked Brad if he would like to attend a play at the Music Center that Sunday evening. For several years the Larry had season tickets to the winter schedule of plays. The tickets renewed each year unless cancelled. Brad said he would like to go and offered to pay for the tickets, not realizing that the tickets had already been billed to Linda.

The rest of the week was uneventful and seemed to drag by. There wouldn't be any classes the following week due to the Thanksgiving holiday. That Wednesday Linda and Brad would leave for Las Vegas, so Brad planned on staying at Linda's Sunday through Tuesday.

Finally it was Sunday. Brad had stayed overnight so he could attend church with Linda. In the afternoon Brad watched football on TV while Linda straightened up the house and then got ready to go to the play.

Brad wore his best suit, a white shirt, light blue tie and shined black business shoes. Linda wore a stunning white knee length dress and white high-heeled shoes. She chose to wear her gold watch on her left wrist and a gold bracelet on the right wrist. Brad thought she looked like a fashion model.

Linda and Brad got to their seats just before the play began at the Music Center. They had planned on getting there a little early, but the show was sold-out, causing traffic to be heavier than expected. Brad joked that he was sorry they didn't have time to look for the Iranians they ran into when visiting the center with Brad's army friends. Brad did notice, however, that everyone was very nicely and appropriately dressed. Most of the crowd was middle-aged to elderly with only a few Brad's age.

The play was entertaining, the costumes were very elaborate, and the actors very professional. Time passed quickly, so it was soon intermission. Linda looked for an opening to stand next to a high table while Brad went after two glasses of wine.

"Linda Wallace is that you?" someone called to Linda.

It took several seconds for Linda to find who called to her. It turned out to be two middle-aged women that Linda knew from several political and social events that Larry had taken her to in the past.

"Hello, Carol and Mary. Yes, it's me, so nice to see you. I assume Ken and Ted have gone after some refreshments," replied Linda.

"Yes, they should show up in a shortly. Mary and I captured a table to rest our drinks on. Please join us. Is Larry here?" Carol Olsen asked.

Linda hadn't expected to see anyone she knew, so she initially wasn't sure how best to answer the question.

"No, you know Larry and I have finalized our divorce. I'm here with my friend, Brad. I'll introduce him to you when he finds me with our refreshments," Linda answered.

About that time Ken Olsen and Ted Williams got to the table. Carol and Mary had asked for wine while Ken and Ted chose scotch and water.

"Linda Wallace, how nice to see you. Is Larry with you?" Ken asked.

"Linda's with a friend that will join us shortly," Carol answered for Linda.

"Nice to see both of you. I hadn't expected to see anyone I knew here. I thought you all normally attend the Saturday night plays," said Linda.

"We usually do, but the boys wanted to attend a football game last night," said Mary.

"That's interesting. My friend plays for football for Cal State. He plays linebacker and sometime something called tight end," said Linda

Just then Brad appeared with two glasses of wine. When seeing the two men were drinking mixed drinks he immediately felt like a wimp drinking wine. He felt like telling Linda he had two glasses of wine for her and that he would go back for his drink. Of course he did not do that.

"Brad, I'd like you to meet some dear friends, Ken and Carol Olsen and Mary and Ted Williams," said Linda.

After handshakes and introductory comments the expected question was asked.

"How do you two know each other?" asked Mary.

"Brad is one of my classmates at Cal State. Now that Diane has started her freshman year at Stanford I decided to finish my last two years and get a degree. We're celebrating the completion of a class project," Linda answered.

The Olsens and Williams couldn't help but notice the age difference between Linda and Brad but didn't seem to be too surprised. Brad also noticed a marked age difference between the men and women. Ken and Ted both seemed to be about twenty years older than their wives. That also didn't bother Brad.

"Linda, going back to college is a great idea. It took me ten years to get a BA degree, but I'm glad I did now. I wouldn't have kept going without Carol's encouragement. What are you studying?" Ken asked.

"I have enough credits from Stanford to be an English major, so I'll probably continue that major. Ted, I'm interested to know if you still like being mayor," said Linda in an attempt to change the subject.

The previous year Ted had been elected mayor of one of the cities surrounding Los Angeles. Linda couldn't remember the name of the city.

"You know it's not as much fun as I thought it would be. Putting up with Mary was hard enough now I have to try to please the whole city even though everyone wants something different. Brad what are you planning to do when you finish college? I hope you don't plan on getting into politics," Ted said.

Brad decided to give a simple answer and then wait for more questions.

"Well, if I ever do get into politics it won't be for a while. I've signed an agreement to go back on active duty in the army first since they are paying for my college education," Brad answered.

"You know a military career wouldn't be so bad if you can stay out of harm's way. I assume you've already served a tour in Iraq," said Ted.

"Brad's actually served two tours," Linda said before she could stop herself.

This caused the group to glance at Linda since her comment made it clear that Brad was more than just a friend.

"Brad it sounds like you have a lot in common with Ken who served in Vietnam and then stayed around for Gulf War I," said Ted.

About that time a bell rang indicating intermission was over. As the group started back to their seats, Joan told Linda she would call her to get together shortly after the first of the year. She said Ken and Brad could talk football and war stories while they discussed fashions and cooking. Linda knew Carol was joking about discussing fashions and cooking, but she could tell Carol really would like to see them again.

On the way home after the play Linda told Brad a little more about the Olsens and Williams. The couples belonged to a charity group Larry joined several years ago. The couples were very easy to talk to and seemed to know everyone in the charity group. They helped Larry meet several people that later became clients of Larry's law practice. The also all got together several times a year for social occasions. They were good friends but not as close as the friendship with the Belsons. Linda mentioned to Brad that Carol and Mary were second wives for Ken and Ted and were about twenty years younger than the men.

Linda was thinking to herself that Carol could tell her somethings about being a military wife. She remembered Carol mentioning that Ken was a retired military officer. If Linda did ask Carol about military life for spouses it would divulge how serious she was about staying with Brad. She thought she could confide in Carol but wouldn't want Brad to know about such a discussion.

Brad also had some ideas about how Linda could experience life as a military wife. Assuming they got along well on the Las Vegas and New York trips they would start planning a summer trip across the United States. Brad hadn't mentioned this to Linda yet, but he needed to attend a two-week army training session in June. The training would be at Fort Carson Colorado or Fort Riley Kansas. If Linda accompanied him she would get a good feel for army life and also live away from a big city. Brad would discuss this with Linda after the first of the year.

Monday morning Linda and Brad didn't get up until around 8:00 a.m. After breakfast Brad left to spend some time working out in the gym and then to shop for some clothes. Linda tided up the house and then started paying bills and reconciling bank accounts. She was still involved with that when Brad returned about noon.

"So, Linda, why are you writing checks to pay all your bills?" asked Bill.

"Well, Brad, you see it I don't pay the bills the utilities will be shut off and we'll be kicked out of the house for nonpayment of the mortgage," answered Linda.

"I know the bill have to be paid, but why not use automatic payments for the utilities and most other monthly bills? Do you know how that works?"

Brad went on to explain the procedure and then set up automatic payments for Linda. He then offered to set up a computer spreadsheet that could take the place of a check payment book. He even offered to write a budget program for her. Other connecting spreadsheets could be written to summarize investments and net worth.

Linda had to think about the request for several seconds. Letting Brad set up such a spreadsheet would let him know everything about her finances. Like most people Linda didn't like to share that information with others. She had disclosed some financial information to Henry Belson when he helped her negotiate divorce financial agreements, but she was sure Henry would never discuss that information with anyone else not even Joan. But then Linda thought it might be good for Brad to know that she was wealthy and could afford to spend her money when they were together and when they took trips. Besides she knew she needed some help handling finances to eliminate wasteful spending and to review investments made by her financial advisor.

"Okay, let's start with a budget. I'll have to tell you I really don't know how much I normally spend for utilities and other items. Larry had all household payments sent to his office. He said something about needing that information so he could write some of it off as a business expense since he did use part of the house as an office."

"So how do you know if you're spending more than you take in?"

"Well, my financial advisor said when my checking balance gets above $20,000 I should buy another Certificate of Deposit for $10,000. Actually since I don't always post payments to my checkbook I just use the month end balance on my checking account."

Brad knew this is not a good practice. Whatever balance the bank statement shows is not accurate by the time the statement arrives in the mail. Any deposits or payments made after the first of the month are not reflected. However, in Linda's case the monthly income appears to have always exceeded her expenses. Even so, it was going to take some time to put her financial transactions in order.

"Okay, for the budget let's first post your annual income. I assume you have some interest and investment income."

"Yes, but I don't use any of that for monthly expenses. I just leave the interest in my savings and the investment income is reinvested or used to buy new stock or bonds."

"Well, that's going to make it easier. Besides alimony and child support do you have any other income like rental property, repayment of loans or anything like that?"

"All I have is alimony. Since Larry is taking care of Diane while she is in college I agreed to not accept any child support. The divorce settlement required Larry to pay $2,000 a month for Diane's support until she is twenty-five years old or marries, whichever comes first."

"Okay, how much should I put down for alimony for the year?"

Linda knew that once she gave out this information nothing else financial could be kept secret. However, she had gone this far, and this may be the best time to see what Brad's thoughts might be as far as their future is concerned.

"I get $480,000 a year. Larry has $40,000 deposited in my checking the first business day of each month."

"It took Brad a few seconds to comprehend how much money that is. He knew Linda was rich, but he was thinking her alimony would be less than $200,000 a year. He had to be careful to not look surprised, but he couldn't stop his voice from shaking when he continued the questing.

"Linda we might want to stop with the budget right now. With that income I doubt you will ever have to worry about overspending. However, if we continue maybe we can find ways to end any wasteful or frivolous spending. Would you like to continue?"

"Yeah, it's important I know where my money is going. Maybe we can also verify that my financial advisor is investing my money the best way."

At this time both Brad and Linda knew that if they were to marry the alimony would stop and Linda's lifestyle would immediately have to change. If Brad did return to the military his income would never come close to what Linda would lose in alimony.

Linda had some additional thoughts however. Her savings interest and investment income along with Brad's earnings might meet her current spending. In other words if she used interest and investment income for living expenses instead of reinvesting it would somewhat offset the alimony loss. The financial review Brad was conducting should tell her if that was a reasonable assumption. The financial review would also reveal an additional cash savings from reduced income taxes, something Linda hadn't yet considered.

The two struggled for the next three hours trying to find relevant financial information to complete the budget, prepare investment and savings schedules and to reconcile the latest bank statements. The budget they came up with is as follows:

Linda Wallace 2005 Budget	
Revenue	
Alimony	$ 480,000
Interest	48,000
Reinvest	(48,000)
Investments	156,000
Reinvest	(156,000)
Total	$ 480,000
Expenses	
Cable TV	3,600
Cash	15,000
Church	12,000
Clothes	12,000
Club Fee & Extras	12,000
College costs	24,000
Contingency	12,000
Donations	12,000
Electric	3,000
Entertainment	18,000
Gas	2,400
Gasoline	3,600
Groceries	6,000
House Maintence	6,000
Insurance	12,000
Mortgage	57,000
Repairs	12,000
Restaurants	6,000
Savings	55,800
Taxes Fed & State	162,000
Travel	30,000
Water	3,600
Total	$ 480,000
Net Income/(Loss)	$ -

Later Linda would rework the budget assuming loss of alimony, using interest and investment income for living expenses, selling the house, and finishing school. Additional expenses incurred by Brad would be covered by Brad's income.

Linda Wallace 2005 Revised Budget		
Revenue		
Interest		48,000
Investments		156,000
Total	$	204,000
Expenses		
Cable TV	$	3,600
Cash		15,000
Church		12,000
Clothes		12,000
Contingency		12,000
Donations		12,000
Electric		3,000
Entertainment		12,000
Gas		2,400
Gasoline		3,600
Groceries		6,800
House Maintence		6,000
Insurance		6,000
Repairs		12,000
Restaurants		6,000
Savings		16,000
Taxes Fed & State		30,000
Travel		30,000
Water		3,600
Total	$	204,000
Net Income/(Loss)	$	-

Even though Linda's revised budged would have to be reworked when actual circumstances were known, it did indicate that the loss of alimony would not be as dramatic as first thought. The most important assumption here is that interest rates would not drop to zero and that the stock market would not crash.

When putting together the investment schedule Brad noticed that there were large amounts invested in tax free government and municipal bonds along with a tax free annuity. Those were safe investments but produced lower returns than equity investments. Reduced income taxes partially offset the lower returns.

The savings schedule included a jumbo $500,000 five-year CD, which increased the overall effective interest rate. Brad didn't have any investment expertise, but he could see that it might be a good idea to move some savings to equity investments where there was a chance for appreciation on the initial investment. Of course you would be gambling that the stocks would not lose value.

Linda explained that Henry Belson recommended a financial advisor that helped her transfer the investments and savings accounts to her name when the divorce became final. Henry also set quarterly income tax payments for her and recommended the amount to submit each quarter. In addition Henry offered to do what she and Brad are now doing, that is setting up investment and savings schedules putting together a budget and reconciling bank accounts. However, Linda didn't want to impose any more on Henry's generosity. It was bad enough getting this much help for free, so she didn't think it right to continue to have Henry help her out. She was grateful for Henry's help and was thankful Henry didn't assign one of his firm's junior accounts to work with Linda.

By this time Linda was in full confession mode. She felt this was a good time to let Brad know some more about Larry.

"You know I never realized how much money Larry was making until the divorce. He had always been a good provider and never challenged any of my spending. Of course just by nature I was never a big spender. Since Larry made all of our money after graduating from law school, I didn't have to understand anything about our financial position.

"Looking back I think the big opportunity for Larry to start making lots of money happened a couple of years after he had started a law practice with his college friend, Fred Farman. It seems at that time Fred was divorcing his wife. Larry was able to buy out Fred's share of the business for a really low price. The net worth of business was close to zero because they were still paying off start-up costs. Fred agreed for the low buyout amount for a couple of reasons. His wife would get half of his assets at the divorce date, so he wasn't interested in taking a large cash payment. Instead Larry promised to direct a prime account and a number of future clients to Fred once he had established a new business. That is the only shady business deal Larry ever made as far as I know. Of course his personal dealings were a different matter.

"About two years ago, Larry's father retired and turned his law practice over to Larry. That required consolidating his practice with his father's and moving to the San Francisco area. I was all right with that, but I wanted to wait until Diane finished high school. Larry said it would take a couple of years to move his local practice to San Francisco, so he would have to travel between the cities every week. The plan was for Larry to spend the weekends here and as many more days as possible here. Larry did spend most weekends here, but most weekdays he stayed up north. That summer Diane and I visited him several times. He had rented a one-bedroom apartment close to the San Francisco office. These visits stopped once Diane started back to high school. Over the next year, Larry began spending more weekends in San Francisco. I really didn't mind. Taking care of Diane took up most of my time, but I found when she was in school I had a lot of free time to do whatever I wanted.

"Cindy came into the picture last spring. One Friday she called me and introduced herself as Larry's administrative assistant. She then said Larry had asked her to call and let me know that Larry had to go to an emergency meeting in Denver so he wouldn't be able to spend the weekend with me. That seemed a little unusual. I knew that there were several female lawyers, paralegals and clerical help in both offices, but Larry had never had anyone of them deliver messages to me. When I gave it some thought later I felt Cindy saying he wouldn't have time to spent the weekend with me was an unusual way to say Larry wouldn't be able to come home that weekend.

"The following Friday I asked Joan to let Diane stay with her over the weekend and then made a surprise visit to see Larry. It turned out the surprise was on me. When I got to Larry's office about noon I was told Larry has just left and was going to do some work at his apartment before catching a late afternoon flight to Los Angeles. Instead of calling Larry I decided to just go to his apartment and surprise him there. Guess what, Cindy answered the door. Larry started to explain that Cindy was there to pick up some papers to take back to the office. Larry had trouble explaining why Cindy's clothes were on the floor in the bedroom and in the closet. At that time Cindy gave a sweet speech saying I might as well know that Larry was going to divorce me and marry her.

"For the next six months Larry kept telling me he didn't want a divorce and never told Cindy he would marry her. During that time I hired a divorce attorney and had Larry served with the papers. Perhaps I wasn't thinking logically, but I never thought of continuing our marriage. I'm now sure that I did the right thing and have never thought of reconciling with him.

"I knew I was at a disadvantage in the divorce proceedings. Larry knew many divorce lawyers and could have made it really bad for me, but to his credit I believe he was fair. He said he just wanted to get the over with because by that time he had decided to marry Cindy. My attorney, Jason Clark said got a good deal, better than expected. I think Larry felt a little guilty about not paying more attention to me during our marriage and about his extramarital affairs," Linda finished talking, thinking she had said enough by this time.

"I'm sure divorces are hard on everyone emotionally, but it seems you have come through it without being bitter. Life goes on, so you can look for good things to happen in the future," said Brad.

"Are you hungry enough for supper? I can have something ready in about forty-five minutes," Linda said wanting to get off the subject.

"Oh, I'm not sure. Maybe I could eat a few hamburgers and a bucket of French fries."

"No hamburgers tonight, will a steak with a baked potato and big salad do?"

"You know it will. How about if I go to the store and get a jug of beer?"

"Okay, but don't be too long."

While Brad was gone both Linda and Brad were thinking along the same lines. Even though neither of them had ever mentioned the possibility of getting married they both had that in the back of their minds. Now that Linda had opened up to Brad with personal information Brad felt he had to let Linda in on some on the things he had planned for the futures. The biggest concern Brad had was how to explain that he would never be rich certainly nowhere near the status Linda currently enjoyed. Going to the grocery did give Brad time to think of what he should tell Linda.

During most of dinner, they talked about the Las Vegas trip. Linda had confirmed all their reservations. Her big problem was what clothes and jewelry to take and how many pieces of luggage she would need. Brad could have gotten ready to leave that night, so he wondered why Linda hadn't already made up her mind. That brought something else to Brad's mind. During the time they were together, they had agreed on almost everything and had never had a fight. Eventually small irritations would result in arguments. How could they handle that?

After dinner Brad decided to forgo watching Monday Night Football so he could discuss his financial status and future plans with Linda. He brought up the subject as they finished putting dinner dishes away.

"So Linda, I should probably tell you some secrets about myself. You probably didn't know this, but my income is also about $40,000. Of course in my case the $40,000 is not monthly but for the whole year. I do have a budget. I put $4,800 in an IRA, $3,600 in savings, and about $5,600 for taxes. That leaves about $2,170 to live on each month. Actually that's more than enough since I don't pay any rent and most meals are free because I'm on the football team.

"For three years when I was in Iraq I saved almost all my pay. In addition, I saved most of my reenlistment bonus except for the cost of my car. I've got about $50,000 in my IRA and about $32,000 in savings. That doesn't make me rich, but at least I don't owe any or anything including student loans.

"As you know I have to spend four years on active duty with the army once I get my degree. As an officer I could afford to support a family at the middle-to-upper-class level. At my age I don't plan on having any more children, but you never know," Brad said as Linda listened.

When speaking of children, Brad had intended to say at his age he didn't think he would ever have any children. At the last minute he remembered Diane, so he changed his comment to talk about having any more children. After he said that, he then wished he just hadn't said anything about having children. For some reason, he didn't want Linda to know he was thinking about what it would be like to be married to her.

Later that night in bed they talked more about themselves and in doing so seemed interviewing for a marriage proposal. No proposal was made that night, but each now felt certain that unless something really bad happened a proposal would be made, probably but not necessarily, by Brad.

Tuesday Linda announced she was all packed and ready to leave for Las Vegas. That evening Brad packed most of the luggage in the car and then filled the car up with gasoline. Everything was ready for an early morning departure. It wasn't until they went to bed that Linda mentioned she had a morning hair appointment but would be finished by 11:00 a.m.

Brad didn't show his displeasure but was upset that Linda hadn't had her hair done earlier. Rain was forecasted for Wednesday, which meant traffic would be that much worse than normal for a holiday. Getting on the road by 8:00 a.m. would have avoided some of the traffic, but by 11:00 a.m. it would be bumper to bumper for the first one hundred miles. Fortunately by morning, Brad had accepted the fact and didn't dwell on it.

Chapter 19

Wednesday morning brought light rain. Not a good omen for starting a trip to Las Vegas.

Brad got up early as usual and was ready to start the trip by 6:30 a.m. Not so with Linda. She had scheduled a hair appointment at 8:00 a.m., which meant she wouldn't be ready to leave until around 11:00 a.m. Joan was also going to get her hair done, so she would drive Linda to the beauty parlor with the understanding that Brad would pick Linda up and then start for Las Vegas from there. Normally the drive to the beauty parlor would take less than half an hour. However, the day before Thanksgiving was not a normal day. Many people would be off work, so a lot of them would be out on the road early in the morning getting ready for the holiday. It seems a lot of people wanted to spend Wednesday window shopping taking note of prices of items they would want to buy at a discount on the day after Thanksgiving, Black Thursday. Because of that and the rain Linda and Joan were fifteen minutes late getting to the beauty parlor. Joan let Linda off at the door before parking the car, which saved another ten minutes or so.

Back at the house Brad was trying to not be impatient by watching TV. That didn't help much since every so often a news bulletin would tell of the continuing rain possibly turning to snow in the late afternoon and building traffic problems, especially on the way to Las Vegas. A little after 9:30 a.m., Linda called.

"In the closet by the front door there is a black umbrella, can you put that in the car before you leave?" asked Linda.

"Okay, but I thought you took an umbrella with you this morning," answered Brad.

"Yes, I have it, but I forgot to get an umbrella for you."

"I'll do it. How is the hair work coming?"

"I was a little late getting here, but they promised me I'd be done by 11:00 a.m. I'll call you about half an hour before I'm finished."

"Okay, I'll see you then. Will I be able to recognize you with your new hairdo?"

"I'll be the lady with a yellow umbrella and plastic bag covering my head standing in the rain outside the hair dresser."

After the phone call Brad thought it nice that Linda thought of getting an umbrella for him even though he hadn't considered it himself. He couldn't remember the last time he had used an umbrella. He was sure he never used one in Iraq. Anyway he decided to put the umbrella in the car before he forgot it. Then since he was going to the car he decided he would just start driving toward the beauty shop. He could stop at a close by coffee shop close to wait for Linda.

The drive to Las Vegas would be a little under three hundred miles. In normal traffic it should take a little over four hours. The reason Brad was so anxious to get started was not to get to Las Vegas early but to get up four thousand feet at El Cajon Pass before it started snowing. That would probably cause the California Highway Patrol to close the interstate. If they got up the pass there was still another four-thousand-foot mountain pass just before the Nevada border. Squeezing out a few extra minutes to get started would pay big dividends as it turned out.

Linda did call around 10:30 a.m. to say she would be ready in half an hour. Brad mentioned it might be a good idea for her to stop by the restroom before leaving since they would probably be in the car for several hours. As soon as he said that he thought that might add another ten minutes before she would be ready. He decided to get there at 11:00 a.m. anyway.

Brad did pick up Linda just after 11:00 a.m. By the time they got to the first stoplight, she had taken the scarf off her head so Brad could admire her hair. Brad said it looked great and that the hairdresser did a good job even though he couldn't tell any difference from the way her hair looked when she left the house that morning. He did notice either Linda or her hair really smelled good however.

Traffic on the freeway was bumper to bumper all the way through downtown. It took almost an hour to go twenty miles. Traffic did ease up a little the next hour as many of the commuters dropped off. By the time they got to the start of El Cajon Pass, it was a little after 1:00 p.m.

As they started up the pass, Brad noticed two highway patrol cars coming onto the road several cars behind him. Both cars had their red lights flashing, so Brad started to move to the far right lane to let them pass.

But before he could change lanes he noticed that the police were slowing traffic behind them and not allowing anyone to pass by zigzagging across lanes. The police were going to have all traffic behind them get off the road at the next exit and return back to lower elevations. The road was being closed to traffic because of the weather. Just then the rain turned to a light snow. However, before they reached the top of the pass, they came out of the clouds and the snow stopped. At the top of the pass all of the cars accelerated as though it was the start of the Indianapolis 500 race. In a few seconds some cars reached speeds of ninety miles an hour, which tended to thin out traffic as most trucks and older cars were left behind.

It was at this time that Linda announced she needed to use the restroom. Brad tried not to grimace when he heard that. He thought to himself that is why he suggested she use the restroom at the beauty shop. If she did, surely she would not have to go again in less than three hours. He now wished he hadn't bought coffee for Linda.

Brad had hoped to keep driving in order to get up the next mountain pass before it was closed to traffic. It would take over an hour of driving time to get to the pass and stopping would add at least another half an hour. However, he agree to stop at a fast-food place just off the interstate in Barstow, which was less than an hour away.

The fast-food parking area was completely full with half a dozen cars circling the lot looking for someone leaving. Brad was lucky to get one of those spots near the side entrance.

"It's hard to believe you managed to time it just right to get the parking spot," said Linda.

"Yeah, well, sometimes I'm able to work a little magic," joked Brad.

"Save your next magic trick for when you start gambling," said Linda.

Inside the four food lines were twelve or more people long, which meant it would probably take half an hour or more to be served. Luckily there was a separate coffee only line with only about six people waiting. Linda suggested they only get coffee. She would go to the restroom while Brad ordered coffee. That is when they noticed the line to the ladies' room extended out the restroom door. Fortunately there was another ladies' room in the shopping area, so Brad told Linda he would meet her back at the car. Linda showed up twenty minutes later. Once on the interstate, it was still light, so they were able to cruise along at about eighty miles an hour since there were only a few cars on the road. Brad figured most of the Las Vegas traffic was still in line for food or the restrooms back in Barstow.

On the earlier part of the trip, Linda had talked about things to do and places to see in Las Vegas. Brad tried to keep up with the conversation as he struggled driving the car in heavy traffic. Since driving was quite a bit easier now, Brad decided this would be a good time to answer a question Linda had asked earlier.

"So Linda you asked about the rules for playing Craps in Las Vegas," said Brad.

"Yes, I understand the players get the best odds on that game, but it seems so complicated," answered Linda.

"Well, I'm certainly not an expert, but I can give you some idea of the basics. As you said the game can be complex, but I like to keep it simple. So I like to think I'm playing a series of individual games against the casino or house. You can walk up to a table and start placing most bets just before a shooter rolls the dice. But for simplicity let's assume you want to start on a come out roll, in other words before a shooter, the person rolling the dice, establishes a point, a number he needs to roll to continue as a shooter.

"Slow down I'm confused already. I think I understand shooter and come out roll, but what is the point. Should I be taking notes?"

"No, the best way to learn the game is to not to read notes but to risk some money playing the game. Believe me when you're using your money you will learn very quickly."

"Okay, but if I do decide to try playing you will have to stand beside me to keep me from doing something wrong."

"You don't have to worry about that the dealers are very good about telling the players if they try to do something against the rules. I'll explain what I meant when I referred to a point in a minute. First let's get back to starting what I'll call individual games."

"I didn't know Craps uses cards."

"They don't use cards, why did you think that?"

"Well, you said something about the dealers."

"Crap table dealers don't have anything to do with cards. That is what you call the guys that operate the game. One guy stays on one side at the middle of the table. He is called the stickman because he uses a long stick with a curved end to capture the dice after the roll and return them to the shooter. He also calls out the number or total of the two dice after the roll. Then two other dealers stand at either end of the other side of the table. Their job is to place bets in the proper place on the table apron. They also payoff wins and collect for losses. A fourth guy is box man. He sits in the middle of the table and watches the action to make sure the players don't cheat and that the dealers don't make any mistakes."

"Aren't there any women dealers or box people?'

"Actually there are quite a few women dealers and at Crap tables now days. I just used the masculine term for ease in my explanation."

"How can the players cheat?"

"First of all don't try it. They will catch you and throw us out of the casino. However, some players have tried to either add or take away chips from their bet depending on if they won or lost. Some players have even picked up lost bets and left the table."

"Don't worry I'm not the cheating kind of girl."

Perhaps her last comment was a message to Brad that she would always be faithful to him. Then again maybe the comment didn't have any special meaning. Anyway the last several minutes of conversation for some reason caused Brad feel even closer to Linda. Maybe this is what it is like to be married.

About this time they had passed the city of Baker and started the climb up the last mountain pass. Traffic had picked up a little and by this time it was almost totally dark. This caused Brad to slow down to around seventy miles an hour. Fortunately, the weather was holding, so the road remained open.

"All right, my darling, I know you are a good girl. Now let's get back to the craps lesson," Brad said

"Okay, my darling. Where did we leave off?" Linda answered, mimicking Brad's use of the term "my darling" since it was so out of character for him.

"You can either bet to win or to lose, but let's only talk about playing to win."

"Why would anyone play to lose?"

"Actually no one plays for themselves to lose. They are betting that the shooter loses. That's called betting the wrong way. Anyway, let's say you want to bet $5 to win your own little game. To do that you would place a $5 chip on the area of the table marked as the pass line. Then if a 7 or 11 is rolled, you win the amount of your bet—or in this example, $5. However, if a 2, 3, or 12 is rolled, you lose your bet, and you start a new little game. If one of the other possible six numbers is rolled, it's a push or tie until the next roll. Let's say a 4 is rolled. That becomes the point, which means to win the shooter must roll another 4 before he rolls a 7."

"So if he rolls a 7, I win?"

"No, you lose. At this time you want a 4 rolled. If that happens, you win your placed bet. If any other number is rolled, it's another push for you."

"Well, does the shooter win if he rolls a 7?"

"No, the shooter and you are playing the same game in this example."

"This doesn't make any sense. One time you win if a 7 is rolled, and another time you lose if a 7 is rolled."

"Maybe it will make more sense if I talk about some other action, or bets you can make. Going back to the pass bet, you can get odds on your bet if you think you are going to win. You do that by placing a bet equal to or greater than your place bet behind your pass line bet. That way if you win, the dealer will pay you odds bet and an equal amount on your pass line bet. So in my example for a winning point of 4, you would get back $15 for your $10 bet and also get back your original $10 bet."

"So if the odds bet pays double, why didn't I win $20 and still get my original $10 bet back?"

"Because as I said you only get paid odds for your odds bet. The pass bet only pays even money. Incidentally, odds payoff is only double for numbers 4 and 10. The odds payoff for a 5 or 9 is $3 for every $2 bet. The payoff for a 6 or 8 is $6 for every $5 bet. However, most casinos limit the amount of odds you can get on a place bet. Usually it's only twice the amount of the pass bet, but some casinos allow up to ten times the pass bet."

"I think I should be taking notes."

"Well, let me mention the come, place and proposition bets first and by then we should be at the casino. The easiest bets to make are proposition bets. They are often called sucker bets because the odds are heavily in favor of the house. You can bet a 7 will come up on the next roll. This a one roll bet. If you win the payoff is 7 to 1. Another favorite is to bet an even point number, which could be a 4, 6, 8, and 10, will come up the hard way. That means the numbers on the dice must be identical. In other words, a hard way 4 is when a 2 shows up on each dice."

"Okay, I get that, but why bet that way?"

"Because you get odds on the payoff."

"I suppose the odds are different on each hard way?"

"You are almost right. The odds are the same for the 4 and 10. The odds are the same for the 6 and 8 but different from the other hard ways."

By this time they had reached the top of the last mountain pass and were about to start down the other side of the pass. Brad sensed Linda had lost interest in the craps lesson, so he changed the subject.

"We should be at the casino in another half hour or so. We should still have a couple of hours before a late dinner," Brad said.

"Oh look, we can see Las Vegas just down the hill," said Linda.

"Actually, that's the community of Jean. It's just inside the Nevada state line. Las Vegas is a little bigger than that."

"Yeah, well, Las Vegas must have grown since the last time I was here," Linda answered going along with Brad's sarcastic comment.

About this time it started to snow, so Brad slowed a little.

"Let's stop at Jean. I've never been there," said Linda.

That is about the last thing Brad wanted to do; however, he decided it best to stop for a short time.

"Okay, do you need to go to the bathroom?" Brad asked.

"Yeah, but I also wanted to find out what would cause people to stop here when it's only a few miles to Las Vegas."

"Well, probably a lot of people think the same thing and have to see for themselves."

Brad took the first exit in Nevada and stopped at the closest casino. He let Linda off at the main entrance saying he would meet Linda at the registration desk after parking the car. The parking lot was almost full, so Brad had to park several hundred feet from the casino. It took him almost fifteen minutes before he found the registration desk. Linda was not there but did show up about five minutes later.

"Okay, I've seen everything there is to see here, so I'm ready to go," Linda said as she approached Brad.

"I had to park the car near pretty far away, so you can stay inside and wait for me bring the car around."

"I'll walk with you. It will be fun to walk in the snow for a short distance."

Part way to the car Linda took Brad's arm. It was getting difficult for her to walk between cars and she was getting cold. Brad wasn't too happy about having to stop and then having to park the car so far from the casino especially since they spent so little time there. However, having Linda hold his arm somehow made him feel it was all worthwhile.

Back on the road, traffic and the snow had picked up a little, so Brad had to concentrate a little harder on driving the car. Linda, on the other hand, thought it was wonderful to see the snow falling. Seeing that Linda was happy made Brad feel it was worth it to put up with the minor annoyances. He figured in the future he would just have to get used to it.

Several minutes later they arrived at the casino where they would be staying and put their previously discussed plan into effect. Brad stopped by the main entrance and got the luggage and Linda's coat out of the car while Linda was getting a bellman to take the coat, luggage and her to the registration desk. Brad would park the car and then meet Linda either in the room or if she hadn't finished registering at the registration desk.

Brad had to park on the fifth level of the parking structure. To save time he ran down the stairs instead of waiting for a slow elevator and then walked quickly into the casino. This took almost half an hour before Brad called Linda to get their room number. As it turned out, Linda was still waiting to register. Well, over one hundred people were trying to check in, so Linda was still several people away from a registration clerk even though the hotel had six reservation clerks checking people into the casino.

While waiting in line, Linda struck up a conversation with the couple in line behind her. In a few minutes, she learned that Rene and Roy Hammond were from Covina, California, and that they had a teenage son and daughter who would be spending the holiday with their grandparents in the Colorado mountains. The Hammonds appeared to be close to Linda's age. Roy had a mustache and a receding hairline. He wore oversize gym shoes, long sports pants along with a sweat shirt with a number and the name of some athletic. Rene wore a form fitting pink pants suit with petite gym shoes. Her naturally blonde hair was combed nicely adding to her sexy look.

Suddenly Linda realized she had given out more personal information than she had intended. She had pointed out that she was recently divorced and that she would be spending the weekend with a friend. Now she wondered how the Hammonds would react to Brad since it would be obvious that he is years younger than her. It didn't take long to find out as Brad arrived just at that time.

"Oh, Brad, these are the Hammonds, Rene and Roy," said Linda.

"Hello," Brad said as she shook hands with Roy and gave Rene a big smile.

The next few seconds no one spoke and it became obvious that the Hammonds were concentrating on the age difference between Linda and Brad.

Finally Brad asked the Hammonds if they were from California. That causes a few minutes of conversation as things previously said to Linda were repeated to Brad mostly by Rene.

"Rene is a pretty name, are you part French?" Brad asked Rene.

"Yes, I am. My mother's parents, my grandparents, came to the U.S. from Paris many years ago. Have you ever been to France?" Rene asked Brad.

"No, but I'd like to visit the country sometime," answered Brad.

"Well, maybe sometime you can ask Linda to take you there," Roy quickly commented.

The crude implication of Roy's comment was that Brad, in essence, was just a gigolo. Brad couldn't think of an appropriate response at that time, so he just didn't comment. Fortunately Linda avoided what could have been an ugly exchange by changing the subject.

"Before you got here we agreed to have Thanksgiving dinner together here in the casino. I can change our reservation to four people later this evening," Linda said to Brad.

"That will be fun. Brad, be sure to give me your room number so we can find out when to meet you," said Rene as she continued to stare at Brad.

At about that time, the registration desk opened, so they said bye to the Hammonds.

After the registration clerk found Linda's reservation she mentioned that Linda could have used the preferred check-in line since her credit history indicated the Wallace's were honored guests. Linda figured that was because Larry used their joint credit card so often in the past on business trips. That started her thinking about traveling with Larry. He had always used valet parking, preferred registration, and always had the bellmen wait with the bags for him to check in. She realized things would be different when traveling with Brad; however, she figured she could easily do without the special perks available to rich men.

The casino had an efficient way of helping guests take luggage to rooms. One bellman would deliver the luggage to the registration area, tag and leave it. He would then be available to take baggage for other guests that had finished checking in to their room. Despite the available help with baggage, most gusts preferred to lug their baggage around with them when checking in. Linda wondered why most people wouldn't be willing to tip a few dollars for bellman's assistance instead of lugging their baggage through the crowded casino area looking for the elevators. The same people seemed to not mind losing hundreds or more dollars gambling.

At the room Brad made sure he was the one to tip the bellman. The room was actually a small suite. There was what could be called a living room, a walk-in closet, a big bathroom with separate shower and tubs. Best of all was the bedroom, which featured a big king size bed with half a dozen pillows. The room probably cost at least $500 per night.

Linda immediately called the restaurant to change the Thanksgiving Day reservations to four people. She then asked Brad what he thought of the Hammonds.

"Well, I though Rene looked really hot in the two-sizes-too-small pants suit. I think Roy is all right, although I think he would have looked better if I had busted his nose when he made that sarcastic comment," said Brad.

"I think Roy was just afraid Rene was flirting with you and wanted to make himself better by somehow making you look bad," Linda replied.

"Well, Roy doesn't have to worry about me. Rene really isn't that hot, and I have no desire to find out what's making those lumps inside her suit."

"Did you have a chance to give her your room number?"

"No, I didn't give her our room number. I figure the hotel operator can connect you to them when you want to call. By the way, if Roy answers, you should mention that we are sharing the room."

"Do you think they've had time to get to their room?"

"I'd bet they are still wondering around the casino looking for the elevators. We'd probably be doing the same thing if we hadn't used the bellman. I wonder why the hotels always set up the registration desk so far from the elevators."

"You're probably right. I'll call the Hammonds later. After I freshen up let's get something to eat. I haven't eaten since breakfast, and I'm really hungry."

On the way to the coffee shop they passed the buffet line. There must have been over a hundred people in line, which meant it probably would be over an hour wait. Near the end of the line they saw Roy and Rene.

"Hey, Linda, look who I see," said Brad as a way of greeting the Hammonds.

"I was just thinking about calling to let you know I was able to change the reservations for the four of us at 5:00 p.m. tomorrow," Linda said to the Hammonds.

"That's nice we'll meet you at the restaurant. You can jump in line with us if you're going to the buffet," Rene said.

"Thanks, but we are on our way to the coffee shop for a light dinner," answered Linda.

"Looking forward to dinner tomorrow," said Brad as he and Linda continued on to the coffee shop.

"Did you notice that Roy didn't say a word?" asked Linda.

"Yeah, I assume he was dreaming about how much he could eat once they got seated in the buffet," answered Brad.

The coffee shop also had number of people waiting for a table, but a hostess was taking names. Linda said they were house guests and showed the room key, which was actually a plastic card. With that they were immediately seated. Brad figured the key must have been color coded to identify honored guests.

Brad hadn't eaten all day, so he had a big dinner. Even though Linda had said she was hungry she didn't have much to eat but did finish off two large glasses of wine.

"So Linda do you want to try winning some money at the crap table after dinner?" asked Brad.

"Not tonight I want to try to remember all the rules before risking any money," said Linda.

Instead of gambling they stopped by the lounge show, which featured a group playing songs from the 1950s. For some reason, maybe it had something to do with the wine, Linda started singing along with the band. She wasn't the only one doing so. It seems everyone except Brad was singing along. After about an hour Brad noticed Linda was slurring her words, so he decided it was time to go back to the room.

Once they got in bed, sex seemed to energize Linda. As was usually the case after sex she wanted to talk. Brad was ready to go to sleep but, as usual, he managed to stay awake and keep up with Linda's conversation, most of the time.

"You know, Brad, I really enjoyed today. I know that sounds funny considering that we spent so much time in the car, but for me it was very relaxing. Once we got here I guess I got caught up in the Las Vegas atmosphere.

"What's your plan for tomorrow?" Brad asked.

"I want to go shopping in the fashion mall on the Strip," answered Linda.

"I'll bet the stores will really be busy. I understand you need to get there really early like just after they open at midnight to get the best deals."

"I don't think that will be much of a problem here, especially since they will not open until sometime around 6:00 a.m. Are you still thinking of spending all day watching football games on TV?"

"Yeah, I may place small bets on the games to make things more interesting. If I get tired I can always go back to the room and take a nap."

Linda was about to tell Brad to charge his lunch and any drinks he may have to the room but then decided not to. It wasn't that she would mind the charges, but instead she didn't want remind Brad that she was paying for most of the costs of the trip.

"Are you planning to gamble any?"

"You mean other than betting on the games? No, I'll be too busy watching the games."

It was almost an hour later before Linda was ready to stop talking and finally go to sleep. Brad was just able to finish saying goodnight before he fell fast asleep.

Brad woke up at 5:30 a.m. After taking a shower and getting dressed he woke Linda up. Just to tell her he was going to get something to eat. Linda wanted to sleep some more, so Brad said he would be back in about two hours.

For some reason Brad headed toward the casino he stayed at last August. He wasn't looking for Kandi. As a matter of fact, he didn't want to run into her. He figured that was not likely to happen since he was pretty sure Kandi wouldn't be working this early. Neither was he hoping to get a free dinner from Art Bartoo. Perhaps he just wanted to relive the pleasant experience he had last summer.

As he walked through the casino area he passed the elevators he had used to get to his room last August. Suddenly, just for a minute, he thought it would be nice if he did see Kandi as she came down from an overnight stay with another special guest. However, he quickly realized that would not be a good idea. So he decided to eat at the fast-food area.

Brad bought a roll and cup of coffee after waiting in line for about five minutes. As he sat down he noticed an older man sitting at the next table. The man was wearing what, at an earlier time, was an expensive-looking gray suit. The suit was now worn, wrinkled and dirty. Instead of a dress shirt he wore a checkered flannel one. As the man finished puffing on a cigarette, Brad noticed he was mumbling something and then smiling broadly.

"Carl you have to stop talking to yourself," the man said to himself and then started chuckling.

Suddenly the man noticed Brad who, without realizing it, was staring at him.

"I wasn't talking to you," the man said angrily.

Brad decided to not acknowledge the comment.

"This is really bad I can't even afford another cup of coffee?" the man then said pretending to be talking to himself.

It cost $3.50 for a roll and coffee, so Brad placed a $5 bill on the table for the man as he left.

Brad hoped he wouldn't be like that when he got older. He figured that if he and Linda did get married that would never happen to him. It made him think about proposing to Linda this morning, but he came to his senses and realized that wouldn't be a good idea. Then again it would really be easy to get married in Las Vegas.

It was time to get back to see if Linda had gotten up and was ready for breakfast.

Linda was up when Brad got back to the room but hadn't finished her morning makeup routine. This was the first time Brad had witnessed how long it took for Linda to fix her hair, and then put on her lipstick and makeup. By the time she finished, it was a little before 8:00 a.m. While waiting, Brad mentioned that he hadn't gambled but instead had just walked around outside to get some fresh air. So they decided to get something to eat together in the casino. There was another long line at the buffet, so they headed for the coffee shop. Once again they were seated immediately after showing the room key.

Over breakfast they went over their plans for the day. Linda would spend the better part of the day shopping but would be back at the casino around 3:00 p.m. Brad would watch the football games on TV in the sports book area until Linda returned. After Thanksgiving dinner they would attend the early show in the main show room. After the show they could gamble or take in the lounge show again.

Around 3:30 p.m. Linda called to say she was back in the room and was getting ready for dinner. A few minutes later after the second football game ended Brad went back to the room to change clothes and get ready for dinner and the show.

Brad started watching the last football game on TV in the living room as Linda finished getting ready, so he hadn't been paying much attention to how she looked. That quickly changed when Linda said she was ready. She was wearing what many call a little black dress. The dress featured a high neck and covered her arms down to the wrists. The skirt stopped right below the knees. She wore a single strand of medium size pearls, probably real, her platinum watch on one wrist and a silver plain bracelet on the other wrist. She was also wearing her large size diamond ring, something Brad had never seen before. She wore solid looking high heal black shoes.

Brad was immediately intimated by her looks and felt he should be wearing something better than his only dark blue suit. No one dresses formally in Las Vegas anymore, so Brad thought they would get a lot of attention as they walked through the casino. He wasn't wrong about that, but he couldn't have imagined how much attention Linda drew to herself.

"Gee, Linda, you really look good," was about the best compliment Brad could come up with.

Before they left for dinner Linda showed Brad the clothes she bought herself. She also bought an expensive bathrobe for him. Something he would have never bought for himself but that he actually liked and would use often in the future.

As they were leaving for dinner, Linda mentioned that the Rene Hammond called to say the buffet was having a gourmet dinner, so they had decided to go there. Rene said Roy wanted to try all the different things the buffet was featuring.

The dinner show was entertaining even though neither Linda nor Brad were able to figure out the theme of the show. The entertainers spent most of the time dancing, singing and jumping around, which the audience really enjoyed. Brad was disappointed that there were no naked girls but didn't mention it Linda.

After the show, the casino area was so crowded, it was almost impossible to walk there without bumping into people. No one seemed to mind, even though a lot of men seemed to go out of their way to bump into Linda. As they were walking, a middle-aged lady bumped into Brad, spilling part of her drink on his trousers. The lady quickly apologized as she tried to dry the area with a napkin by forcibly rubbing Brad's pants just below his belt buckle. Suddenly she realized how this must have looked to a small crowd that stopped to watch.

"It's all right, she's his mother," the lady's husband said jokingly.

"I wish I had a mother like that, or even a wife," an older man said as he glanced at his wife who was not amused.

"Hey, lady, you can spill the rest of your drink right here," said a younger man as he pointed to his crotch.

"I hope I didn't ruin your pants," the lady said to Brad.

"No, there're okay, but it's a good thing you stopped rubbing when you did. Otherwise I might have wetted my pants myself," Brad joked.

It took a few seconds before the lady figured out what Brad meant. She then blushed noticeably before walking away.

"Brad, I think you embarrassed that lady," Linda said.

"Me embarrass her? What about her groping me?" Brad replied.

"I can tell you enjoyed the groping by the big grin on your face. Maybe I should try groping you later tonight," Linda said surprising herself by her sexy comment.

"Why wait until tonight? Now is as good a time as any,"

About this time they had reached the elevators to their room. Brad was ready to go upstairs, really ready, but Linda seemed to want to wait awhile. Actually Brad didn't mind as he liked showing Linda as they walked around the casino floor.

At one of the bars, they found a table separating them from the people walking in the casino by only a three-foot wall. Linda faced out toward the casino, so everyone walking by was able to get a good look at her. So many people slowed down, or some even stopped to look at Linda that she felt as though she was window dressing in a department store window. A couple of people took pictures, probably thinking Linda was someone famous. After a few minutes, they quickly finished their drinks and went to their room.

Friday morning they took a tour from the casino to Boulder Dam. Linda wore a black midcalf leather coat with a fir lined hood. Brad didn't have a winter coat, so he wore his camouflaged colored army field jacket with his name on it. This caused many of the tour group to thank him for his service, something he hadn't expected. Many of the older men mentioned that they were veterans, but none of the middle-aged or younger men said anything about ever being in the military service. Fortunately no one said anything to Linda about how she should be proud to have a son in the army, something both Linda and Brad secretly worried might happen.

That afternoon Linda wanted to look at some houses or condominiums in the Las Vegas area. She said her financial advisor had indicated real estate might be a good investment. They visited several new housing tracts where prices for new houses ranged from $300,000 to over $650,000. Then they were shown some high rise condominiums that started at over $1,000,000.

Linda had never discussed her financial status with Brad and he had never asked. Brad did think Linda was wealthy, but after considering the value of the jewelry she wore Thanksgiving evening and the fact she had a financial advisor suggesting she invest perhaps over $1,000,000 in real estate he figured she was really wealthy. That would cause Brad some concern about the effect it would have on their continued relationship. He knew the subject would have to be addressed in the near future.

Back at the casino Linda wanted to take a short nap before dinner. When she was ready they decided to have dinner in downtown Las Vegas where Brad said it was less expensive to gamble. By the time they finished dinner it was after 11:00 p.m. They walked through several casinos before stopping at one Linda seemed to like. The place was crowded and noisy with mostly older gamblers, all of whom seemed to be smoking.

They were able to find room at one of the crap tables, Brad stood immediately to the left of the stickman with Linda to his left. An older heavyset man with a full beard stood to Linda's left. After buying in for $100 each they played conservable for a few rolls of the dice. Linda bet exactly like Brad.

Suddenly just before a roll of the dice, an arm poked out between two players and a couple of dollars along with a handful of change was dropped on the table. The man with the arm loudly called out that the money plays the field. A field number was rolled, so the man with the arm should have won a three-dollar bet. It took several seconds before the dealers could pick up the losing bets and start paying the winning bets. Just before the payoff to the man that made the field bet, the box man called out no bet. The stick man quickly used the stick to pull the man's hand away from reaching for the winnings.

"What do you mean, no bet? I got the money down before the dice were rolled," the man at the end of the arm asked.

"The minimum bet is three dollars. You only bet $2.94," the box man answered.

"Hey, man, I just got out of jail, and that's all the money I got. I'm just trying to get enough to get something to eat."

The jail, which is across the street from the back of the casino, lets inmates out at one minute after midnight on the day of their release.

The crowd at the crap table became quite for a few seconds. Then several people shouted out to pay the guy.

"Pay the man," the box man reluctantly said to the dealer.

"Let it all ride," said the man.

Bad decision. The number rolled was not a field number, so the man lost his $6. Then a couple of gamblers each tossed him a five-dollar chip, saying the money was for something to eat and not for gambling. With that, the man thanked his benefactors and left.

That action seemed to energize the crowd, and more gamblers started making comments to encourage all the shooters.

When it was Brad's turn to roll dice, he made his first 2 points, then lost on a 7. Now it was Linda's turn to be the shooter.

Linda first rolled a winning 7, then a winning 11. The next roll was a 4. At that time Brad took odds on his pass line bet, placed a bet on the 10, and another bet on the Come. After rolling several more numbers, Linda rolled a winning 4. By this time there was a lot of chatter at the table encouraging Linda to keep rolling winners.

"Come on, baby, throw a 7 this time," a man with a Southern accent called out.

Linda did just that.

"Good girl," the bearded man beside her said as he gently slapped her on the back.

"You have to hit the end of the table when you throw the dice," the stickman said to Linda.

Because she had to lean over the table and toss the dice with her left hand, it was difficult for her to throw the dice all the way to the end of the table. Therefore when she started to roll the dice again, she turned toward the left end of the table. Immediately seeing that, the box man, dealers, and stickman all yelled out, "No roll!" in unison.

"You have to throw the dice to the other end of the table, lady," said the stickman as he pulled her hand with the stick.

"But earlier people were throwing the dice this way," Linda responded.

"Look, lady, your half of the table throws it this way. The other half throws it toward your end."

"All right, here goes."

Linda then continued to roll several numbers other than a 7, which won money for almost everyone at the table. Eventually she rolled a hard 10, something the bearded guy had money on.

"Good girl, good girl," the guy shouted quite loudly as he absentmindedly hit her on the back rather hard.

"Come on, good girl, keep rolling numbers," shouted a couple of men picking up on the bearded guy's comment.

Then everyone at the table began yelling, "Good girl!" as Linda rolled several more numbers before rolling a 7, while absorbing several more pats on the back.

The bearded man was next to shoot the dice. His first two rolls were 6s.

"Did we win?" Linda asked Brad after the second 6 was rolled.

"Yeah, everyone won."

With that Linda wound up and hit the bearded guy hard on the back while shouting that he was a good boy. The hit surprised the guy, causing him to drop the chips he had just picked up.

"Oh gee, you got my good arm," the bearded man said as he feigned being in pain.

"Hit him again, lady. Maybe you can put his shoulder back in place," someone shouted.

For a few seconds, Linda wasn't sure the man wasn't really hurt. She put her around his shoulder and asked if he was all right. The man said he would just have to use his other arm when rolling the dice while winking at her to let her know he was not serious

The man then rolled a winning 7, which immediately caused everyone to shout out, "Good boy!"

"Come on, lady, give him a good whack this time," someone called out.

The bearded guy tightened his body as if he were getting ready to be hit with a baseball bat. Linda took an exaggerated swing but just barely tapped him on the back.

"Oh gee, you got me again. I'm not sure I can hit the end of the table now," joked the bearded man.

This seemed like a good time for Brad and Linda to leave, so they exchanged their many small denomination chips for a few larger denomination chips. They would then exchange those chips for real paper money at the cashier's cage. Linda cashed in about $300 of chips, and Brad won almost $1,200.

"You can't leave now, lady. You were bringing me good luck. Let me apologize for hitting you on the back, but I got a little excited because this is the first time this month I've won any money," the bearded man said.

"That's all right, this was a lot of fun," Linda answered.

Then without knowing why, Linda kissed the guy on his forehead. This immediately caused a number of hoots and hollers from the crowd, along with a number of people pleading Linda to not leave.

"We have to leave now, we have to go to bed," Linda said innocently.

This caused more hoots and hollers from the crowd.

"Ride um, cowboy," called out the guy with the Southern accent.

"Hang in there buckaroo," someone else called out.

Linda couldn't help but smile broadly, thinking about what she had just said as she waved bye to the crowd.

"That's a lucky guy to have a woman like that. It would be great to be young again. I wonder how long they will stay together?" a man asked the woman next to him.

"I don't know, but I think they really love each other. I could tell by the way the guy explained how to place bets to the lady," the woman answered.

The bearded guy asked the stickman if there was any lipstick on his forehead. When told there was some, the guy declared he would never wash his forehead again.

There was a pause in the action as the crowd grew quiet, thinking about the nice couple that had just left.

CHAPTER 20

Saturday, November 26, 2005

Saturday, Linda and Brad had intended to sleep late. They didn't get to bed until after 2:00 a.m. and then talked for about an hour before going to sleep. Around 8:30 a.m. Brad couldn't sleep any longer, so he got up. He figured he could watch college football games on TV while Linda was sleeping. Besides he wanted to buy a gift for Linda using some of his gambling winnings. He also planned on using most of the rest of his winnings to buy a new suit and top coat sometime before the New York trip.

Linda woke up before Brad left and told him she wanted to sleep a little longer and then would call her travel agent make arrangements for their New York trip. She said she would try to find Brad in the casino sports book section around 11:00 a.m.

By the time Brad had gotten coffee and a donut the first games had started. He couldn't bet on those games but did place bets on four games that would be played that afternoon and evening. While watching the games he tried to think of a nice gift for Linda.

By 10:00 a.m. the casino stores were open, so Brad started shopping. A beautiful ring in a jewelry store caught his eye. He thought that would be a nice gift if he only had $25,000 to buy it. He quickly decided jewelry was out. He couldn't afford anything that would complement the expensive jewelry Linda already had. Flowers and candy were not appropriate and he wasn't about to shop for lingerie in a woman's store. Finally he decided on an expensive silk scarf. Linda could use that in New York.

After finding Brad back in the sports book area Linda and Brad headed toward the coffee shop for brunch. While waiting to be served Linda wanted to know what was in the bag Brad was carrying. Brad decided he might as well give the scarf to her now, so he did. Although this wasn't a romantic place to give a gift Linda seemed pleasantly surprised and appreciative. She said the scarf would come in handy in New York.

After they finished brunch Linda said she would drop the scarf off in the room and then spend a couple of hours shopping in the many stores in the casino. Brad said he would be in the sports book or back in the room the rest of the afternoon.

Linda had only intended to only drop the scarf off in the room, use the restroom, and then leave for shopping. However, just as she was about to leave, she got a phone call. It was her mother calling from Chicago.

"Hi, Mon, I wasn't expecting a call from you until tomorrow. Is everything all right?" asked Linda.

"Yes, everything is good. That is why I'm calling. I have some good news. We've sold the house. The buyers agreed to pay our asking price if we they could move in by Christmas. We decided this was just too good an opportunity to pass up," said Ethel Dowling, Linda's mother.

Linda's parents had been planning on living with her for a few weeks or even months while they looked for a new home somewhere in California or Arizona after selling their house. The original plan was to not put the parents' house on the market until after the first of the year. That would give Linda time to ease her parents into the idea that Brad would often be staying overnight. Linda also hadn't told Brad about her parents moving in with her. Despite the initial shock, Linda was careful to enthusiastically say she would be happy to have her parents move in before Christmas.

"Gee, that's great news. I'm sure you will enjoy being in California over the holidays. Have you made arrangements on when you can get here?" Linda asked.

"Yes, we'll arrive Monday, December 19. That will give us a few days to see you before you leave for New York,"

"Mom, I don't remember telling you about our New York trip. How do know about that?"

"Diane called yesterday from Hawaii. When I told her we would be able to spend Christmas with her and you, she said Larry was taking her skiing since you would be going to New York."

This was really upsetting to Linda. She had left three messages with Diane, who hadn't called back. Why would Diane call her grandmother but not her real mother, she thought. A few weeks later she would have that thought answered, and it would not be what she expected. Linda was having difficulty keeping her composure, but she didn't want to get into an adversary discussion, so she was careful to speak calmly.

"Mom, as usual Diane didn't tell you the whole truth. We had planned on Diane spending Thanksgiving with me at home while Larry and Cindy went to Hawaii. A week or so ago Diane suddenly wanted to spend Thanksgiving in Hawaii. I said then she could spend the Christmas holidays with me instead of going skiing. She said she couldn't do that since Larry had already made arrangements for the three of them to spend the holidays together. So I didn't plan on either the Thanksgiving or Christmas trips until after Diane said she wouldn't be spending either holiday with me."

"I suppose you're thinking about taking that boy with you to New York. I think it's about time you stop looking foolish by being seen with some guy half your age. We can talk about it more before Christmas."

Linda knew she would have to have serious discussions with her mother, her father and Brad about her future relationship with Brad. What Linda didn't know was that her mother would have another big surprise in store for her and that there would be more serious discussions with others.

"Mom, let's leave that discussion until later. If Dad is there, maybe I can say hello to him."

"Your father is out making plans for our furniture to be stored. I'll call you next week. You can talk to Ralph then."

"Okay, Mom. Before you hang up, how is Diane? Does she seem to be enjoying herself?"

"Yes, she is fine. Larry is taking good care of her,"

"Okay, we'll talk again next week. Good luck on getting ready to move,"

"Looking forward to talking with you next month, bye now,"

After hanging up the phone Linda seemed to be in a daze. A thousand thoughts raced through her head about what she would be faced with the next few weeks.

First she had to think about how to tell Brad about her parents coming to live with her. Linda knew what she wanted, which was to have Brad continue to stay overnight at her house and to go through with the New York trip. She wasn't sure what Brad would want to do however. He may not like the idea of having the parents around when he visited her. If he didn't want to continue to stay overnight with her or go on the New York trip, it probably would mean the end of their relationship. That would solve one problem by making the parents happy but would make her miserable.

Linda hadn't realized how serious her relationship with Brad had become. Since they wouldn't be in a class together next semester Brad may just lose interest in her thought Linda. Even if their relationship continued for the next two years what would happen when Brad went back on active duty. If their relationship ended at the end of next month she knew she would be deeply depressed. She had grown accustom to having someone to go places with and to just talk to. She wasn't interested in starting all over to find someone to have a relationship with and she really didn't want to have her mother take over control of her life. She decided she would just have to bite the bullet and tell Brad about the situation. She figured it best to discuss this with Brad Sunday on the way home. That would give them time to have a full discussion.

Now if Brad didn't object to staying overnight with Linda while the parents were there the next problem for Linda was how to get her parents to accept the situation. The last thing she wanted was to alienate her parents and have them decide to stay somewhere else. She decided to not let her parents know Brad would be staying overnight at her house until the parents arrived. Brad could meet the parents at the airport with Linda and then disappear for a couple of hours after dropping them all off at Linda's house. Linda would let the parents know Brad would be back for dinner.

Linda knew her mother would want to talk to her about Brad before he returned, so that is when Linda would let her parents know that Brad would be staying overnight that night and frequently in the future. She was sure her mother would object, but she was not sure how her father would react. She had a feeling that her father and Brad would get along well after they got to know each other.

The next big problem was Diane. Linda was sure that Diane would do everything she could to make the situation as difficult as possible. Linda wasn't sure if Diane was afraid of Brad, jealous of Brad for getting Linda's attention away from her or just upset over the age difference. Whatever it was Linda was determined to keep her relationship with Brad, assuming he felt the same way.

While Linda was thinking about Diane some thoughts about her mother came into her head. For the first time Linda realized Diane and her mother had many of the same traits. Beth has a strong personality, always thinks she knows what is best for Linda and is not shy about demanding Linda do what she wants. Diane also has a strong personality, always thinks she knows what is best for herself, and is not shy about demanding what she wants for herself.

It's an amazing phenomenon that what seem like innocent comments at the time, get lost in time and then suddenly pop back into a person's head. Linda experienced that when thinking back to how her parents treated her when she was a child. One incident seemed to define how her parents interacted with her.

Linda recalled that one summer when she was seven years, her father took her to two afternoon baseball games at Wrigley Stadium. Her mother didn't want to attend either game. The evening after the second game Linda remembered overhearing a conversation between her parents. It seems Ethel told Ralph that Linda was not a boy. She was a girl and should be doing girl things, not going to ball games. Ethel said she didn't want Linda to be a Tom Boy. After that Ralph rarely took Linda anywhere without Ethel going along and that meant no ball games or other boy type activities. Even so, her father actively participated in her upbringing. He was always there when needed, but she realized that she related more closely with her mother than her father.

It was a different story with Diane. She definitely was daddy's girl. Larry certainly spoiled Diane by always taking her side when Diane didn't want to do what Linda asked. Larry always brought gifts for Diane when he returned from business trips. Until now Linda never thought much of the fact that Larry normally did not bring gifts for her.

About that time her thoughts were interrupted by a phone call from Joan.

"Hey, Linda, I just called to see if you've won any jack pots," said Joan.

"No, but I did win about $300 playing crap. I've got to tell you about it when I get home," answered Lind.

"Hope I'm not calling at a bad time, but if you have a few minutes let me know if you have been able to see any good shows,"

"I am in our room getting ready to go shopping, but I've got plenty of time right now. To answer your question we only saw the show in this casino. I liked it although I have no idea what the story line was. Brad seemed to enjoy it even though there weren't any naked girls. I've got to tell you some big news."

"Let me guess. You and Brad got married."

"No, we didn't do that, although it would have been really easy to do so. What I wanted to say before you called is that I just got off the phone with my mother. My parents sold their house in Chicago and are coming to live with me until they decide where they want to live. They will arrive the nineteenth."

"I thought you said they wouldn't move until after the first of the year. Have you told Brad yet?"

"No, I just found out myself. Brad is in the casino watching football. I'll wait to tell him in the car when we start home tomorrow. I don't know what his reaction will be."

"I'm sure he will be okay with that. I don't know about your mother, but I think your father will be impressed by Brad. How will you tell your mom that Brad stays overnight sometimes?"

"Well, I need some advice on my plan. I think Brad will go along with meeting the parents at the airport. After Brad drops us off at the house he will go work out or something for a couple of hours. Then he will come back for dinner and spend the night with me. While he is gone I can explain the facts to my parents. I don't want to sneak around or keep secrets, so I think it best to make sure everyone understands the situation right away. What do you think of my plan?"

"It's a great plan. I hope it works. I agree it is a good idea to tell your parents the whole story right away. However, I don't think that will be much fun for Brad at least until he gets in bed with you. Maybe I can come over and watch the fireworks. I'd also like to watch the action in bed."

"You know I probably could use your help in talking to Mom, but I definitely do not need any help in the bedroom."

"When are you going to break the news to Diane? It's going to be really awkward next time she comes home and finds out Brad will be spending the night."

"Yeah, well, that is a future problem. I'm going to try to get her to visit over the MLK holiday weekend. I'm sure Mom will help me convince Diane to show up."

"Besides gambling and attending a show what else have you done the last couple of days?"

"Yesterday we toured Boulder Dam and then spent an afternoon looking at real estate. There are some really nice high rise homes here that I might be interested in as an investment. The most fun, however, was playing crap downtown. Brad taught me the rules, which are really complicated. I learned just enough to keep from embarrassing myself most of the time. All the people at the crap table were very nice and very funny. Almost all the players were old guys and everyone was smoking and drinking beer. "I'll have to give you the details when I get home."

"Let me get this straight, you've only been in Las Vegas a couple of days and already become a gambling real estate queen.

"Well, I haven't progressed that far yet, but I'm really enjoying myself. Look Joan it's time I meet Brad downstairs. I don't want to leave him along too long because the casino keeps giving the players free drinks and Brad probably can't drink more than fifteen beers."

"Okay, I'll be interested to hear about your crap table fun when you get back. Bye now."

After talking to Joan, Linda felt confident that things would work out well with her parents. However, there would be two more huge surprises for Linda before the New York trip.

Before going downstairs she called Diane once more hoping to be able to talk to her.

"Hello, Mother," Diane said in a flat tone voice as she answered the phone,

"Hi, Di, glad I could get ahold of you. Are you enjoying Hawaii?" asked Linda.

"Yeah, it's great over here."

"Your grandmother, Ethel, said you talked to her recently. Did she tell you they sold their house and will be staying with me while they look for a new house somewhere in California or Arizona?"

"Yeah, Dad thought it would be nice if I called both grandparents for Thanksgiving."

Linda realized Diane wasn't interested in talking, so it would be difficult holding a conversation with her. Therefore she figured it best if she just ended the call.

"Well, I think that is nice that you called them. I just wanted to say I'm thinking about and hope you are having a good time. Let's plan on getting together early next month."

"Sure, Mom, bye now."

After talking to Diane Linda's mood changed again. Instead of feeling really good she suddenly felt not so good. Fortunately her mood would change positively as soon as she saw Brad.

"Hey, mister, is this seat taken?" Linda jokingly asked Brad as she sat down beside him in the sports book.

"Well, lady, I was saving it for a good friend, but since you look so good the seat is yours," Brad said going along with the joke.

"Is your team winning?"

"They are ahead right now, but the other team is almost in scoring position. There is only about four more minutes left to play. Did you like any of the stores here in the casino?"

"I didn't have time to go shopping but talked on the phone for almost two hours. First my mother called, which took over an hour, then Joan called. Finally I was able to talk to Diane,"

"Is everything all right with everyone?"

"Yeah, I was worried about Diane, but she seemed happy. If she wasn't I'm sure she would have let me know. I always like to talk to Joan, she always sounds so cheerful."

At that time a cocktail waitress asked Brad and Linda if they would like to order drinks. Brad said he would like one more beer.

"I'd like that drink I had last night," Linda said to Brad.

"I don't know what you had last night lady. Maybe you would like to try a Shirley Temple," the waitress said thinking Linda's remark had been addressed to her.

Okay, that sounds good to me," Linda said to the waitress even though she had no idea what she was ordering.

After the waitress returned with the drinks, Brad tipped her $2 and then excused himself saying he had to go to the restroom and make room in his body for his next beer. When he returned a commercial was showing on the TV, so he asked Linda what had happened while he was gone.

"Well, a guy on the team with the red pants ran across the zero line, but something went wrong, so the judge punished him. Then the red team hero threw the ball to the wrong guy. Now the team with the white pants is starting to go the other way," Linda said.

Even though she had watched several of Brad's football games Linda still wasn't familiar with football terminology. Brad's interrupted of her comments were that the team Brad did not want to win appeared to have scored a touchdown, but because of an infraction the play was called back. The next play the quarterback threw an interception in the end zone. The team Brad wanted to win now had the ball on the twenty-yard line with only a few seconds left in the game.

"You know Brad something else must be wrong. You said there were less than four minutes left in the game, but that was ten minutes ago and the game hasn't ended," Linda said.

"Yeah, well, the four minutes was for playing time, not elapsed time," Brad answered.

"Got it," said Linda even though she really didn't get it.

It was only about 4:30 p.m. when the game did end a few seconds later. Linda had finished her Shirley Temple drink in two swallows, so Brad asked if she wanted another one. Instead she suggested they walk along the Strip and visit some other casinos.

Maybe because it was a little chilly outside, Linda hugged Brad's arm as they walked along. For some reason Linda seemed to enjoy watching people in the crowd. After walking for almost an hour, they stopped at a sidewalk coffee shop, where Linda continued to watch the people walk by. By the time they got back to their casinos, it was close to 7:00 p.m. They had a light dinner and then went to their room. The plan was to go to bed early so they could wake up early and then start back home in order to get ahead of heavy traffic.

Linda had a lot to talk about before going to sleep but was careful to not mention when her parents would arrive. Instead she talked about how she liked getting away from home and how much she would enjoy the New York City trip. Surprisingly Brad showed a genuine interest in the activities planned for the trip. Linda finally went to sleep feeing that everything was going to work out well.

They were able to start back home by 8:00 p.m. The traffic was light and the weather clear but cold. This made driving easy, so Brad could concentrate on what Linda was saying.

"You know, Brad, we have to go over our environmental class presentation tomorrow. Remember we have to gives it in class Tuesday and it is supposed to count for half of the entire course grade," said Linda

"Yeah, we can do that Monday afternoon after I get home from school. I'm sure we will get a good grade, but even if we don't Scott Watson already promised us an A grade for the work we did at his party," answered Brad.

Linda wasn't sure if Brad was serious, so she quickly asked him to promise to not do that. By this time they were passing the town of Baker, California. Linda figured they would stop in Barstow, which was less than an hour away, so she decided this was a good time to tell him about when her parents would arrive.

"Brad, I was thinking it might be a good idea if you stayed at my place the Monday and Tuesday before the Wednesday we leave for New York. We still need to decide if we want to try skiing or use the time to visit Washington DC. You can help me decide what clothes I pack for the trip. I don't want to take more than two suitcases, so I don't want to take any clothes I won't wear."

Linda felt it best if she worked up to the big announcement about her parents moving in while Brad was spending nights with her rather that coming right out with the news.

"Yeah, I like both ideas, spending nights with you and not taking any extra luggage. You know I'll only need one suitcase, so you can use another one if needed."

"Brad, you know my mother had a long conversation with me yesterday. Well, she said they just sold their house and the new owners want to move in before Christmas, so they will be staying with us for a couple of days before we leave for New York. I think they should know about our relationship right away instead of trying to keep secrets. Of course if you won't feel comfortable sharing the house with my parents you don't have to do that."

"I won't mind your parents moving in. School classes will start just after we get back, so I'll be away from the house all day during the week. If things get too awkward I can always move out. Besides, there will be a few days when I'll have to stay in my room to make sure the billet administrator doesn't give my room away. Of course if you don't think I should stay overnight while your parents are there, you can always stay at my place."

"Thanks, but I'd rather you stay at my place. I don't think Dad will care, but Mother will probably let us know she doesn't approve. If she does, I'll just tell her I'm an adult and own the house, so I'll set the rules."

Of course Linda knew she would never talk to her mother that way. She still respected her mother and therefore would find a more diplomatic way to address the situation if needed.

"We're almost to Barstow. Do you want to stop for a snack?" asked Brad.

"Yes, guess what else I need to do?" said Linda.

"Well, if you just want to use the restroom I can stop anywhere so you can use a ditch."

"I'd rather stop in Barstow. You can use the restroom too unless you want to stop by the road later and use a ditch."

Both Linda and Brad were quiet for the next several minutes. Linda knew having Brad stay at her house was taking a gamble. She would just have to risk alienating her mother. The other big risk is that Brad may lose interest in her after the first of the year.

Brad also had some thoughts about the arrangement. What if Linda's parents convinced her to end their relationship? He'd just taken it for granted that they would stay together for as long as he was going to school. By then they would both know if they should stay together when Brad went back on activity duty.

The rest of the way home was uneventful. They got home before Linda's mother called. Brad stayed overnight and was able to get almost eight hours of sleep. They went to bed early, and Linda was tired, so she only wanted to talk for about forty-five minutes.

Brad and Linda got an A grade for their environmental presentation. They both got good grades in their other classes and finished the semester on Friday December 9, 2005. They would start the second semester the second week of January 2006.

Sunday, December 11, they attended the early church service. Brad watched football on TV while Linda completed some household chores.

Most of the rest of the week Brad stayed at his room in the transit facility. He spent several hours each day working out in the school weight room. He also found time to shop for a top coat, which would be needed in New York. Starting Saturday, Brad would stay overnight at Linda's until leaving for New York.

Linda spent most of the week in deep thought. She went over plans for the trip and which included deciding which clothes to pack. She also spent a lot of time thinking about how to get her parents comfortable with Brad. A couple of days she was able to have lunch with Joan. She enjoyed talking to Joan and always felt better after doing so. It was probably a blessing that Linda didn't have to think about two new issues, which would arise next week.

Sunday morning Brad and Linda went to church, stopped for brunch at the club, and got home before Linda's mother called. That evening Linda left a message on Diane's phone asking her to call before leaving on her skiing trip.

"Mom said they would arrive Tuesday, December 20, on a 2:00 p.m. flight from Chicago. She said we should be receiving several packages with clothes and some other items that they sent ahead. Mom also said she had some very good news she will tell me after they arrived," Linda said to Brad at dinner.

"I wonder what the good news is. Do you think she's pregnant?" asked Brad.

"No chance of that," Linda said laughingly.

Tuesday Brad and Linda got to the airport about thirty minutes before the parents' plane was scheduled to arrive. Linda suddenly wished she had told them Brad would be meeting them. When the plane's arrival was posted on the flight arrival board, Brad noticed Linda started shaking as if she was shivering from the cold. He put his arm around her.

"Don't worry, your parents are not going to scold you for not telling them I would be meeting them. I'm sure we all will get along well. I promise to not tell any jokes," Brad said.

"I know it is so silly that at my age I'm still worried about getting Mother's permission to do something I want to do,"

As they waited by the baggage claim carousel, Brad held Linda's hand hoping it would relax her. After a few minutes, passengers from the flight started coming out of the plane arrival doors. Linda's parents were among the first group. Linda pointed them out to Brad.

The parents looked just like Brad thought they would. Ethel Dowling wore a dark blue dress, high heels, and an attractive necklace. She appeared to be slightly shorter and slightly heavier than Linda. She had a pleasant smile on her face, which both Linda and Brad noticed and appreciated.

Mr. Dowling wore a dark blue business suit with a light blue tie. He appeared to be a little shorter and a little heavier than Brad. He had flashed a big smile when he saw Linda.

After hugging her parents and exchanging greetings, Linda introduced Brad. Mr. Dowling shook hands with Brad and said it was nice to meet him. Mrs. Dowling said nothing, but she did smile. They made small talk about the flight and weather before the baggage carousel started up. The Dowlings' luggage was among the first to show up. Brad assumed that was because they probably flew first class. There were four large luggage pieces and a golf club set in a big leather holder.

Brad piled the luggage on an airport cart. Mr. Dowling slung the golf holder over his shoulder, and they started toward the exit. When they got outside, Brad excused himself to bring the car around. While he was gone, Linda explained that Brad would drop them off at the house, and then he would leave to work out at school. He would be back in time for dinner.

As soon as the car arrived, Brad opened the trunk and started loading the luggage with Mr. Dowling's help. Mr. Dowling was especially careful with the golf clubs. While they were doing that, Mrs. Dowling told and then virtually shoved Linda into the back seat of the car and then climbed in beside her. Mr. Dowling sat in the front seat.

"So, Brad, what do you do for a living?" Mr. Dowling asked.

"The government is paying for my schooling and living expenses since I signed a contract to go back on active duty with the army as a commissioned officer after I get my degree," Brad answered.

He figured it best to tell the whole story right away instead of trying to be secretive about his status. Mr. Dowling seemed surprised at the answer. He knew Linda was seeing someone named Brad and that Brad was a jock, but apparently Linda had never mentioned anything about Brad's army commitment.

"Are you going to try and get in some golf over the holidays, Mr. Dowling?" Brad asked, changing the subject.

"Call us Ralph and Ethel. Yes, as a matter of fact Linda has reserved time for me tomorrow morning at the club's golf course. Are you a golfer?" Ralph asked.

"I haven't played golf in over a year. I don't even have any clubs now."

"Look if you can get up early tomorrow, why not join me for nine holes? Maybe Linda still has Larry's clubs. If not, we can rent some at the golf shop."

Brad had to think about that before answering. He really didn't want to go golfing, but he realized that Ralph just wanted to have time to talk to him man-to-man.

"I can make it if you wouldn't mind the fact that I'm a really bad golfer."

"That won't be a problem. I'm not so good myself, so we can give each other mulligans if we get anywhere near the greens."

When they got to the house, they found that four large boxes had been left at the door. After taking all of the Dowlings' luggage, except the golf clubs, upstairs to their room, Brad started to take the boxes upstairs one by one.

"Oh, Brad, you don't need to do that. We may not need to unpack some of those boxes. When time permits, Ethel and I can take whatever we need upstairs piecemeal," Ralph said.

Brad was relieved to hear that. Then again if he had struggled to get the boxes upstairs, he wouldn't have needed to work out at school. As planned Brad said he was going back to the school weight room to work out for a couple of hours.

"Brad, on your way back, will you pick up a quart of pecan ice cream at the store," Linda asked.

Brad realized Ethel had heard Linda's request, so if he forgot to get the ice cream, it wouldn't look good. He was so worried about not forgetting, he had to exercise control to not buy the ice cream right away. Instead he wrote himself a note and then taped it on the steering wheel. He also wondered if he should pick up two quarts since he could eat one quart by himself.

Linda had prepared coffee and cake for her parents, so they all sat down around a kitchen table. That seemed like a good setting for the serious discussion that Linda knew would follow.

"Linda, why did you invite that boy for dinner? You know Ralph and I have some private important issues to discuss with you," said Ethel.

"Brad will be staying for dinner and overnight with me until we leave for New York. We can talk now. I'm interested in the good news you said you have," said Linda.

"This will make you really happy. Larry is going to divorce Cindy and wants to get back together with you. He will call you tomorrow night to explain when that can happen. He hasn't told Cindy yet."

Linda was surprised to hear that—not that Larry would divorce Cindy but that it would happen so soon. What shocked her was that Larry was confiding in her mother before he contacted her. Thoughts raced through Linda's head like lightning bolts. She hadn't given this much thought, but she knew she wanted to stay with Brad. The risk is that he may not feel the same way. If she didn't take advantage of Larry's offer now, it may not be available in the future.

"Mom, why do you think that is good news? I have no interest in getting back with Larry. Since you seem to be his messenger, you can let him know it would be a waste of time for him to call me."

"Linda, you should do what you want, but first let's at least consider some important concerns," said Ralph.

Ralph then stated the risks she would be taking if she didn't agree to get back with Larry at this time. Did she want to get married to Brad? If she got married, could Brad support her, certainly not at her current lifestyle? What if she should get pregnant? Does she want to be an army wife and move every two years? What would she do when Brad was stationed apart from her for a year? What if he got killed in Iraq, a real possibility? Finally, what kind of a relationship would Brad have with Diane, who was only a few years younger than him?

Linda had considered most of the things Ralph mentioned. She had saved enough to support her and Brad conformably, and she knew how to keep from getting pregnant. She really didn't know about being an army wife, which would be a test. Her main concern though had to do with Diane. Would Brad help take care of her. How would Brad and Diane get along together, as father/daughter or as lovers?

"Look, Dad and Mom, I really have thought of all the things Dad just mentioned, along with many other potential problems. You're right, it's best if I talk directly to Larry. I assume he will continue to support Diane's college education," said Linda.

The group continued to rehash concerns over Linda's relationship with Brad until it was time for Linda and Ethel to start making dinner. Brad returned, letting himself in, a little before 7:00 p.m. dinnertime. He asked if he could help with dinner arrangements but was told everything was ready. In the kitchen Ethel asked Linda where that guy was going to sit.

"Mom, that guy's name is Brad—B-r-a-d, Brad. Is there any reason you can't call him by his name?" asked Linda.

Ethel didn't answer.

At the dinner table, Brad sat to Linda's left. On the other side of the table, Ralph sat opposite Brad. Ethel sat to his left across from Linda. The conversation was friendly even though Ethel never said anything directly to Brad except for short answers to a couple of questions he asked her. Brad and Ralph helped clear the table after dinner and then were told they should go watch TV as Linda and Ethel washed the dishes. When the ladies finished washing the dishes, Ethel and Ralph said they were going to bed. Ralph and Brad had agreed to meet in kitchen at 6:00 a.m. and then head off to the golf course.

The next morning nothing was said about Brad and Linda's relationship until Ralph and Brad had passed the first hole of golf. Then Ralph decided to bring up the subject. Brad realized the next hour would be like an interview to see if he was fit to continue seeing Linda. Brad decided to be honest and not act any different from normal.

Ralph asked Brad the expected questions—how did they meet, how long had he been seeing each other, and did he want to go back on active duty with the army. Ralph then got right to the point.

"Brad, I think you know I still have some responsibility to protect my daughter. I don't want her to be hurt by a short-term romance. Linda has a good brain but is very naive about many worldly matters. Are you in love with her?" asked Ralph

"Yes, and I have been for a while. If you are asking if I can still love her ten years or more from now, I believe I can. To be honest no one knows what the future holds. Linda might lose interest in me, but I believe that would be less likely the longer we stay together. The big challenge would be for Linda to adjust to me going back in the army. It's possible she may get some experience in that regard this summer. I will have to spend two weeks training at Fort Carson or some other army base. Housing will be provided on base for Linda and me if she wishes to accompany me," Brad said.

Ralph seemed to appreciate Brad's answer, which indicated he had given the future some thought and felt comfortable staying with Linda. Because neither of them seemed interested in the golf game, Ralph suggested they stop playing and have something to eat in the bar.

In the bar, discussion continues about Brad and Linda's relationship for a while. The subject then changed to sports, which was of interest to both men. Ralph also got Brad to talk a little bit about his duty in Iraq. Over the next hour, Ralph had three scotch and water drinks. Brad almost matched him with three less alcoholic rum and Coke drinks. Brad felt he passed the interview and believed Ralph actually liked him. He felt Ralph and he could become good friends.

As soon as the men got home, Linda and Ethel took over Linda's car and left for shopping. Ralph said he was going to take a nap. Brad drove his car back to his room at the transit facility.

A little after 2:00 p.m., Linda answered a call from Ralph, who let her know Diane had just shown up at the house. Ethel was several feet away looking at some blouses, so she hadn't heard the phone ring. Upon hearing the news, Linda walked a little farther away to be sure Ethel didn't hear the conversation.

"You say Diane is at home now. Maybe I'd better talk to her," Linda said to Ralph.

"Well, she's taking a nap now. She said she was tired and wanted to take a nap," said Ralph.

"Is she all right?"

"Yeah, I think so. She seemed mad about something but didn't want to talk. I think it best if you talk to her."

"Okay, Mom and I will be home shortly. If Diane does come downstairs ask her to call me. No, on second thought it's probably better if we wait to talk until I get home."

Once again Linda was blindsided by something unexpected. Thinking fast she knew the first thing to do was to tell Brad and assure him she needed him to be with her that evening. Her call to Brad was short and to the point. Brad said he would get to the house by 6:00 p.m. By then Ethel was looking for her, so she gave her the news without mentioning Brad.

Linda went directly to Diane's bedroom when she got home. Diane appeared to be asleep, but Linda could tell she was just pretending. That made no sense to Linda. Diane must know her mother would be concerned about her, so why not talk to her. It was hard for Linda to control herself as she gently shook Diane instead of grabbing her by the neck.

"Diane, you surprised all of us by not letting us know you were coming home. Is there anything wrong?" Linda asked Diane.

"No, I'm all right. I just wanted to come home for Christmas. Didn't Grandma Dowling tell you I was coming?" Diane answered, trying to speak in a sleepy voice.

"No, she did not. Is there anything else she should have told me?"

"Well, I guess you know Dad is going to divorce Cindy. He hasn't told her yet, but I think she knows."

"Will you be all right next semester at school if Cindy doesn't visit you during the week?"

"Oh, I'm not going back to school at Stanford. It isn't fair for me. All the other kids went to better high school than the one you sent me to. They learned things that weren't taught to me, so of course I had trouble keeping up. I think it is best that this fall I enroll at Cal State for a couple of years. I know I won't have any trouble there. Dad said I can finish my last two years at Stanford or some other first-rate school."

"Well, Larry is going to call tonight. I can discuss your schooling with him then."

"Oh, Mom, I guess Grandma didn't tell you. Larry is going to spend Christmas with us. He'll be here tomorrow."

Linda had been upset with Diane and her mother. Now she was madder than hell at both women as well as Larry. Apparently none of them felt any need to ask her to change her plans. They all knew about the New York trip. She really didn't like Larry, Diane, and Ethel making plans involving her without consulting with her. She had been sitting at the foot of the bed but got up before talking with a controlled voice.

"Well, Larry will just have to change his plans. I'll tell him so when he calls. Brad and I are not going to change our plans for the holidays in New York. Incidentally Brad will be staying overnight with me tonight and tomorrow night."

This caused Diane to scream loudly, "Mom, how can you do that. Didn't Grandma tell you to get rid of that guy? If he stays here, that will spoil my entire Christmas."

A few seconds later, Ethel opened the door and took one step inside. "Is anything wrong?" Ethel asked.

"Go outside and shut the door. Everything is fine here," Linda said.

Ethel didn't move for a second until Linda started toward her. Ethel then quickly left but slammed the door. Linda then turned her attention to Diane.

"Don't scream at me. That shows that you are still a child and haven't learned anything from college or your good friend Cindy. Your lack of courtesy toward me and immature thinking has caused unneeded problems for Brad, your grandparents, Larry, and me. Of course all you can think of is yourself. This time you are not getting your way. Brad is staying here tonight and tomorrow night. Brad and I are leaving for New York Friday morning. You can stay here with your grandparents, go back to Larry's house, or go stay with Cindy wherever she is. Stop crying and get cleaned up. I want you downstairs in fifteen minutes, or by God, I'll come up here and drag you down just as I find you," Linda said.

Linda now went downstairs looking for Ethel. The few seconds' delay before Ethel came into Diane's room after Diane screamed was not time enough for Ethel to walk more than a few feet. Linda knew Ethel must have been listening outside the door. When Linda got downstairs, she noticed that Ethel had been talking to Ralph. The both stared at her wide-eyed.

"Diane said she told you she would be here today. Did she tell you?" Linda said to Ethel.

"No, I don't remember her saying anything about that," Ethel answered.

"Diane also said Larry told you he would be here tomorrow. Is that true?"

"No, Larry didn't say that to me."

"I'll tell you right now and Larry when he calls that he is not going show up here tomorrow. If he does, I'll have Brad throw him out the door like he did Bernie Mitchell."

"Did Brad really throw Bernie Mitchell out of the house? I would have liked to see that. Larry introduced me to Bernie once at a legal convention. I instantly disliked him," Ralph said, speaking for the first time.

"Yeah, he really did. He'll be here in a few minutes, so, Mom, I hope you are able to remember his name is Brad, not that guy. It would also be nice if you would talk to him for the first time about something tonight. Diane is sure to be disrespectful toward my friend, so I hope you don't join up with her and try to make Brad feel unconformable," Linda said to Ethel.

"Brad and I had a good talk this morning. I told Ethel he is a very mature and I'm sure he has strong feelings for you. I'll mention this only once, the age difference did bother me initially, but after talking to Brad, I'm over that. I'm sure you two will get along fine," Ralph said to Linda.

Linda then started upstairs to get Diane. Unexpectedly, Diane had just left her room and was on the way down. She passed Linda without saying a word. She did warmly greet her grandparents though when she saw them.

By then it was time to start dinner preparations. They planned on eating early so they would finish before Larry was expected to call around 8:00 p.m. Diane and Ethel both helped out. Ralph watched TV.

Brad did arrive a little before 6:00 p.m. He rang the doorbell but let himself in. Linda came out of the kitchen to greet him. Brad gave her a hug and quick kiss on the mouth.

"Brad, it's time you formally meet Diane. You remember seeing her at the Stanford football game," Linda said to Brad.

"Nice to see you again. It's also nice that you can spend Christmas with your grandparents. As you know your mother and I will spend the holidays in New York," Brad said to Diane.

Diane said hello and smiled. She said dinner was ready, so everyone could sit down at the dining room table. Brad noticed that Diane was gorgeous and had a great body. However, he quickly erased those thoughts from his mind. He reminded himself that he should never be alone with her, not because of what he might do, but rather because of what she may accuse him of doing. This was going to be a problem for a long time.

Brad sat at the head of the table with Linda to his right and Diane next to her across the table from Ralph and Ethel. Most of the discussion at dinner centered on personal matters of the four family members. Linda did explain the absence of a Christmas tree and presents. Since her parents and Diane were not expected and since she and Brad would be away, she didn't see the need of setting up a tree. She had sent Diane's present to her apartment.

Ethel did ask Brad if he had ever been to New York. This stimulated a lively discussion about things to do and see there. Everyone had something to say except Diane. At the end of dinner, Ralph said the five of them should have dinner at a nice restaurant the next night since Brad and Linda would be leaving the next morning. It would be his treat.

By then it was close to 8:00 p.m., so Ethel suggested they wait for Larry to call before having dessert. Linda then shocked everyone by saying she wanted to put Larry's call on the speakerphone so everyone could listen in. She said since everyone had an interest in what would be said, it would be best if everyone heard it firsthand.

That being the case, dessert was served while waiting for the call. It seems everyone except Brad knew Larry enough to know his habits, which included certain things such as making phone calls at certain times. Therefore no one was surprised when Linda's phone rang just after 8:00 p.m.

"Hello, Larry, I was told you would be calling," Linda said.

"Yeah, well, it's been a while since we talked. I understand you are well," said Larry.

"Mom and Diane told me why you are calling. Did you know Diane is here?"

"Yeah, she left me a phone message, but I wasn't able to call her back before she left."

"Because you've already discussed your plans with everyone but me, it's best everyone hear this conversation. You're on the speakerphone. Mom, Dad, Diane, and Brad are all listening."

"Well, I was hoping we could have a private conversation. Would you like me to call back later?"

"No."

After a long pause Larry continued, "Well, I have some good news. I'm going to be able to spend Christmas with you, all of you. I should get there in the early afternoon. Linda, you and I can talk more after Christmas."

"Larry, you know Brad and I are spending the holidays in New York, so there is no need for you to come down here. If you show up tomorrow, Brad will throw you out the door just like he did Bernie Mitchell. If you come down here after Brad and I are gone, Dad will throw you out the door. To be clear, I don't want to see you. If you have anything to say, say it now before I hang up."

"Well, this is a little awkward, but you know I'm going to serve Cindy with divorce papers early in January. So I'd like to talk to you about getting back together again."

"I have no interest in getting back together again with you, Larry. Did you have anything else to say?"

"Yes, I do, but it will wait until you are in a more reasonable mood."

"Since you didn't ask, Diane does not want to go back to Stanford. She is thinking of going to Cal State this fall instead. She'll be staying with me but can visit you anytime she wants after Cindy leaves. After the first of the year, Diane and I will pick up her things from her apartment. After that you may want to stop renting it."

"All right, I'll talk to you later."

"Good-bye."

"Good-bye, Dad!" Diane shouted just before Linda hung up.

The group finished dessert pretty much in silence. The three women then retreated to the kitchen to clean the dishes and to talk. Ralph and Brad watched the latest news on TV. One of the news stories talked about how the Iraq war was not going well and there was no end in sight.

"Brad, do you think you'll have to go back to Iraq when you finish school?" Ralph asked.

"Yeah, I probably will. The army needs more experienced men at the junior officer level. Fortunately the heavy fighting by American forces seems to be over. Most of our troops will be in advisory roles," answered Brad.

Ralph didn't ask the follow-up questions, which were "What would Linda do while you were gone?" and "What would happen if you got killed?" Both men knew it was important to have plans for those possibilities.

Most of the stress had left Linda after Larry's phone call. So she decided it a good time to apologize for the way she talked to Diane and to her mom. After some discussion, most of the bruised egos were repaired.

In bed Linda and Brad talked for almost two hours about the day's events and about what to expect next after returning from their trip.

Thursday morning, Brad called an auto service company to change the battery in Diane's car and get it running. He then drove it to the local gas station to inflate the tires to the proper level and fill it up with gas. Later that day Brad would leave his car at the transit facility while he was in New York. Linda would pick him up there in time for dinner.

Linda had a long discussion with Diane, telling her she had to mind her grandparents while Linda was away. She also gave Diane $100, which should last her for the next two weeks. Larry had given a low-balance credit card to Diane, which was maxed out for the month. Diane said Cindy often used the card for personal purchases she didn't want Larry to know about. Diane went on to say Larry found out Cindy was having sex with a number of Stanford students while waiting for Diane to finish her classes. That's why he wanted a divorce.

Later Linda called Joan to bring her up-to-date on recent activities. Joan said she was going to drop Hannah off at an afternoon movie and wanted to know if Diane would like to go along. Diane and Hannah had always been friends but hadn't palled around with each much after Diane started high school. However, Linda though Diane would like an opportunity to tell Hannah about her Stanford experience, so she asked her. Diane agreed to go to the movie.

In the afternoon Linda did some shopping by herself. She bought presents for everyone and had them Christmas wrapped at the store. Ethel and Ralph spent the afternoon opening the packages they had delivered to Linda's house. They unpacked some clothes but decided most of the items could remain in boxes downstairs. The clothes they wanted were placed in one box that Brad would take upstairs when he returned.

Dinner turned out well. Everyone joined to some extent in discussions about future activities. Ethel and Diane both called Brad by his name. Ralph ordered expensive wine, which tasted good to Brad even though he couldn't tell it from any other wine he had drank.

Friday morning went quickly. Soon it was time for Ralph to drop Linda and Brad off at the airport. After checking their bags, they had some time to relax. Linda spent some time thinking about why she didn't cancel the trip. The initial plan for the New York trip would not have presented any problems for Linda's family members. When Linda's parents arrived early, Linda thought of cancelling the trip. Then when Diane showed up, Linda knew it would look really bad if she didn't spend Christmas with her parents and daughter. However, she could justify not cancelling the trip because no one told her about their change in plans. She would try to make it up to them when she returned.

Brad thought about the problems he and Linda would face in the near future. Larry was not going to give up on Linda. Diane would be a permanent problem. Then there was something else Brad hadn't mentioned to Linda. The army said Brad could immediately come back on duty as a commissioned warrant office helicopter pilot. That was attractive to Brad for a number of reasons. Because progression in the officer ranks would be limited, he could leave the army after a few years with training to qualify for a well-paying private helicopter pilot position.

About that time, boarding was called for their flight, so all thoughts turned to the trip. They would leave their problems behind them. Brad and Linda were going to have a Merry Christmas and a Happy New Year.

Printed in the United States
By Bookmasters